# RETURN
## OF THE
# SHADOW

# RETURN OF THE SHADOW

## SHADEBOUND

# LIV EVANS & ZAC PILOT

Return of the Shadow
First published by Liv Evans and Zac Pilot in 2024
ISBN 9781763514942



For any enquiries please visit www.livevans.com.au

Cover design: MiblArt

Editing: Tracy Kisgen

*Zac's Dedication-*
*To my amazing wife Liv, without her hard work, persistence, and dedication, we would not have been able to deliver this incredible tale. I look forward to the next and many more to come.*

*Liv's Dedication-*
*I would look terrible if I didn't dedicate this one to Zac after his lovely comment above. I've already dedicated two other books to him, but third time is the charm, right?*
*To everyone who says that working with your spouse is a bad idea... I could not disagree more. Three jobs, two kids, one dog, and two books later, I can confidently say I am grateful for every wonderful and challenging second of working with my darling husband.*
*Thank you for wrangling my chaos, Zac. You're a legend.*

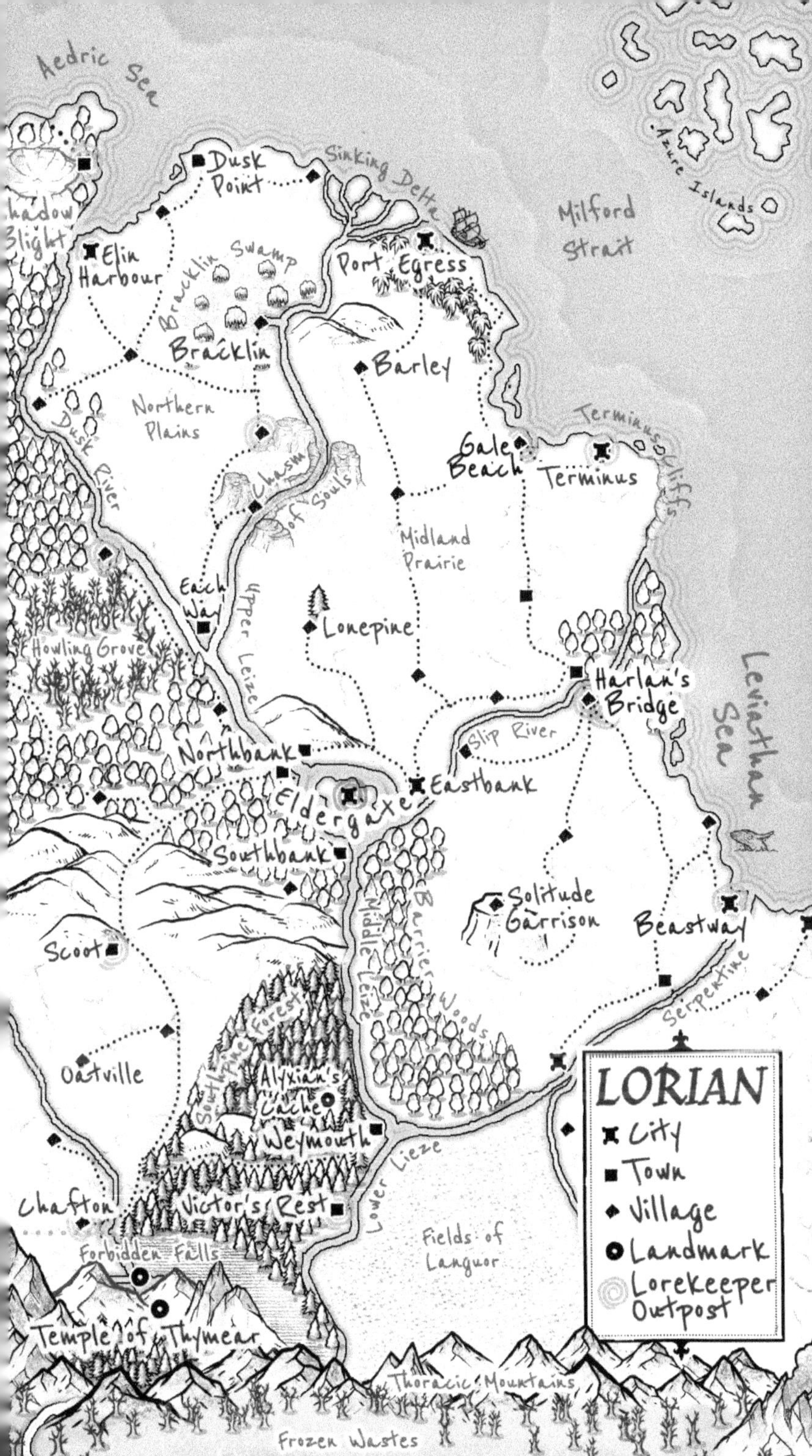

Aedric Sea
Azure Islands
Milford Strait
Dusk Point
Sinking Delta
Shadow Blight
Elin Harbour
Bracklin Swamp
Port Egress
Bracklin
Barley
Northern Plains
Gale Beach
Terminus
Terminus Cliffs
Dusk River
Chasm of Souls
Midland Prairie
Each Way
Upper Leize
Lonepine
Howling Grove
Harlan's Bridge
Leviathan Sea
Slip River
Northbank
Eldergate
Eastbank
Southbank
Solitude Garrison
Beastway
Scoot
Middle Leize
Barrier Woods
Serpentine
Oatville
Southpine Forest
Alyxian's Cache
Weymouth
Lower Lieze
Chafton
Victor's Rest
Fields of Languor
Forbidden Falls
Temple of Thymear
Thoracic Mountains
Frozen Wastes
LORIAN
City
Town
Village
Landmark
LoreKeeper Outpost

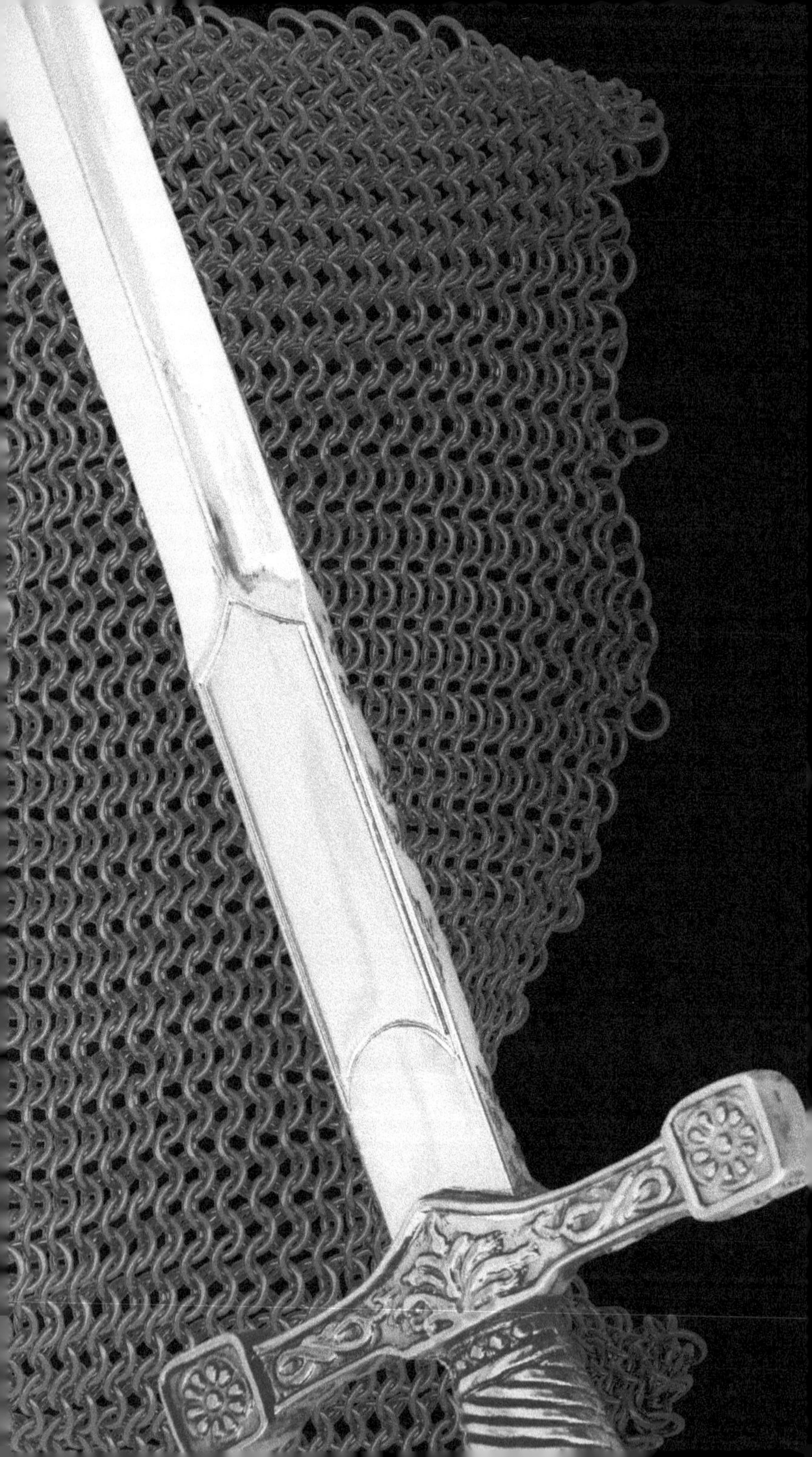

# RIVEN

Riven gawked at the yawning cavern before him. He found it hard to believe that this was the entrance to an ancient temple. To him, it looked like a large hole in the side of a mountain. Standing beside him, brown curls bouncing as she scribbled busily in her leather-bound notebook, was Miri, his friend since childhood.

It could take him a lifetime to understand all the unique symbols and drawings Miri copied down, but he trusted she knew what she was doing. After all, she was a senior archivist now, and it was her knowledge of ancient scripts that led them to the long-forgotten ruins.

When they were young, Miri displayed a knack for understanding different languages, both verbal and written. Her passion for age-old history was rivalled only by her sense of adventure. Miri worked for the Lorekeepers. They were responsible for cataloguing and securing dangerous magical artefacts of the past. Several years ago, Miri left Riven and their small town behind to study in Eldergate, the capital city of Lorien. They exchanged letters occasionally, but nothing more than that. Not until she knocked on his door a couple of weeks ago and asked him to provide her and her colleagues with his protective mercenary services on their mission.

Riven, on the other hand, had enjoyed the simple life. He trained with the local militia, but after a few years he decided to work for himself and became a private mercenary. Recently he had been accepted to study as a revoker; a specialised member (within the Enforcers), taught elite skills to eradicate the illegal use of magical artefacts.

Riven's work was not as exciting or adventurous as Miri's, but he was afraid of leaving the home he knew, of leaving the people and friends from childhood. Seeing Miri again after all these years brought a sting to his heart; he regretted not going with her when she asked. Given another chance he would not make the same mistake.

Riven's mind returned to the present. Instead of her notebook, he focused on Miri's expression. She had a cute wrinkle in her forehead that always warmed his heart. When they were little, she had a habit of getting so lost in her work she barely noticed the outside world. He felt the corners of his mouth spread into a wide grin as he saw that same quality now.

With a slight shift of her hips, Miri adjusted her stance. The movement caused her woollen cloak to ease from her shoulders. The black fabric was thick, decorated with meandering red swirls. Its colour scheme matched her Lorekeepers uniform beneath; a black, embossed satin skirt paired with a white chemise layered under a shimmering red and black bodice. Miri's clothes were all adorned with the brass chains that the Lorekeepers favoured, and the black belt around her waist contained a pouch full of oddities and supplies, with straps on the bottom to hold the notebook which seemed to be a permanent fixture on her person.

As Riven watched her, Miri glanced up and caught his gaze. She smiled at him, and he spluttered, "The entrance is huge. How has it not been discovered until now?"

"During the purge they buried a lot of these temples under hundreds of tons of rocks, but I'm guessing the decades of erosion, and a few rockslides must have expanded the entrance over time, so for many years it may have been smaller or hidden." Miri let her gaze linger on her scrawling for a moment longer before she shrugged and closed her notebook. "Do not forget, this area is also off-limits. We had to get special permission to be here." Miri gestured toward the rest of their group. They were labouring their way up the cliff face.

Riven smiled to himself. His years of combat training had shaped his body into a fit, lean fighting form; his strength and stamina were ideal for long and arduous treks such as this. Even weighted down with armour, Riven was able to travel easier than the rest in their lightweight, cloth uniforms. Riven adjusted his pauldrons and checked his steel bracers for any damage, but even though they were old, they had fared well. He wished he had the money to buy steel greaves to replace his leather ones, but he supposed his outfit was a work in progress. Not that it would matter, because Riven was sure the Revokers would provide him with new armour upon his return.

Heading back to Chafton was not a welcome thought right now. Not with Miri a few meters away. Determined to take advantage of the only real alone time they had since starting their journey, Riven steeled himself and decided to lead into a conversation he had been wanting to start ever since he saw her again. "Remember that time we went to the Forbidden Falls? That was fun."

Miri tilted her head to the side, long brown ringlets

falling over one cheek. Her smile curved into something more mischievous. "Oh, right! I remember we went skinny dipping there."

*Skinny dipping?* Riven choked on his next breath and tried to cover it with a cough. It was the last adventure they went on together before she left. He would have remembered that if it had happened... wouldn't he? "I, uh, I don't remember that. Are you sure?" Riven knew, for a fact, that would not be something he could forget.

Miri chuckled in response. It was a light, melodic chiming that sent goosebumps along Riven's skin. "Oh, I know I went skinny dipping there. Maybe it wasn't with you, maybe it was with ..." Her voice faded as she turned and walked away.

With a jolt, Riven chased after her. What did she mean, *'maybe it was with'*? Had she taken someone else to their spot?

Before Riven could speak to Miri again, a loud and exasperated voice broke their exchange. "Miriam, you did not tell us we'd be doing so much climbing." Gareth, one of the older Lorekeepers' members, collapsed onto a nearby rock, breathing heavily.

Eyes wide, Riven glanced at Miri. Even though he had grown up with her, he had only heard her full name used twice; once when her parents were mad with her, and another time when a child in the village had used it to tease her. Based on how ferociously Miri had responded to both events, Riven had never dared call her that. In fact, he had banished the name from his vocabulary.

"My name is Miri." She jabbed a finger in Gareth's direction. "And what the darkness did you expect? If it is so—"

"My apologies, good sir." Riven interrupted, placing

himself between Miri and Gareth, in hopes of intervening before she lost control of her temper. "Since this area is off-limits none of the cartographers have been able to map the zone. However, from this height, I think I already know the best route home. I guarantee there will be less climbing on the return trip."

"Well, there better be. We did not pay you for sightseeing," Gareth growled, mopping sweat from his receding salt and pepper hairline with a pristine handkerchief.

"Yes, sir," Riven replied automatically. He had been a mercenary for five years now and, in that time, he had learned that no matter how he was treated, 'the customer is always right.'

Riven had not been hired by Gareth. It was Miri who was guiding the mission, and who had offered him the job contract. However, Gareth liked to act as though he was the one in charge of the group.

The other two people in their party included Fiona and her son Willis. Fiona was a middle-aged woman with hair as lovely as her frame, and was pleasant enough. She seemed to act more as a support for Gareth than a senior archivist in her own right, but she had demonstrated her experience in different ways. Willis was an apprentice archivist . Fiona had brought him along as part of his training. He was a tall, gangly fellow with red hair and freckles. In his late teens, he had only just joined the Lorekeepers.

Riven walked to the ledge and peered over to check on them.

The mother and son pair were trudging up the embankment; clearly, neither of them had prepared for the trip. Both wore their red and black archivist garb, which had become filthy during the long journey.

Assuming they would arrive shortly, Riven returned

to Miri's side. She hummed with appreciation as she ran her fingers over the rows of inscriptions that were chiselled into the stone walls of this area. "At the very least, these symbols are telling me we are definitely in the right place."

Riven massaged his close-cropped hair as he stared at the wall. He was in awe of Miri understanding the complex characters. "What does it say?"

"This says it is Thymear Temple," Miri said as she tapped a few of the curling, graceful glyphs. "And the rest translates to something along the lines of 'great evil,' 'dangers lurk inside,' 'death awaits.' You know, all that doom and gloom stuff. Blah, blah, blah."

"Evil? Dangers? Death?" Riven's voice bounced around the cavern, creating an ominous echo.

"What was that?" Fiona called as she and Willis finally joined them. Gareth trailed behind them, huffing and puffing, complaining about how much time the pair wasted by taking so long to get up the cliff.

"Nothing, I was just telling my friend a funny story," Miri called out, without peeling her eyes away from the inscriptions.

With the mystery of the glyphs unravelled, Miri turned and clapped her hands together as she looked at her peers. "So, this is a secret entrance. Well, it was a long while ago. I imagine there was some intricate incantation and key needed to open the door, but time has done all the work for us." She gestured to the gaping cavern they entered through.

"So, what do we do?" Willis asked.

"Oh, that's simple." Miri turned her back on the passage leading farther into the mountain. She let her fingertips settle on a decorative line between a row of glyphs, then tapped several in a pattern that Riven was unable to discern.

"I doubt that will—"

Gareth's protest was cut short as the loud grinding of stone on stone sounded. The glyphs all separated into individual blocks and rolled back to reveal an archway in the wall with a deep well behind it.

"Ladies and gentlemen, I welcome you to the Temple of Thymear," Miri said with a bow.

Riven was stuck on the fact that the rocks just *moved*. He blinked and looked around, trying to find gears or pulleys, but finding nothing of the sort. The others did not seem to share his concerns as they all peered into the black abyss.

"You! Get me down there." Gareth gestured to Riven.

Bamboozled by the appearance of the curved entrance, Riven did not argue, but took the rope from his pack and tied it to a nearby rock formation. Once complete, he went to the edge of the well.

"I'll go first," Miri announced. She grabbed onto Riven's bicep as he passed her.

"What?" Riven and Gareth asked at the same time, but with completely different tones.

It was not that Riven thought Miri could not handle herself, but it was his job to escort them safely and so far, he had not done so.

Gareth sniggered. "Oh, I know what this is. You want the glory and credit for this. I have been a senior archivist for longer than you have been alive, girl. It is *my* right to this discovery."

"Of course, Gareth, where are my manners?" Miri unhooked the rope from Riven and presented it to Gareth.

Riven was surprised she gave in so easily.

Gareth snatched the rope from her.

Then, Miri added, "Oh, and please be a dear and disarm the automated traps on the way down."

"Traps?" Gareth dropped the rope, letting it coil on the ground in a puff of dust. "On second thought, you are the *lead* archivist on the expedition, perhaps you *should* go first." He shuffled away from the arch. Fiona and Willis followed.

Miri pursed her lips. Riven grabbed the rope and handed it to her. He leaned in closer and whispered, "Are you sure you want to go first? You know... the traps. Danger. Death."

"It was only a vague translation. Besides, it has been hundreds of years. I doubt anything is still alive, or working, down there." Her face shone with the charm and confidence he recalled from their youth.

Riven knew there was no point arguing with Miri. Once she made up her mind there was no changing it. He contemplated the fact, that if it were not for Miri, he would never have seen the Forbidden Falls.

Shaking off the memories, Riven helped Miri to unravel the rope. Disappearing into the darkness they watched the rope, inch by inch, until there was a dull thump of it landing. *At least it is not some bottomless pit*, Riven thought to himself. He helped Miri prepare to climb down then watched as she vanished from their sight. "Call out when you reach the bottom."

Riven stood back with arms crossed, waiting with bated breath with the others. Miri's progress seemed to last forever as she worked her way down the rope. Riven knew she was still moving by the way the rope shifted.

Finally, Miri's voice echoed up to them, "I'm done!" A torch flared to life and Riven peered over the edge of the chasm to see light glowing a dizzying distance below, and Miri's tiny face grinning up at him.

"Excellent. Me next." Gareth surged forward, then hesitated as he saw the drop. "Although, rope climbing was not covered in my training." He turned and glared at Riven expectantly.

Riven considered his options. It was not feasible that he could carry the man down the shaft. Then, an idea occurred to him. "I, uh, I could tie a harness for you and lower you down?"

That seemed acceptable to Gareth. And to Fiona and Willis who requested the same treatment. Riven nodded and got to work. When Gareth was safely secured in a harness and sitting at the edge of the well, Riven called out, "Lowering Gareth down now!"

Just as he started, Miri yelled, "Don't touch anything with a symbol on the way down. I think that I disarmed most of the traps, but I may have missed some."

After Riven ensured that the archivists were safely down the shaft, he shimmied down the rope himself. It was a long descent, and thanks to lowering the other three folks, his biceps were burning with the strain by the time his own feet touched a stone floor.

Ahead, an archway opened into a long hallway. Small spheres of warm light dotted the walls, bouncing off stone polished so smooth it had reflective properties. On closer inspection Riven realised the light produced was emanating from glowing crystals within the spheres.

Riven's mouth dropped. He had never encountered anything like this, which led him to wonder about the source of the crystal's power.

When he looked ahead the others had already moved farther down the tunnel. Riven followed in amazement.

The architecture was unlike anything he had seen before; it seemed ancient yet untouched by time. When he got to the end, the others had continued, but Miri fell back and waited for him.

If he had thought the hall was impressive, it was nothing compared to the temple's interior. It was a vast, cavernous chamber, with a ceiling that was at least ten metres high. Several large pillars, ornately carved with sinuous curves and flourishes, supported the ceiling. Hundreds of shelves and tables formed a maze around the space; some of them were damaged and others had items stored on or in them. Just like the hallway, luminescent crystals littered the area. The interior walls appeared worn, as if no one had stepped foot in the cave for over a hundred years.

"Pretty amazing, huh? Can you believe there are hundreds of these Shadow Temples buried all around the world?" Miri asked, sidling over to Riven, her eyes dancing.

"As impressive as it is, I'm glad they buried the temples. Can you imagine if they let the Shadows continue their reign of terror?"

Miri's expression was difficult to read. "History isn't always as it seems."

"What do you mean?"

Miri met Riven's inquiring gaze. For a moment, something flickered in her eyes. She opened her mouth, then closed it, shook her head slightly, and said, "Never mind. Look, we better catch up to the others before they 'take all my glory'." Amusing herself, she frolicked deeper into the chamber.

A laugh rumbled in Riven's chest as he followed her. The others had not gone very far as they had become distracted by the multitude of treasures littering the space.

By no means a scholar, Riven was taken aback by the sheer volume of items. Everyone seemed excited, as though presented with glorious gifts.

"This is the find of the century! The council will be pleased," Gareth crowed as he shovelled several glowing objects into his bag.

The rest of the team was doing the same but with much less enthusiasm. Fiona would touch an object, close her eyes briefly, and the glow would dim, then she would put it away. Willis was apprehensive about touching anything and would take several test taps before copying his mother's behaviour. To Riven, the objects resembled ordinary household items; cups, plates, bags, mirrors, etc. The objects seemed familiar at surface level, with the exception of their indistinct designs, and being made of unknown materials.

Miri caught Riven's eye and gestured toward the main chamber. "I'm going to look around for a while; you're welcome to join me. That is, unless you have got something else you would rather do."

"Uh sure, I mean I could protect you from that broken chair over there—" he pointed to what looked like a throne that was listing forward, thanks to two broken front legs. "But I think it's safe for now."

Riven patted his own back, pleased with his joke.

Miri responded with a gratuitous "Ha, ha."

They walked around the cavern for some time. Like the others were doing, Miri picked up small objects and performed the same strange procedure, but unlike her crew, she also sketched the items and wrote notes after observing each one. Along the way, she stopped to read the script on the floors, walls, and pillars marking the area.

Miri noticed an intricately designed box. She read the inscription, then fiddled with the object for a few minutes, then after manipulating what appeared to be the controls of a locking mechanism, it opened with an audible click. Inside was a necklace. Hanging on a copper chain was a pendant with wire wrapped around a glowing red cabochon gem that pulsed, glowing brighter than everything else they had discovered thus far.

Thrilled with her find, Miri clutched the box tightly. She took note of the location for each of her companions. Fortunately, they were busy with their own treasures and so she returned her attention to the necklace. Riven watched as she lifted it gingerly from the box, enclosed it in her fist, then closed her eyes. When she opened them, the glow bleeding between her fingers had dimmed.

"What are you doing?" Riven whispered. "Why is that glowing?"

Miri did not answer right away, waiting until the radiance dissipated completely. "It is called the Reformation Ritual. Shadow relics can be highly volatile, especially those that have not been used in a long while. Anyone untrained in the art could activate the item incorrectly and cause untold chaos, or worse."

"Worse?"

"It could explode in a torrent of uncontrolled magic, disintegrating everything around it."

Riven's eyes widened as Miri spoke with such calm. He could not tell if she was joking.

Miri reached for Riven, squeezing his hand and beaming. "Do not worry I am fully trained. You kept us safe out there; I will do the same for you in here. But I would not touch anything glowing if I were you."

"Thanks, how long does it take to train for—" Riven stopped, realising that Miri was not listening anymore. She was staring intently at a nearby wall with a large inscription.

Scrunching her face, she seemed to be lost in some internal debate.

When she did not say anything further, Riven felt obliged to break her concentration. "What is it, Miri?"

She flinched, then turned and offered him a smile that did not reach her eyes. Then, looking away she spoke quickly. "Oh, it's probably nothing. Do you mind checking on the others to see how they are going, please?"

"Uh, sure." Riven was not convinced. Miri was usually a very confident person, almost always sure of herself. He rarely saw her concerned. However, he was not able to question her, so he did as she asked, watching her even as he backed away. Miri returned her attention to the back wall, and began copying the inscription into her notebook.

Satisfied that Miri's behaviour had returned to normal, Riven turned to find the others. Gareth and Willis were nearest in proximity to Riven. Gareth was inspecting an interesting staff, mumbling something under his breath, as Riven approached.

"What is it?" Riven asked, noticing how strangely they were all behaving amongst the relics. Gareth had been dismissive of his concerns before, but there was such an air of secrecy to things now.

"None of your business. Willis, put this with the others, now!"

Willis hastily tied the staff to one of the already full bags. Riven felt sorry for the boy. For Riven, even though Gareth had been rude to him, at least when the job was over, he could say goodbye. Willis would be stuck with Gareth as his unbearable instructor.

Suddenly, Riven heard a loud creak from behind him. He whipped around, with his battle instincts on high alert. The wall where he left Miri had opened, revealing a hidden room. Gareth pushed past him. "What have you found girl? Trying to get the glory again, no doubt."

Willis and Fiona came over, and Riven joined them in following Gareth. Miri was already in the newly opened room. It was a small space, barely five metres square. Miri studied a cylindrical dais made of the same polished stone as the wall. It held a single item. It was hard for Riven to see it over the shoulders of the archivists, but he caught a glimpse of another item made of copper wire, and a red gem. Its glow was enormous. In fact, it was the only source of light in the entire room.

"What do we have here?" Gareth rubbed his chin. "Can it be?"

"Be what?" Miri asked, buffing the surface of the inscription clean.

"I already know what it is." Gareth shoved her out of the way and reached past her.

Just as he was about to touch the item, Miri called, "No, wait! There's a—"

Aside from the gem, all light sources disappeared, leaving the group swimming in near darkness. A deafening rumble filled the temple. The ground shook violently and the walls creaked with strain. Riven was barely able to keep his balance. Miri yelped and grasped the podium to keep upright. The rest of them fell to the ground in a mess of groans and flailing limbs. Boulder sized rocks began falling from the ceiling in the main chamber, crashing down onto the shelves of artefacts below with deafening booms.

"The temple's caving in on us!" Riven warned.

"Get the relic!" Gareth had already jumped to his feet. He launched towards the podium, but Fiona gripped the edge of the black and red cloak he was wearing.

"Leave it," she wheezed. "We have more than enough in our packs. Let's take what we have and leave while we can."

This seemed to break Gareth out of his obsessive actions. He glanced around them as an odd glow flickered along the walls. He snarled with frustration before storming out of the room, pushing past Fiona, and knocking her to the ground.

Riven pulled the older woman up as Miri moved to help Willis stand. The younger man winced as he put weight on his ankle. Without a word, Miri slipped her arm under his. Riven joined her, and they helped Willis to hobble into the main chamber while Fiona followed. It was a perilous trek, as the boulders continued to fall, and the ground shook so tremendously that it took all their concentration to keep from falling.

Inside the main chamber they found Gareth, who had already made his way to the other side. It seemed impossible for him to move that fast considering the obstacles of shelves and tables, along with the fallen debris that now littered the area, but the selfish man did not even look back to see if they were safe.

A rock pelted down from the ceiling, striking Riven's pauldron with a loud ding and bouncing off against the wall. He grunted and worked his shield from his back, bringing it up to protect their heads from injury. Even with that, they all received scrapes along their arms and legs, due to the exposure of their limbs to the raining rubble.

It was difficult to keep track of their shifting path through the cavern, so Riven focused on following Gareth. He seemed to know where he was going. As Riven watched, a jagged shard of rock shook loose from the ceiling directly above the older man. Riven tried to yell a warning, but Gareth raised his hand and the rock exploded with a loud crack. The shattered pieces fell to the ground behind Gareth. There was an eerie whoosh, and awful scraping sounds as the ground between the team and Gareth caved in. They skidded to a stop just before they tumbled over the edge of the dark abyss.

Gareth stared back at them, clutching something to his chest as he assessed the situation. Somehow, he was uninjured. Riven was unsure of what had transpired, of how that rock had cracked, but he did not have time to think about it.

"Oh, darkness!" Miri cursed.

The only way to get to the same side of the chamber as Gareth was to walk across a ledge against a nearby wall which connected to the exit. But the ledge was crumbling, and rocks from the ceiling continued to pour down. The chances of them making it over without getting bludgeoned or falling to their death was minimal.

"Fiona, I'm going to need some help to stabilise this place," Miri said. She reached into her pack, yanking out a golden ring with a large faceted onyx that glowed when she slid it onto her finger. Fiona, seeming to understand her obscure request, tugged a jewelled silver comb from her pocket and raised it triumphantly into the air.

Just as Riven was about to point out that they had more important things to do than play with their stolen artefacts, Miri whispered something, and the items that she and Fiona had plucked from their bags pulsed with light.

The shaking cave stilled, and the sudden silence was only broken by the scrapes of settling rocks and dirt.

"What just happened?" Riven asked, worried he was seeing things. This whole situation had gotten so out of hand.

"We must go across one at a time because I doubt that

ledge will hold all four of us at once," Miri said, ploughing through his confusion with a call to action.

"Willis is the most injured; he should go first," Riven suggested.

Miri and Fiona nodded in agreement.

As a group, they helped Willis onto the narrow walkway but due to his uncooperative ankle, he could only crawl. He slipped a few times, and the rim of the ledge crumbled away as he moved along. Finally, he managed to get to the other side, then collapsed onto the ground, breathing heavily.

Gareth glanced down at him, then back over his shoulder towards the exit. He did nothing to help the young man get to his feet, but instead backed away slowly, one step at a time.

"Fiona, you're next," Miri urged. "Will you need help?"

"No, I will be fine." Fiona lowered her glowing artefact. The light spluttered and she shared a wary look with Miri as debris began falling again.

"Go, we don't have much time." Miri nudged her gently. She glanced down at the ring on her finger, and Riven noted that the glow had dimmed slightly and that there was now a small crack at the edge of the stone.

"We'll be right behind you," Riven promised, sensing the urgency even if he was not quite sure what was behind it.

Fiona remained upright as she traversed the ridge, keeping her arms outstretched to maintain her balance. She got around half way across before their makeshift bridge collapsed.

Everything seemed to move in slow motion as everyone watched in horror.

Fiona screamed as the stone crumbled beneath her feet.

Her arms flailed, and she looked around wildly, hands and fingers clawing, desperate to find something to slow her fall.

Instinctively, Riven reached out. His eyes met Fiona's as her hand wrapped around his bracer. She was still struggling for footing and Riven slid as close to the ledge as he could without being pulled in by Fiona's thrashing limbs. His muscles strained as he battled to hold her. He was about to adjust his position when the bracer started slipping from his forearm.

"Mother!" Willis cried, his eyes widening with terror as he watched his mother sliding. He turned and gripped Gareth's shirt. "Help her!"

Riven felt for the boy's desperate plea; he was not sure what Gareth could have done to assist considering their distance, but Willis seemed to expect action of some sort.

"It's too late!" Gareth took hold of Willis' hands and pulled him back.

With a grunt, Riven did his best to readjust the angle of his arm to keep his bracer in place. However, with the exertion and stress, beading sweat caused the strap to loosen and it slipped off.

Fiona let out a heart-wrenching scream as she fell back into the abyss, still clutching Riven's bracer.

"No!" Miri howled. Riven whirled around to face her and saw the light from the amulet she was clutching flicker. As if on cue, the rocks from above began to fall again, but with a much greater ferocity. Riven grabbed his shield to deflect the new wave of debris and made his way over to Miri to help protect her.

"We'll have to find another way out," she yelled, eyes glimmering with determination as she grabbed him by the hand and pulled him along with her.

"Is that even possible?" Riven asked as they sprinted

back through the chamber. By now, most of the tables and shelves were destroyed, crushed beneath boulders and debris. They were even able to duck under some of it and use it as shelter. There was little point in using his shield now as it was a dented mess, so he ditched it, relying solely on the remaining bracer on his left arm.

Miri led Riven to the vault. The walls and ceiling were cracked all over, but it remained steady, as if some mystical force was holding everything in place. Riven spared a moment to look at the object on the podium; the cause of all their woes. It was nothing more than a cuff made from copper wire, with a red cabochon stone in the middle. If it were not for the faint pulse of ruby light emanating from it, he would have thought it a mundane item. A strange beckoning tugged at his muscles as he ventured toward it, urging him forward.

"Help me look for symbols on the wall." Miri's voice broke his reverie.

"Right, what exactly am I looking for?" He forced his eyes away from the cuff and turned his attention to the walls.

"Any symbol you can find. Once I see it, I will know."

Riven obliged her request, however vague, and scoured the walls for any type of symbols or etching in the stone. The walls had been perfectly smooth before they had cracked, so Riven searched with optimism. He and Miri ran around the room, quickly scanning every surface. The chamber outside was nearly collapsed and the faults in this room kept growing. It would give way at any moment.

After what felt an eternity Riven spotted some of the curling, stylised script on the wall. "I found something!"

Miri was at his side in a flash. She leaned past to look at

the etchings and then let out an excited cry. "Blazing! We are getting out of here."

There was an odd break in this part of the wall that ran vertically from the ground to ceiling in almost a perfectly straight line. Miri threw her backpack down and dove into its contents. She spoke while rifling through her belongings. "I was wrong before. This is not a vault, it's a prison."

"For who? There is no one here." He glanced back at the cuff on the pedestal. Did it just glow brighter?

"Not who, *what*. That thing up there is a Shadow. We set off a trap. But there should be another way out. A service tunnel to check on the prisoner," she explained while digging through her pack.

Riven wanted to shake her shoulders, to make her focus on getting out instead of searching for whatever it was she was she was trying to find. "Prisoner? What prisoner? Miri, it is a bracelet, what could it possibly..." His voice trailed off as he realised, he had been walking closer to it, lured in by it once more.

"Blazing! I found it." Her voice broke through whatever was pulling at Riven.

"Huh? What did you find?" He looked at her, expecting to see her holding some kind of excavation tool, though he did not believe that would help them in such a short space of time.

Instead, she plucked out another ring. She placed the delicately twisted platinum and diamond piece onto her finger beside the now fully cracked onyx. It began to glow brightly at first but then the light spluttered out. She seemed confused as she shook her hand and gritted her teeth. "Darkness! This should be working. Argh ... stupid thing!" Miri smacked her hand, and the ring, against the wall in frustration.

"What should be working? It's just a ring!" Riven was bewildered, his head was spinning.

"I don't have time to explain. We just need to pull this door apart. It was not designed to be opened from this side but with enough force we should be able to get it open long enough to slip through." She hissed all sorts of things at the ring, to no avail, before slumping against the wall. As if to make things even worse the ceiling inside the vault was starting to collapse. "It should have plenty of Aedris left, I made sure of it."

Riven had no idea what 'Aedris' was, but he could understand the part about the door. "Let me try."

Before she could continue, Riven drew the sword from his scabbard and wedged the blade into the gap in the wall. Using it as leverage, he managed to ease it open enough for one person to fit through, when suddenly, the blade snapped. Riven reacted in time, using all the strength in his arms to prevent it from closing.

Miri darted inside, barely able to squeeze past him.

"Okay I'm in." She beckoned him from the other side and clutched at the pendant around her neck. "Your turn, I'll hold it!"

Riven doubted Miri was strong enough to hold this amount of weight. His own muscles shook under the strain. He wanted to use the last of his strength to say something, anything, but he could barely breathe.

Miri screamed when, from above, Riven was struck by something heavy, and everything went black.

# CHAPTER 2

# MIRI

Typically, a journey to a destination felt longer than the return trip. Miri decided that this was, categorically, not the case for her trek from the Thoracic Mountains back to civilisation. She was not sure if it was the weight of the fact that they had failed their mission, or the horrid, dull, and empty ache from the knowledge that her best childhood friend, Riven, had died to help her escape.

As they hiked out of the mountains and into familiar terrain, Miri felt disconnected from the world around her, and from herself. She relived her final moments with Riven, and she kept picturing the look on his face as that rock hit him, sealing the chamber between them. She tried so hard to find a way to get to him. Miri pulled out every item in her bag, ready to bust through the stone, but the walls rocked and rumbled and she had to run. When she finally found an exit, she had collapsed on the ground. She did not realise it was at the base of the cliff they had scaled, until Gareth and Willis stumbled across her.

"It's time to go," Gareth told her.

She protested, but it was a whisper from Willis that had gotten her moving. "No one could have survived that."

Advancing on their journey, it was clear Miri was not alone in losing the drive to return to Lorekeepers Tower. Willis was, understandably, devastated by his mother's death. From what Miri knew of the family, they were not close in the way she had been with her parents, before their abduction. It was more about prestige and pride for them, but it clearly left the young man feeling directionless.

"Can you two quit dragging your damn feet!" Gareth snapped, glaring at Miri and Willis over his shoulder.

He had given them a couple of days to "mope about" but since then, he had shown little patience for their losses. When he was not barking orders at them, he was grumbling about "useless novices" and "know-nothing upstarts." Once, Miri suggested finding somewhere to purchase mounts, and Gareth had balked. He reasoned that they needed to get back to Eldergate, and he was not wasting any more of the Lorekeepers' precious coin when they had six perfectly good legs between them.

"I wouldn't have to drag my feet if they were off the ground in a set of stirrups," Miri hissed behind Gareth's back. Miri wrapped her hand around the stone pendant dangling from her neck, the copper wire warm from resting on her skin. Oh, she was so tempted to channel some Aedris through the charm. Just enough to heat the back of Gareth's robes. Make him sweat a little. See how he liked traipsing through the wild while feeling discomfort.

As Gareth continued ahead, Willis kept pace with Miri.

The silence between them was disconcerting. Miri had found it difficult to find the right words and eventually chose to say, "I'm sorry about your mum. I should have done more to save her."

"*You* did everything you could." Willis scowled at Gareth's back. "I saw you restrain the rocks with that relic; it was amazing. I wish I could channel that kind of power. Maybe then *I* could have saved her."

"Keep up with your training and you will be just as able as me, maybe more so," Miri said, because talking about learning new skills was far easier than delving into their losses.

Willis scratched his cheek. "I doubt it. I don't even understand how it all works. I mean, how is there even magic inside the relics?"

"Wait, what was your mother teaching you?" Miri asked, shocked that Willis did not know the basics.

"She never taught me about controlling a rockslide, that is for sure. The council kept her busy with Nexus Point research. She drilled in me that the birthplace of the Shadows is the most fundamental part of our history."

Miri smiled at him and playfully bumped him with her elbow. "So, she did teach you something."

"Not about the interesting stuff. I know that Aedris is a mystical force that allows a wielder to control the elements, or create illusions, or do other amazing things, but I have no practical experience with it," Willis said. "Mum said that splitting my apprenticeship between her and Gareth would help fix that, but Gareth is always too busy talking about himself and telling me to fetch this, and do that. Nothing about training. I'm just his errand boy."

"I get it. Gareth's favourite topic really is himself. I think he would implode if he didn't stroke his own ego at least once an hour," Miri said. "Could you imagine the mess?"

Willis quickly disguised the guffaw he let out behind a

cough when Gareth whipped around and narrowed his eyes at them.

"If you have time to whoop it up, you are not walking fast enough! I am twice your damn age and I am ahead of you!"

As Gareth refocused his attention on the path forward, Miri and Willis shared humour with a smirk. Gareth had just proven their point spectacularly. Miri walked closer to Willis and whispered, "Since we have some time now, maybe I can help you with some basics."

Willis nodded. "I'd love that."

Miri removed her necklace and handed it to Willis. "Hold onto this and concentrate."

Willis held the pendant in his palm, his face screwing up as he focused on it.

"Do you feel the warmth?"

"I do."

"That is the Aedris stored within; it represents the amount of magic available. Now look closer; do you sense anything else?"

Willis focused his attention back on the necklace, then after a few moments he responded. "Yes! There's a hum or something, almost like a musical beat."

"Right! Spells stored in relics have a unique pattern, their own signature that defines its abilities. Now, reach out with your senses even further. This time, I want to see if you can increase the sound of the beat."

Willis swallowed and took a deep breath. The gem began to glow.

"Okay, now hold one of your hands out and direct the pattern toward the centre of your palm."

The intensity in Willis' expression was palpable. Then, a thumb-sized flame came to life in his hand.

"I'm doing it!" The fire grew larger and larger, covering his entire palm and edging closer to his sleeve.

"Uh…" Miri snatched the relic from his other hand to break the connection. The magic dissipated, extinguishing the flame. "Well done. You do have to be careful when you are playing around with spell stored inside a relic; it can easily get out of control."

They spent the next few hours practicing control until Willis was conjuring a controlled flame instead of growing unruly fireballs.

"Haven't we passed this tree already?" Gareth's voice interrupted their travel. He walked over to an ancient oak. It towered above them and had several lower branches that twisted back towards the ground, as if the tree regretted growing so tall.

After staring at the tree, Gareth rounded on Miri. "Why weren't you looking at the map?"

"You yelled at me this morning for trying to pull the damned thing out!"

"I did no such thing."

For the first time since leaving the Thoracic Mountains, Miri's grief morphed into rage and she retaliated. "I am no fool, Miri! I know my way around these woods. I do not need your blasted map," Miri whined in an exaggerated mimicry of Gareth's pompous air and dialect.

Gareth raised his hand and pointed at Miri. "When we get back to Eldergate, girl, I swear—"

"Here! I have the map." Willis stepped closer, waving a rolled-up piece of parchment between them, cutting off the start of what was undoubtedly a disgruntled rant from Gareth.

Miri took the map from Willis, and ventured over to one of the lower, twisted branches of the tree. Gently, Miri unrolled the delicate paper, stretching it across the rough bark. From the purse at her hip, she extracted two gold coins, placing them at either side of the map to hold it in place.

"Do you even know how to read that thing?"

Ignoring Gareth's snide comment, Miri looked down at the map. Given they were still at the edge of the forest, and had been walking east from the mountain pass, she had a general idea of their present location. She traced her finger over the map, and noted they were quite far from the highway that would give them a clearer trek back to Eldergate. However, the actual distance was unclear. Miri took in the details of this oak tree and shucked off her bag.

Wilis frowned as he watched her. "What are you doing?"

"Getting our bearings, for where we go next," Miri told him matter-of-factly. She jumped onto a taller branch and began climbing the tree for a better vantage point.

It took several minutes to reach higher elevation, to see past the other trees, but when she did, Miri was pleased with the view.

Just as Miri expected, much forest lied between them and the main highway. They had passed the plains at the foothills of the mountains, and off to their right was the winding blue sheen of the Lower Leize River. Miri cupped her palm over her eyes to protect them from glare before she spied rooftops peppered amongst the trees along the riverside.

"There's a town over there! About half a day's walk to the east," Miri hollered to her companions. She shimmied down the trunk.

As Miri landed in a pile of fallen leaves, she saw Willis

was hovering over the map. He inquired, "Is the town you saw by the water?"

Miri nodded.

"Says here it's ... Victor's Rest. What is the meaning if there's a little spiral shown above the town?"

"A spiral?" Gareth shoved Willis out of the way and looked down at what the younger man had just pointed out. "That means that the Lorekeepers have an outpost there."

Miri perked up at the sound of that. "So, we can go there, and they will provide us with transport back to Lore-keepers Tower, right?"

"Precisely," Gareth said, sounding uncharacteristically positive. "They are obliged to provide return transport to visiting archivists."

That was the first bit of good news that Miri had received since Riven agreed to accompany them on their journey. Although, she would much rather have Riven with them and need to walk the rest of the way to Eldergate than have lost him in that cave-in.

"That sounds good," Miri said, straightening up and offering, "Why don't we stop for an early lunch, and then just push through the rest of the way?"

The other two archivists agreed with her suggestion and they ate their meals while sitting on the low, twisted limbs of the ancient tree. Given how many weeks they had been on the road, the dried-out travel crackers and beef jerky was hardly appetising, but being so close to Victor's Rest gave Miri hope that they would be able to get some real food soon enough. As with the rest of their travel, there was minimal conversation over the meal, but Miri did not mind. She was far too busy thinking about what her next step would be now that she would not get the money she needed from the treasures she was hoping to find. It had been a key part of her plan to gather the resources to learn where the Lorekeepers were keeping her parents imprisoned. Recalibrating her plan was a far easier thing to stew over than the fact she lost her childhood best friend along the way.

Victor's Rest was a picturesque town. As Miri and her party approached, they walked past moss-covered stone fences and fields of wildflowers. The sound of river rapids was easy to hear from a distance away, and the homey scent of smoke from cooking fires wafted over them with each shift of the wind.

The quaint farmsteads and cottages soon gave way to more densely populated streets and a view of the river. The community was busy, even in the late afternoon. Miri knew by the number of ships, at the row of docks on the water, that the main business of this town was trading and fishing.

On their first pass through the town, Miri, Willis, and Gareth were unable to locate the Lorekeepers outpost. It did not help that most people were too busy to even notice them. Even with their distinctive black and red patterned cloaks, they remained unremarkable. In most smaller towns and cities without a guild building, the sight of a Lorekeepers member was a novelty. Whilst the majority of folk felt the Lorekeepers, and their role in society, had changed over the past few centuries with the increasing rarity of magic and relics, there was still a mysticism that clung to the striking uniform, and knowledge that they were keepers of history and magical lore.

"Did you come here to walk in circles, or are you looking for something special?"

Miri stopped and turned to face the source of the unexpected comment. She was an older woman, with a braid of greying brown hair spilling out of the hood of her brown cloak. Just as Miri was about to answer, the woman pushed herself off the barrel she was leaning against and drew the edge of her cloak back over her shoulder to reveal the black skirt and shimmering red and black bodice of the archivist uniform she was wearing beneath.

Miri exhaled, relieved to find help. "We're looking for wherever you are settled in this town."

"Oh, thank goodness, someone civilised. I cannot tell you how long we have been travelling through backwash areas." Gareth puffed out his chest and walked towards the woman. He extended his hand. "I am Senior Archivist Gareth, hailing from Eldergate. With me, I have Apprentice Archivist Willis, and ... Miriam."

"It's Miri, actually." Miri shoved her hands in her pockets to resist the urge to punch Gareth for using *that* name while refusing to use her title. "We are on our way back to Eldergate after a quest for the guild. We were hoping to please use your facilities to contact our seniors," she explained, figuring that anything they could do to get closer to their base would be well worth it. She was done playing Gareth's stupid, snobbish little games.

"My name is Jamela, Senior Archivist, and leader of the Victor's Rest Outpost. Luckily for you, our communication orb is still in working order, so you can use that. Come, follow me." She turned, the hem of her cloak fluttering as she moved. The edges of it shimmered black and Miri sensed the Aedris powering the glamour that made the fabric appear to be brown.

The trio were shown out of the marketplace, and down a street that led away from the docks. Shops selling all sorts of homewares and fabrics lined either side of the uneven cobblestones. People milled about, browsing the wares, or moving from store to store and using the area as a thoroughfare. Jamela led them down to the end of the street, to where it opened into a generous square, complete with a fountain and what appeared to be their Town Hall built from river stone. To the right of the Town Hall, Miri spied the Lorekeepers spiral logo etched upon distressed wood hanging above the modest shingle-roof cottage.

Miri had learned that most Lorekeepers outposts were found in simple, understated buildings. Initially, their humble façade created the illusion of ordinary venues. In the olden days, people were not fond of the idea that one guild had so much knowledge about magic and its nature. Over time, as the previously copious supply of relics dwindled, people cared less about the Lorekeepers, and more about whatever silly politics were happening in Lorian at the time. The only exception was Lorekeepers Tower. As the original base for the group, in the busiest city in the land, it was built within the Council Keep in Eldergate. By comparison, that outpost soared into the skyline of the city and, at night, the fires at the top could be seen for miles.

Of course, the idea that all they were doing was cataloguing relics was a pile of utter horseshit. The notion of maintaining the annals of history and storing the valuable artefacts was really a cover for an illegal underground relic trade, but they did not like that information getting out. That kind of shady dealing was why they took Miri's parents from her when she was younger and imprisoned them. Somehow, they must have drawn too much attention to themselves.

Here, the cottage was just as simple within as its exterior implied. The entry room was a quaint space with four bookshelves on one wall, and two well-worn, overstuffed velvet couches draped with hand-knitted throws. It was a far cry from the stone halls and vaulted ceilings Miri knew in Eldergate. Having been to half a dozen outposts, she knew they still held many secrets despite their mundane appearances.

"Please lock the front door, Willis," Jamela requested, as it shut behind them. Willis complied, and the group were led to one of the bookcases.

It was pristine, even with books that were likely as old as the cottage itself. Delicate and brittle with age, their spines had never been cracked. Jamela reached up to the high, fifth shelf, and tugged on the top of a leatherbound tome, its spine stamped with "The Use of Acid for Wart Removal." As the book moved, there was a high pitched scraping followed by a definitive click. The side of the bookshelf, where it met the corner wall, slid back to reveal a dark passage.

Stepping into the secret tunnel caused lights to flare to life in wall sconces that led down, and around, a spiral staircase. The space below reeked of damp stone and earth, and Miri knew they were going a fair distance underground as they descended the twisting, and seemingly never-ending, steps.

Finally, the group emerged into a large stone room, lit by similar magically powered sconces. The use of Aedris-based lighting was a luxury, and unheard of anywhere other than the dens of the Lorekeepers. Still, after her years studying, Miri could not deny the sense of comfort the familiarity brought.

"Our orb is through the door to the right. You are free to use it at your leisure, or to get some food and take a rest before you reach out to Eldergate," Jamela offered.

With a gratuitous bow, that was as fake as it was repulsive, Gareth said, "I appreciate the offer, but we have been fluffing about long enough. We need to report immediately."

"We will take a break first," Miri said, shaking her head. "We haven't had proper food or a comfortable place to sit in weeks."

For a moment, Gareth looked like he would argue. Then, he just huffed, "Very well. Where is the lavatory?"

Jamela gestured down the corridor. "Fourth door on the right." Gareth unceremoniously dumped his pack on Miri's toes. She swore under her breath, but he was already striding towards the door.

Jamela said, "You two can come with me. I will get you something to eat and drink." She leaned over, picking up Gareth's pack and giving Miri a wry smile. "He seems ... cheerful."

"That's an overstatement," Willis grumbled.

"I hope you don't think all Archivists of the First Order are as stuffy as that," Jamela said, an apologetic tilt to her head.

"Oh, we know Gareth's special," Miri promised.

Miri and Willis followed the woman out of the corridor to a dining room with plush furniture. After a few minutes of comfortable waiting, Jamela returned with steaming bowls of warm beef and rosemary stew for them, along with a basket of fresh bread, and a pitcher of cool water.

As Willis and Miri consumed the welcomed meal, Jamela explained that she was amongst a small group of five archivists at this outpost. The reason for the glamour on her cloak earlier, she shared, was that the townsfolk had come to resent the Lorekeepers. As a fishing and river port village, servicing the local farms, there were very few people who valued the archiving and recordkeeping role which the Lorekeepers provided. Jamela described how, as the town grew, the real estate of their headquarters also became increasingly more coveted. There were plenty of companies and individuals who thought that an organisation of more utility should be located beside the Town Hall.

Growing up, Miri thought the same thing about the Lorekeepers; that they were simply historians. After all, she had watched her parents live their lives as the only Lorekeepers in town. It never made sense to Miri that there was an outpost in Chafton. It was too small, and unimportant. It was not until their home, and the ones around it, were burned to the ground and her parents were dragged out of town by multiple black-cloaked figures, that Miri learned their truth.

Searching for her parents, Miri had uncovered the facts about the Lorekeepers and how they had peddled Aedris-infused relics in illegal commerce. At least, Miri knew they were perceived to have been involved in this kind of smuggling. Miri had learned her parents were marked in the Lorekeepers' books for "Incarceration," and she was determined to save them. She had spent years going on quests and helping the Lorekeepers with their dealings to get information from the inside, and to find more about where they were keeping her parents so she could free them. This last journey to Thymear Temple was supposed to earn her enough money to pay off an important bribe to get her that information. For a while Miri felt she was getting close, but recent events were a setback.

Jamela was smart and, Miri assumed, had been with the guild long enough to know not to question the pair. Not that Miri or Willis would have provided information. Competition amongst archivists, to find valuable artefacts, was high. No one asked for information, and no one volunteered it. Instead, Miri and Willis continued to enjoy their delicious dinner while they spoke about the town and its economy. Miri realised that Gareth had been absent for some time, but she was unconcerned, and more grateful to have a break from him.

Just as Miri was biting into a particularly tender piece of beef, the kitchen door opened and there stood Gareth at the threshold, looking more smug than usual.

"Girl, they want to speak with you," he spat, eyes glinting with amusement.

The warmth of the stew that had been sitting so comfortingly in Miri's stomach chilled. She did not bother addressing the disrespect of calling her *girl*. "What have you done?"

"You did not contact them immediately, as per the regulations for debriefing. So, I did." Gareth's superior attitude was on full display.

Miri wanted to punch his stupid face.

He laughed. Miri should have been surprised, but felt contempt because Gareth, the bastard, actually laughed. "You better get in there. They are already furious with you."

Pushing past him, Miri marched out of the room and down the corridor. As she made her way to the door Jamela had indicated earlier, her mind reeled. She could only imagine Gareth had given their superiors a rundown of the severe blunders of the mission and pinned every single problem on her. She stood outside before making entrance, trying to decide the best approach, but it was impossible to predict how the leader of the Lorekeepers would react to such devastating failure.

There was no point in delaying the inevitable. Miri held

her breath and, gathering her courage, pushed open the door to the chamber. Inside, at the centre of the space, rested a large, translucent, quartz orb, sitting atop a carved stone pedestal. Not fully crystal-clear, the sphere was filled with the wavering, light-projected face of Head Archivist Nina, one of Gareth's closest conspirators.

Miri resisted the urge to groan at the visage of the wizened woman. During the early years of Miri's training, Nina, Gareth, and the other senior archivists had delighted in making Miri's work harder for her, trying to gauge her skills against that of her uniquely talented parents. It had been Nina who slipped up one day, saying that she hoped Miri would not be foolish enough to get captured like her parents. At that point, Miri believed her parents were dead, but those words revealed the depth of corruption within the ranks of the Lorekeepers. Not only was Miri faced with the heart-shattering discovery that her parents were still alive, but they were being punished for some sort of transgression.

"Your Grace," Miri said, bowing her head. As much as she hated Nina, there were certain social expectations within the Lorekeepers she must follow. *For now, at least.* "Apologies for the delay. Senior Archivist Gareth said you wish to speak to me?"

"Yes, child," Nina said, her piercing blue eyes narrowing, her image wavering in the crystal light.

Miri bit the inside of her cheek. She hated how condescending the older archivists could be. She was nowhere as old as them at twenty-three, but she was no damn child.

"Senior Archivist Gareth has explained the situation in which you and your party found yourselves. I understand not only did you not retrieve any relics, but Senior

Archivist Fiona perished in your failed expedition and the entire temple was lost to a cave in?"

*Oh, so now it's 'Miri's expedition' because it failed? How convenient,* Miri thought. She wanted to inform the head archivist that they also lost the life of a kind and caring mercenary, but that would only make matters worse.

The stolen pendant hidden against Miri's chest hummed with power. She wondered if it would be valuable enough to save her hide. Then again, bringing it up now before she knew the penalty might make it worth less if she had to bargain, or make amends. Miri was aware of how these things operated. The Lorekeepers functioned on magic, money, and knowledge. She had two of those things. She was still valuable to them.

"I am also of the understanding that you squandered the funds allotted to your expedition. Including the emergency fund given to Senior Archivist Gareth—"

Miri's eyes widened. Gareth had not said anything about having extra funds. If he had, they could have used them to pay for transport days ago. Then again, if he had not mentioned it, Miri was willing to bet there was a reason. Had he squandered it? Or was there something else going on? She was about to say Gareth had not told her about the extra money, but the head archivist continued, unperturbed by Miri's wide eyes and open mouth.

"The Lorekeepers have little time for people who blatantly waste knowledge and funds. Not to mention the fact that your actions destroyed an entire trove. Therefore, the cost of the expedition must be either recouped or struck off. Given that Willis lost his mother, we are willing to negate his part of the debt. Gareth is high ranking, and we cannot afford to lose his political influence in Eldergate. That leaves you ..."

Rage surged in Miri as she realised how much of a scheming rat Gareth was. He had lived a cushy life in Eldergate ever since he was a child. She should not have been so taken aback by the fact that Gareth, a sycophant, managed to worm his way into a pardon through privilege.

Miri did not have enough value to the organisation to plead a case for striking off a debt. As for the money, she had gathered enough artefacts in her pack to help with a bribe, but that would not come close to cover repaying an entire temple's worth of value.

"I ... I cannot pay," Miri said.

"Then, given this expedition was such a failure, and you clearly are incapable of interpreting the runes well enough to have prevented the destruction of a priceless trove ... we have no choice but to demote you."

Shock rippled through Miri in a wave of nausea. "Demote me? I have worked tirelessly in Eldergate for years!" If she lost the position, no matter how hard she had fought to attain it, she would lose the influence needed to find her parents.

"Please do not act so surprised. You are just lucky we are not imposing a higher penalty," Head Archivist Nina continued.

*A higher penalty?*

Suddenly, Miri was fourteen again. In her mind's eye she relived the experience of watching her house burn down. The smoke was thick and noxious, making her eyes burn and her lungs seize as she watched her home being destroyed. At the time, she thought her parents died in that fire.

Years later when she joined the Lorekeepers, after her seventeenth birthday, she learned the truth. They were not dead; they had been taken to the capital to serve time for betraying the Lorekeepers (in some way).

"You are to return to that backwash hometown you came from. Reopen the Chafton branch of our organisation and await further orders. If we hear that you are making any kind of trouble, or taking advantage of our mercy, we will make you wish that you had died in that collapse," Nina sneered.

Miri chewed the inside of her cheek. She had a feeling "further orders" would never come. Still, it would give her time to come up with a new plan. They could not keep an eye on her forever.

As much as Miri wanted to swear at Nina, she knew that would not help. Not now. She had to play this right and pretend to be suitably compliant. So, she offered a low bow and, through gritted teeth, muttered, "Thank you for your lenience, Head Archivist Nina."

"You'd do well to remember this kindness, girl," Nina said, voice sharp as a dagger. "Dismissed."

*Oh, I will remember it*, Miri thought to herself as she turned and walked out. She let the door slam. *And I will be sure you remember it, too.*

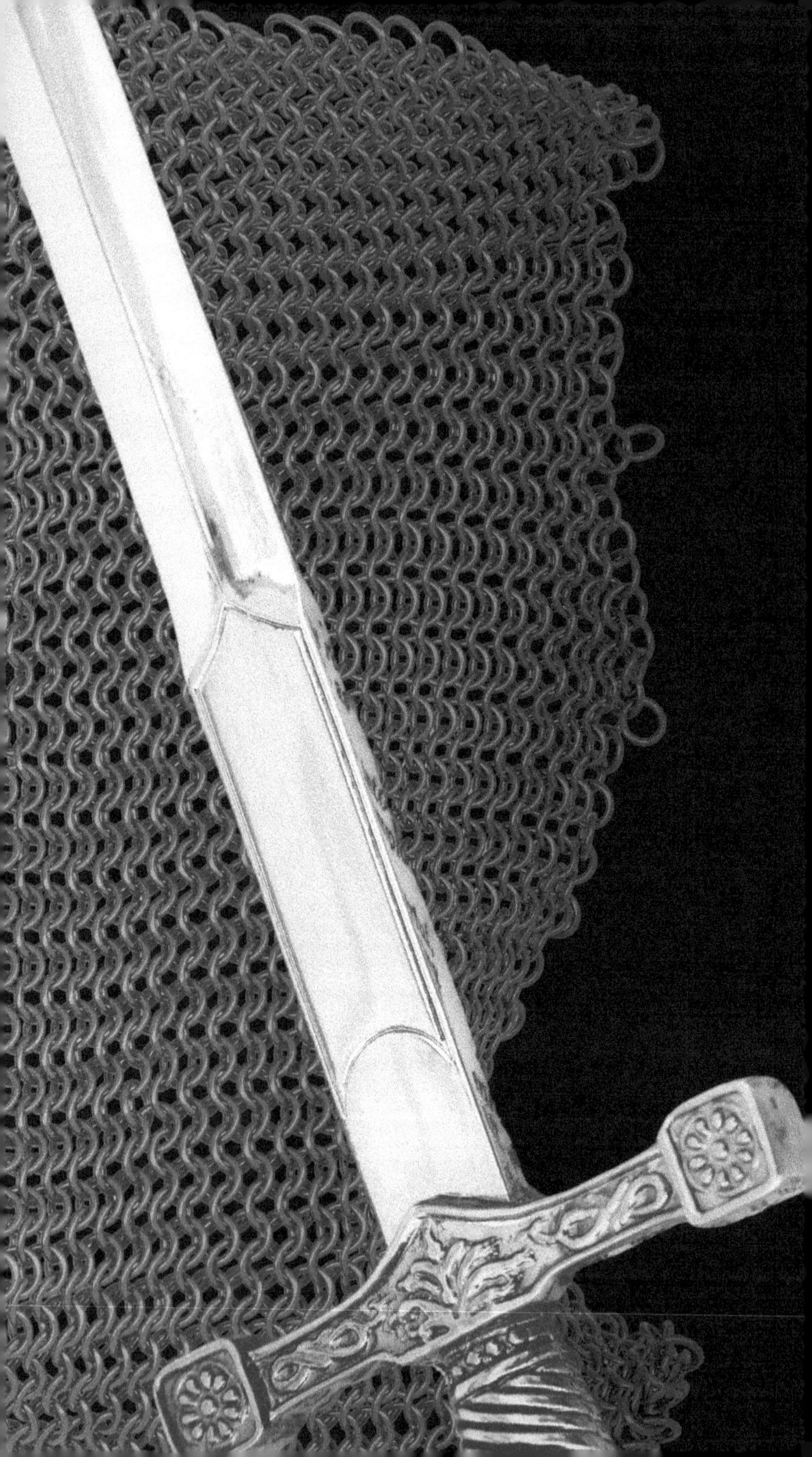

# CHAPTER 3

# RIVEN

Unexpected agony ripped through Riven's side as he made his way along the trail to the Forbidden Falls. Miri was pulling him along, her smooth hand in his. It seemed strange that his ribs hurt just from walking but perhaps it was something else, something he had forgotten?

Miri's voice interrupted Riven's thought process. "What are you thinking about?" The bright light of the day filtered around her face, dancing and shimmering against the waterfall behind her. Miri's grin was just as he remembered.

*Remembered?*

*Why was he remembering it? She was right—*

"Ummm, I was thinking how crazy it is that we are here," Riven said aloud. Another sharp pain pulsed in his head now. He rubbed his forehead to try and alleviate it. When his hand came away there was blood on his fingers.

*What? How?*

"Don't be silly." Miri moved closer. He tried to focus on her face, then on the hand that held his. Something was wrong, everything was out of focus, and now her voice sounded miles away.

"You just need to wake up." She laughed, as if it was something normal to say in that moment.

"Wake up? What do you mean?" Suddenly, Riven felt aches all over and throbbing pains, as if his entire body was on fire. As if he had stepped out of an ice bath and into an inferno.

"You need to wake up!" Miri yelled the last part; now her voice was not just muffled, it was masculine.

"Huh? I need to—" he began but the pain was too much, and he collapsed to the ground. The crashing sounds of the waterfall faded.

*"Wake up .... wake up ...."*

Riven's eyes shot open. He was suffering terribly, lying on his back, pinned to the ground by piles of rocks. His legs were buried beneath the stones, and his right hand was wedged in a gap between boulders. He tried to wiggle his fingers and toes, but he could not feel them at all.

Memories flooded his mind.

*The temple?*

*The artefact?*

*Miri!*

*"Ah, Riven! Finally, you are awake."* A voice spoke to him. It was a deep baritone, soothing yet commanding. Riven was unable to see who produced this voice as he let his gaze wander through the chamber's rubble. Riven marvelled at his luck though, as the rocks had just happened to drop from the ceiling, landing in a dome shape around him, rather than falling and crushing him.

"Who are you?" The whispered words cracked as they left his parched lips and throat. "Where are you?"

*"Over here, Riven."* The voice was much clearer than before, as if its owner were beside him.

Riven twisted his head, wincing at the pain, as he tried again to spot the man who spoke. It was then he realised there was a subtle glow emanating from an area in this underground tomb. A faint crimson light.

Riven squinted. "I don't see you." This pocket where he found himself held no room for another person.

*"Here. No, here. Back this way."*

Riven's eyes darted around the space, looking left and right, up, then down. The voice continued to guide him until Riven settled on a metallic glimmer. He peered into the rubble, spotting a single metal wrist cuff. At its centre was a glowing crimson gem. He recognised it from somewhere, but it took a moment for him to realise it was the very same object that was on the pedestal in the chamber, before the cave in.

*"Yes. You found me."* The luminosity of the cuff pulsed in time with the spoken syllables.

Riven's eyes shot wide, and he tried to scramble away. He cried out in agony as his limbs pulled uselessly against the rocks holding him down.

*"I would not move if I were you. Unfortunately, a lot of this area has collapsed on top of us and you were quite injured in the process. Luckily for you, I was able to form a temporary shield to protect you while your broken bones mended. You are welcome, by the way."*

It was then that Riven realised that it was not luck that formed the safe space around him, it was that *thing.*

*"I would prefer if you called me by my name. 'Thing' is not a very respectful term,"* the voice chided.

Riven ignored the rebuke. He needed answers, not a reprimand. "What is going on? Am I still dreaming?"

*"No, Riven, this most certainly is not like the pleasant dream you were having. You are very much trapped underground, and that pain is real. I am Zyndraxis, Lord of Thymear, Grand Vizier to the Archmage Lorian, Keeper of the Hold."*

Riven's forehead creased. He heard the words but had no idea what they meant. "Lord? Vizier? What are you talking about? You're a piece of jewellery."

For several long moments, there was silence in the cavern, aside from the dust settling against the walls of the rock dome.

Riven doubted himself when there was no answer. *Maybe I am hallucinating.* Riven considered that perhaps his injuries were both mental and physical. *Clearly my mind is shot if I am talking to a decorative piece.*

Suddenly, the space felt ten degrees colder. As if a sense of frigid ire filtered through the room, making Riven's breath fog in front of his face.

*"I am more than just an attractive accessory!"* Zyndraxis yelled, the sound piercing the tense quiet.

Riven winced at how the voice reverberated in his mind, exacerbating his splitting headache. *Oh great, it is back, and twice as loud, too*, he thought. Then, he could swear a sigh trembled from that source. Only, it felt like he was hearing it in his mind more so than through his ears.

*"Tell me Riven, are we still in the Age of Betrayal?"* It inquired.

"Age? What are you talking about? How do you know my name?" Riven shot back.

*"First tell me the Age, Riven. What era are we in?"* Zyndraxis repeated his request. *"Are there any nearby Nexus points? If we are to escape our current predicament with any haste, I will need to draw on more Aedris. Also, the*

*remains of the prison are still nullifying my power somewhat.*"

"Uh ... era? Nexus? Aedris? I don't understand anything you are saying!" Riven cried, his frustration getting the better of him.

"*What kind of servant does not know their history? First there was the Age of Dawn, then the Age of Enlightenment, after that the age of Glory; and my personal favourite, the aforementioned Age of Betrayal, the one in which I was mistakenly imprisoned,*" the voice lectured.

Riven could not make sense of these words. His confusion grew as more and more questions mingled with his agony.

"*A Nexus Point is a place where Aedris, the power source of all magic, spills from the earth. Sha ...*" Zyndraxis cut himself off and paused for a moment. "*Wait. Riven, do you know what I am?*"

Riven wanted to scream. If he did not know about the rest of the rubbish the voice was blabbing on about, how was he supposed to know that? He really wished Miri was with him. She would understand exactly what was going on and how to deal with it.

"*Indeed, your mate would have made much better company. I assume she was the beautiful maiden of your dreams. It is hard to tell in the dreams of humans sometimes; it is so blurry while you sleep.*"

"Wait! How do you know about my ma—" Riven stopped and shook his head. She was not his mate. "I mean Miri. Is she here? Is she still alive? How long have I been down here?"

The memory of the panic on her face as she stared at him through the crack in the wall surged to the forefront of his mind.

*"She is fine. Well, as far as I know. After my prison was broken, I was able to warn her as the last parts of the temple fell into the sinkhole. The very one in which we find ourselves. As for how much time has passed, it is difficult, if not impossible, to tell. I have kept you in a form of stasis so your body could heal. Well, I did my best. Healing magic is not my forte."*

Having to wade through what felt like a wall of words and issues, Riven tried to pick out the most pertinent information. "You spoke to her?"

*"Unfortunately, I was unable to establish a proper connection. With all the rubble and protection spell residue in the way, I have no way of knowing what happened after her escape. I did sense her lifeforce leaving the zone, however."*

Riven sagged against the hard stone ground; his efforts had not been in vain. At the very least, Miri survived the temple collapse. His next concern was how long he had been buried under the rocks. From his basic first aid training, he knew it took one to two months to mend bones. If it had been that long, Miri likely thought him dead.

*"Let us return to the important topic, Riven. Do you know what I am? Do you know why I can read and speak into your mind?"* Zyndraxis brought his attention to their present reality, which felt more like a dream than the one he had previously been enjoying.

"You are ... you're a ..." Riven trailed off, stalling for time.

Then it dawned on him. He had heard tales of them as a child, immortal creatures that possessed and enslaved.

"A Shadow ..."

*"We prefer 'Shade'"* It tutted. *"Shadow is a pathetic, shallow human interpretation of what we are."*

Riven thought to himself, *"Shade? But weren't they all destroyed during the Obsidian War?"*

*"Ah, so that is what your kind named it. As far as I was aware your people started it, and I suppose we lost considering you barely know what I am. Or anything else for that matter. Personally, I never liked the idea of war. I was perfectly happy enjoying the world the way it was."* Zyndraxis spoke as if it was an event from only a day ago, but as far as Riven knew, the war had long since passed. There were still remnants from their kind in the form of relics, like the ones Miri and her companions had been seeking.

*"So, the Age of Betrayal gives way to the Age of what? Idiocy? Boredom? Mediocrity?"* A derisive laugh bounced around the ache in Riven's mind. *"Your memories are so bland! Working on a farm and training to fight dummies is hardly exciting. Miri is probably the most interesting thing in your past."*

"Stop that!" Riven spluttered. By this point Riven was aware he could just talk inside his own head, but he still felt more comfortable voicing his words.

*"My deepest apologies, I would very much like to meet your Miri, she seems very ...."* Zyndraxis did not finish the sentence with words, but instead emotions washed through Riven. Longing? Desire? *"When we get out of here, of course."*

"I'm not so sure about that, Shadow." Riven snarled, protectiveness flaring in him and pushing away the distraction of the aches and pains. If this creature thought it was going to get anywhere near Miri, it had rude shock coming. "Firstly, you are a creature of evil. I would not let you out of here, let alone near Miri. Secondly, we are trapped underneath a fallen temple. And thirdly, *I* am injured and *you* are a trinket. We are stuck here."

*"Indeed, it has been too long. Your kind have forgotten so much. Riven, my friend, if I were to bind with you, we would have just enough power to escape the rubble and get to the surface,"* Zyndraxis explained.

Riven was about to tell the Shadow how ridiculous it was when his mind snagged on something it had said. "Wait, bind with you? How does that work?" Riven asked. Was it truly possible to get out of this tomb and back to— "No! I would not allow you the chance to escape. We shall die here together."

The creature was evil. He would not unleash it upon Lorien, no matter the gilded promises it whispered into his mind.

*"Die with you?"* The creature purred into his mind. *"I think not. You see, I am immortal, in time I will be free."*

Riven glanced at the rocks that were pinning down his left wrist. Maybe if he tugged it free, he could grab a stone and smash the cuff. If he could destroy the cuff, maybe he could destroy the Shadow. With a grunt, he rolled his torso in that direction and tried to shift some of the rubble, but he was too weak to move even a smaller one.

*"You are in no condition to stop me. Besides, my power is the only thing keeping you alive right now. Without me you will die,"* the Shadow explained in such a way that Riven knew it was true.

Riven hated the situation in which he had found himself. Bitterness roiled through him. "Why even ask for permission? Don't your kind just possess humans anyway?"

*"It saddens me to think how much knowledge has been lost ... a Shade cannot bind with an unwilling participant. It must be an agreement between both parties, after which our souls intertwine, forming a personal Nexus Point, from*

*which we can directly draw Aedris. Don't you see? We could access enough power to set us both free!"*

Did it really need his permission? That wasn't at all like the stories Riven had grown up hearing. "So, without me you are trapped down here, too?"

*"For a time, maybe. Now that my prison is destroyed I can either slowly break my own way free or wait for another to come along, one who does not reject my gifts. Perhaps if it has not been too long, I could even visit Miri when I am free. She will need another male to take your place ..."*

Riven was furious. This creature thought itself worthy of her attention? *Preposterous!*

Riven toiled in his mind to find a way out of his predicament. Given what he had seen so far, he did not doubt the Shade's ability. The fact that it was able to stop several hundred tonnes of rocks from crushing them would have taken a significant amount of power, and keeping him alive probably was not a small task either.

Riven needed time to think, though. He knew that Zyndraxis had an unnatural interest in Miri and despite his distaste for it, he needed a way to mask his thoughts. He focused on bringing an image of her to the forefront of his mind. It was a memory from their time at the waterfall. He remembered thinking how crazy it was that she had managed to convince him to break one of the oldest rules in their town, to go there. She was adventurous, even after slipping on the rocks she persevered, climbing to the top of the falls. He remembered the breathtaking view from that height. The way the light from the sun slowly fell into the horizon as dusk approached, silhouetting Miri in a golden aura. It had made her appear ethereal. Otherworldly. His heart hammered at the thought of her. Of her smile, her laugh.

Riven thought of being able to see her one last time …

"Okay," Riven blurted "I'll do it, but you have to promise that I will remain in control."

"*Of course, my friend. I promise to respect your need for control,*" Zyndraxis replied smoothly.

"Wait, that's not what—"

"*Normally this ritual is performed by trained initiates, but we will have to make do with what I remember. First, you will need to empty your mind. That should not be too hard. Then, you will open your soul to me,*" Zyndraxis began, rattling off directions the way one might recite a simple recipe for potato soup.

"Hold on. If you don't know how to do it, perhaps we should stop."

"*I recall enough.*" If Zyndraxis had a hand, Riven imagined him using it to wave away his concerns. "*Besides, if I fail, we will both perish. I am far too important to die here, so I will make sure it is done properly.*"

"That's reassuring," Riven grumbled sarcastically, then closed his eyes and tried his best to not think about anything.

As he relaxed, his pain faded and his mind settled. There was an odd, but warm, energy coiling around him, soothing him with deep, thrumming, ancient power.

"*Good, the bonding has begun. Our souls are becoming one. Focus on your breathing. Allow the Aedris to flow through you.*"

It took a great deal of restraint for Riven to keep from flinching at the mere thought of ancient, forbidden magic touching him. Then, Riven felt a gentle nudge against his body, almost like an animal edging for a pet, but in the centre of his heart. He let out a slow breath, and allowed it to enter.

*"Now say the words 'Ethos, Mias Betran.'"*

"Etos, Mion Bedrad?" Riven said, trying hard to copy a language that felt foreign on his tongue.

*"Close enough. I'm sure it's not that important."* Riven's lips parted in protest, but Zyndraxis cut him off. *"Your service is appreciated."*

Riven's breath caught in his throat, and when he opened his eyes, the entire space was filled with light. A powerful force slammed into his body. There was a scrape, and the copper cuff floated in the air, coming toward him, and latching closed around his right wrist. Then his world turned black.

Riven realised that he must have lost consciousness, because he felt himself waking again. The dim crimson glow pulsed weakly around him, but this time the source was at his wrist.

*"Oh, good you are awake. I need you fully aware for the next part. We are going to draw upon a lot of Aedris to break free and it is going to take much out of us,"* Zyndraxis explained, not waiting for Riven to fully rouse. His voice was much clearer now. It felt almost the same as Riven's voice in his own head.

One thing Riven did notice was that his body felt different. Better. Healthier than even before he was injured. "Wow, I fe—"

*"Amazing. Yes, I know. Our bonding was much stronger than I anticipated. Normally, the bondees must be closer in personality and temperament for an ideal connection. At the very least, I hoped we would be able to break through one layer of rock at a time, but I think we can do the whole thing at once."* Zyndraxis seemed giddy at the thought, the tone equivalent of what someone might say when they were cracking their knuckles in preparation for a good bar brawl.

Alarm bells flared in Riven's mind. *"Wait — is that safe?"*

*"Safe, hardly."* Zyndraxis hummed with amusement. *"Fun? Absolutely!"*

Riven's arm moved of its own accord and his palm facing the rocks above them. A surge of warmth seeped through his entire body and then settled on his hand. Then, without warning, a burst of power erupted outward.

# CHAPTER 4
# MIRI

"Wench, I require more ale!"

Miri jumped back as the burly woodsman slammed his tankard down on the rough bar and the remnants of his ale splashed out. The man let out a long, low belch and Miri nearly fainted at the stench of his breath as it wafted over her.

With a speed that made the man blink his bleary drunken eyes, Miri snatched the tankard off the bar and glared at him. "I'd say you've had more than enough to drink tonight, Borrin."

Borrin's face sagged with confusion. He was not used to being told "no." He growled and slammed his fist on the bar. He opened his mouth to yell something, but Miri held up a hand to silence him. "I can see that your ale-addled brain is processing just how loud you'll need to yell to get me to do what you want," Miri whispered, causing him to lean nearer. "Maybe you're even tempted to grab my collar and try to intimidate me."

Borrin's mouth flapped open, then shut, as he failed to find words.

"Now, here's the deal, Borrin Hartkin." Miri reached out across the bar and grabbed *him* by the collar. "I do not like being called a wench, and I *hate* when brutes like you forget their manners. So, I am going to give you one chance to turn around and walk out of here with your dignity intact before I get one of the boys to get that sweet mother of yours and have you dragged out by your big dumb ear."

Borrin's eyes widened at the mention of his mother. He inherited her impressive build, and a life as a baker had ensured she had just as much practical muscle as her son. Still, the oaf looked between Miri and the keg behind her, licking his lips hungrily.

"I said—" The large man squared his shoulders and glared at Miri "—I want—"

"And I said," Miri interrupted, not caring that he could crush her with the next slam of his fist, "Leave!"

Miri wished she was wearing the bracelet she had hidden back in her apartment, one that was spelled to increase her strength. She did not wear it to work, as she was concerned it would be seen or damaged. But right now, she regretted that decision, as a good punch in the jaw would do Borrin a world of good.

Instead, Miri concentrated on the amulet she was wearing, hidden beneath her simple cotton shirt. The warmth of the Aedris tingled against her skin, and she siphoned a sliver of magic and flicked it towards the cuff of Borrin's shirt. The worn linen fabric caught fire.

It took a couple of seconds for Borrin's drunken senses to register that something had happened. Then, Borrin gawked at his arm and let out a comical yelp. He jumped back, his arms flailing as his foot caught on the leg of a bar stool. Miri reached out and grabbed his shirt to stop him from falling. She summoned more magic to extinguish the flame. The instant Borrin was standing upright again, Miri released him. Then, he turned and fled.

"Oh no, Borrin givin' you trouble again?" The elderly owner, Jarvis, patted Miri's hand as he joined her at the bar.

"Nothing I can't handle," Miri promised. It was true, too. She had faced far worse in her travels. She untied a cleaning cloth from her belt and wiped up the spilled ale.

As much as Miri hated every moment of working in this nearly crumbling tavern, Jarvis was kind. He paid her well and did his best to keep her safe from the more brutish customers. Given his age, Jarvis was also happy to have help from anyone who was not trying to swindle him.

After returning from her mission empty handed and without her best friend, many of the townsfolk had mourned the loss of Riven. They had held a memorial ceremony for him, and Miri was touched by the attendance of farmers, shopkeepers, and Enforcers alike. Though the only person to offer Miri any practical help was Jarvis, ensuring she came to the tavern every night for food and a drink, and eventually employing her, helping her to get back on her feet. Reopening the Lorekeepers outpost in the apartment she shared with Riven as a teenager was her day job, if she could call it that when she had yet to see receive a single payment or directive from Nina. Jarvis' much needed kindness reminded her of how he had insisted on feeding her and Riven when they became orphans as teenagers. She would forever be grateful for him, so scamming Jarvis was out of the question. She resolved to keep her roguish tendencies for another time.

As Miri pushed through the swinging doors and into the kitchen to wash a small collection of tankards, she took a deep breath. It was nearing the end of her shift, and the thought of going back to her empty apartment made grief gnaw at the edges of her mind. She wished, not for the first time, that she had made a hundred small decisions in her past differently. If she had known that Riven's life would have been the cost for trying to discover the secrets of Thymear, she never would have paid it.

Gareth's life, however?

Well, Miri would trade that for a freshly baked loaf of bread.

"Traitorous pile of horse shit ..." Miri muttered under her breath as she scrubbed the tankards more violently than necessary. It was far easier to be angry about what had happened than to let herself cry over it. So, she put all her energy into getting the dishes cleaner than they had ever been and finding new and increasingly profane names to call Gareth. When all the tankards were washed and set aside to dry, Miri wiped her hands on the stained white apron tied around her waist and went back to the bar.

"I think that's the last of it for tonight, Jarvis," she said, voice louder than it needed to be so that her boss could hear her. Usually, she tried to get his attention before even bothering to talk, but this time the room was quiet enough she did not have to.

"Oh, thank you m'dear." Jarvis turned and gave her one of his crooked, gap-toothed smiles. "Now you make sure you walk home safely, you hear me? Did you want me to get Vincent to escort you?"

Looking over to where a middle-aged bard was lazily strumming on a lute, Miri suppressed a shiver. Vincent had always been polite enough to her, but the thought of being alone on the dark streets with him did not sit well.

"No thanks, I'll be fine." Miri plucked her cloak off a hook by the kitchen doors and hung her apron in its place, mentally reminding herself to bring it home with her the next day to give it a good wash. "I'll be back tomorrow."

Miri shook out her cloak and frowned. The black wool embroidered with red circles was a hallmark of the archivist uniform. Not feeling particularly loyal that night, Miri turned the cloak around so that only the black lining showed, and she fastened it around her neck. She turned and walked through the kitchen, figuring it would be easier to escape that way than to go through the busy dining room.

What had been a chilly day had turned into a down-right icy night. She tugged her cloak around herself tighter. Her teeth chattered and her breath formed puffs of frost before her face as she walked through the town. Thankfully, the trip to Miri's small apartment above the tailor's shop was short and familiar. She and Riven had grown up in Chafton. Their first homes were on the outskirts of town, where their parents lived side by side. Her parents were Lorekeepers and would walk into town with her every day to the small space above the tailor's shop, which they were using as their outpost. Riven's father hired out his labour to various farms and businesses in the area, lending a hand wherever he was needed. That left Riven's mother to care for him, and she also helped by looking after Miri, too. At least, on days when her parents could not take her to their outpost.

When Miri's childhood home went up in flames, Riven's house swiftly followed before the town could rouse enough people to form a chain, using buckets of water from the local well to extinguish the burning buildings. Riven's parents had died in that fire, and Miri thought hers had, too. Following the tragedy, the previous head archivist sent their apologies for her loss, and told the mayor that they would donate the premises of the outpost back to the town, as they did not wish to assign new archivists to maintain it.

Luckily, Miri and Riven were quite liked by the mayor. Instead of reclaiming the outpost, he had the locals help refit it as an apartment, and in their mid-teens, the two shared it for a few years. Right up until Miri received an invitation to join the Lorekeepers after her seventeenth birthday.

Returning to the apartment was always bittersweet. The walls of the old place held so many wonderful memories of the days she spent watching her parents read old texts and tinker with relics. There were also the more visceral recollections of how she and Riven had spent their time by sharing their dreams, playing dice games, and trying to make a living to keep them both fed and healthy. However, as rose-tinted as those memories were, all they did for Miri was remind her of exactly how much she had lost.

How alone she felt in the world.

It just made her want to find her parents and free them from the Lorekeepers' custody even more desperately.

Miri pulled down her hood as she reached the door of the tailor's shop. She reached her icy, trembling fingers into the pocket of her dress to retrieve her key. She opened the door then ran up the steps two at a time to warm her body faster, and used the same key to open the apartment door.

Inside, the temperature was very cool but not unbearable. Still, Miri undid the clasp on her cloak and cast it aside. She strode over to the fireplace and reached one hand into her blouse to grasp at the amulet resting against her skin. She could light the fire manually, but it wasn't worth the effort when using Aedris would barely put a dent in the reserves of her necklace. With a combination of intent and magic, sparks jumped from the fingers of her free hand and onto the logs in the hearth, setting them ablaze.

Perhaps, Miri thought, it would have been better to just jump straight under the blankets. The light only seemed to highlight just how much of a mess the small apartment was. The scrolls stretched out across her only table, and the dozen books laying open on the floor, served as timely reminders of how she found herself back in Chafton.

The temple had been far more lethally protected than Miri and her colleagues had anticipated. The Lorekeepers had invited her to study with them as her parents had been the only ones who had deciphered the southern dialect of Shadow runes. As Miri had grown up around the work of her parents, and she had access to their notebooks and ciphers, she was able to help translate the location of the Temple of Thymear from some old maps in the archives. She had picked up on the hints of several traps in the area, but there was nothing that spoke to the sheer scale of the potential destruction.

The sound of the ancient rocks crumbling and hitting the ground haunted her in her sleep, as did the look on Riven's face when that final boulder slammed against his head and the concealed door shut between them.

"Enough... that's enough," Miri chided herself before her emotions could get the better of her. She sucked in a breath, and then exhaled slowly as she released the tension in her shoulders. "Miri, get your shit together."

Instead of being lured over to the runes marking those ancient pages, she went over to the small kitchen and unwrapped some bread and cheese she had bought that morning. She sat down cross-legged on the only free floor-space beside the hearth, soaking up the warmth of the fire as she ate. When she was finished, she stripped off her work clothes. Then she used a jug of water kept by the fireplace, which was now pleasantly warm, to clean herself and wipe away the bitter smell of ale and spirits.

Even though Miri was exhausted from the workday, when she looked over at her bed, she could not bring herself to sleep yet. So, eyes gritty with fatigue, she walked over and sat at her dining table in nothing but her shift. The fact that the fire was still working hard to warm the room meant that there was enough of a chill to keep her awake as she pulled her parents' journal closer. She let her eyes fall on the familiar runes.

Her father's looping script and her mother's untidy scrawl was punctuated by Miri's own plain, but easy-to-decipher, block letters. She had spent the last few years whilst working with the Lorekeepers sifting through her parents' journal and archivist records to learn what it was they had done to anger their superiors and get them taken away. It had taken some time, as the runes they used in the south were different to the ones most archivists used. Whilst reading, Miri had come across some references to items they owned and traded that had not been catalogued, but she had not met a single archivist who did not keep a little extra for themselves. If they punished her parents for that, they would have to punish everyone.

As she did every night, Miri poured every ounce of herself into studying those pages. She could almost recite each sentence, word for word at this point, but she kept searching, hoping, that maybe tonight she would finally find the clues she had been missing all this time and be able to make a real plan to get her parents back.

Try as Miri might, she was only human. As the hours wore on, and her determination kept her upright, her fatigue fought for control. Slowly, and without her even realising it, the exhaustion started to win. The fire raged in the fireplace and gave the room a warm, humid air that addled her senses. The symbols on the page blurred into one another, but Miri's tired mind failed to notice. Instead, her eyes grew heavy, and her posture sagged until her forehead hit the table with a loud "thunk" that she would feel in the morning.

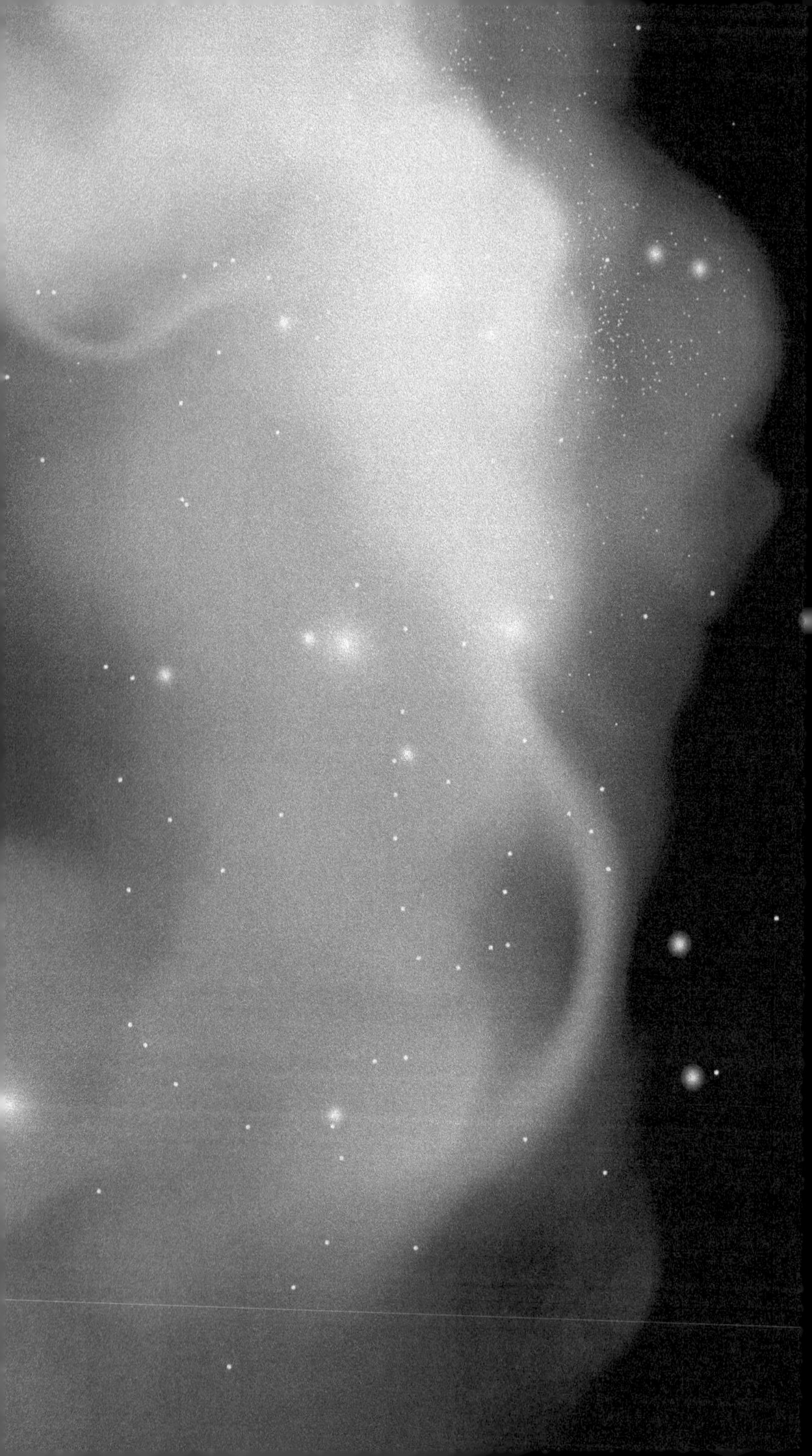

# CHAPTER 5

# ZYNDRAXIS

Zyndraxis did not have time to explain the ins and outs of using Aedris. Under normal circumstances, the one he was bonded to would have had prior training and understanding of how to work with a Shade to shape magic into spells. For Riven, it would be like teaching a toddler. Also, with their bond so new, it would require a lot more of their power reserves for him to take control of Riven. Luckily for them both, their current predicament did not call for finesse. Only raw power.

The rocks above them creaked as they shook and gave way until a small opening appeared. It would be just large enough for them to slip through, so Zyndraxis wasted no time commandeering Riven's body and forcing him to move.

The freedom of being able to use such power, and finally breaking through to the surface, was exhilarating. As soon as they had moved through the narrow tunnel the Aedris had carved through the side of the mountain and into the forest beyond, Riven collapsed to the ground. Zyndraxis understood that it was not by choice; he could sense that their reserves of Aedris were drained, and Riven's injured body was weak and shaking.

"Hey, what happened? I thought you said I would be in control!" Riven grunted as he rolled over onto his stomach and pushed himself to his feet. They might have been out of the temple, but it was cold outside. They still needed to get somewhere Riven could get food, water, and shelter.

*"Would you have preferred to have stayed down there?"*

"Well, no, but don't do that again."

*"I may have overestimated our initial power reserves. It takes extra energy for me to control your body without permission; it might be some time before we can gather that amount again, anyway,"* Zyndraxis explained.

"So, you need me to be able to access your own magic?"

*"For the most part, yes. I can use Aedris to enhance your natural strength and abilities, but for anything else it is much more efficient if you do it."*

"So, how would I—" Riven began speaking, but then seemed unsure of himself. "—actually, never mind. It's not important. We need to see where we are—ah!" Riven stopped in his tracks, the all-consuming pain returned, and he doubled over, dropping to one knee.

*"Ah yes, your body isn't fully healed, and you have been immobile for some time. We do not have enough Aedris to help you heal, so I suggest we take it slow."*

Riven did not answer right away. Instead, he inspected his clothing and armour. Zyndraxis noticed his line of attention and followed it as Riven discovered that his breastplate was destroyed. Zyndraxis' cuff was wrapped around his right wrist, and his battered bracer was on the left. The right pauldron was dangling from his shoulder and the strap was holding on by a single busted rivet.

"Well, this isn't going to work." Riven began undoing

the straps around his chest and shoulder. He dumped the damaged breastplate and pauldron, and then removed the scraps of his disintegrated shirt, leaving his bare chest exposed. Then, as if becoming aware of their surroundings for the first time, he looked around. "When did it get so cold?"

It appeared as if they were moving into the Season of Ice. Most of the leaves had fallen from the trees and although it was daylight, the chill invaded their body. Zyndraxis had nearly forgotten the physical sensations of a human body. He had been trapped, as a prisoner, in suspended animation for so long he never imagined he would feel anything again.

Sensations were different for a Shade. Because of their nature, their physical and emotional experiences were proxied through their host. The bonding process was symbiotic in nature, meaning that whatever their host felt, the Shade felt, too. In the early stages, the connection was new and fuzzy. Over time, as their bond grew, those shared perceptions would become stronger.

Also in the early stages, when taking control of the body, things like movement and magic wielding could be awkward and uncoordinated, especially if the human and Shade tried to work in tandem. That is why most Shade preferred to remain in a support role, channelling their magic through their Dyad rather than taking direct physical control.

"All right, let's keep going. I know the way." Riven began limping onward.

As he piloted their journey home, Riven kept his words and thoughts to himself. Zyndraxis inwardly congratulated him; after all, the bonding process normally gave both parties access to each other's thoughts and memories, but

Riven found a way to remain silent. Unless he had no thoughts. Zyndraxis would not have put that past him.

Zyndraxis was finally free of his jail, so he did not mind being a passenger of sorts. He had been kept underground with no light, or access to the outside world, for longer than he knew. The prison gem allowed only a fraction of his consciousness to remain aware, but even then, he still felt time passing. Without a frame of reference, there was no way to calculate how many years he had missed. Surprisingly, Riven broke his inner thoughts with a question.

"So, there is something I don't understand. I thought the Revokers destroyed all the Shadows. Why were you in prison?"

*"Revokers?"*

"Yeah, the anti-magic enforcement force. They handle the illegal usage of magic. I am — well, was — going to be a revoker."

*"Really, how's that working out for you?"*

"You didn't answer my question."

*"I was in prison because I was betrayed."*

"Betrayed? How?"

The memory began to surface; but it was too painful for Zyndraxis to relive, so he buried it.

*"You know, I did not care for war. I was happy just experiencing all the world had to offer, but the ones in power wanted to keep said power. She—"* he paused, not ready to reveal that yet. *"—They asked me to fight but I had no interest, so I went into hiding. Unfortunately, according to the Grand Syndicate, I was deemed too dangerous left free. Powerful enough to turn the tide of battle. So, they imprisoned me."*

"What happened to your bonded human? Bondee? Bonder?"

*"My consort,"* Zyndraxis confirmed. *"After Gathlyn and I were separated, he was forced to retire on a distant farm."*

"Consort?"

*"Yes, you are my consort, and I am your Shade."*

"I am *not* your consort. That is a terrible word for it. The meaning must have changed over the years."

*"Really? What does it mean now?"*

"Sexual partner," Riven stated flatly.

*"That is unfortunate. It was a perfectly good explanation for what you are. What would you prefer?"*

"I don't know but not 'consort.' I don't care what it used to mean, now it would send the wrong message."

*"Human language is so confusing. You change the meaning of things with every generation. Fine; perhaps we should brainstorm ideas on our journey."*

"Gee, that sounds riveting," Riven said.

Despite the sarcasm in Riven's tone, Zyndraxis forged on. *"What about soulmate?"*

Riven laughed. "That's just as bad. I'm not in love with you. Never will be."

Zyndraxis supposed that was fair. *"Just mate, then?"*

Stumbling over his own feet, Riven spluttered, "Absolutely not!"

*"I meant as in 'friend'."*

"And I meant when I said absolutely not," Riven retorted. From the way his muscles tightened, Zyndraxis could feel his growing frustration.

*"Fine,"* Zyndraxis conceded. *"Why don't you try suggesting something?"*

To his credit, Riven did spend time considering it. "Partner might work."

*"And give off the impression that we are equals?"* Now it was Zyndraxis' turn to laugh. *"Apologies. It was foolish of me*

*to presume you were capable of finding a suitable term. Allow me to try again. How about escort?"*

Riven replied with a flat, "No."

For the next few hours Zyndraxis continued to suggest new and inventive ways to describe what Riven was to him, only to have Riven shoot down every option.

Riven did not ask any more questions. Zyndraxis instead used the time to reminisce about his past, and then compare it to his current situation. Riven was nothing like Gathlyn. Riven was all brawn, and no brain. A simple soldier trained for one thing; to fight.

Zyndraxis reflected on when he first became properly aware of Riven's group in the cave. It was when Miri opened his vault. Even though his magical abilities were nullified by the prison enchantment, it still allowed him to observe his surroundings. When the temple started to collapse, he watched helplessly as they scurried out of his room, only to return when their exit was blocked.

Zyndraxis was bemused to see Riven desperately trying to pull open the service tunnel doors, as if mere muscle could do the job. However, despite all logical bounds, he succeeded ... and all to save her; Miri. At the time, Zyndraxis' prison blocked his ability to read Riven's mind, but his final act of heroism convinced Zyndraxis that he should save the human. If Riven had the fortitude for that, then he would certainly be useful in getting to the surface.

A minor flaw in the design of the prison meant that the spell, holding him in stasis, failed just before the vault collapsed, and he was barely able to keep them both safe under the failing structure.

In the present, Riven stumbled before bracing himself against a tree.

*"Do you know where we are going?"*

"Yes, I navigated on the way here. There are certain landmarks that show me the direction we need to go," Riven explained.

Zyndraxis was mildly impressed. He himself had never paid much attention to the topography of the land. In his time, much of it had been mapped, showing roads and paths leading in and out of the mountains.

*"You want to go home?"*

"Of course, why wouldn't I?"

*"There is no need to speak out loud. I can hear you very well inside here."*

*"I'm not used to talking inside my own head. It feels strange,"* Riven thought, his mental voice tentative but effective.

*"Trust me, once we are outside, it will look strange talking out loud. Anyway, why do you want to go home? We should venture outward. I am completely unfamiliar with this new world you have brought me to, and I wish to see it."*

"No, we need to go home. Miri might be there," Riven explained.

*"Why would she go back? I have seen your memories. Our girl is an adventurer. She would not settle for that pathetic excuse for a town. After all, she left for a reason,"* Zyndraxis reminded him.

*"I know her better than you do. Even if you can read my thoughts and see my memories, she would have at least stopped by on the way. Besides, if we are to travel beyond Chafton we will need rest, supplies, food, armour, and weapons."*

*"Riven, you have much to learn! Aedris is all of that and more,"* Zyndraxis boasted, reminiscing on the lavish lifestyle he and his consort had lived in their time.

"Really? Then why do I feel so cold, tired, and still sore from my injuries? Why hasn't Aedris taken care of that?"

*"As I explained earlier, our supply is quite low. It may take some time before I can call upon enough to do much more than summon a breeze."*

"Well, until then we will require the supplies I mentioned. We will need to make camp soon too. I can forage some berries from those bushes there and I guess you can take care of the fire."

*"I suppose that will have to do. But no armour. It interferes with my channelling."*

"No armour? How will I protect myself? I mean, us?" Riven was aghast at the suggestion. He then looked at his left shoulder, at the remains of his once pristine armour held on by the last remaining strap over his chest.

*"When our Aedris returns we will have no need of it ... although, I suppose you can keep those parts if you must,"* Zyndraxis said, exasperated, referring to Riven's pauldron and bracer, which were both dented and filthy, but still serviceable.

"What about a shield? I lost mine during the cave-in."

*"I can create a shield of magic. Besides, you have your left bracer. If you put one on your right and cover the relic, it may impact the strength and accuracy of my magic."*

Riven looked over at his right wrist, to the cuff made of copper wire and a red cabochon gem. He marvelled at the special piece linking this Shade to a human; himself. From the cuff, a trail of darkness painted a mark on Riven's wrist, like a snaking tattoo shifting ever so slightly on his skin.

"Woah, what is that?" Riven jolted as he spotted the patterns.

*"Oh, those are mementos... marks left behind every time*

*you channel my power,"* Zyndraxis explained nonchalantly. *"The more we invoke the power, the more they will spread."*

"Wait, this will cover my whole body?"

*"I am not sure why you are worried. In my time the mementos were an honour for all Shadebound,"* Zyndraxis replied, not understanding the fuss Riven was making. *"In fact, they were quite the status symbol."*

"Things have changed since then." Riven pushed the cuff farther up his arm, but it only half covered the mark.

*"I see. Well then, shall we be off?"* Zyndraxis sensed Riven's fear and distaste at mementos. He tried to search the human's thoughts, to delve deeper, but Riven was surprisingly good at evading notice. Without responding, Riven started to walk, resuming their journey home.

The next few days were spent in relative silence, with occasional outbursts from Riven. He seemed happy to share the history of his town, Chafton, and the folklore and stories around it. However, his simple upbringing did not reveal much about the wider world or their country's history. All he knew was that Shade were evil slavers that subjugated the human populace.

The perceptions of bonded pairs asserting their control and dominance over the human population were not entirely over exaggerated. Several groups of Shadebound had become complacent about their role in society and had taken things too far. However, Zyndraxis, and many of his own consorts, believed that the relationship between them should be symbiotic, and both Shade and humans would only thrive when they worked together. Not all humans could be Shadebound, and there were far fewer Shade than humans. And so, as a divide grew within the community, so too did the disparity of power and influence. A certain group of Shadebound acted more like gods than associates or consorts. It led to a war with humans and Shade taking sides. Zyndraxis was imprisoned before the dispute could be resolved, but from Riven's history lessons, it seemed the human victors drove the Shade to extinction. It was a disturbing notion for Zyndraxis, and he hoped they would find more of his kind out in the world, once Riven had gotten his fill of his lacklustre hometown.

As they made their way from the mountains, snow fluttered around them. Riven was exhausted from his recovery, and from the long trek, and he stumbled across the wild landscape. He did not seem to notice the cold, and Zyndraxis was quite pleased about that. Human bodies tended to run warmer when they were bound to a Shade, and it was a good sign that he was, at least, passively accepting the bond. It was especially lucky given his lack of clothing and supplies.

From the base of the mountains, they travelled through a thick forest, to emerge on the other side amongst fields of corn and wheat. Zyndraxis sensed relief take the edge off Riven's fatigue. The small settlement of squat brick cottages and run-down stores was surrounded by farms, and buildings were lit by simple candles or lamp lights. This town certainly had not existed in Zyndraxis' time.

*"Quaint little village you live in. I see your people no longer use our glowing crystals as lighting. It seems you have regressed to the primitive ages,"* Zyndraxis commented as they entered Chafton.

Riven ignored him and made his way over to the tavern. It was late enough at night that the warm light from inside made the windows glow, and the buzz of a busy trade spilled out onto the street. Riven marched right up to the door and pushed it open. He stumbled over the threshold, holding his arm up over his face to ward against the sudden brightness. The heady aroma of stewing meat and the smooth floral honey notes of mulled mead made his stomach growl. Many of the customers gave him wary looks or turned their backs. Zyndraxis could not blame them. Riven was dirty, dishevelled, and his clothing was tattered.

Despite their dramatic entrance, the elderly man who was standing at the bar, polishing a tankard, gave them a welcoming wave. "Hello, weary traveller! Come, rest your feet. We have hot soup and cold ale. What fancy you?"

"Jarvis!" Riven croaked, his voice raw and stilted from so long without water and vocal conversation.

The elderly man's hands froze in their repetitive work, his eyes widening. "Riven?" The disbelief in his tone was quickly replaced with relief. "Oh my, it *is* you! My boy, we thought you dead!" Jarvis made his way from around the bar and placed his hand on Riven's shoulder. He leaned in close, as if trying to take stock of him. Clearly, whatever he saw concerned him, as he guided Riven to rest on a nearby stool.

Riven eased into the seat and his travel-worn joints creaked with strain. Jarvis disappeared behind the bar and then returned with a mug of water. He offered it to Riven, who gladly accepted. He took several moments to consume the drink, letting the coolness soothe his gravelly throat.

Jarvis sat beside him and patted his back. "You look terrible, Riven. What happened? I thought you were dead!"

*"Perhaps you should not tell him the truth. I know that you are old friends, but given the history you have explained to me, he might not accept it,"* Zyndraxis advised.

"That is a story for another time. I promise to tell you

one day when I am not so tired. Do you know if my apartment is still free?" Riven inquired.

"In a fashion, my boy," Jarvis said, stroking his white, wiry beard. "Miri has taken up residence there."

"Miri?"

*"Miri?"* Zyndraxis echoed in his mind.

"Yes, she came to town a while ago and told us what happened. She said she watched you die."

"I nearly did. Is she still here? Please I need to see her." Riven turned and held the old man's shoulders, his drink left forgotten on the bar.

"Here? No, she finished her shift just before you walked in. Unfortunate timing, really."

Before Jarvis could say more, Riven leapt up from his seat, his energy renewed. They might have just missed Miri, but the fact she was working here and living in their old apartment meant he was so close to being able to see her again. It broke his heart to think of her lonely and mourning. Mumbling a goodbye to Jarvis, he rose from the bar stool and left the inn in a hurry.

Zyndraxis let out a low hum of intrigue in Riven's mind. *"Mmmm, this anticipation is enticing. I wonder what she will think, seeing us again after all this time."*

*"There is no 'us',"* Riven reminded him. *"It's just me she'll see."*

*"So, you intend to hide me from her? I think you will find our girl is much more perceptive than you predict."*

Riven's determination had him rushing through the town with a speed Zyndraxis had not witnessed. He thoroughly enjoyed the zing of energy singing through his consort's body at the thought of seeing his heart's desire again. It was not something Zyndraxis wished to interrupt.

It was evident they arrived at Miri's residence from the

way Riven's heart hammered against his chest. Zyndraxis pictured him raising his fist and banging against the door before bursting in and proclaiming his lover for her.

Instead, Riven raised his fist ...

And then froze.

*"What are you waiting for?"* Zyndraxis blurted. *"It has been months. You must burst in there and declare your undying love for her!"*

Riven lowered his hand. *"It's late, she might be asleep. I should return in the morning."* Riven was about to step back but Zyndraxis decided now was the time to act. He had been gathering a small amount of Aedris, which allowed him to move Riven's legs and arms forward, in an attempt to knock on the door. Unfortunately, Zyndraxis was not accustomed to using his consort's limbs. He ended up slamming Riven's whole body against the door instead.

"Hey stop that!"

Zyndraxis ignored him, repeating his actions. He already sensed Riven was too tired and exhausted for this. But if he waited any longer, Riven would likely pass out where they stood. If he could just try one more time ...

Zyndraxis summoned a bit more Aedris, and charged Riven into the door with such force that before the door fell in, the hinges let out a ghastly creak, and then they crashed into the apartment.

# CHAPTER 6

# MIRI

Miri woke suddenly, and with the intense conviction that something was wrong. She blinked; her bleary eyes barely able to discern objects from furniture in the light of the dying fire. She moved her hands to rub her face, when there was an ear-splitting crack, and the door to her apartment collapsed inwards, with a tumble of limbs and torn fabric flailing over the once-solid timber.

"What the—" Miri cried out as she launched off her seat and scrambled back against the wall. "Do not come closer! I am armed and dangerous!" Her hand flew past the crumpled clothes and wrapped around her pendant, ready to light the invader on fire if they dared come nearer.

The man was wearing weather-torn pants and black leather greaves, and his shirt was hanging from his waistband in tatters. His beaten steel pauldron clung to his chiselled torso with a single leather strap, and his torn and frayed brown cloak was nothing more than a useless flap barely dangling from his shoulders. He raised shaking, weather ravaged arms towards her and she held her pendant higher.

"Wait! Miri, it is me. Riven."

Miri's certainty wavered at the sound of that voice.

It was scratchy, as if he was parched, but ... she would know that voice anywhere.

"That is impossible. I saw you—" Miri stopped as the figure – no, Riven – took another stumbling step. His foot caught on the edge of a rough floorboard, and he tumbled.

Miri rushed forward to try and catch him, but even as emaciated as he was, she struggled with his weight. All she managed to do was slow his fall and stop his head from banging against the floor.

"Riven!"

Upon impact, Riven passed out. His head lolled to the side and his chest shuddered as he took a deep, gasping breath. As Miri held his arms, she felt his skin was cold as ice.

Miri took a good look at her dear friend. Riven looked unwell. When she met up with Riven to invite him on their mission, he had been tanned, healthy, and strong. Now ... his frame was lean with wasting muscle.

"Oh, Riven, what's happened to you?" Miri swallowed a lump in her throat. She shook her head, guilt running through her at the very real knowledge he would not be in this state if she had just left him to live his life.

Miri gently lowered Riven's arms back to the floor. Even if he had shrunken somewhat, she did not have the strength to lift him on her own. Instead, she got to her feet and walked over to the pantry in her kitchen. She opened it, and pulled out some small sacks of flour, sugar, and a pile of cracked pottery vases so she could reach the loose plank on the back wall. When it came free, she reached into a small hollow space, which was home to a couple of pieces of Aedris laden jewellery, including a bracelet imbued with extra strength. Growing up, she had seen her parents stash all sorts of relics in the various hidden nooks and crannies in this space, so she was glad some of the items she left behind, when moving to Eldergate, were still there.

Miri's fingers clutched at a familiar, thick silver bracelet set with a blue stone. She fastened it around her wrist and was pleased with access to a new reservoir of Aedris, now opening within her. Miri strode to Riven's side.

"Let's get you somewhere more comfortable." Miri bent over, sliding her hands under Riven and grasping his arms. With access to the relic's magic, she was easily able to drag him to the bed. Even with the Aedris now running through her, she knew that her muscles could be easily strained if she was not careful. Of course, there was enough power that she could hold his weight, but in the past, she had used this trinket often enough to know how it combined with her own body, and the limitations.

Miri hauled Riven up and onto the bed, so his top half rested on the blankets. Then, she moved down and grabbed his legs, lifting those and settling them over her covers, too. She inspected him and his shredded linen pants and single shoulder pauldron. The remainder of his exposed skin was covered in dirt and grime, but was remarkably unscathed. It was an odd contrast; his clearly damaged clothing but otherwise unharmed skin. Something about his appearance stirred her memory, but the combination of her sleepiness and her shock at seeing him took priority in her mind. She would figure the rest out later.

Miri's next goal was to clean Riven. There was no way of knowing how long he would be asleep, so she wanted to make sure he was comfortable. She returned to her kitchen area and poured some water from a bucket on the floor into a bowl, then dipped her fingers into it. Thanks to the fireplace, the water was a decent room temperature, but she channelled some of the heat from her necklace amulet to warm it faster. When it was ready, she retrieved a washcloth from where she kept her linens and moved back over to the bedside to get to work.

Growing up in close proximity to Riven, and then living with him for some of their teen years, meant that Miri was not unfamiliar with his body. When they shared the apartment, he had often gone shirtless in the Season of Fire's peak months. Looking at him now made Miri feel as though she was looking at a stranger, and she winced while running a washcloth over the muck on him. She wondered, *where have you been all these months?*

Stroking his hair, Miri's thoughts took her back to that day, to that treacherous moment when the wall closed between them. "How did you get out of there?" Miri whispered as she worked. She remembered that the prison chamber was holding up well as the temple fell, but surely not *that* well?

Miri shook her head. She would hopefully find out when Riven woke. As she wiped away the dirt, she glided across his exposed chest and towards the strap holding his remaining pauldron in place, and then she paused. His skin felt warmer than it should. Miri noticed because he had felt so cold initially. Now he was a furnace, but not in a sickly, clammy way ... he was just *hot.*

Miri undid the stiff leather strap of Riven's armour and eased it from his shoulder. She also removed his belt so it would not be uncomfortable as he slept, then took off his shoes.

"Oh, darkness!" She dry-retched at the stench coming

from his feet. It took her several minutes to gather her courage and wash his heels and toes as best she could before covering them with a blanket.

Next, Miri carefully removed Riven's ruined cloak from his shoulders. It was then that she realised where she had seen it before – at the tavern, just before she had left.

Miri had a vivid memory of the dark, dishevelled stranger stumbling into the inn, and she now severely regretted leaving. The man was her Riven. Perhaps if she had stayed longer, she would have been able to help him and he would not have passed out.

Guilt was gnawing at Miri's gut as she retrieved a fresh pot of water and a new washcloth and began scrubbing his arms. She picked up his right hand, the one he wielded his sword with. His palm was calloused against hers as she turned his arm and then—

A gasp slipped from her lips. "What in the darkness?"

Miri stared down at Riven's wrist; at the cuff wrapped tightly around it. The copper wire band and the red cabochon gem were familiar. They had haunted her dreams for months now. She remembered the first moment she had laid eyes on it after opening that chamber in the temple. She recalled the way it seemed to lure her closer, how it felt like an inviting portal that could connect her with an abyssal level of Aedris.

Miri desired to learn how the powerful relic wound up on Riven's wrist. For a moment, she considered trying to remove it. However, given his precarious state and how he had shown up on her doorstep when she believed him dead, she did not dare touch it. *What if this is keeping you alive?* Miri would not risk messing with that.

So, instead of trying to claim the relic for herself, as she had been doing for the past five or so years, Miri left it right where it was. As she rubbed the dirt and grime off his fore-arm, she saw dark, swirling lines extending five centimetres from Riven's wrist to the edge of the cuff.

"What do we have here?"

Riven was never a tattoo-loving kind of guy, but she had an idea of what these markings could be. She would need to research it, of course, but that would have to wait. She wanted to make sure Riven was clean and comfortable first. She smirked to herself as she cleaned her way up the ropey muscles of his biceps. "Well, well, well, Riven, looks like you have brought back an intriguing mystery with you."

Miri went to a hidden compartment in the floorboards and retrieved an old journal. It was an account from before the purge that contained some obscure lore that was not known to the general population. The Lorekeepers were permitted to preserve such tomes in their archives, so long as they were kept away from the public. That meant that this particular book had escaped the fate of being destroyed by the Revokers in the name of cleansing.

The leather-bound book was over a hundred years old and very delicate. In an ideal world, Miri would have donned a pair of cotton gloves to leaf through the old parchment paper, but she did not have that luxury. Instead, she took her time to open it with caution.

*Property of Ceralak*
*Consort to Mikaleous.*

She kept turning the pages, skimming the words as she went along. She knew exactly what she was looking for. She just hoped she was not imagining having seen the information in this book.

> Day four, Season of Fire
> I am so excited, today is the day of my bonding ritual. I cannot believe that Mikaleous picked me out of all the other acolytes. He is one of the oldest Shade on record. I cannot wait to learn from the thousands of years of experience he has.

> Day five, Season of Fire
> The bonding ritual went exactly as planned. I have heard stories where it fails and the acolytes are burned by the power of the bond ... but not for me. Well, not for us. We are now a Dyad; consort and Shade. Mikaleous is a little annoyed that I must write everything down. He would prefer if we practice magic, but I need to record my thoughts while they are still fresh.
> Firstly, the bonding ritual. It was held in a small chamber with two stone slabs in the centre. Mikaleous was laying with his consort Oroth on one. Oroth was near the end of his life, and if Mikaleous did not move on, he would risk dying with him. Hence him

selecting me to be his new consort. I was laying on the second slab for the transfer.

Several other acolytes of the Dawn were performing the bonding ritual. They were transferring Mikaleous' essence into his conduit, the magical ring on Oroth's finger. When the ritual finished, they moved the ring from Oroth's dying body onto mine. I spoke the words of bonding "Ethos, Mias Betran." I had practiced the pronunciation for weeks to make sure it was perfect. It would be embarrassing if I had gotten it wrong, especially in front of Mikaleous. Even more worrying, perhaps, is what might have gone wrong if I did. Who knows what might have happened.

The acolytes responded with, "Thank you for your service."

Then I felt the bonding lock in place. The depth of Mikaleous' wisdom and power became a part of me, and the vastness of it took my breath away. I was not sure that such an honour would ever be mine, but it has happened...

I am Shadebound.

Miri's stomach filled with a swarm of overactive butterflies. Her head spun as she read Cerelak's words between glances at Riven. He was still laying on the bed, eyes closed, chest rising and falling steadily as he slept. She bit her lip as she dragged her eyes over to the markings on his arm, then forged on in her search through the journal.

Finally, she came upon a diary entry that was bordered on all sides by sketches of dark, sinuous lines that looked familiar. Miri gasped. Her research about the Temple of Thymear had spoken of many great wonders, and she had hoped, but ... *don't get ahead of yourself, Miri*, she chastised herself. She needed to get out of her head and keep reading, there was no point theorising when the answer was probably on the pages before her.

Day 9, Season of Earth
I have been learning so much from Mikaleous; there is so much more to Aedris than I had learned even as an acolyte. The more we use magic the more I see the marks of power forming on my arm - they are up to my elbow now. Every time I see the memento I am reminded of how I am forever changed, altered by the powerful, wise being I now share my body with.

Miri stopped reading and sat back. The pages of the ancient book fluttered shut before her, but she had seen everything she needed to confirm exactly what the sight of that cuff and those marks on Riven's arms had made her postulate …

Riven was Shadebound.

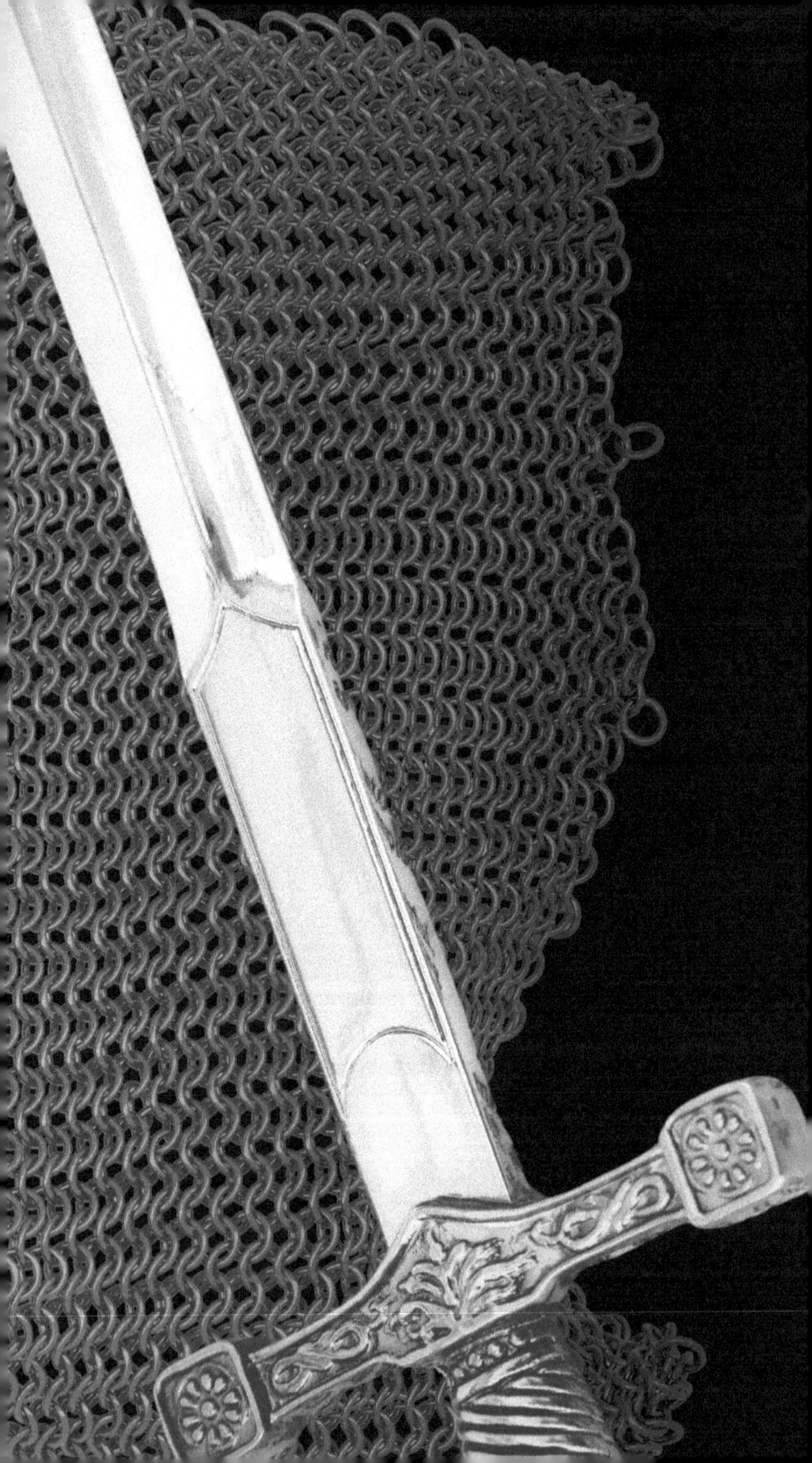

# CHAPTER 7

# RIVEN

The first thing Riven noticed as consciousness returned was the softness of the sheets around him, warm and comforting against his bare skin.

*"I think she enjoyed undressing us,"* Zyndraxis' voice broke through the haze of sleep. So, it was not a dream.

Riven's eyes shot open, and he found himself staring at a familiar timber ceiling. He blinked as he tried to remember how he had gotten home.

Then, a soft scratching stole his attention, and he turned his aching head to the side to see—

"Miri?" his voice cracked.

She set down the pencil she was scrawling notes with and turned to face Riven, her eyes bright with joy and relief. "Good morning! Or, should I say, good afternoon." She rose from the dining table, laden with the small scroll and notebook, and approached him.

As Riven observed her movements, he was pleased to see her healthy and well. Riven appreciated the subtle orange light filtering in through the window and silhouetting her form. From what he could recall he arrived at her place in the darkness of the night. *How long have I been sleeping?*

*"The whole day. It was very boring, except when Miri was playing with us,"* Zyndraxis teased as Riven pushed himself into a sitting position.

Riven felt his cheeks flush, and he tried to avoid letting his mind consider what it would be like to be "played with" by Miri. He might have been naked, but also felt clean. He was sure whatever Miri did was purely clinical.

Miri drew her friend into a comforting embrace. Withdrawing slightly, she left one hand on his shoulder as she reached up with the other to caress his cheek. "I never expected to see you again, but I'm so glad you're here," she whispered, searching his face, her own filled with disbelief. "How did you survive?"

Riven considered what he was going to tell her. He'd never lied to Miri, but what could he say that would make sense? That he had survived certain death by becoming the host to an ancient long forgotten creature of evil?

*"I'd prefer you use my proper title,"* Zyndraxis interrupted.

Riven ignored him. "I, uh … there was another exit," he stammered.

*"That is a pathetic excuse. Tell her that you were rescued by a gallant hero of old, and you now possess the power of a god,"* Zyndraxis told him, his tone irritatingly commanding.

"Shut it! I am not saying that," Riven hissed under his breath, then turned to Miri.

She scowled at Riven and retreated, her hand falling from his face. "Are you okay? Here, lay down."

She grabbed Riven's forearm, helping him to recline. He chose not to protest, for that would lead to explaining himself, and to revealing the truth about what had just happened.

"I'm just tired, I think. So much has happened since—" He paused, not wanting to get back into that headspace again. "I'm just glad you're okay."

*"Our Miri is far more resilient and resourceful than you think Riven,"* Zyndraxis explained with a hint of something behind his voice that Riven could not quite decipher. He did not want to ask, either, and give the Shadow the satisfaction.

"Me?" Miri choked. "You're the one that was trapped. I got out fine, thanks to you. How did you make it through that cold out there?" She pointed at his shirtless torso, as neither of them had pulled the blankets up to cover him. If it were anyone else, he might have moved to respectfully hide his body, but Riven found he enjoyed Miri's eyes on him.

Miri noticed Riven's gaze, and a cocky smirk curled her lips. "Oh, I hope you don't mind, I cleaned you up – you were so dirty – I wanted you to be comfortable." She gestured lower. "I can heat more water so you can finish up the areas I haven't washed. Yet."

"Oh?" His brows raised a moment, and Riven stroked the beard that had formed on his chin and cheeks. It was neat and trimmed, so that, obviously, was not what she was talking about.

This time, Zyndraxis did not say anything, but instead conjured images in Riven's mind. It was a vision of Riven sleeping in this very bed, lying on top of the sheets. Wearing his single remaining pauldron and pants, he was covered in dirt and blood, and was able, somehow, to smell himself. In this image, Miri did not seem disgusted as she undressed

Riven with deft fingers and cleaned his wounds. Zyndraxis ended the vision before things became any more graphic.

*"Do not fret Riven, you did not miss anything. Sadly, she was very respectful. I was hoping for much more."*

Riven must have been silent for too long because Miri stared at him as if waiting for his response. "Sorry, what?"

"I was just wondering how you survived the cave-in and then the cold."

"I took shelter in some nearby caves," Riven blurted, but it really was not a great answer, and even he knew that.

"Do you know how long you were gone?" she asked, walking over to the small kitchen, and picking up the wash bowl. She dipped it into the bucket to retrieve some water, then set it on the bench. She turned her back to Riven and after a minute steam started to curl in front of her.

*"Hmmm ... do you see that our Miri is using Aedris to heat that water?"* Zyndraxis sounded almost ... impressed?

"She wouldn't ... using Aedris is illegal!" Riven whispered.

*"Says the man with a literal source of it inside him."*

"Miri is just an archivist, why would she be using Aedris?" Riven pressed his lips together as he watched her back.

*"You should ask her ..."* Zyndraxis suggested.

Miri turned around as if she caught the last part of his conversation. She scooped up her bowl, the water sloshing as she walked.

"That was fast ..." He was unable to keep the suspicion from his voice.

Miri retrieved a dry cloth from a rack by the window. She then set both items on the table beside him. She gently massaged the washcloth over the skin of his neck and shoulders. Riven's earlier inspection of himself had revealed that those parts were already clean, but he was not about to turn down her slow and purposeful touch.

"Do you know how long you were gone?" she repeated.

"How long? Uh ..." he began to answer, then paused. *"Zyndraxis, how long was I down there?"*

*"Difficult for me to tell, we were underground. If I were to guess I would say a few months, but details will not matter if she continues to touch us like that..."*

The Shadow was right. Miri's ministrations were distracting. "A few months? I, uh, I don't remember exactly. You see—"

Riven froze again, breath catching in his throat and eyes widening as her bare fingertips grazed the skin just over his rapidly beating heart. It was more than just a warm touch, though. As he tried to determine what was different about it, Zyndraxis purred into his mind, *"Mmmm ... clever girl."*

Was that arousal? Could Shadows get aroused? Riven wanted to ask more but he was just as preoccupied as the magical entity.

"You see ...?" Miri said, softly urging him on. She kept her skin against his.

Zyndraxis was utterly distracted by her touch now, so Riven continued. "I had to dig my way out of the ruins. That took time."

"Is there a lot about it you don't remember?" One of Miri's hands slipped down and took his, and by extension, the arm wearing the cuff. She threaded their fingers together.

Internally, much more was happening with Riven and his Shadow.

*"The way she touches us, like a lover's massage ..."* Zyndraxis' words devolved into a foreign language Riven did not recognise. What he did recognise, however, was the

way his own body was reacting as he strained against the sheet. Somehow, he felt her hand on his, but her proximity and the warmth of her breath fluttering over his skin made it seem as though she was connecting with him on a whole other level. It was deeper. More intimate. More ... primal.

Riven did not want to lose any more control so he snatched his hand away and the moment shattered. Heat flushed through him as he saw her eyes, heavily-lidded and full of determination a moment ago, clear with what looked like disappointment. "Sorry," he blurted. "I, uh—"

*"Why did you pull away?"*

There was a yearning in Zyndraxis' tone that made Riven distinctly uncomfortable. Riven did not want to allow the evil being to share the pleasure of Miri's touch, especially since she was unaware of his true nature.

"You should have something to eat." Miri got to her feet as though nothing had happened. She walked back to the kitchen and went about the business of preparing a plate of food.

Zyndraxis growled at him. Actually growled. Riven ignored him. He had no intention of letting the Shadow intimidate him. It was his body. He was in charge. Well, he would be when he allowed it to calm down. He took some long deep breaths in attempt to get himself back to a sense of equilibrium.

It was only a few moments before Miri returned with some bread and cheese, which she set down on the table for him. "Eat, please," she urged. "Sorry, I know it isn't much, but it's been hard getting decent food lately."

The simple meal may as well have been a luxurious feast for Riven. It was the first proper food he had had in months. During their journey back to town he had only managed to scavenge for small berries and tree nuts.

"No, you don't need to apologise," Riven reassured her between bites. He looked around as he noticed that she had spread scrolls and parchment across every available surface. Riven had gotten rid of the second bed they had squished into the space as teenagers not long after she had moved out, and he doubted there would be any place to fit a new one in now. In the short time that this apartment had gone from his home to hers, she had thoroughly claimed the space with her belongings. It did not feel right to think of it as *his* place anymore. "I do not want to impose upon you. Perhaps I can find accommodation in town."

Miri chewed on her lip as she looked around, eyes trailing over the organised chaos.

"There's no need for that," she said with a slight shrug. "We are adults; we can share the same bed if we must. Besides, you are going to need to be careful around town now."

"Careful? What do you mean?" Riven was too desperate to finish his meal to wait until his mouth was empty to talk, but she seemed to understand him all the same.

"Well, with that Shade you are carrying around and the way you keep arguing with it, you must make sure people do not get suspicious. It's safer just to stay here," she said casually, as she broke off a piece of bread and nibbled on the crust.

Riven choked, and bread went flying across the room. His mouth refused to close again as he tried to understand what she had just said.

*"She really is quite brilliant, our Miri. Ask her how she knows."* Zyndraxis' tone held a note of confidence that Riven did not appreciate.

"Uh, what do you mean 'that Shade'?" Riven tried to

play innocent. The last thing he needed was for Miri to know about his bond with the creature.

An instant after the words left Riven's mouth, his own right hand slapped him in the forehead. Hard.

"Hey!" Shock and annoyance rippled through Riven as he shoved both of his hands under his butt to contain them, just in case the Shadow thought to take the same liberty with him again.

A laugh spluttered from Miri, and she leaned forward. "It can control your movements, too? That is blazing!" She lashed out, grasping his right wrist, and pulling it out from under him. She held up the limb, her attention narrowed to the black tattoo-like swirls on his skin as her gaze traced them until it met the cuff. The red gem pulsed with light in a way that felt nothing short of triumphant.

Somehow, she *knew*. Riven considered playing dumb about it, but then he got a feeling that the Shadow would only make life harder for him. "It does not control me. Well, most of the time," he said. "I promise that I won't let it hurt you," he added, moving to cup her cheek, wondering if being in the presence of such power would scare her.

*"There are many things I would love to do to Miri, and hurting her is not one of them,"* Zyndraxis reminded him. *"Now ask her* how *she knew."*

"Fine, I'll ask." Riven exasperatedly returned his attention to Miri. "It wants to know *how* you knew."

*"Use my name!"* Zyndraxis' voice roared through Riven's mind and made him jump. The ferocity of the demand was unlike anything the Shadow had spoken before. There was an odd foreboding in his gut as the creature summoned a flicker of Aedris.

"Sorry, I misspoke," Riven said through clenched teeth. "*Zyndraxis* wants to know how you knew."

Miri perked up at the Shadow's name. "Well, there's that bracelet you're wearing. I remember that on a dais at the temple," she said, gesturing to it with a shrug. "You're not really one for jewellery. Especially not jewellery that hums with Aedris and appears to have left a memento on your arm." She traced her finger along the dark marks on Riven's skin as she gazed into his eyes.

Riven murmured in annoyance looking down at his arm, cursing it for giving him away. "Wait a minute! You can sense the Aedris? How?"

*"She can do more than sense, Riven. Let her touch us again, then you will understand. It was very pleasant for the both of us,"* Zyndraxis suggested, his cockiness returning.

"You will not go near her," Riven said, a protective urge rearing up inside him.

Miri leaned in closer, her eyes wide with wonder. "Are you arguing with it? Zyndraxis, sorry. Are you arguing with Zyndraxis?"

Riven could not help but think that she looked far too excited about the whole situation.

"He and I are having a civil discussion. He seems to want me to ask how you sensed him," Riven said.

"I did some research on the bracelet and the marks along your skin." She went over to her desk and retrieved the book she was reading. "This text is not something you will find in the regular libraries. I *borrowed* it from the Lorekeepers' collection." She began reading passages from it explaining the history of the original Shade, including vague detail around the bonding ritual.

After she finished, Miri scooted towards Riven, and asked. "What is it like ... being bound to a Shade? Can you feel the power? It must be immense."

"It's ..."

*"Stupendous! Amazing! Transformative! I provide you with experience and power like you have never known,"* Zyndraxis offered, preening.

"Crowded," Riven muttered.

The excitement in Miri's eyes dimmed. "I suppose it is for someone who didn't—" she stopped then, looking at him with renewed interest. "Wait ... did you want it? I thought bonds had to be consensual. Did Zyndraxis force you? Or did you not know what you were getting into?"

"I wanted to ..." Riven trailed off, afraid of how he would be received.

*"Just tell her how you feel, Riven. Her answer might surprise you,"* Zyndraxis urged.

Riven twitched at the idea, then pushed it aside. "I just wanted to get out of the rubble."

"Oh." Miri's shoulders slumped and Riven wondered if he had made the wrong choice. "I suppose Zyndraxis was eager to escape that temple, huh? How long was he there? Was he conscious the entire time?"

*"It was difficult for me to track time in my prison. You see, I was in a form of suspended animation. Although my power was frozen, my consciousness was mostly intact, part of me had a slight sense of the passage of time and—"*

The Shadow would go on for a century if Riven did not interrupt. "He doesn't know."

*"I did not say that! I was explaining that it was difficult to determine and perhaps I might be able to calculate—"*

"It's okay to just admit you don't know something," Riven replied, as though he were talking to a small child.

The feel of Miri's gentle hand covering his forearm drew Riven's attention away from his argument with the being. "I'm sorry. This is probably overwhelming for the both of you. I should be letting you settle in, not interrogating you. Really, I am just so grateful to see you alive. Losing you ... it hurt."

Riven sat and stared for a moment. Her words spoke directly to his heart.

*"You see, she does care for us."* Victory rippled through Zyndraxis, and he let it bleed out until Riven sensed it, too. *"Now, ask if she would agree to a courtship."*

"I'm not asking that!" Riven yelped. He wished the creature would just leave him so he could have a few minutes alone with Miri. "Sorry ... I'm so happy to see you again."

Miri shook her head. "I do not mind if it—he—wants to ask questions. A lot must have changed. This must be just as disorienting for him as it is for you. I will not take offence, I promise." Miri's voice was gentle, and kind, reminding him of all the times he confided in her during their younger years.

*"Riven, allow me to speak with Miri directly. If we could converse one to one it would be far more efficient, not to mention convenient for all of us,"* Zyndraxis suggested. Riven felt a pang of jealousy hit his gut. All he wanted was to spend one last night with her, but she and Zyndraxis kept trying to talk about things that did not matter to him.

*"You make it seem like this is the end. Your injuries are not that dire; they will either heal on their own or when I have gathered enough Aedris I may be able to accelerate your natural abilities. I promise I shall be a complete gentleman around our Miri. It would be just as detrimental to me, as for you, if she turned away from us,"* Zyndraxis reasoned, his tone taking on that polite edge he used only when he was trying to persuade Riven to do something he did not wish to do.

Riven had to admit that he was grateful the Shadow

was, at least, waiting for his permission. Given the power it seemed to hold, drained though it was, Riven had no doubt he could seize control whenever he wished.

*"I would like to remind you I did hold up an entire temple to keep you alive. But alas, it is not about power. It is not my intention to control or command you, for this I have little desire. It is just difficult communicating. I can feel your frustration rising as well as my own,"* Zyndraxis stated.

*"Fine, you can speak to her."* Riven slumped against the bed. *"But the instant I say it's over, you give me back control. Got it?"*

*"Understood,"* the Shadow responded, with a hint of condescension.

An odd numbness spread across Riven's face, then down his neck, and over his shoulders and arms. It was almost as if he had become disconnected from his own skin. Just as it became unnerving, Riven's mouth opened and words that were not his own poured out.

# CHAPTER 8

# MIRI

The change that came over Riven was instantaneous and complete. Miri was amazed as she observed the physical transformation as the Shade took charge. Riven's shoulders rolled back and he straightened. The tentativeness that Riven portrayed in his usual posture and expression melted away, and the being that looked back at her with a discerning gaze was someone she had never met. This was someone comfortable taking up space, and who drew attention to themselves with their demeanour rather than shrinking away from notice.

"My lady Miri, it is a pleasure to speak with you, at last." The voice that came from Riven's mouth was undeniably his, but it contained a new vibration. An added depth, formality, and sense of confidence that caused Miri to take seriously the ensuing conversation.

He reached a hand out to her, palm facing up.

"Riven—no," Miri corrected herself— "Zyndraxis, there is no need for the *lady*," Miri told the Shade as she reached across to shake the offered hand. Riven's skin was still hotter than it should be and calloused under her touch, just as she remembered. "I trust that Riven will remain safe and conscious while we are speaking."

Instead of tightening Riven's grasp around hers, Miri's eyes widened as Zyndraxis lifted her hand to Riven's mouth and brushed a gentle kiss across her skin. She was startled by the gesture, and then Riven's hand spasmed and jerked away.

"Of course, Miri. We can fluidly switch between who is speaking at any given time," Zyndraxis explained. "Riven, say hello."

Riven's shoulders fell, and he ducked his chin. "Sorry about that, Miri. I asked him to not be so forward." Here was the man she knew, the one who would apologise for breathing too loudly.

"It's fine," Miri said dismissively. In fact, her skin still tingled pleasantly from where Riven's lips had been a moment ago. So, for her, it was *more* than fine. "I'm happy to speak to Zyndraxis, so long as you are safe in there."

Again, Riven's posture changed, and that sheepish expression of apology was replaced by a dashing smile. "I told him you would not mind, but he does worry, this Riven of yours," Zyndraxis told her.

"He certainly does," Miri agreed, but really, if she had this time to talk to an ancient Shade, she did not want to spend it discussing the intricacies of Riven's personality. "Are you aware of how things in the outside world have changed since you were imprisoned, Zyndraxis?"

There was regret in Riven's dark eyes as Zyndraxis shook his head. "Alas, I was blind to the surface world. From Riven's mind I can only ascertain that my kind are no longer as revered as we once were."

"*Revered*? No, you are not. In fact, I would highly recommend that you and Riven do your best to conceal your presence," Miri said, voice hushed even though they were alone in the room. Then, she pointed to the cuff on his wrist, with its glowing red stone and hammered wire bindings. "Even being seen with a relic like that could draw the wrong kind of attention. Luckily, most people won't know what the memento marks are, so that should be fine. But perhaps ... I should find you some clothes." Her eyes dipped down his naked chest, to where the bed sheet had bunched around his waist. She was reminded that it was not just her childhood friend inhabiting that well-honed body.

"I rather like our current attire, and I have a feeling you do as well," Zyndraxis noted, making Miri snap her eyes back up to Riven's face "You see, weaving Aedris is much easier without the hinderance of clothing, or armour. Have you tried channelling naked? If not, I highly suggest it. I can give you some pointers now, if you want to disrobe and—"

Zyndraxis was stopped mid-sentence, and Riven's shoulders twitched, as if he was going through an internal struggle.

Miri marvelled at what she was seeing. Was that glitch Riven trying to take back control? It was fascinating to watch. She knew she should have checked in with her friend, but she needed information, and she needed it from Zyndraxis. She went to ask a question, but there was a flash of Aedris, and Riven's uncertainty was replaced with a wide grin as his shoulders straightened.

Zyndraxis continued, "On that note, how is it that you have developed such a talent for manipulating Aedris? Even humans of my time lacked that capability and relied solely on the bonding."

"I have some relics. They contain Aedris, but no Shade," Miri explained, as she rolled up her right sleeve, revealing the bracelet she had put on the night before to give her enough strength to move Riven by herself. "This is something my parents had. They were Lorekeepers, too."

Then, Miri lowered the neckline of her dress. Zyndraxis used Riven's eyes to follow the motion smoothly as she said, "This came from the temple where we found you." She dragged her bodice, and their attention, lower and lower, until the copper and red gem pendant was visible between the swell of her breasts.

"That pendant... I know it." Zyndraxis breathed reverently, looking between her face and the red stone as it glinted against her skin. "That was a gift created for me by my dear friend, Alyxian. She gave it to me, and my consort, before my unfortunate imprisonment. I can sense the amulet still contains a wealth of power."

Miri's gut twisted with disappointment. If it belonged to Zyndraxis, she did not want to give him a reason to use his power against her to retrieve it. It was valuable, but it was not worth more than her life. "Oh. Do you need it back, then?" Miri asked, clutching it in her hand.

"No, you should keep it," Zyndraxis replied, unperturbed. "Knowing her, she would have wanted someone like you to have it. Though you have not answered my question. How do you wield the power stored within the amulet?"

Miri shifted on her seat as Zyndraxis questioned the obvious, and she reorganised the fabric of her bodice, covering the amulet. She was fine with him demanding answers if it meant he would let her keep the pendant. "Humans have become a little more resourceful since your time. Particularly the archivists in the Lorekeepers."

Zyndraxis' poise faded and those searching dark eyes flashed with concern. "But it is illegal Miri! You could get into so much trouble if someone catches you," Riven interrupted in a rough whisper.

"Don't panic, Riven," Miri said, her features softening as she took his hand. "It is just something I picked up while studying with the guild. Nothing unusual in their halls. Nothing that will cause problems."

"I don't understand—" Riven began.

"—I do." Zyndraxis interjected. "There is more to our Miri than meets the eye, Riven. I look forward to seeing more of what she can do."

Riven's face was reclaimed by Zyndraxis' amused set of his jaw, and Miri preened. She liked witnessing Zyndraxis' faith in her... and how his hand tightened around hers.

"*Our* Miri?" She leaned in as her gaze dipped to his lips.

"He misspoke," Riven replied both verbally and physically as he snatched his hand away and sank back into his seat. He grunted as the fast movements aggravated some of his injuries, then continued, "You are not *his*. I think the years of imprisonment have made Zyndraxis crazy."

The Shade's expression returned, but the cockiness was soon replaced by outrage. "I resent the implication—"

"Stop! We have talked about this, I do not—"

Miri pinched the bridge of her nose. "Did you two want a little privacy?" She felt the same as when she was a child, sneaking into the kitchen at night, to steal a snack, only to find her parents arguing.

"No!" Riven blurted, followed by a calmer, "That won't be necessary," from Zyndraxis.

Miri was just about to suggest that they take a short break to gather themselves when the sound of bells pealed through the apartment. Looking at the window, Miri swore as she saw how the sky outside had turned a delicate ombre of pastel pinks, blues, and purples. Evening had arrived after hours of exciting research followed by the opportunity to speak to a Shade.

"As much as I would love to stick around and hear you two argue," Miri said, sliding off her seat. "I must get to work. Jarvis is counting on me, and I think you need more calories than the bread and cheese that I have here."

"You have to work?" Riven sat up a little straighter before wincing and putting his hand on his ribs.

"I've got to get money for firewood and food some-how," Miri told him as she walked over to the corner of the room. She retrieved her cloak from the hook by the door. She was about to swing it over her shoulders when she realised Riven was without a shirt, and none of her clothes would fit him. She untied the cape that formed a top layer over the cloak and offered the thick, woollen, red, and black fabric to him. "Here, take this. It's best if you stay inside, but this should keep you warm as evening falls."

Riven accepted the material, and gladly fastened it around his shoulders. "This is better," he said, pulling it to cover his chest. Then, his fingers twitched and flicked at the edge of the cape. His attention seemed to turn inward. "No, I will not uncover my chest. I do not care if you can keep me warm."

"Oh dear, is Zyndraxis asserting his preference for existing in the nude?" Miri teased.

"Are you sure you won't need it for yourself?" Riven asked, concern causing crow's feet to appear in the creases of his eyes. "It was snowing something terrible when we came into town."

"I'll be fine," she promised, putting the full-length cloak around her shoulders, and fastening it. "I've got other clothes to keep me warm." She winked at him. "I will be back with some hot stew for you just after midnight. Please, make yourself at home. Maybe finish cleaning up." She waved her hand in the direction of the bowl of water she had abandoned beside the bed, and it warmed up instantly, steam coiling off the surface once more.

Riven crossed his arms disapprovingly over his chest at the casual display of Aedris use.

Ignoring his discontent, Miri leaned over Riven and tapped a panel on the wall above his head. The old timber popped out of place to reveal a small cavity full of different trinkets. She retrieved two matching silver and opal rings.

"W-what? Has that been there all along?" Riven stuttered. He had never been the observant type.

"This used to by my parents' Lorekeepers outpost, remember? There are hidey holes with relics all over the place," Miri said, extending a one of the rings to Riven. When he did not accept it, she added, "Go on. It will not hurt you. You've already got the cuff, so this is nothing by comparison. It will allow you to communicate with me if anything goes wrong."

Riven was still and silent. There was a shift in his posture, and Zyndraxis clumsily assumed control of his hand to take the ring from Miri. She slipped the matching ring onto her own finger and smiled at the memories she had of her parents wearing them over the years.

"They are nearly drained, but I'm sure they have enough for an emergency," she said.

Riven gave in and put the ring on. "How do I—"

"—Don't be ridiculous, Riven," Zyndraxis interrupted. "I can teach you how to use it. It should be easy for a simple-minded lad like yourself."

"It has got nothing to do with me being simple! Did you think that perhaps I do not want to use it? It's bad enough that ..."

Miri slipped away before being subjected to yet another argument. She closed the apartment's front door, shaking her head as she left. Miri had never heard anything so ridiculous as someone having a disagreement without an audible second party.

Regardless of the strangeness of it all, there was a spring in Miri's step as she walked the familiar path to the tavern. For years she had tried to earn enough money, or clout, to buy information about where her parents were being kept, and now ... she had the best leverage possible. Miri would research how to extract Zyndraxis from Riven, and then she would have more than enough to save her folks and get them all set up somewhere nice and safe.

The snow might have stayed away that night, making the walk to work an easy one, but it meant that most of the townspeople showed up at the tavern for a meal. It did not help that another wandering bard had stopped by to ply her trade for the customers. Any other time, Miri would have cherished the array of toe-tapping tunes, and the charismatic lass who was playing them, but tonight was not any other night. The music and the raucous cheers and sing-alongs were a distraction from the plan she was trying to form in her head.

Miri's main obstacle was that Nina warned her to stay in Chafton. Given the fact the Lorekeepers seemed to value their reputation, and their trade, above human life, it was no empty threat. Having Riven return to her, now in possession of, or rather, possessed by, a Shade, presented an unexpected opportunity. The ancient spirits were unheard of in present day, and would fetch a pretty reward if she handed over the Shade to someone who knew its worth. However, Miri knew the Lorekeepers well enough to know that she could not involve anyone else in this mission. She could not risk communications being overheard or falling into the wrong hands. She had no doubt that there would be a long line of back-stabbing, self-serving archivists willing to slit her throat, and drop her in a river with a bag of stones, to turn Zyndraxis in themselves for monetary gains.

Miri accepted the responsibility of working alone. She had to be the one to keep an eye on the Shade, so to speak. Its agenda was unknown, so she dared not take chances with saying, or doing, anything to frighten it away. The Shade's value had the potential to reunite Miri with her family. The stakes were high.

"Oi! What's a man got to do to get a drink around here?" a disgruntled voice grumbled, forcing Miri out of her plotting and drawing her into the present.

"I think starting by paying your tab might be a good idea, Larry," Miri countered, even as she dragged a tankard off the bar and walked over to the barrel to pour some ale.

Business for the rest of the dinner service remained steady thanks to the bard. Most nights, Miri would have welcomed the distraction of the constant stream of mind-numbing tasks, but she had an enigma at home in the form of an ancient magical being inhabiting the body of her best friend.

It was a relief for Miri when the oil lamps needed to be refilled, signalling the end of her shift. She hung up her apron and ducked into the kitchen. She walked over to Jarvis, who was checking on potatoes roasting in the oven, the garlic and rosemary butter on top filling the kitchen with a mouth-watering aroma.

"I'm going home now. Is there anything you need me to do before I leave?"

The elderly man shut the oven door and straightened, greeting Miri with a pleasant tone. "Just one thing, dear." He hobbled over to the bench and opened the lid on an earthenware dish, sitting on top of the timber counter. He sniffed it before humming, apparently satisfied with the aroma.

Miri mentally checked the orders placed in the kitchen all evening and was sure she had not missed one.

"Riven is staying with you, I assume?" Jarvis lifted the pot from the table and turned around to her, holding it out. His hands trembled with age, so she dashed forward and gently took it from him. "Take this home. Feed that boy up. He looked dreadfully worn when he stumbled in here last night."

Holding the warm pot to her chest, Miri could not help but feel something akin to love for this man. Jarvis was so caring and maybe too good for a place like this. "Thanks, Jarvis. I am sure he will appreciate it so much. Stews are Riven's favourite."

Jarvis patted her hand before retrieving bread wrapped in a scrap of linen from the counter, placing it on top of her pot. "Take that, too. Bread is always good for filling the belly."

Balancing the pot in one arm, Miri reached for the coin purse at her hip, but Jarvis shook his head and waved her away. "The only payment I need is knowing you will be going home and sharing that meal with that young man. I do not know how he survived after what you said he went through, but he fought a battle to get back to you."

Riven did not come back for her. He just wanted to get home. With the smile that Jarvis gave her, Miri decided it was pointless to argue. Instead, she said, "Thank you. I will tell him about your kindness. He has always had such great respect for you."

Miri set the food down long enough to retrieve her cloak and fasten it around her neck, before braving the cold. The night was alive with flurries of snow marring the view of the sleeping, worn downtown of Chafton. However, a fog was settling over the buildings, and Miri had a feeling it would hang around well into the next morning. With the pot hugged against her chest and keeping her warm beneath her cloak, Miri wound her way through the familiar streets.

The trip home was steps and turns based on rote memory, allowing Miri to get back to the conundrum of the Shade waiting in her apartment. The knowledge of the rewards he would bring if she were to turn him over to the Lorekeepers plagued her thoughts, and she wondered what Riven would think of her if she did that. He had always been such a rule-follower that she knew he would not hate her. Would that change when he learned of the personal gain she would receive? Or perhaps it would not matter once she finally brought her parents back home. He would understand then, wouldn't he? He had to.

*"Miri..."*

Miri stumbled and looked around; eyes wide as she heard a voice.

No, that was not possible. She was alone on the streets. There was no—

*"Come swiftly!"*

This time, Miri *was certain* she heard something. The ring on her finger grew uncomfortably hot. She had never heard that voice before, but somehow, she knew, for a fact, that it was Zyndraxis. Whether it was the tone, or the inflection, she was not sure. But it was definitely him.

"Wait, what?" Miri whispered as she dropped the food and ran towards her home. Her footsteps echoed noisily on the stone-cold cobbles. When there was no answer, she realised she had spoken out loud. She tried funnelling her thoughts through the stone in the ring instead. *"What's going on?"*

Just as Miri turned onto her own street, her vision spotted and the image of the town farrier's workshop flared in her mind, accompanied by a distinct sense of urgency. Her boots skidded on the stones as she dropped the pot, whirled around, and ran in the opposite direction.

*"Zyndraxis? What is it? What's happening?"* Miri thought, willing the mental words to spin through the air as if she were yelling.

There was no response.

No projected visuals. No words magically whispered into her head. No sense of anything ... which was perhaps more alarming.

The only thing left to do was to run as fast as she could.

For such an out of the way place, Chafton was well organised, with the farrier's property on the very edge of its layout. It was a great location for travel to the market to gather supplies. The only downside for Miri was the fact it was on the opposite side of the village to her apartment.

When Miri finally drew close to the farrier's, she slowed to a walk and peered around the premises. As the icy wind whipped and ruffled her cloak, she wondered if she had made a mistake. If all the drama of the past twenty-four hours had her imagining things. She was just about to leave when a glimmer of light caught her attention.

*There!* Off to the side, illuminated by the moonlight, was a flash of silver; it was the opal ring she had given Riven. Only, it had been crushed, the stone shattered and metal mangled. It sat there, destroyed at the mouth of a dark alley. The same one that led to the small stone cottage used as the Revokers headquarters in the town.

Then, the cogs clunked into place. She recalled the sense of urgency. The quietness of the thoughts projected into her mind.

The fact it was *Zyndraxis* who had contacted her.

"Oh, darkness," Miri gasped, launching into motion once more.

He was going to turn himself in.

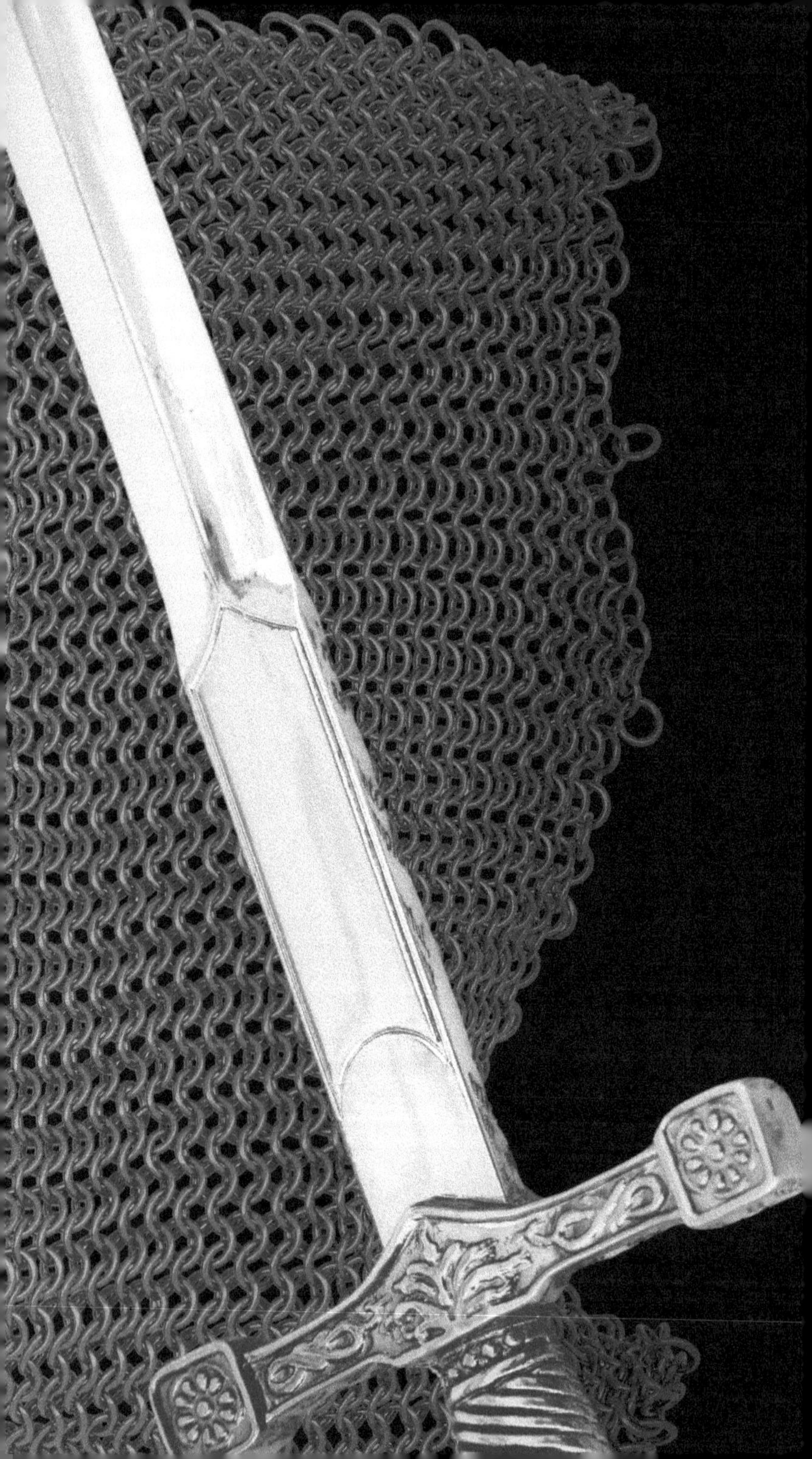

# CHAPTER 9

# RIVEN

"*I should congratulate you Riven,*" Zyndraxis droned, his voice dripping with disdain. "*As a master of knowledge and wisdom, I must say, I'm impressed. How did you hide your inner thoughts from me so well?*"

Riven's chest puffed with pride It was a challenge, but once he had realised that Zyndraxis had an infatuation with Miri, he decided to hone in on that. He kept his innermost thoughts private whilst quietly plotting his next move. Ironically, it was a trick he had learned at combat school; feign your attacks, let your opponent think they can predict your next moves, and then strike when they least expect it. Riven did not appreciate the lesson at the time, he always preferred a straightforward and fair fight, but for a Shadow, nothing was fair.

"*As I said before I prefer Shade, and I think I have been more than fair.*"

Riven ignored him.

He had already witnessed, and felt, the power Zyndraxis commanded and knew that a creature of his calibre could not be allowed to run free. If holding up an entire temple and breaking out was him at his weakest, then Riven did not want to imagine the Shade's power at full strength.

*"No, please do think about it Riven. There is no need to hide your thoughts now. Here we are, my power is depleted and I cannot stop you. Think about all the horrible things I would have done!"* His tone held a hint of melodrama, but Riven would not be fooled.

"I will not play any more of your foul games, evil creature. You will be stopped here and now!" Riven declared as he strode across the walkway toward the Revokers headquarters.

Riven was familiar with the building, of course, having signed up to join their next training program before he went on his final mission with Miri. This was not the condition he was hoping to return to them in, but at least he could live true to their ethos of eradicating evil from the world.

Riven's footsteps scuffed on the stone pavement outside the Revokers' cottage. From the outside, it did not appear to be the headquarters of the famed Revokers. Like everything in Chafton, it was far quainter and more unassuming than it might have been if it were in another town. It was clean and well-kept, though, with a small garden that had frozen over in the winter, and a shovelled path that led right to the front door. There were no guards, or soldiers, posted either, the only indication of the building's purpose was the old mahogany sign above the door, carved with the symbol of a shield and a hammer. It was old and worn, and creaked slightly as the cool night wind whistled past it.

As Riven lifted his hand to knock on the door, his arm felt leaden and it took all his will to force it.

*"Please Riven, this is our last chance. If you turn yourself in now, they will not only destroy me, but you as well. The*

*Revokers of my time considered the consort of a Shade just as guilty and had no qualms about eliminating both."*

"Don't call me that," Riven hissed. However, he was pleased to finally hear the Shade humbled. He had already considered the outcome. In fact, he was counting on it. It was a well-known fact that Revokers' final judgement had a totalitarian response. His memory darted back to his younger years, the body of a relic user hanging in the town square; a warning to those who would follow. Riven had known the man his whole life; he was the town baker. He was a bully that often yelled at children and argued with everyone else. One day, Riven and Miri snuck into his shop. They found strange symbols and idols littered around. Miri told him they were Shade artefacts. She was excited, and he was scared. They left just before getting caught and ran home. Riven was too afraid to tell anyone, too afraid that the baker would come after them.

The next day, the town councilwoman was arguing with the baker about his prices. She ordered him to lower them to a reasonable fare; they yelled at each other for a long while before she threatened him with exile. After she walked away, Riven heard the man curse her in a strange language. Miri joked that he was casting magic. The next day, she was dead. Her cause of death was unknown to the local town healer, but Riven knew the truth. He left an anonymous note at the Revokers headquarters, telling them about what he had witnessed at the baker's house. He did not even tell Miri he had done it, but he regretted not acting earlier. He could have saved that woman's life.

Suddenly, another memory followed: an army of soldiers bearing the Revokers symbol crashing into a small cottage, but it was different, was as if from a different time. They dragged a screaming woman onto the street, someone

Riven had never seen before; her crimes were announced to everyone witnessing the event. Worshiping evil, cavorting with Shadows, they proclaimed, then, in front of the other townsfolk, they beheaded her.

Riven froze. That was not something he remembered. The armour, the symbol, everything about the Revokers looked wrong. *"Zyndraxis? Was that your memory?"*

*"Her name was Glenara. She begged Gathlyn and I to stay ... told us they would come but we did not want any part of the war, it was not our fight. She was not even a consort, just another acolyte devoted to the Shade. She flaunted her opinions and support without censorship. There was no trial, no appeal. They acted as judge, jury, and executioner that day."*

Through their bond Riven could feel some of the melancholy in Zyndraxis' words. Riven took a deep breath. It was the past and during a time of war. It was not like that now. In Riven's opinion, Zyndraxis' inaction made him just as guilty, as if he had killed her himself.

"Then we both deserve this ..." Riven whispered resolutely. He broke through Zyndraxis' resistance and the loud banging of his fist on the door echoed into the frigid night.

Footsteps sounded behind the door and within seconds it opened to a large, burly woman wearing the tabard of the Revokers. She sported short black hair, peppered with grey, framing a face scrunched with impatience.

Riven knew this woman as Nyrelle, the commander of their local Revokers detachment, as evidenced by the shield with the hammer on it, embroidered on her tabard. He remembered admiring the Revokers symbol on her uniform when he had spoken to her and asked to join them.

"Yes?" she looked down on Riven as if seeing a disgusting piece of dirt on the ground. Then after a moment of hesitation her expression changed to that of curiosity. "Is that you Riven? I thought you were dead!"

"Uh, yes. It is me. I am here to, uh, turn myself in," Riven proclaimed, his confidence waning at her disdain.

"What for? I'm very busy and I do not have time for games," she warned.

Riven steeled himself and coughed to clear his throat. "I have become host to a Shadow."

Nyrelle stared him for a while before she raised a single brow and burst into a fit of laughter.

Riven was confused. Wasn't she supposed to arrest him, now? He was a real threat to their society!

*"Well, that went well, I suppose we can go home now,"* Zyndraxis mused, sounding far too entertained by his failure.

"I am serious! The dark entity now inhabits my body," Riven continued, trying to break through her mirth.

Nyrelle's laughter turned to a howl. Then, she turned and called over her shoulder, "Oi! Yacob, Smythe. Come 'ere. Riven is back from the dead and he thinks he has been possessed by a Shadow."

From around the corner, two men appeared. One younger, one older, but both wearing the same tabard.

"What are you on about Nyrelle? You interrupted my reading time," the older man grumbled.

"Riven, tell the others what you said." Nyrelle urged. Riven found the grin on her face unnerving. She jabbed his chest with her elbow.

*"Use my name and title this time; they are sure to recognise me then,"* Zyndraxis suggested. Was he also mocking him?

"I have become host to the Shadow known as Zyndraxis, Lord of Thymear, Grand Vizer to the Archmage

Lorian, Keeper of the Hold," Riven announced, tipping his chin high and puffing out his chest.

*"Aww, you did remember my title. I knew I meant something to you,"* Zyndraxis cooed, only further enraging Riven.

Nyrelle laughed again. The older man, who Riven assumed to be Yacob, looked puzzled. Smythe stood there, devoid of expression, as if he was tired and waiting for the whole ordeal to be done.

"Riven, there hasn't been a living Shadow reported for more than half a century. Now, if you have been actively using illegal Aedris magic, then we will most certainly detain you. Otherwise, go home." Yacob turned to leave, while Nyrelle started to close the door.

"I can prove it!" Riven clenched his fists as he became more desperate. He remembered what it was like when Zyndraxis drew upon the mysterious force known as Aedris. It felt like retrieving water from a well, only Zyndraxis emptied the entire well. Riven did not need that much, as he called upon his inner connection to their Aedris. A light breeze ruffled through his hair and sparks of light fluttered in his hands, tiny arcs of warm energy trailed from the bracelet upward along his arm. The memento markings grew ever so slightly as he channelled more power.

The signet rings the Revokers wore, on their right hands, glowed brightly. They stared at their rings, eyes wide with shock that quickly morphed into outrage.

*"So, you* have *been paying attention ... if you were not using this newfound skill against me, I would be impressed,"* Zyndraxis purred.

Nyrelle recovered from her surprise, pushing the door open again and drawing the longsword from her back scabbard. "Foul creature! We shall end your evil."

Smythe fumbled around, trying to draw his own weapon while Yacob raised his fists in a defensive stance.

Riven did nothing to defend himself as the large woman swung the sharp edge toward his head. He closed his eyes and allowed himself one last thought of Miri as he let the Aedris slip from his grasp.

But nothing happened.

He peeled one eye open, to see a confused Nyrelle, frozen in place and straining against an invisible force. The other two also appeared to be locked in place, trying to make sense of the situation.

Riven opened his eyes properly before cursing, "Zyndraxis!" He thought the Shadow would not have enough power to muster a defence. He certainly could not feel the telltale tingle of Aedris being woven and expelled through his body.

*"That wasn't me,"* Zyndraxis said before he could ask. *"Although I'm glad I'm not the only one upset about your little trick."*

Riven was confused by Zyndraxis' comment, then he realised that Smythe, Yacob, and Nyrelle's attention was no longer on himself; they were staring past him. Riven turned slowly to see Miri holding out a small metal rod in her hand, directly pointed at the three Revokers. Her face was full of a terrifying mix of rage and determination.

"Let him go!" Miri lowered the rod and the trio of Revokers tumbled, free-falling to the ground, as they were released from the magical hold.

Yacob reacted first, squeezing past Nyrelle and with his blade raised high above his head, he charged at Miri. "You too? I always knew you were trouble, girl!"

With lightning reflexes, Miri pulled another trinket from a pocket inside her cloak. It looked to be a small round ball. With a gesture of her wrist, she directed a blast of wind toward Yacob. The force knocked him back only a few metres away.

Nyrelle sensing a new threat in Miri's power gave up on Riven and turned her attention to Miri instead. She charged past Yacob as he got to his feet. Miri sent another gust of wind at her, but Nyrelle was prepared. She raised her sword just in front of her like a shield and braced herself against the ground. The weapon began to glow and the wind Miri cast buffeted against it. Somehow this act seemed to weaken the blast, and Nyrelle was able to push forward, slowly, toward Miri.

*This is not how it was supposed to go. They were supposed to attack me. Miri was supposed to be safe at the inn!*

By this time Smythe finally found his weapon, a crossbow he had just finished loading. He shoved Riven to the side, barely even caring he was there anymore and fired a bolt toward Miri.

"No, Miri!" Riven cried.

The necklace around her neck flared to life. A ball of fire appeared from nowhere and hurtled to intercept the bolt mid-flight. The bolt did not appear to have the same properties as the sword, and was engulfed by the flame. As this happened, Yacob finally pulled himself up, and cautiously circled around Miri, closing in for a flanking manoeuvre.

*"As much as I think our Miri can handle herself. Perhaps we should so something to assist,"* Zyndraxis urged.

"Stop!" Riven screamed. He tried to summon more Aedris around him to get the Revokers' attention. The power flowed through him. It still felt awkward, almost like he was trying to pick up sand.

Miri, Smythe, and Nyrelle were too engaged in their

own combat to notice him. Yacob, however, turned back toward Riven. Yacob reloaded his crossbow and fired toward Riven.

Riven panicked and released the Aedris he had been holding. Instead of blasting Yacob, it misfired and Riven flew backward instead. Luckily for him, the timing meant that the bolt flew over him, narrowly missing his body. Riven landed flat on his back, his head slamming against the stone of the path.

*"Ten out of ten for effort, zero for execution,"* Zyndraxis remarked dryly.

"You are not helping!"

By this time, Nyrelle and Smythe had closed in to flank Miri. She was doing a respectable job deflecting their blows with barriers of wind and fire, but the Revokers' glowing swords made them seem far more menacing than earlier.

*"Dyads are supposed to work together. I shape the Aedris into a useful spell and through careful gestures and movements of your body, you deliver it onto the world. You, weaving and shaping Aedris on your own, is like me trying to fight with a sword. It does not work."*

Riven was becoming increasingly frustrated at Zyndraxis' lecturing, so he tried to block him out. For the moment, Riven's trained battle senses allowed him to evaluate the situation as if in slow motion. Yacob had pulled a new bolt from his quiver, while Nyrelle and Smythe coordinated another attack, but Miri used Aedris to deflect them both. He could tell she was not combat trained, because her entire strategy centred around her magic. She did not even try to avoid the attacks. Riven knew little of how magic worked but he did know how combat functioned, and given time, Miri would be overwhelmed.

*"Okay, let's work together,"* Riven spoke into his mind.

*"Now, since you've squandered so much of the Aedris I'd kept in reserve we don't have many options."* This time Riven sensed Zyndraxis shaping Aedris from within. *"I am shaping a spell that we can use, in front of us, to form a protective barrier of force."*

*"Like a shield?"*

Before Zyndraxis could confirm this, Riven positioned his left forearm between himself and Yacob. Zyndraxis then released the stored energy around Riven's bracer; concentrating the new power in the shape of a circle.

Yacob fired another bolt. Riven blocked; it worked. But instead of harmlessly falling to the floor, it was reflected, straight towards Miri.

Miri raised a barrier of ice just in time. The bolt slammed into the frozen shield, and clattered uselessly to the ground. "Riven! What in the darkness?" she grunted while trying to fend off her own assailants.

He winced. "Sorry!" Unfortunately, deflecting the shot was a moment of distraction that Nyrelle used to slip past Miri's defences and slash her blade across her left leg.

Miri cried out and fell to her knees, barely avoiding a follow up attack from Smythe on her other side.

*"When you use a force shield the amount of energy used is directly proportionate to its reflective capabilities,"* Zyndraxis scolded him.

"Why didn't you tell me?"

*"I was trying, but you were too quick to act. Now we are out of power!"*

Riven gritted his teeth. He did not need the ill-timed comments, especially not as he watched blood pouring down Miri's leg as she defended herself from one knee. Her opponents were nearly on top of her. Yacob had also followed the flight of his bolt and when he turned to face

Riven again, he took his time loading his next bolt, as if he thought they had already won.

Riven panicked. It was the first time he had truly felt useless. Even when trapped, with the temple and the entire roof collapsing on them, he still had one last thing to offer.

His body.

Riven did not waste more time. He launched himself toward Yacob. The older man was so surprised by his sudden change in strategy he could hardly muster a defence. He raised the crossbow between them, which Riven happily grabbed. Using his continued momentum, he grappled Yacob to the floor. Despite his shock, Yacob recovered swiftly. He rolled over so that Riven was on his back and used the crossbow to gain leverage in the tussle. Under other circumstances, Riven knew he could have overpowered the man, but the drain of using Aedris, and the wound on his head, had exhausted him too much.

*"He has a knife!"* Zyndraxis warned.

He was not sure how, but Yacob had managed to retrieve it during their scuffle. With one arm across the crossbow, and the other raised and ready to stab, he plunged the knife toward Riven. Zyndraxis' warning gave Riven enough time to anticipate the attack, and he shimmied to the side. The blade clanged against his pauldron instead.

Yacob tried again, but Riven rolled the two of them at the same time. The knife found the flesh of Riven's bicep, but it was only a minor graze. Now Riven had the advantage; he hastily grabbed into Yacob's wrist and applied pressure, causing him to drop the knife. With a well-placed head butt he slammed his forehead into Yacob, whose head jerked back, blood pouring from his nose; the fight was over. Then Riven heard a scream.

It was Miri.

Riven looked up, expecting the worst. Miri was on her knees, with her hands and wrists crossed in front of her. She was grasping the metal orb, and a jewelled dagger he had not yet seen. They glowed brightly, along with her pulsing necklace. A burst of power erupted from Miri in a wave of blinding light and fire. Nyrelle and Smythe were flung back. Riven took advantage of the situation, overpowering Yacob and throwing him into the path of the blast.

The Revokers were thrown against the wall of the cottage, and slammed into it with audible thuds. They collapsed to the ground, and there was no movement from any of them.

The acrid odour of fire and brimstone filled the air. When the pain and brightness faded from Riven's vision, he saw Miri still on one knee, breathing heavily, and surrounded by a plume of rising smoke. A second later, she slumped over as her trinkets dropped to the ground.

Riven gathered what strength he had remaining and rushed over to her. He pulled her arm over his shoulder and stood, helping her back to her feet, and she winced at the pain her leg.

"You are blazing!" Riven said, his voice full of awe as she leaned against his side, panting.

"Indeed, you truly are a wonder." Zyndraxis spoke through him. Riven did not even try to hold him back; he was too tired and relieved to bother.

"Well, that was a once off. We need to get out of here before they can recover." Miri sounded exhausted.

They both surveyed the remnants of their fight; all three Revokers were still crumpled on the ground. Nyrelle still appeared to be breathing, but Yacob and Smythe were deathly still.

Riven nodded. She was right. They needed to get away

from there, and fast. He started guiding Miri, but she stopped in her tracks.

"Wait, I think they still have some Aedris left. I should get them so the Revokers do not." Miri gestured at the dagger and orb on the ground.

Riven wanted to argue, but given that those relics saved them, he held his tongue. Manoeuvring carefully with Miri, they walked over, then Riven helped her bend down so she could gather the magical objects. She placed the orb into a pocket in her cloak, and hitched up her dress to secure her dagger in a calf-sheath. Riven's eyes almost popped out of his head as he took in that sight; it was not something he ever expected to see on his Miri.

Riven spied Smythe's sword also on the ground. Riven had lost his own weapon in the tunnel collapse, and this sword was the same style. Riven decided to take it.

Their trip through the dark, deserted streets was quiet. The tension between them was as thick as the fog hanging heavily in the air. Riven wanted to say something to Miri, but from the way her jaw was set, it was clear she was silently seething. Growing up with her had taught Riven that speaking to Miri when she had that expression on her face would only earn him a brutal tongue lashing. In all fairness, he realised he probably deserved her anger. He was still dismayed by how poorly his plan had gone but, if he was honest with himself, he could not be mad as Miri clutched his side.

*"Not such a bright idea after all, huh?"* Zyndraxis hummed.

*"Oh, shut up,"* Riven snapped back, letting out a heavy sigh.

# CHAPTER 10

# MIRI

Miri's head was still spinning from the turn of events. Her heart thundered beneath her breast from the rush of the fight, but her mind stalled on the fact that *Riven* had been the one to start it. By trying to turn himself in.

"Where are we going?" Riven asked, breaking the silence between them. After their departure, Riven managed to stop and bandage Miri's leg. The injury from the blade was not as bad as Riven had feared, and Miri had started walking on her own once they emerged from the alley, but Riven was keeping pace with her, his hand on the pommel of his stolen shortsword.

"Shh!" Miri snatched up his wrist, attempting to quicken their steps. She glanced around warily, certain that someone would catch them hurrying over the cobbles. Or that the bell at the Revokers' headquarters would ring, signalling a disaster.

"Miri, where are we going?" Riven insisted.

Arm jerking painfully against her shoulder at his change in pace, Miri swore under her breath as she stopped and whirled to face him. "Riven, shut up and move! We do not have time to mess around. We need to get out of town—"

"Get out of town?" He shook his head. "No, no … I need to turn in the Shade, don't you see—"

Miri choked on her next breath. "Turn him in? Darkness, you are an idiot sometimes." She dragged her hands down her face. "They'll kill you; you fool!" She whisper-shouted, shoving his muscled chest with both hands. "Not only are you bonded with a Shade, but we knocked one Revoker out and killed two others! What in Lorien made you think that was a wise idea?"

"Agreed, dear Miri. This is why I warned you. I feel our simple Riven does not yet fully understand the true wonder of the gift I am," Zyndraxis said. It was easy for Miri to discern the smoother, deeper tone coming from Riven's body when Zyndraxis was in charge. "I also am quite concerned about his ability to understand basic information. Going to turn himself in without your aid was a foolish way to approach things. I was quite impressed by how you wielded Aedris back there. I say, why don't we return? There will be nothing to run from if they are *all* dead. No witnesses, so to speak."

"Are you serious?" Miri jabbed Riven in the chest. Well, it was Riven's chest, but she was intending to poke Zyndraxis. He was being just as dumb as Riven right now. "You have no idea what you are up against. This is not your ancient time where you were revered as a god. You are nothing here but an enemy. You will have the entire might of Lorien against you if word gets out!"

Zyndraxis took control of Riven and grasped Miri's hands. His skin felt like a burning brand against her ice-cold fingers. "Let them come!" The fervour in his tone was undeniable. When Miri met Riven's eyes, there was nothing in them of the man she knew. Instead, she found herself staring into a vortex of power. "Together, we can run away and explore this new and wondrous world!"

The heady, tempting sensation of spiralling into the depths of that Aedris ground to a sudden halt. Miri shook her hands free of his grasp. She did not want to take over the world. She just needed to get him to Eldergate so she could find her parents. "What in Lorien is *wrong* with you?" she asked, shaking her head. "Put Riven back in charge. I am done with you."

Genuine disappointment wavered in Zyndraxis' expression before the set of his jaw relaxed and Riven's gaze darted away from hers. The way that shame weighed on his shoulders told her that she had her friend back. "Well, what do you have to say for yourself?"

"I just wanted to ... uh—" Riven spluttered his way through an excuse. From the way he was stuttering, she knew he would spend minutes, if not hours, trying to find something to say that would not get him into more trouble.

"You know what? It doesn't matter. We need to get out of here. Now." She clutched his shoulders. Even in the frosty night, she could feel the heat of his nearly naked chest radiating just a hairsbreadth away from her clothed one. She pinned him with a narrow-eyed glare. "Shut up. Follow me. Don't you dare try and pull anything else."

"But Miri—"

"No buts!" She released him as her attention slid to his chest and exposed arms. A new kind of heat radiated in her core at the sight of the black memento that had expanded from his wrist, farther up his forearm, edging closer to his elbow. It was an entrancing contrast against his tanned skin that kindled a more carnal interest in her. She wrapped his cape around his torso. "Keep that on. It's darker than your skin. It will help you blend into the shadows."

Before Miri had to admit that she was more concerned about hiding Riven's body from herself than any onlookers, she resumed her careful trip through the town. She trusted Riven to follow this time, and did not look back to ensure he was keeping step with her.

The closer they got to the heart of the town, the lighter and noisier they were walking towards. They could skirt around the edges to get to her apartment, but the extra time it could make all the difference. She reached into her bodice and wrapped her hand around it and called on the Aedris. She urged the fog nearer, causing it to thicken and better conceal not only herself and Riven, but the buildings closest to her. She was grateful it was the middle of winter, as no one would really question the weather phenomenon.

Riven gasped at her back. "Is that more Aedris?"

"Of course it was! Do you really thing our Miri can spontaneously conjure weather? Pah!" The whispered tone and clear disdain left no doubt that Riven and Zyndraxis were having some kind of argument behind her. "Have you tried any illusion magic Miri? It might be more efficient."

"None of my relics have those kinds of spells," Miri replied.

"Let me have a look at your supply, I am sure I can come up with an alternative solution. Weather magic is so cumbersome."

"I think we should just let her do what she needs to do, Zyndraxis. We messed up, okay?"

"I believe it was your decision to try and turn yourself in, not mine."

"Yes, I know, I thought it was the—"

"Can the two of you shut up?" Miri glared back at them. "If they catch us, we're dead."

Riven looked as though he might argue.

"*All* of us," Miri said, putting a hand against her own chest. "You two may be willing to get yourselves killed, but I still have a lot more life left in me."

Riven's dark eyes wavered with regret. "Miri, I'm so sorry."

Miri let out an exasperated huff at the genuine regret on his face, and the way he was now watching her with so much concern. "Just ... don't try and pull that again, okay? We are in this together now. We can talk about it more once we're safely on the road, out of town."

Riven's mouth hung open at the at the word "road."

Miri was not sure why he was surprised. Really, what was he expecting after that stunt?

As much as she would have loved to sit down and discuss their plans over a warm cup of tea, they did not have time to mess around. So, with the Aedris still fuelling the fog, she kept moving.

Getting past the streets around the town square was difficult, as some of the patrons from Jarvis' tavern had spilled out into the courtyard, crowding around a barrel with a roaring fire, warming themselves. From the sound of it, they were singing bawdy, drunken songs that had Riven blushing.

"It is good to see that your people still share their sense of humour in their music," Zyndraxis whispered from behind her.

"There is a difference between humour and crudeness. Those songs are just crude," Riven muttered.

As they neared Miri's apartment, the town was well

shadowed, and Miri was able to drop the fog. Still, she kept alert for the sound of pursuit.

At the apartment building, Miri took the stairs two at a time. She threw the door open and called back over her shoulder, "We need to pack up and get out of here right away. Take the pillowcase off my bed and use it to store anything you brought with you."

Then, Miri went about the business of packing up for herself. Instead of going straight for her clothes and the like, she walked around prying up floorboards, looking beneath jars, and sliding loose wall panels aside to reveal various Aedris-filled trinkets she and her parents had gathered over their years. She set them all on the dining table before she walked to her bed, grabbed the end of the mattress.

"Oh, here. Let me help." Riven raced over. The instant he grasped the end of the mattress, the load became significantly lighter. Miri thanked him and gathered the notebooks and gold coins stashed under there.

Riven asked, "Uh... Miri, what is all of this?"

Miri paused to look at Riven. He watched with great interest as she added to the growing horde of artefacts on the dining table. "Just things I want to take with me."

"Well, I gathered that, but—"

"What I believe he is asking, dear Miri, is why you have so many relics in your possession?" Zyndraxis offered. Immediately, Riven stiffened, and Miri knew he'd resumed control.

"Oh, that? We will discuss that later. What would be helpful, though, is if you would pack suitable foods for the road. Thank you both."

Without giving them a chance to converse, Miri turned away. She grasped the back of a chair, dragging it across the room, the legs scraping against the timber floorboards. She set it to a spot just behind her front door, gathered up her skirts, and jumped up onto the seat. She grunted as she reached up, punching a panel in the ceiling, shoving it out of the way.

"Please don't tell me that you've got something hi—"

Riven's voice was muffled as Miri gripped the edges of the gap left in the ceiling and pulled herself through the opening. She coughed and spluttered as dust and soot billowed up in her face. She gave herself a moment to adjust before sweeping her arms around until her fingers closed around the familiar leather of her parents' notebook. She had so many trinkets and titbits in her apartment, but the notebook was the thing she valued above all else.

Miri dusted it off in the ceiling before she dropped back down onto the chair.

"You hid a book in the *ceiling*?" Riven blurted, his hands stalling as he wrapped a piece of bread in a tea-towel.

"Clearly it is a very important book. May I look?" Zyndraxis asked, Riven's face turning more curious as he took over.

Stuffing the book in the internal pocket of her cloak, Miri shook her head. "What part of 'we need to get out of here right away' has escaped your consciousness?" She jabbed her finger in the direction of the bread. "You have until I pack my bag to get the food sorted. If you don't, then we'll all starve."

Miri's annoyance seemed to spur Riven into action. She genuinely felt that haste was important, but she would have been lying to herself if she said that her motives were completely innocent. She was keen to buy more time to figure out exactly what she wanted to tell Riven, and what she was planning to do with Zyndraxis. And she also wanted to give him a job so they would both shut up. Even a few minutes of silence would be bliss.

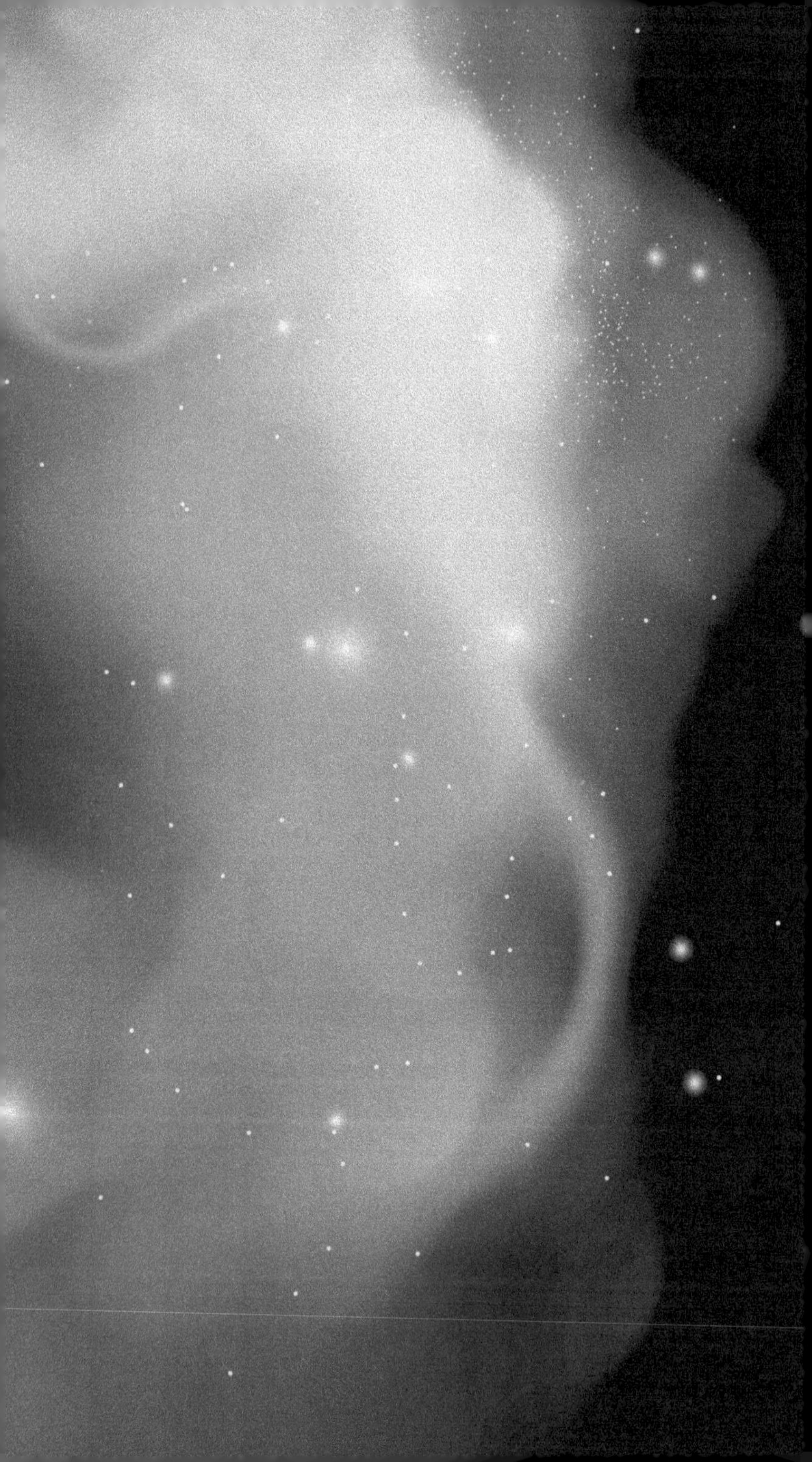

# CHAPTER 11

# ZYNDRAXIS

Zyndraxis was happy to let Riven do the manual labour as he fumbled around Miri's small living space. It seemed to be the only thing he was good at. Once the makeshift bag he was packing had been filled, Riven slung it over his shoulders.

Miri walked over to her bed, reached underneath to retrieve a pack containing a tent, and handed it to Riven. Then, she took one last look around the room before declaring, "Okay, time to go."

Zyndraxis cleared Riven's throat, pleased that Riven was more liberal with giving him control after his little escapade. It was only some parts of his body, and only for a few moments, but anything in excess was inefficient for him anyway.

"My dear, I believe we are forgetting something." Zyndraxis guided Riven's gaze toward a ritualistic chanting symbol hanging on the wall above what appeared to be a cooking table. It thrummed with a wealthy supply of Aedris. Miri must have been so busy finding her hidden trinkets, she had forgotten the one directly on display.

Miri grimaced. "My name is Miri, not 'my dear'." Then, she followed his line of sight, and her eyes widened. "Oh, right. Thank you. Grab that too, please, Riven."

"The frying pan?" Riven asked incredulously as he pulled the symbol off the hook and turned it over in his hands. "Huh. Who knew?"

A snort erupted from Miri, and she shook her head. "It's not a frying pan. It's a relic."

*"Frying pan?"* Zyndraxis spoke directly into Riven's mind. He did not want Miri to overhear and think him unknowledgeable.

*"Yeah, we use it to cook things. You did not have these?"* Riven replied.

*"Of course we did. But I had servants to cook for me. In my time, relics like this were used in a bonding ceremony between two lovers. Each participant would ..."*

"Stop! Do not say anything else!" Riven cried, voice spilling from his throat.

Miri, who had moved to stand by the door, jumped at his sudden outburst. "I didn't say anything."

Riven winced. "Sorry, I was speaking to Zyndraxis."

"Oh, I see," she grumbled. "If possible, could you please speak aloud? Especially if it's important. It is just too confusing trying to understand these conversations."

"Sorry. It was nothing. Zyndraxis did not know what a frying pan was, now he does."

*"Riven!"* Zyndraxis was insulted by Riven's desire to shame him. "My deepest apologies, my lady. I was simply attempting to educate Riven on the finer points of—" He choked on the next word as Riven asserted control back over his own voice. Riven gave him a mental nudge. "— cooking implements."

"Right, well, we're in a bit of a hurry so if you're

finished sharing recipes we should go." She did not wait for them as she turned and walked out of the door. Riven hastily packed the 'frying pan' in the sack and chased after her.

They followed Miri through the streets of the quiet town. Even though it was an unseemly hour of the morning, Miri summoned another fog cloud to cover their escape. Zyndraxis kept to himself and allowed Miri to take the lead, believing her to be far more capable than Riven during a crisis. Despite her simple upbringing and lack of bonding, her mastery of Aedris was quite remarkable.

As they crossed the town limits Riven finally spoke up. "Uh, Miri. Where are we going? This road just leads to the next town. Won't they follow us?"

She paused a moment and glanced around. "Normally I have more time to plan and execute my exit strategies," she huffed. Then, she slid her pack from her shoulders to her front and started rifling through it. "Damnit, I can't see a thing!"

"What are you looking for?" Riven stepped beside her. Zyndraxis raised his right hand and tweaked their Aedris so the gem on the bracelet cast a warm glow of light.

"I don't know exactly, maybe something to make us invisible?" She began as she pulled out a metal bird whistle. She focused on the object.

Now that he was more aware of her capabilities, Zyndraxis paid closer attention to how she manipulated Aedris. She seemed to be drawing out a minuscule part of the magic to test the type and power of it.

It was an inefficient and wasteful technique.

Still, Zyndraxis watched with interest as she finally discovered that it was not the right kind of relic and threw it back into her bag.

"Or maybe something to make us travel faster?"

Miri pulled out another small artefact that looked like an hourglass. Zyndraxis could immediately sense that it held a spell of minor levitation.

"That does not have what you are looking for. Unfortunately, I barely have enough energy at present to keep this light going, let alone casting a spell. I can, however, assist in identifying which one of your trinkets can help us without drawing upon too much Aedris," Zyndraxis offered.

Pausing, Miri glanced over at him. "You can do that?"

Riven shifted scuffing his shoes against the dirt. "Or maybe we could just travel the regular way?"

Miri continued to dig through her bag, apparently ignoring him.

"Riven, I think you should leave the thinking to the experts," Zyndraxis said, only half joking. Then, he saw the next item Miri pulled out. "No, that one is for keeping food warm."

"You might be ancient and magical, but you have not been in our world before. I know what I am doing!"

Zyndraxis was taken aback by Riven's conniption. It was not his usual argumentative tone; it was full of exasperation and genuine anger. Miri stopped looking through her bag and looked into their eyes, but Zyndraxis sensed she was only searching for Riven.

"This night has been stressful for everyone, Riven," she said in a low tone. "Right now, we need to focus on getting somewhere safe to rest for the night. The sooner we do it, the better. You need to put aside your ego and let Zyndraxis do what he does best."

Zyndraxis felt Riven shift awkwardly.

"I understand that you and *him* know all about Aedris, and magic, and throwing fire around, but I know about travelling. I have trained for this. Please let me help." Riven's tone was one step short of begging. Zyndraxis could hear the guilt in it. If it were not for him, they would not be in this mess in the first place.

"They don't use regular tracking methods. They will be tracking the Aedris that we leave behind. More specifically, they will be tracking him and I," Miri informed them.

"Actually, there is something I can do about that." Zyndraxis straightened Riven's spine. "Though I do not have the reserves to summon anything powerful right now, I can dampen the magic I exude, and mask the items in your pack."

"Incredible! Where were you when I was running from the Zohran?" Miri winked at Zyndraxis.

Riven grumbled, but conceded, "Fine, do it."

"While Zyndraxis works on that, why don't you cover the good old fashioned tracking methods?" Miri suggested.

The tension in Riven's shoulders and the frustration in his thoughts were enough for Zyndraxis to know that he took exception to the idea of his methods being *good old fashioned* ones, but he let it go. This time, Riven took the lead. He explained how a hunter would normally track their prey using their tracks. He made them double back slightly and then blend their tracks into some of the existing trails. He also took them off the main road and for a time to follow a game trail. Zyndraxis could tell that Riven was really enjoying himself, truly in his element. He could also sense how much Riven enjoyed holding Miri's hand as he helped her climb over some rocky terrain. Her touch was intoxicating for them both, it seemed.

Riven led them through a forest path so far off the main road, that Zyndraxis lost his bearings. His consort showed no signs of concern and spent most of the time telling them stories about his training and how surprising it was to him that many of his clients were so unprepared for travelling in the bush, despite their desire to travel inconspicuously. Miri seemed content to listen and follow along which was far preferable to her previously heightened state. His only concern now was that she might fall asleep due to Riven retelling the same stories.

"Did I tell you about the time I—"

"Yes!" Zyndraxis interjected before Riven could finish the sentence "You have told us all the stories of your life twice over. Or, three times when it comes to that blasted cleric's pony."

"It was a horse," Riven mumbled.

"Really? It feels like it gets bigger every time you tell the story," Zyndraxis needled. "What will it be next, a dragon?"

"What are you saying?" Riven's feet were planted in the ground, their shared body refusing to move, as a tremor of outrage trembled through his limbs.

Miri rubbed her face. "There is no need to argue. Riven has interesting stories—"

Zyndraxis went to argue, to tell Miri that Riven's stories were nothing in comparison to his own, but Miri surged onward.

"—however, Zyndraxis is right. We have heard that one already." The dappled moonlight falling through the trees on either side of the road illuminated Miri's face, and the quirk to the corner of her lips.

"Sorry." Riven sounded crestfallen and Zyndraxis could sense his disappointment.

He had not intended to send his consort spiralling into a pit of self-abasement, he merely wanted a break from the inane, repetitive chatter. Given that it was his line of protest that triggered Riven's current sulking, he felt responsible for fixing it.

"So, we've heard a lot about Riven's past but not much about yours, Miri," Zyndraxis noted, smiling over at his beautiful companion. "Please tell us how you learned to harness the power of Aedris."

There was an immediate shift in Riven's mood. A spark of curiosity leaping in his chest.

Miri paused in her tracks; her eyes shifted to the side as if she was contemplating an answer. Then, her smile was back, and she shrugged. "It is nothing, really. Just a few little tricks I picked up over the years."

"You just 'picked them up'?" Riven asked, in a mix of surprise and confusion. "Using Aedris is illegal, though. I didn't think you would be into…"

"Be into what?" Miri paused, fixing him with a sultry smile that made Riven's legs go weak. "Be into naughty things?"

Zyndraxis could not believe Riven doubted her interest in him. Miri was so flirtatious that it was impossible to ignore.

Even though Riven seemed to be scraping the recesses of his mind for a witty comeback, he was too stuck on his prior line of reasoning. "Do all archivists know how to use Aedris?"

Miri took several small steps forward until she was directly in front of him. She placed her hands behind her back looking up at him, a dashing twinkle in her eyes. "It is the duty the Lorekeepers to ensure that every Shade artefact be identified and quarantined."

She spoke as if reciting a mantra.

"That's what I thought." Riven's forehead creased. "But that does not equate to *using* the artefacts, does it?"

"After the war, that is what we told everyone, especially the Revokers. The Shade were beaten, wiped from existence. All that remained was their legacy, their power, their magic." As Miri explained, she settled her hand over Riven's bare chest. Riven became unnaturally still at her touch, as if not wanting to startle her into ending the contact. Zyndraxis sent a small pulse of power towards her palm, just so she would feel it and know the touch was welcome.

Miri closed her eyes and bit her lip as she sensed that magic, as her mental energy caressed it and tried to gently coax it out; as if she was asking silent permission to channel some of it. The thought of Miri channelling some of Zyndraxis' Aedris made him lean closer, into her touch. He wanted their essences to coalesce, to entwine with one another, to—

"They were evil, Miri," Riven interjected, pushing her hand off his chest.

"Were they?" She gave them a long stare. This time, Zyndraxis sensed she was looking at him instead of Riven. Her expression was not one of accusation, but curiosity.

Zyndraxis held her stare and kept Riven's chin high. "Some were."

"And were you one of those?" she whispered.

Taking control of Riven's hand, he guided Miri's palm back to their chest, over Riven's beating heart. "I admit that I indulged in the pretence of godhood and even now I do miss the reverence given by your people. Some of our kind wanted full dominance over humans, worship without question. They used that power to justify cruelty of the worst kind. I would never condone their actions, or their desires."

"What did interest you, then?"

Miri's voice felt like a special magic of its own.

Zyndraxis leaned nearer, unable to resist her allure. Their lips inched closer together.

*Snap.*

The sound had them springing apart. Immediately, Riven was back in control, slowly and smoothly moving his hand towards the sword in his scabbard as they came face to face with a dire wolf. It was a queenly beast, with thick brindled fur, that was shaggy and raised.

The wolf stepped forward, body slinking low and moving like liquid. Its tail twitched, and the intention to pounce flashed in its eyes.

Zyndraxis growled at the animal, and it responded in kind. In the corner of his eye, Zyndraxis spied Miri, slowly reaching into her bag, likely looking for a solution to their immediate problem. Zyndraxis took stock of his power reserves; they were still very low. However, given Riven's prowess in combat, he was certain they could defend Miri long enough for her take care of the wolf.

"She isn't going to hurt us," Riven whispered as he took a step back.

The wolf continued to watch them while letting out a low, spine-chilling howl.

"Doesn't look like she wants to invite us in for tea…" Miri hissed.

Zyndraxis wholeheartedly agreed with her.

Riven nodded towards a nearby copse of trees. There was a small yipping that Zyndraxis had not noticed earlier, overshadowed by the wolf's warning. "She is just protecting her pups. If we move away, slowly, and keep going, she will leave us alone," Riven said, sounding far more confident of the wolf's willingness to back down than Zyndraxis felt.

Riven gently grasped Miri by the arm and pulled her away from the mother wolf, one step at a time. He kept the palm of his other hand facing outwards as they backed away until the light from his bracelet no longer illuminated the protective creature.

Thankfully, Riven had been right. The wolf let them go without any trouble. However, it was a stark reminder that they were in woods that belonged to the beasts. The flirtatious mood had been extinguished, and they agreed to travel in silence to avoid attracting further attention from the wildlife. The farther they travelled, the more difficulty the moonlight had in piercing through the thick forest canopy. They had the ruby red glow of the Riven's cuff, but overall, the lack of lighting made navigating in the uneven terrain increasingly challenging.

Finally, they reached a small clearing in the woods that ran alongside a dark, but gently bubbling stream. "I think we are far enough from the path now; they won't be able to track us," Riven said as he stopped and stretched his arms.

Miri let out a groan of relief. "Thank goodness, because these shoes weren't made for this much hiking." She hobbled over to a low rock, at the edge of the clearing, and took a seat on it. She shifted so that her feet were off the ground.

"Worry not, Miri. Riven and I will look after you," Zyndraxis offered, walking over to stand beside her.

Riven shrugged the pack off his shoulders for the first time that night. It landed on the ground with an unceremonious thud, and he leaned over to fish out some nuts that they had packed earlier. He split them into two portions and offered one to Miri.

After finishing his share, Riven gathered several branches and kindling and set them on the ground.

"I can help with that." Miri grasped the pendant that hung between her breasts.

Riven looked up and gulped as he saw where her hand was. "Uh, no need. Better to avoid using it, right? No sense risking the Aedris if they could track us with it. If I can just start a fire, like this."

Riven took some flint and steel from his pocket, but the cold, dewy night had made the conditions for starting a fire less than ideal. His frustration seemed to grow as flames eluded him.

Miri placed a warm hand on Riven's shoulder. "Thank you for getting us this far, but I am sure a tiny spark won't hurt." She clutched her pendant tighter. It glowed briefly and a small flame spluttered to life on her palm. She stretched her arm outward toward the pile of kindling and shot the fire toward it.

"Thank you." Riven organised the rest of the wood until they had a healthy campfire going.

With the flames now warming them all, Miri reached into her pack and retrieved a couple of carrots, a sweet potato, and some mushrooms, as well as a small packet of thyme and wild garlic leaves. She looked around, trying to find a cooking container. Riven produced the bonding relic and held it over the fire for her.

"You were right, Zyndraxis, this frying pan is handy," Riven said.

"As I tried to explain before, it's not used for that."

"Right, you said it was for—" Riven paused, vague thoughts of naked bodies moving together and a fantasy of Miri's dark hair falling onto his muscular shoulder flashed through his mind. He gulped. "Never mind, I remember. You explained it well enough."

Unable to help himself, Zyndraxis said, "You would understand much better if I *showed* you. What do you think

Miri, care for a demonstration?" Zyndraxis teased, feeling Riven's eyes open wider.

Zyndraxis heard Miri titter, seeming tickled by the exchange as she cut the vegetables with a pocket small knife and set them in the pan.

"Now isn't the time." Riven shook his head. Zyndraxis detected a subtle change in his mood. There was interest there, and a warm blush of embarrassment crept up on his cheeks.

*"Perhaps another time, then?"* Zyndraxis offered, directly into Riven's mind. *"You just say the words, and I will show you how you can use the relic to... deepen your relationship with our Miri."*

Clearing his throat, Riven said, "Maybe since we have a moment, you could both explain how these artefacts work?" He nodded towards the frying pan as Miri poured some water from her waterskin in to help cook the vegetables.

"The artefacts, or relics, are simply objects crafted by Shade and imbued with a spell or two," Miri told him.

Zyndraxis hummed in agreement. "Although in my time, normally only the bonded were trained in the art of Aedris manipulation, which was necessary to cast the spells. On rare occasions, unbonded humans were trained by the lazier Dyads."

"Interesting, that lines up with some diaries I was studying. According to them, the first rebels were, in fact, trained servants that hoarded relics in large numbers for their uprising."

"Before I was imprisoned, I'd heard of many rumours of a rogue group of Dyads that worked with the rebels and taught them how to use Aedris."

"Maybe it was both?"

"In any case, your talent with the art is remarkable, Miri. Any Shade would be proud to be bonded with you."

"It still takes time and training," Miri said, brushing off the praise. "The first test is being able to detect the presence of Aedris. Not many of us can even get that far. After that, a lot more training is required to be able to manipulate it. The real trick is using the right amount of Aedris. Expel too much at once, and you risk it exploding, or burning out."

"And how about you, Zyndraxis," Riven started as he took over stirring their dinner from Miri so she could have a break. "If your kind make the artefacts, do you also use them in the same way?"

"We used them for their intended purpose, unlike Miri. She has gotten creative with them. They were designed as a method of storing our magic in a more convenient way. Instead of casting a spell on demand, we could store it for later use. Also, they have a limited amount of Aedris. Meaning, after repeated use, it will eventually devolve into a simple object with no magical properties."

"You told me that while we are bonded our magic works differently. You shape the Aedris into a spell, then I deliver it. How does Aedris work for Shadows without a human?"

"Shade without *consorts*," Zyndraxis corrected, "shape raw Aedris into spells directly. We have no need of relics because we are already a source of Aedris."

"What spells do you know?" Miri chimed in.

Zyndraxis spent the next half hour happily listing some of the different spells he was capable of casting and many anecdotes around their usage. As he spoke, Riven cooked, and Miri retrieved the tent. She strung it up between two trees, near the fire. As much as he wanted to watch her build a shelter, Riven seemed determined to keep his eyes on the vegetables he was stirring. He was also, for the first time, keen to hear the stories Zyndraxis shared with him. Even though he often recoiled at any mention of Aedris, he remained calm and open to what Zyndraxis had to say.

Still, something seemed to be bothering him. "If you are capable of all that then why would you need to bond with humans?"

"Following the bonding, there are many experiences that humans allow us to have."

"Such as?" Riven asked.

"Don't try to get us killed again and perhaps there will be opportunities to show you," Zyndraxis said, only half joking.

Riven stiffened at the comment. "I grew up believing Shadows were evil and needed to be destroyed."

"And what about now?" Zyndraxis asked.

Riven shrugged as he pulled the frying pan from the fire. "I am not sure. You do not seem evil, but you could just be good at hiding your true intentions."

"What do you think, Miri?" Zyndraxis wrestled enough control from Riven to turn his head. At some point during the discussion, she had finished setting up the tent and had laid down at the entrance. He was about to ask his question again, but he noticed the steady rise and fall of her chest, and her tightly shut eyes. "Oh, look Riven, you put her to sleep with your riveting questions."

Riven snorted. "I'm pretty sure it was your stories."

"*In any case, we should get some rest after you eat,*" Zyndraxis suggested, noting how Riven's stomach rumbled at the aroma of the root vegetables and spices.

Riven leaned forward, taking a spoonful of the contents

of his pan and blowing it softly before trying it. The sudden pain of his burned tongue let Zyndraxis know it was still too hot, but Riven tried to cover the sensation with a casual cough. "I thought you didn't sleep," Riven said, clearly trying to draw attention away from his own mistake.

*"Not in the same sense that you do. However, my source of Aedris is linked to your own stamina, so it benefits both of us if you rest. Also, if you are well fed,"* Zyndraxis explained, speaking in Riven's mind so he could eat.

*"So, are you still alert while I am sleeping?"* Riven asked, pushing through the burn to eat as his stomach grumbled ferociously.

*"Sometimes. I can remain alert, or I can enter a meditative state, but I did that for so long, I would much rather be aware."*

*"Oh, good. That means you can keep watch, then."*

The way Riven spoke made Zyndraxis wish he could slap the man across the back of the head. *Presumptuous human.* Of course, given that they were in the wilds, and he wanted to ensure Miri's safety, Zyndraxis would comply. Also... as annoying as Riven was, if Riven died, he himself would cease to exist.

When Riven was finished his share, he set aside the leftovers for Miri to reheat in the morning, tidied up their campsite, and then walked over to the tent. He stood uncomfortably, shifting his weight from foot to foot as he looked at the small size of their accommodation for the night.

*"Guess we're going to need to sleep up close to our Miri,"* Zyndraxis thought, with far too much glee.

He felt Riven's face and neck flush. *"Maybe I should bring my bedroll outside instead."* Riven gestured towards the fire.

*"Do not be stupid, Riven. It is far too cold out here. I certainly do not wish to waste precious energy for heating your body all night. Not when sleeping beside Miri will provide warmth for both of you."*

With a forced modicum of false reluctance, Riven stepped over Miri, and settled down onto the blanket she had spread on the ground for them. He laid down behind her, curling around her but not letting any of his body touch hers. It was a rather respectful move, and it made Zyndraxis wish they had discussed sleeping arrangements prior to Miri falling asleep. He was certain she would not hate them if they contacted her body, but arguing with Riven about it was pointless.

It did not take Riven long to fall asleep after he got a second blanket from his pack and draped it over him and Miri. During the night Zyndraxis kept watch using his preternatural senses to remain alert for any life essences entering or exiting their vicinity. He spent some of that time contemplating recent events. The world had changed so much since his imprisonment. He considered the implications of his actions before his capture. His own people thought him a traitor for not fighting with them. He had zero interest in asserting dominance over anyone, or freeing anyone else. What Zyndraxis wanted was to experience all the world had to offer.

Now he was the only Shadow; the last Shade left.

This truth was not where he wanted his thoughts to linger, so Zyndraxis focused his attention on their surroundings. There was no activity at all. It seemed that Riven had done an excellent job hiding their trail.

In the stillness, he allowed himself to drift into Riven's sleeping mind. Most of the time, he dreamed of mundane things; training, hiking, eating. However, every now and again Miri would feature in his dreams, quietly watching him work or running errands in Chafton with him. These pleasant clips seemed like memories, and showed how Riven saw Miri.

This was how Zyndraxis initially became familiar with Miri. Zyndraxis knew that his own attraction toward the fiery brunette was part and consequence of the bonding process with Riven. However, now that he had gotten to know her better, the interest had intensified. Miri's knowledge and power were beyond any human he had ever known, and the mysteriousness of her past made her even more appealing.

At some point in the early hours of the morning, the fire died down to embers. It was not long before Zyndraxis noticed Miri shivering, within inches of Riven's body. He mulled over his options; deciding between summoning some Aedris to warm Miri or scooting Riven's body closer for contact; both efforts would drain him equally. As Zyndraxis pondered his choices, Miri moaned in her sleep and shifted until her back was pressed along the curve of Riven's chest. She yawned with relief, and Zyndraxis moved Riven's arm so that it was draped around Miri's middle. The alluring honey and vanilla scent of her hair was arousing and the warmth from her body radiated to Riven's.

Miri mumbled something incomprehensible before asking, "Riven?"

"No." Zyndraxis whispered, "It's me."

"Zyndraxis." His name sounded like a lover's on her lips, and Miri relaxed against him, pulling his arm tighter around her. Then, she fell back to sleep.

Instead of thinking about Riven's dreams, Zyndraxis

spent until dawn contemplating the way Riven's body warmed and responded to Miri's closeness, and how the soft rise and fall of her breathing felt against his chest. It was a good way to spend the quiet hours.

# CHAPTER 12

# MIRI

When Miri woke, she had the sleepy realisation that while her mattress felt hard beneath her, it was also extra toasty. The air that caressed her cheeks was cool, but the blankets around her radiated heat, and it was bliss.

Groggy, Miri snuggled deeper under the blanket. Then, she became aware of the solid presence against her back, and the arm draped around her waist. Her eyes flew open, and the events of the previous night tumbled back to mind.

The last thing she remembered was sitting at the edge of the tent and listening to Zyndraxis and Riven speaking amongst themselves. It was odd to see, almost like Riven was talking to himself. However, Miri had caught onto the different inflections and pronunciations that marked Zyndraxis' speech, so it had been easy for her to follow.

That did not explain how they ended up under the same blanket, but despite the confusion, it was nice being embraced by a pair of strong arms. She did not dare try to think of how long it had been since she had had some kind of intimacy.

*It is not like I have ever thought of Riven like that before,* Miri thought to herself. Then, she froze. *Before?* That specific word held an implication that, maybe now, she would consider thinking of Riven like that.

As Miri sucked in a breath, she was acutely aware of Riven's firm body at her back, and the Aedris radiating from the powerful Shade inside of him. It was intoxicating. Although, she could not tell whether the headiness was from the strong body or the Aedris contained within.

*Speaking of Aedris...*

Miri sucked in a slow breath as she let her eyes close. With great difficulty, she tried to push away her awareness of all the tingling points where her body was in contact with Riven's. Once she had reduced that distraction, Miri let out a slow breath and searched for that powerful core of Aedris that was throbbing at her back. Reaching for it was almost like sinking into the energy reserves of a relic, only this felt *deeper*. It was as if Miri was standing on the precipice and staring down into a fathomless well of power.

Tentatively, Miri crept with her own consciousness brushing against the boundaries of Zyndraxis.' She had thought of attempting this before, when he and Riven tumbled into her apartment, but she did not know if he was keeping Riven alive, and had not wanted to risk his life to get an answer. Then, she had come close while talking earlier, but Riven had pulled away. Had he sensed what Miri was doing?

"Well, well, you're a curious one this morning, aren't you my dear?"

The gravelly whisper was husky with sleep, but the voice itself was deep enough Miri knew who she was speaking to immediately.

Miri kept her energy where it was, poised to brush up against his. "Is Riven still asleep?" Miri whispered back.

"Yes. I am borrowing his voice, because I can feel your desire," Zyndraxis replied.

Licking her lip, Miri let her tentative tendril of consciousness unfurl to rest against the presence of Zyndraxis.

An aroused groan rumbled in her ear, and Riven's strong arms pulled her tighter against his body.

It sent a wave of need coursing through her, a primal mix of yearning and curiosity.

"Come now, Miri. I can tell you want more than that." There was a soft rustling as he moved Riven's head closer to hers, so his hot breath flirted over her skin as he added, "You are drawn to power, aren't you? You want to feel how deep my reserves are. Go on, my dear. I promise, I will behave."

It might have been a trap, but Miri did not care. When she handed Zyndraxis over to the right person, she would probably never see him again. She also figured it was highly unlikely she would ever get to meet another Shade. It was a once in a lifetime experience. Besides, the being seemed to have some sort of interest in her. If it had wanted to hurt her, it could have done so a hundred times over already.

So, Miri let herself indulge. She focused on the energy she had resting against his presence, and then *pushed*. At first, nothing happened. Just as she started to wonder whether she was doing it right, she burst through a thin veneer of resistance and plunged into his power.

"Oh, darkness," Miri breathed as she felt herself engulfed by raw energy. Aedris thrummed around her, crackling with potential. The metaphysical landscape pulsed with waves of awareness, and she felt Zyndraxis' presence coiling around her. It was not restrictive, though. More like an anchor in the wellspring of power.

"You like what you feel, don't you?" Zyndraxis whispered. The brush of Riven's breath against her neck reminded Miri that she was more than just that energy.

"How deep does it go?" Miri asked, tempted to slip from Zyndraxis' embrace and dive into the abyss to find out.

Riven's hand tightened on her skin, and his hips pressed against hers. It seemed this foray had awoken the needs of both the Shade *and* his host.

"Deeper than you can fathom. Perhaps one day, I will show you," Zyndraxis told her, voice cracking as Riven shifted again. "For now, I will retreat. Riven will wake if we are not careful. He can sense your desire, you know."

Before Miri could question what Zyndraxis meant, her consciousness was gently tumbled back into her own body. The morning light was startling as she blinked against the stream of it. Riven rolled back, and the lack of his warmth was a crisp reminder of where they were, and what they were doing.

As curious as Miri was, she was aware she could easily get lost in the promise of that power. She had never been good at controlling her impulses, and right now she was playing with fire. Instead of pushing, and risking getting burned, she shoved the blanket off herself and sat up. The morning air was just the slap in the face she needed to fully wake, and she was secretly grateful for Zyndraxis' restraint.

Miri stepped out of her tent and looked around. Whilst it had not snowed overnight, there was a natural light fog in the trees. She walked around the perimeter of their small camp to stretch her legs. When she got back to the remnants of the fire, she saw that some vegetables Riven had left in the pan from the night before had frozen over. Deciding she did not want to restart the fire, she scooped them into a tin in her bag for safe keeping so they could reheat them that night. Then, she retrieved some dried apricots and nuts from her pack to have for breakfast. Just as she was finishing her light meal, she heard the bedroll rustling nearby.

Riven came to sit beside her as he rubbed his eyes. "You're up already? This must be the first time you have ever woken before me."

Miri glanced over warily. It was not all that long ago that Zyndraxis was speaking through him. Was he truly unaware of what had transpired between her and the Shade? "We are on the run. As much as I would have loved to sleep in, I felt it more important to get ready." Miri handed him the pouch with her trail breakfast in it.

"I—er... I hope you didn't mind that I shared the tent with you last night. I figured it was better to conserve our body heat."

"I don't mind sharing body heat." She winked at him.

Riven's shoulders sagged with relief and he scratched at the back of his neck. "Did Zyndraxis come out at all? He said he does not really need to sleep."

"Yes, he did," Miri admitted. "Although it was fleeting, and he was very polite."

"Oh, thank the darkness, I was worried—"

"It's almost as if you do not trust me," Zyndraxis interjected. "That wounds me, Riven. Wounds me to my core."

From the way Riven clawed back control and his expression hardened, Miri could tell he did not, in fact, trust Zyndraxis.

"You only woke up a few minutes ago, and already you're arguing?" Miri shook her head.

"Ugh, no." Riven yawned. "It's even worse in here." He tapped his head, before he started eating.

*Given that he grew up hating the idea of Aedris*, Miri thought, *Riven is taking all this remarkably well.* As much as she knew it would complicate things, Miri almost wished that she had been the one to bond with Zyndraxis.

"For someone who was insisting on hastiness, you are taking an awfully long time to eat." The smooth voice of the Shade broke Miri from her thoughts.

She laughed. "I am good at telling other people what to do. Not so good at following rules myself." Then, she dug into her meal, finding that everything that had transpired over the past day had made her hungry.

After several minutes of blessed silence while Riven was shovelling porridge into his mouth, he finally asked, "So, what's the plan now?"

"Well, we should probably get you some real clothes." Miri jutted her chin towards Riven, acknowledging his bare torso, partially visible beneath the cape. He barely seemed cognizant of the fact he wore little more than his boots, pants, cape, and pauldron. Miri, on the other hand, was dressed in several layers of fabric, topped with a woollen cloak, and she could still feel the chill.

Riven shrugged dismissively. "I find I'm running surprisingly hot ever since being possessed—"

"—bonded—"

"Whatever." Riven shook his head. "Besides, that is not what I mean. I was wondering what the plan was for everything else."

Miri cursed inwardly at the fact he had neatly dodged her diversion. Luckily, she had an answer prepared. "We need to get to Eldergate," she explained. "I have a contact there that should be able to help us resolve your little predicament."

"I happen to like this arrangement," Zyndraxis said, porridge spluttering out of Riven's mouth as the Shade took advantage of his distraction to steal control.

Riven wiped his mouth on his arm. "Well, that makes one of us."

"There is plenty of time for you to piss each other off, enough that you both come to agree that it may be better to part ways."

That seemed to quiet the pair down, and the rest of breakfast time was a silent affair. Externally. Riven seemed distracted as he finished a second helping, and Miri knew he and Zyndraxis were likely having some sort of internal debate.

As much as she wanted more information from the Shade, Miri had plenty of time to build his trust. However, for now, she appreciated that Riven was keeping him distracted. Miri needed more time to consider how to best avoid detection until they reached Eldergate. She had grown proficient at deception over the years, but she had a feeling that Zyndraxis, with his age and experience, would be able to see through her if she spent too much time speaking with him.

Their simple camp arrangement meant that it took next to no time for Miri and Riven to pack everything up and get on their way.

Walking through the forest, in the middle of winter, rather than taking the main roads, meant their journey was far longer than necessary. However, it was worth it as they managed to get through the forest without further incident.

Each morning for the next four days, Miri woke in Riven's arms. They did not speak about it. She had not reached out to Zyndraxis again, but she felt his presence keenly.

As they walked, Zyndraxis explained to Riven more about how Aedris worked, and the two took turns sharing amusing anecdotes from their own lives. Between the pair, Miri was unable to get a word in, but that suited her just fine. Especially as they were too busy nattering to one another to bother asking her why she had chosen to go in the direction they were headed. They left her to lead.

When the travellers finally stepped out of the forest, they heard the rush of white water over rock and felt the warm sun shining down on them. On this side of the trees, there was no snow on the ground, merely a ground coating of shining, crunchy frost. They followed the river for a good hour, leaving behind the sounds of rapids, trading them for the calls of sailors coming into dock. In the distance, they could see the small, but critical, river port town of Weymouth.

The outskirts of the town were a mix of stone and timber cottages, surrounded by orchards or farming plots. A gravelled highway ran perpendicular to the river and was playing host to an array of produce wagons, mounted horse traffic, and stagecoaches and carriages of all sorts of quality.

When Miri, Riven, and Zyndraxis joined the traffic on the highway, they were the only people on foot. No one seemed to mind, though, and those moving faster just went around them. Miri found relief in the fact she that could not spot a single revoker in the crowd.

"Where exactly are we going from here?" Riven finally

asked, walking close to her side and eyeing everyone around them warily.

"We are going to try and take a boat to Southbank. As much as I want to go directly to Eldergate, there is no way I will get us passed the gate guards without a little help."

"Help?"

Dismissing his concern, Miri nodded in the direction of Weymouth. The gravel road was slowly turning to cobbles, and they were now surrounded by squat stone warehouses and storefronts rather than cottages. "I have got a contact here that should be able to help us. Although, he is ... well, he is a lot. Just let me do the talking, okay?"

Miri took Riven's arm before he could reply, taking a sharp left. The road ahead would lead them passed a Revokers' headquarters. Whilst the law enforcement group had a holding in this town, they were probably the most corrupt group within Lorian. They had to be, to let the sheer amount of smuggling that Weymouth was known for, past their doors.

Vaguely aware of the growing tension in Riven's posture, Miri tried to focus on her own issues. One of which, was the very unfortunate fact that she was not sure how her contact at the docks would react to seeing her. They had enjoyed a rather tumultuous relationship, but she had managed to worm favours out of him so many times before. Why would this one be any different?

"Are you sure we're in the right place?" Riven asked as the street opened to the shore, and the series of docks along the waterline. Each one had trade vessels moored to it, and the sailors were busy loading up goods that had come in with the morning rush.

"Please, Riven, I have been here enough times to know where we're going," she reassured him. If there was one thing she had become more certain of over the past few days, it was that Riven believed her to be naive and innocent. He still pictured her as the same young girl he had been best friends with; mischievous and bright-eyed.

A lot had changed since then.

"Ah, there." Miri took Riven's forearm and led him around to the front of a store near the mouth of the longest dock. There were piles of crates and stacks of barrels obscuring the entrance. All nine panes of window glass were dusty in the corners, but the worn doorstep spoke of a high trafficked area. "Guess the Wayfarers are keeping busy. Good for them."

"The 'Wayfarers'?" The incredulity in Riven's tone and the way he stopped dead on the spot almost made Miri stumble.

She turned around, raising an eyebrow at him. "Where did you think we were going? Surely not to the passenger port. We are potentially wanted fugitives, Riven."

"So, you're taking us to the foremost guild responsible for travel through Lorien?" He threw his hands in the air. "You might as well just walk us right back to the Chafton Revokers."

"Oh, you'd like that, wouldn't you Riven," Zyndraxis interjected. "It would fit right into your gallant plan to sacrifice yourself for the greater good."

Miri stifled a snort. "Please don't worry. I have this handled. Just like me, the Wayfarers are not quite what they seem." She grabbed Riven's hand and yanked the door open before he could argue any further.

A jolly bell tinkled when the door flung back, and Miri plastered a pleasant expression on her face as she looked around. Inside, there were three tired looking ship captains standing around a counter, covered with ledgers. They seemed to be deep in conversation with a young man who was wearing a much nicer shirt and breeches. He looked up, eyes narrowing. Miri watched him closely and wracked her brain for memories of him but could not find a one. She decided he must be a new recruit.

"Can I help you?" he asked, leaning forward, and resting his elbows on the table, conveniently covering the ledgers with the billowing sleeves of his shirt. The smile he gave Miri was brighter than the summer sun.

The kid had charisma; she had to give him that.

"No, I am afraid *you* cannot. Dace can, though." Miri then grasped the right-side neckline of her shift and pulled it to the side to reveal her shoulder and collarbone. There, peppered on her light olive skin, was a spray of tiny star tattoos, all arranged in a replica of the constellation known as the Swift. Shaped after the birds, living their life almost exclusively in the air, it was somewhat of a brand for people who chose to live their lives in an elusive manner. "I'll just go straight through, shall I?"

The young man's eyes widened at the sight of the tattoo.

So did Riven's. His mouth dropped open too, and Miri winked at him as she covered the markings. She was certain he would ask about them later, but right now she had more pressing matters to consider.

"Ah, yes, madam. I believe he will see you. I will take you through when I am finished serving these gentlemen," he said.

Miri had no intention of waiting. She was already striding towards a door at the back of the room as he spoke. Dace had been one of the first contacts she made on the shadier side of the world, when she had left Chafton. As a member of the esteemed Wayfarers Guild, his dodgy dealings and smuggling tendencies had been a good reminder for her that all the organisations that held the power in Lorien had their own dark sides. For the Wayfarers, it was the fact that they were so eager to turn a blind eye to people wishing to move illegal goods over the waterways, under the nose of the Revokers. They had a headquarters back in Eldergate, like every guild worth its title did, but outposts like this, led by knaves like Dace, was where their real money and influence was derived.

Miri gestured for Riven to follow her, as she was determined to find the scoundrel who owed her a favour. When they reached the door, she pulled it open without bothering to knock. The room beyond was far more chaotic than the front. One wall was full of pigeonholes with ledgers, another was lined with crates of all shapes and sizes, and there was a round table in the middle with six chairs around it. Seated at the table was a man who wore a long raven braid, a plain red shirt, and tight leather trousers. He looked up as they entered, well-defined black brows narrowing over deep blue eyes.

"Leiton, I told you I didn't want to be—" Dace paused as he saw Miri. Then, he glanced at Riven He was about to say something when the man from the front desk skidded into the room.

"Forgive me, sir. I would have warned you, but I was with a customer and she just helped herself."

Miri presumed the young man's name was Leiton.

Dace held up a hand to silence the lad as Miri strode towards the table. She walked right up until she was standing beside his chair. She leaned to the side and rested one hand on the table, covering the document he had been reading, and put the other on her hip.

"Come now, Dace. Is this how you greet an old flame?" Miri purred, smiling at him the way she used to.

His cerulean eyes flashed and, the next instant, his hand was around Miri's throat and he threw her down onto the table, pinning her against it.

When Miri's head slammed against the tabletop, she tore at the Aedris from her pendant, and frost crackled along Dace's hand. He sneered as orange sparks danced from the hand gripping Miri's neck.

Then, heavy footsteps and a warning growl drew his attention.

Miri glanced over to see Riven standing with his hand on the pommel of his sword. *Or... is it Zyndraxis?* She wondered as Riven's cloak blew back off his shoulder to reveal his carved chest. His body seemed to *glow* with a menacing kind of energy. "Remove your hand from our Miri, or you will die."

The voice that spoke was a combination of Riven's tone, and the deep baritone of Zyndraxis. Hearing the two mingling together produced a sound that made Miri's stomach flutter.

It seemed to have the opposite effect on Dace, piquing his interest as he assessed Riven and the power he seemed to be radiating. Miri already knew where it was coming from, of course, but she had a feeling Dace was trying to identify where Riven's relic was, and whether it was worth trying to take.

Still, Dace pulled his frost-covered hand off her neck and stepped back. A casual toss of his head had his long black braid sliding off his shoulder, as he eyed the bonded Riven and Zyndraxis.

"No need to make threats," Dace said smoothly,

offering his frigid hand to Miri. "We are old friends here. Come, Miri. Apologies for my uncouth greeting."

Despite the urge Miri had to slap Dace's hand away, she needed him more than he needed her. So, she took it. She released some Aedris to rewarm it as she got to her feet. "I'm here to call in that favour," she told him.

Dace cocked an eyebrow at her. "A favour? On our last job you left me chained to a boat, and sailing away in nothing but the clothes I wore."

*One that clearly did not sail far enough away*, Miri thought to herself. She resisted the urge to express as much, and instead said, "You mean the ship that we were stealing? The one you got to keep?"

"After I escaped the chains."

"I knew you would."

"I thought we were a team! I had plans, you would be my business partner, and we could take over the Wayfarers together."

"They were *your*, plans not mine," Miri reminded him. Then, she added, "So, can we talk about that favour now, or do you want to hang around and flirt a bit more?"

"I believe I said we were—"

"Sorry, what was that?" Miri cupped a hand around her ear. "That sounds an awful lot like arguing. I thought we were talking like old friends."

There was a sharpness in Dace's eyes then. Not the dangerous kind, though. The kind she remembered from the times where she let him tie her up while he—

"Let's speak in private," Dace interrupted that memory as he gestured to a side door.

Miri straightened her clothing and approached Dace.

The sound of Riven's footsteps started, but then

stopped, almost as suddenly as Leiton pointed the tip of his sabre at Riven's back.

"It's fine, Riven," Miri promised. "I've got this."

"No, I—"

"I said it is fine," Miri snapped, with a little more bite than she intended.

The way Riven's features fell made her feel like a proper bitch.

Dace chuckled. "I see you still like to treat your men like pets." He shook his head.

"No," Miri said, looking down her nose at him, even though he was almost a foot taller than her. "That was reserved just for you."

Then, she strode by him, pushing the door open without waiting for Dace's permission. Inside, she held it, as if inviting Dace into his own office. It made him narrow his eyes as he walked past her.

The room was just as messy as she remembered. Although, she knew that was the point. If a Revoker happened to come into the place, they would find nothing amiss amongst the whirlwind of ledgers. All the good stuff, from memory, was hidden in an Aedris enchanted box, underneath a loose tile in the fireplace, behind the giant mahogany desk. Still, that did not stop her from moseying over to his desk and leaning against it. As she did, she let her hand drift to a fancy gold paperweight in the shape of a riverboat. It held down the edge of one of his scrolls. She slipped the heavy object into her pocket as Dace shut the door and rounded on her.

"Of all the people I thought I would be seeing today, you were not at the top of the list," Dace drifted closer, almost if he was taking his time so he could size her up. She let her arms hang loosely by her side, the picture of relaxation. "You know, despite how you left me, I can't say I'm disappointed to see you."

Dace's cool fingertips brushed against her neck as he swept her hair over her shoulder. He was standing at her back, their bodies almost touching. His warm breath tickled her skin as he took in a deep breath of her.

"But you're here for business, not pleasure, aren't you?" Dace asked in a tone that told her he already knew. Still, he gently held the neckline of her shift aside and brushed his lips over her tattoo before straightening himself.

"Why not both?" Miri asked, turning around to face him.

The feelings she had suppressed at waking up in Riven's arms for the past few nights resurfaced. Her body ached at the reminder of unmet needs. Her memories flitted back to the moments she had shared with Dace, and she found herself wondering if it would be terrible if she let him have his way with her one last time.

"Oh, you're a fun one, Miri," Dace whispered before pressing his lips against hers.

Just as she was about to deepen the kiss, he pulled away. He walked around her, and moved to sit on his desk, his hands gripping the carved edge tighter than was strictly necessary.

*Good*, Miri thought to herself. *He wants me... should make it easier to negotiate.*

"So, about this favour—"

"I don't owe you anything."

"—it is really rather simple. My companion and I need to get to Southbank. That is it. We can work on the ship if needed. I can help with their ledgers or stock, and my companion is good at physical labour—"

"I'm sure he is," Dace grumbled, glancing at the closed

door. "But he seems the rather simple type. I do not imagine he can hold your interest for long, beyond a rushed romp here and there. Does he even know how to really pleasure you the way you deserve?"

"Oh, please. You think too highly of your skills."

That was a lie, and they both knew it.

There was a reason that Miri kept finding herself in Dace's bed over the years, despite his abhorrent cockiness.

"I also happen to think too highly of *your* skills," Dace said, pushing himself off the edge of the desk and stalking back towards her.

Miri let him hear the way her breath caught at the return of his proximity.

"I am feeling rather generous today. You see, I may not owe you a favour, but I do have a use for your particular skillset," Dace said, his gaze calculating.

"I've told you before, Dace, I do not pay for services with sexual favours."

"Not those skills," he said, even as cupped her cheek. He ran his thumb over her lower lip. "Although, if you want to throw a favour in, I might even be able to make it so you don't have to work on the ship."

Miri turned her face just enough to catch the tip of his thumb between her lips and nibbled on it. The act earned her a strangled moan from Dace and he kissed her. Hard.

With a grunt of need, Dace wrapped his arms around Miri. He pulled her against his body, and turned them around so her arse hit his desk. She let out a surprised squeak, but he reached down. He grasped her backside and lifted her to sit on the edge.

Every part of Miri wanted to let Dace continue. Her head was spinning, her heart thundering, and other parts of her were waking at the attention. However, she knew this would only end poorly if she let it continue.

It always did.

So, Miri slid her hand up Dace's back and grasped his braid, pulling him back from the kiss and guiding his lips to her neck instead. "What do you need me to do?" she asked, reminding him that she was there on business.

"There's a cache of relics I'm trying to retrieve just outside of town," he murmured against her neck. His hands moved from her arse to her front, one sliding up to run over her breasts, while the other moved down her leg to start gathering the hem of her dress. "I have lost three men to it so far. It is beneath a cursed stone. You—"

"I can read the enchantments and counter them," Miri supplied, knowing exactly where that was going to lead. As his hand moved higher up her leg, she knew where *this* was going to lead, too.

"Get me the cache and the trip is yours." Dace moved his mouth further down her neck, towards the swell of her breasts where they spilled out of her bodice. "I might even forgive you for screwing me over last time."

"Where is the stone?" Miri asked, trying to not let the way her body was reacting get the better of her.

"In a clearing in the forest, just north of the apple orchard, on the highway outside of town," Dace's breath tingled against her skin.

"Perfect!" Miri pushed him away and jumped off the desk. She let her skirts fall back down into place as she grinned at him. "See you soon. Make sure the boat's waiting. I do not want to waste any time."

Somewhat dazed, but unsurprised, Dace ran a hand over his raven hair to smooth it; he licked his lips as he watched Miri. "We'll finish this later," he said, his words filling Miri with anticipation.

*No, not anticipation*, Miri thought. *Desire. As much as I may want it, I am not going there again.*

She aimed for the door but stopped when Dace let out a huff.

"Miri," he said in a quiet, warning tone. "Where's my paperweight?"

Miri reached into her pocket. She threw the golden riverboat up in the air and caught it once, before throwing it back at him. Instead of scrambling to catch it, a breeze of Aedris-summoned wind caught it, settling it back on the edge of his desk. Dace shook his head as she walked out.

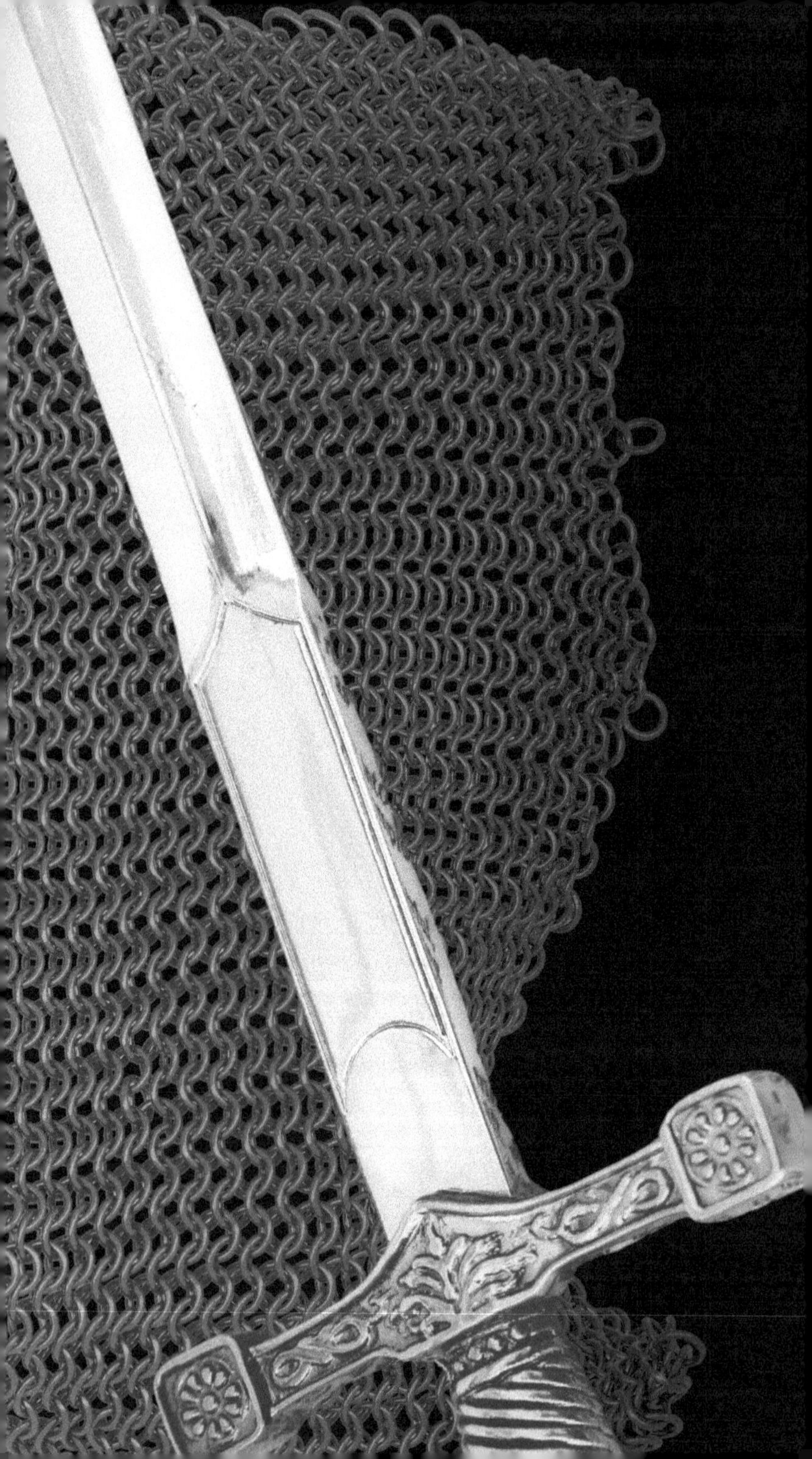

# CHAPTER 13

# RIVEN

Even though Miri had asked him to stand down, both Riven and Zyndraxis remained alert as they waited in the backroom with Dace's lackey. The boy kept his sword pointed at Riven's back. Of course, he could have taken the man down if he wanted to, but he had a feeling Miri would not have appreciated that.

Once Miri and Dace had disappeared into Dace's office, the customers in the front room resumed their business, counting out coins over the table. Riven could just see through to that space out of the corner of his eye. He was in a state of disbelief as he observed them muttering to each other about some goods they were smuggling and complained about the price that Leiton had called out to them over his shoulder. It seemed completely surreal to Riven that the Wayfarers Guild would be involved in shady operations, yet here they were.

As a mercenary, Riven had prior dealings with the Wayfarers. His clients would sometimes require passage across the waterways and would need to procure the paperwork required for the travel. The Wayfarers were responsible for managing the requests and organising the travel; nothing in the past had ever hinted at anything other than a respectable business.

One of the captains in the front room grumbled to himself before calling out, "Oi, Leiton. Get back here an' help us out. My goods ain't gonna catalogue themselves."

Leiton responded without turning away from Riven. "As soon as this scum is gone, I'll come back to help you."

Another of the captains says, earning a guffaw from his companions. "Don't bother. Look at him; all muscles and no brain. Do not worry; if he plays up, we can melt him in an instant."

*"They have no chance against us. We have had several days of rest now and our power has been restored. They have some skill, but nothing like our Miri's."*

A smirk formed on Riven's face at Zyndraxis' astute assessment of the situation. He let his posture soften and even turned slightly away from Leiton as if to say, *I do not even consider you a threat.* A wave of energy roiled off him as Zyndraxis got in on the act.

The change in stance seemed to unnerve Leiton, and his sword arm began to shake.

A muffled bump coming from the room with Miri and Dace snatched both of their attention. Leiton's lips pinched together with concern, and Riven swallowed at the unexpected sound.

*"I do not trust Dace. He does not seem like an honourable man. Especially toward our Miri,"* Zyndraxis hissed in his mind.

Riven agreed. There was something about the way Dace looked her that gave him chills. Part of him considered busting down the door right then and there, but the other told him she would not want that.

*"She would call out if she needed us, right?"* Riven asked, keeping his eyes on the door that Dace had shut between them.

*"I believe so. I will keep my senses open, just in case,"* Zyndraxis replied. Riven was pleased that they could at least work together on this.

They did not have long to wait though, as the door was yanked open and Miri stepped out, readjusting her clothes as if she had been in a fight, or perhaps something more carnal...

"Come on, we've got work to do," she told him, as if nothing untoward had transpired.

Miri strode out of the building confidently, and Riven had to jog to catch up to her.

"Wait, Miri, what happened in there?" Riven panted, ignoring the amused looks from the ship captains they passed.

"I've secured passage to Eldergate."

"Really? That was fast. Wouldn't it normally take much longer and a considerable amount of gold?"

"I have my ways." She shrugged as they stepped back on the busy street, and she turned towards the road they had taken into town. "But first, we need do a wee side quest."

Her words and her tone made Riven grimace. He had heard that kind if mischief in her voice before. It never boded well. "Side quest?"

"I made a deal with Dace. If we get him a few little artefacts, he will give us passage to Eldergate."

"We don't trust him Miri," Zyndraxis said, speaking for both he and Riven.

Miri stopped and turned to stare at them. "We?" She raised an eyebrow.

"Yes, we don't trust him," Riven confirmed.

"I think that might be the first time you two have agreed on something." She placed her hand on his chest.

Riven froze, so Zyndraxis took over.

He placed Riven's hand over Miri's and leaned toward her. Riven hated to admit it but allowing Zyndraxis these small bouts of control was becoming easier and easier. He was not sure what was more frightening, how easy it was to let go or the fact that he was beginning to accept it.

"I've met men like Dace before Miri, just be careful, he will just as likely help you as use you." Zyndraxis whispered.

Miri held his gaze, and they appreciated her warm brown eyes. Riven found it hard to tell whether she was looking for him or the Shade.

"You can trust me." Her lips formed a casual, knowing smile. Riven felt Zyndraxis leaning in closer, but then Miri patted his cheek and turned away again. "Follow me."

They made their way outside of the town, following a road until they reached what would be a lovely orchard of sorts when spring came. For now, the rows of trees were nothing more than spindly skeletons of their usual glory. It gave them little cover as they jumped the low stone fence and moved towards the forest at the far edge of the property. Miri seemed content to be quiet for the walk, but the farther they got from the town, the more difficult Riven found it to keep his concerns to himself.

"So ... you and Dace know each other?" Riven asked, knowing the question would claw its way out anyway if he did not speak now.

"Yep," Miri said, keeping her pace.

She did not seem inclined to volunteer any information.

"*In all fairness, she did answer your question. Why don't you ask her what you really want to know?*" Zyndraxis drawled in his mind, as if Riven's first question was stupid.

Riven cleared his throat. "Sorry, I meant to ask how you and Dace know each other."

Miri shrugged. "It is a long story. We used to work together."

"But he is a Wayfarer, and you're a Lorekeeper. I didn't know those two organisations were connected." Riven scratched his jaw as he struggled to find a reason they would ever have reason to work together. He would understand more if they met in transit, or because Miri was requesting passage somewhere, but that would not be *working together*.

"There's a lot more to the world than the general public is unaware of," Miri said, as if that answered his question.

"Indeed. They also appear to have similar gifts to you, Miri." Zyndraxis' comment to Miri was far more enthusiastic than his critique of Riven a few moments ago.

"Yes, good point." Riven jumped onto that line of thought. "How many organisations deal in illegal relics?"

"Are you sure you want to know?" Miri paused and glanced over her shoulder at him.

He nodded.

"More than you think."

Riven grunted in annoyance at yet another non-answer, but Zyndraxis' laughter echoed in his mind. He was tempted to ask the pair if it would be better off if he just made himself scarce, and they could bond over their illicit activities together. No, it was clear Miri was being deliberately evasive. He was just going to have to be more direct.

"*That's the spirit!*"

Ignoring Zyndraxis, Riven pushed further. "What

about the Reclaimers? The Artisan's Guild? The Hearth-builders? The Economists?"

"Hmmm..." Miri tapped her chin. "Yes, sometimes, no, and definitely."

Mouth falling open, aghast, Riven had another more alarming thought. "What about the Revokers? Please tell me they don't!"

That made Miri laugh, her soft voice dancing on the cool winter breeze that whistled as they approached the edge of the forest. "Well, I didn't think so. But then I saw that sword—" she pointed to the borrowed Revoker shortsword hanging at his hip, "—and now I know they must. I am guessing they don't trade, but there is no way that the Aedris siphoning function did not take Aedris to create."

That shook Riven to the core. The Revokers' original purpose and overriding goal was to rid the world of Aedris. How could he go on knowing the truth of their hypocrisy?

"I believe the rings they wore were infused with Aedris as well. Simple detection spells, but spells nonetheless," Zyndraxis added, mirth dancing on his voice. It was clear from the smug satisfaction pulsing in Riven's body that he was thoroughly enjoying Riven's discomfort at this news.

"I don't believe it," Riven insisted. Too much of his worldview had been torn to shreds. He would not allow his pride in the Revokers crumble around him.

"Too bad. It's true. They're nothing but a bunch of overzealous pricks!" Miri hissed, glaring at him with a sudden and intense rage.

"But they saved us from the tyranny of the Shade," Riven argued. Perhaps that would counteract the fact they were probably unknowingly using their relics.

"Riven, they tried to kill us," Zyndraxis reminded him,

an image of the fanatical attacks of Nyrelle and her colleagues flashing through Riven's mind.

"No, they tried to kill *you*," Riven corrected.

That made Zyndraxis laugh. "I don't think they could distinguish the difference."

Miri pinched the bridge of her nose. "The Revokers are arseholes. We can agree on that much. They would rather the world burn down than use the power around us."

"Agreed. Plus, not all of us Shade were bad," Zyndraxis offered.

Riven looked at Miri to see what she thought of Zyndraxis' claim.

Catching the question in his expression, she chewed her lower lip. "The historical records are mixed. All I know is that the Revokers do not tell the whole truth, so it is impossible to get an accurate picture of what really happened."

"After all we've been through, I'm shocked you still think I'm evil, Riven," Zyndraxis said, sounding genuinely disappointed.

Riven threw his hands up in frustration. "You are literally possessing my body! I do not know how else you can define evil."

"Possession would imply you are no longer in control. I can assure you Riven, you have far more control than you know. You have access to all my power and knowledge and yet you spit it back at me!" Zyndraxis snatched said control of Riven and whipped his head around to face Miri. "And you! After all we have shared, my dear Miri, how can you let him say I am evil? Tell me truthfully, do you believe I am evil? Are all Shade evil?"

Miri's nose scrunched. Her face showed a mix of apology and pain.

"There are several accounts detailing the positive effects

the Shade had on our society; medicine, travel, weaponry, technology. The Revokers destroyed a lot of that information, but the Lorekeepers managed to save some and they now hold it in secret."

"You did not answer my question, Miri." For the first time, Riven noticed hurt in Zyndraxis' words.

Stopping in her stride, Miri turned to them. Riven almost tripped over her, but Zyndraxis let out a wave of Aedris to buffet his steps and help him maintain his balance. Miri rubbed her face. "For the time being let's just try and get along. After we get to Eldergate, you'll both be separated, and you won't need to worry about this anymore."

Riven looked into her eyes, and remembered the anger in her voice when he tried to turn himself in. How he had nearly gotten her killed in the altercation with the Revokers. He saw that frustration again, and it broke his heart because of his part in it. "Fine."

They continued in silence as they hiked through the thick trees. Riven was not sure how long they were walking but he did not want to question Miri and risk upsetting her further. Finally, they came to a clearing. The leaf-covered ground had char marks. Miri warily skirted around them and moved to the centre of the area. She closed her eyes, knelt, and appeared to enter a mild trance as her body stiffened and her eyes glazed over.

*"Do you feel that Riven? There is Aedris in this area. That is why the trees do not grow past this point."*

At first, Riven assumed the clearing was natural, but when he stepped back, he realised they were inside a perfect circle. He felt a small tingle. Like a light breeze that he only just sensed with the tips of his fingers.

"I *can* feel it," he replied, just as the sensation dissipated.

He was not sure how to feel about being this close to the power he had spent his life fearing.

Miri shook herself out of her meditation, shuffled back slightly, and began to scrape at the ground beneath her. Riven joined her to inspect her work. She uncovered a disc shaped stone that was embedded into the ground. Runes were etched around the outer rim, and there was a large, deeply carved symbol in the middle. Riven recognised none of it, of course, but Miri let out a puzzled hum.

"It's a lock that needs the right key," Miri said as she got to her feet and brushed crunchy leaf litter off her knees.

Riven scratched the back of his neck. "Do we have the key?"

"No, but I have used one like this before. There is usually a way get around it if you know what you're doing." Miri shrugged her pack off and dug through it, apparently unperturbed by the obstacle.

"Careful Miri, I recognise the writing here. If what I am seeing is correct, this was designed by my friend Alyxian, and from what I know about her style, it will be secured against brute force attempt," Zyndraxis warned.

"Wait, Alyxian, as in the same Shade that gifted you this necklace?" Miri asked, holding her pendent aloft.

"One and the same," Zyndraxis replied, nostalgia rippling through Riven at the words. "That symbol in the middle represents her name."

Glancing back at the cover, Miri's eyes widened. "Of course! You can read this, too. I am not used to someone else being able to read the ancient text."

"Well, it is not ancient to me, but I accept the sentiment all the same. It is not normally my field of expertise. However, if Riven would allow me, I can assist."

Miri bounced on the spot with excitement, reminding

him of when they were children, and she would keep watch while he climbed into his parents' pantry and stole treats. It was her idea, of course, but he had always found her eagerness endearing and impossible to refuse.

"Fine." He allowed Zyndraxis to guide his movements. Riven threw the red cape over his shoulder, exposing his bare arm.

Miri positioned herself directly beside him, their shoulders touching. It seemed odd to Riven, being so close yet not controlling his own body. Together, Miri and Zyndraxis began talking in a language Riven could not comprehend as they deciphered the script. They would touch different sections of the disc, which lit up periodically in response. Sometimes Miri would try a something and Zyndraxis would guide her in a different direction while explaining why.

Riven was jealous of how animated she had become. Zyndraxis brought out a part of Miri that Riven had never seen. Riven knew in his soul there was no way he could compete against the Shade, not in this field... if any.

*"Do not fret, Riven, I have absolutely no intention of stealing Miri away from you. I respect the bond you have with her and only wish to strengthen it. I am certain that a woman like Miri has enough room in her heart to love you, even while I am here."*

Hearing those words in his head pleased Riven. The sincerity was moving. He could feel Zyndraxis' intention so strongly it almost felt like his own thoughts.

*"When it comes to Miri we are aligned in our desires. I have thousands of years of experience; you can trust me,"* Zyndraxis added.

An involuntary shudder ran through Riven's reminder. *Thousands of years?* It was easy for him to forget the age of the Shade when they got lost in their debates, so it was good to have that reminder of exactly what he was dealing with before he softened too much to the being.

"And I think we've got it!" Miri cried out pressing a symbol and sitting back, her body tense with anticipation as she watched, waiting for something to happen.

The symbols that had started to glow just faded.

A thoughtful hum echoed through Riven's mind. "My dear, try channelling some Aedris from Alyxian's amulet as you touch the symbols again in sequence. We have the order right, but I think it may just need an extra push."

"Oh, you're brilliant!" Miri leaned over and did as she was instructed.

Internally, Zyndraxis preened at the compliment.

Riven rolled his eyes.

Sure enough, this time when Miri tried the sequence, her hands manipulated wisps of purple, glittering energy, and it worked. The symbol in the centre glowed a bright purple that matched Miri's magic, and the disc began to spin on its own.

They all stood and scrambled back from the stone to allow it to continue. The forest around them quaked, shaking some of the remaining leaves from the trees, as a pillar of light shot up from the stone to the height of the trees. It covered the entire diameter of the disc, which was seemed to Riven, approximately three metres across.

"Is that what I think it is?" Miri gasped. She looked at Riven.

"If you think it is a portal, you would be correct," Zyndraxis said, his obvious affection for Miri's wonder tickling Riven's heart.

"I have only ever read about these. I never thought I

would get to see one!" Miri stepped closer and walked around the thick light in a slow circle.

"What is a portal?" Riven asked.

"It's a doorway to the Nexus dimension. The origin of all Shade, the source of Aedris!" She looked expectantly at Riven... well, not Riven. Zyndraxis.

"Knowing Alyxian, it is probably just a pocket dimension. She was brilliant, but a Nexus portal would require a Nexus point and we are nowhere near one," Zyndraxis explained. Miri's expression soured.

Riven was too busy analysing the lingering admiration within him, after Zyndraxis called Alyxian *brilliant*. These words held a fascinating warmth and... affection? *Interesting*, Riven thought, filing that information away for later.

"However, she was also an unparalleled Aedris weaver, so this likely will lead to one of her secret caches," Zyndraxis added, earning himself a grin from Miri.

"So how does it work?" Riven asked.

"Like this." Zyndraxis pushed them forward and into the pillar of light.

Having your body torn apart, and then put back together, did not properly describe the feeling of being transported through the portal, but Riven felt it was a close approximation.

*"Don't worry, it gets easier each time. Also, I am shielding you from most of the effects. We will need to watch Miri, because she will not have the same protection."*

"Each time? I am never doing that again!" The only reason Riven did not fall flat on his face was Zyndraxis controlled his legs. Once steady on his feet, Riven turned to find Miri following them.

"Wow, that was an experience." Miri's face was somewhat green as she tumbled through. Riven managed to catch her before she fell onto the ground. She was shaking, and did not seem capable of standing on her own. Riven swept her off her feet and looked around for somewhere for her to sit.

Calling the space a room was not an adequate description. The space had the illusion of four walls and a ceiling, but the way that lighting seemed both to emanate and reflect the surfaces made it impossible to tell how large the space really was. Even the floor had a semi translucent appearance to it. Every surface shimmered, the colours cycling through each shade of the rainbow, never quite settling on a single tone.

The only item in the room was a large chest in the distance. From what he could see, it was carved of a rich, deep coloured timber. Given that there was nowhere for Miri to sit, he checked with her to make sure she was okay before he gingerly set her down on her feet.

*"She will be fine; place your hand on her back. Direct contact will help me channel a spell to help her."*

Riven was grateful to Zyndraxis. He considered asking the Shade if it would be beneficial to send Miri back through the portal. He pushed that thought away as they approached the chest, and he reached out to see if it was solid enough for Miri to sit on, so she could catch her breath before they checked inside of it.

"Wait!" Miri and Zyndraxis cried at the same time.

It was too late. As soon as his fingers made contact with the polished wood, a loud voice boomed through the chamber.

*"Droshi! Droshi! Droshi!"*

A burst of energy erupted from the chest and sent them flying backward. Riven lost hold of Miri, and she went skidding off in a different direction as he tried to tuck and roll.

When he skidded to a stop, he jumped to his feet, head spinning. After he regained his bearings and looked back toward the chest, he spied a large form swirling in front of it.

"Alyxian was a brilliant Aedris weaver, but also very paranoid!" Zyndraxis yelled, so complimentary in his warning that it only enraged Riven as the menacing twisting form swelled and howled.

"Why didn't you stop me?" Riven barked, reaching for his sword.

"I was busy helping Miri!" Zyndraxis retorted, as if it were obvious.

"I'm fine. We have bigger problems," Miri said as she got to her feet, now a few metres away, and side-stepped over to them. She pointed at the vortex of energy, before the chest, as it solidified into a solid, shining creature made of what appeared to be clockwork machinery. The automaton was twice as tall and twice as wide as Riven, and it loomed over them with an eerie, faceless head; an unnatural aura glowed around its edges giving it a foreboding presence. It raised a gigantic fist above its hulking form and its repeated warning grew to a harrowing cacophony.

"Droshi?" Riven yelled over the alarm.

"I think it means 'unwelcome'?" Miri yelled back.

"Intruder," Zyndraxis corrected.

At that exact moment the golem creature lurched forward at a speed that defied its gargantuan form. It lashed out with one of its arms, aimed directly at Riven. With trained reflexes, he raised his shield arm to defend himself, only realising in that moment that he was not wearing one. He had lost it back in Zyndraxis' temple. Luckily, Zyndraxis seemed to notice and empowered his bracer with a magical disc of force that deflected the blow. It was still heavy enough to send a shockwave of pain through Riven's body... but he had not been crushed.

*That was close!*

The automaton was unfazed by this manoeuvre and moved around Riven. A strange tingle ran through his arm as the black memento markings unfurled higher up his skin.

Taking advantage of the construct's distraction, Miri threw a bolt of fire directly at its smooth featureless face. The blast was so intense that even Riven felt the heat kiss his skin. The creature paused for a short moment; its mighty head completely undamaged. As if it could see, the monster turned back and forth between Riven and Miri, clearly trying to determine who was the greater threat. Riven drew his sword.

Its attention settled back on Riven.

With a series of quick strikes, the creature continued the assault. Riven narrowly avoided each punch. Though fast, its moves conveniently telegraphed through its predictability, giving Riven enough time to avoid being pummelled. From behind, Miri slung several more combinations of magic at the being's solid back. Riven spied bursts of ice, electrical bolts, and blasts of water, but none could deter its relentless assault. In fact, the aura around it glowed brighter.

"Miri, you will need to access the coffer and retrieve the control crystal! You are only *empowering* it with your attacks," Zyndraxis coached.

Riven blocked the next strike with his Aedris-laden shield. Miri summoned a gust of wind that allowed her to flip with inhuman agility from one side of the room to the other, falling to one knee as she landed before the chest.

"There's some kind of lock on it. I will need some time to understand it," she called back.

"The lock on the lid uses the Genatra cypher system, start with Unara One!" Zyndraxis suggested. Riven ducked below another strike.

"Genatra, I know that one. It—" She kept talking, but some of her words were lost over the resounding thud of the automaton's fist slamming into the ground between them. "What about you two?"

"Don't worry about us, we'll be fine," Zyndraxis replied in a chirpy tone completely inappropriate for the situation. Especially since they were being pushed farther and farther back towards the portal.

*"Will we be?"* Riven asked. He switched to inner thoughts since he had no intention of letting Miri know he was afraid of losing this battle.

*"I have the utmost confidence in your abilities. Besides, what better way is there to learn how to fight together, than with the motivator of imminent death?"*

Riven fell to the ground, and rolled to the side, avoiding a downward strike. The floor of the room did not break under the power of the giant, but instead warped like putty before sucking itself back into a smooth, solid state.

*"You're crazy if you think I can learn how to beat this thing before it kills me!"* Riven thought with a grunt as he dove between the construct's legs. The move earned him a second to catch his breath before it turned and found him again.

*"Kills* us,*"* Zyndraxis corrected. *"And no, you won't let it kill us because if you do then Dace will have his way with Miri when she gets back, and they will make sweet, passionate love on top of the treasure she finds in that chest."*

Riven felt a surge of rage, but not at Zyndraxis. He raised his blade and charged at the golem, swinging wildly, instead. The automaton did not flinch, but merely executed a series of defensive manoeuvres matching Riven's sweeping motions, blow for blow. Unfortunately, Riven managed to only make small dents in the beast's fists as it blocked his sword. This was the first visible damage.

*"While I admire your renewed vigour, we will need more than that. Alyxian was as talented she was paranoid. For some reason she always thought that other Shade were constantly trying to steal her creations. I, for one, do not see why. I mean, if someone tries to steal something seven times in a millennium, one would hardly call that 'constantly'."*

*"Zyndraxis, I'm too—"* Riven jumped out of the way of a brutal uppercut *"—busy for one of your lectures!"*

The automaton found a break in Riven's attacks and smashed him directly in the face, blood spraying from his nose. Riven quickly switched to a more defensive stance and alternated parrying with the sword and using his energy shield.

*"It looks like we have our shield technique down."*

*"Concentrate!"* Riven ordered.

*"My apologies. Yes, where was I?"*

Riven wheezed as the construct slammed down on his shield again. This time it leaned into the attack, slowly pushing him backwards.

"I think I've nearly got it!" Miri cried, her voice sounding so far away amidst the intensity of the fight. "Oh wait, not quite. Hold on just a little longer."

*"It appears Alyxian designed a lot of her defensive mechanisms with other Shade in mind. That is why magic is mostly ineffectual against it, and your blade is the only thing that has been able to make a literal dent. I think that is partially because it is a Revoker blade, and because she never imagined a* human *would dare fight her creation."*

Riven managed to feint a strike to the left, allowing him

an opening on the construct's side for a powerful blow. Again, it did not stop the creature, but did blemish its armour.

"*What's your point?*" Riven asked, too focused on the fight to bother with any sense of politeness.

"*It would take hundreds more hits like that to take it down. However—*"

"*The short version!*" Riven's patience waned as the aches in his muscles increased.

"*Next time I prepare the spell, channel it into your blade at the same time as you strike, and it should give the spell a catalyst to break through that thing's defences.*"

At this point, Riven was desperate enough to follow any harebrained plan. So, he did as he was asked. Instead of flinging the power outward, he focused it into the Revoker's sword in his hand. The blade glowed an ominous red, and something about it felt more lethal. Not questioning the change, he renewed his assault on the guardian. This time when he struck, his blows hacked large chunks out of its fist.

"It worked!" Riven cheered. He kept going, though. Hacking and slashing until one of its arms fell off clean, clattering to the ground. Riven was about to hack the other when the creature retreated. It paused a moment before its arm magically regrew.

"*Great, just when I thought we had it.*"

"*Don't fret, Riven. I am sure we will figure something out.*"

"Okay, got it!" Miri announced.

The alarm was silenced and the construct froze. The apparent three-dimensional monster Riven had been fighting suddenly liquefied, melting into the floor. Riven let his sword arm drop and he doubled over, panting.

"Phew, that was close." Miri ran over to him and grasped Riven's shoulders. She leaned in close, eyes scanning him, taking in the various cuts and the broad red spots that would bloom into bruises. "Are you okay?"

Miri's concern warmed his heart, and Riven let the adrenaline fuelled rage from the life and death fight dissipate. "Just some scrapes and bruises. Nothing I cannot handle."

Miri's hand moved from his shoulder, her fingertips brushing along the bottom of a graze on his chest. His head spun at the sensation of her skin on his. "I do wish Aedris could heal."

"There are only a few Shade I know who can reverse the penalties of mortality; the best I can do is accelerate his natural healing," Zyndraxis stated.

"Guess we'll have to do this the old-fashioned way," Miri replied. She shrugged her pack off and dug into it, retrieving some pre-torn strips of fabric to use as bandages, and her canteen to wet one piece. With tender, considered movements, she cleaned Riven's wounds and then bandaged the bigger cuts.

Riven relaxed at her touch. The warmth of her skin was the perfect remedy for injuries. He would be willing to do that fight repeatedly if it earned him her tender ministrations.

*"Oh, darkness. You really are smitten with our Miri, aren't you?"* Zyndraxis crooned.

Before Riven could tell him to shut up, Miri pulled back and rinsed off her hands. Without saying anything else, she walked back to the chest. She leaned over, peering into it. After a moment, she pulled out a crystal, slightly bigger than her fist.

Turning to Riven, she looked at him.

"You said I would know what it was when I saw it, and I did. This thing was controlling that construct. Luckily, it was not hard to turn it off," she said, excitement shining in her eyes.

Riven's shoulders fell. She was not looking at *him*, she was looking *past* him.

"You should keep that. It could come in handy later," Zyndraxis suggested, his tone warm with affection and pride.

Annoyance — or perhaps, jealousy — surged in Riven. "Are you kidding me? That thing nearly killed us!"

"Nearly killed *you*," Zyndraxis clarified. If he had a physical presence, Riven would have punched him. Zyndraxis continued. "Putting your self-preservation aside, can you imagine what it could do to your enemies?"

"He's right." Miri tucked the crystal into her cloak and patted the wool. "In fact, from what I can tell, everything in here is really powerful. It would take me months to properly catalogue all of it."

"As much as I'd love for you to do that, Miri, Alyxian never had a single form of security in her caches. I suggest we take what we can, and leave as soon as possible," Zyndraxis urged.

"That's the first good idea you've had since I met you," Riven grumbled, kicking the corner of the chest.

Miri simply squeezed his hand, in a quiet show of tenderness, before she turned her attention to the chest. Wanting to get out of the vault as soon as he could, Riven put aside his frustration and assisted. They gathered everything they could fit into the small packs they carried. Whether by luck, or magic, they managed to get most of it. Zyndraxis chimed in at the end to help them prioritise.

After looting the cache, it took hardly any time for

them to reactivate the portal and return to the forest clearing. They left the strange area, and after walking for half an hour, Miri paused to spread their treasure across the leaf-covered forest floor.

"One for him, one for me," Miri said as she sorted their spoils into two piles.

Riven cleared his throat "Uh, wasn't the deal that we would retrieve all of the items for him?"

The confusion on Miri's face took a few good seconds to clear. "Oh, right. I forgot you're new to this." She raised her hands in the air and said, "As far as Dace is concerned, this is all we found." She patted the pile on the left. "And this—" she split the second pile into two uneven groups. She patted the smaller one. "—is what we'll give him when he thinks we're withholding stuff from him."

"Won't he notice that our bags are fuller than they were before?" Riven asked.

"Nah, I can be wonderfully distracting when I need to be." She winked at him suggestively.

Riven baulked. "That's not what I—"

"Ooh, this is pretty!" Miri purred as she snatched up a palm-sized silver item, encrusted with multiple deep blue sapphires. She pushed a button on the side, and it flipped open to reveal two mirrors.

"Ah, Alyxian loved using that to keep track of her lovers," Zyndraxis said.

"Like some kind of scrying device?" Miri asked.

Riven's head nodded of Zyndraxis' accord.

"How do you use it?"

"You need to attune it to your target, then you just channel Aedris and think of them. It is quite simple," Zyndraxis informed her in a tone that could be construed as bored. He used Riven's hand to reach for the item. He ran his finger over the cool metal, and it vibrated with power as he sent a sliver of his own Aedris into it. "See? Just like that. Now, if Riven ever tries to run away from you while I am bonded with him, all you need do is imagine his handsome face and you will know exactly where he is. You're welcome, by the way."

Riven was embarrassed on Zyndraxis' behalf at the Shade's shameless attempt at flirting.

*"My efforts are helping you, Riven. Embrace it,"* Zyndraxis reminded him.

Riven wanted to tell Zyndraxis where to shove his efforts, but he would not risk him redoubling them. Instead, he made himself content with watching as Miri did her thing. When Miri was finally done with her pilfering, they resumed their trek back to Weymouth. Miri spent most of the time inspecting some of the new artefacts while they walked. On occasion, Zyndraxis would comment on the item as she brought it out. Again, Riven was left out of the conversation. As much as he had resented it at first, he came to realise that it gave him the opportunity to contemplate recent events.

Even though Riven had never considered fighting with magic, especially after he had tried and failed back in Chafton, the new technique they had found was incredibly effective. With the empowered Revoker blade, combat felt more fluid than it ever had. It was almost like the weapon was an extension of his arm rather than an addition to it.

He watched Miri as she walked ahead of him. As always, his eyes were drawn to the curves he could see, as she had removed her cloak and was walking with it tucked over the strap of her pack. His mind drifted to that pretty, delicate arrangement of tattooed stars sprayed over her shoulder and collarbone. *The Swift*, she had said. He did not know much about the constellation, or the bird it was named for, but he wanted to find out. Between that and the obvious chemistry between her and Dace, as well as this whole Aedris business, Riven was quickly learning that Miri was not the playful, sweet woman he had thought her to be. That truth was an intimidating one, and as he listened to her happily discussing artefacts with Zyndraxis, he was not sure if he was excited, or apprehensive, to learn more about her.

# CHAPTER 14

# MIRI

On her way back to Dace's, Miri consciously subdued the exhilaration that surged through her veins thanks to her acquisitions from the vault. It was lucky she did, too, as they spotted several questionable characters lurking outside the building.

While Miri had focused on her own thoughts, it had opened a window for Riven and Zyndraxis to engage in yet another one of their little debates. From what Miri heard before she tuned them out, they were bantering about their fight with the construct, arguing over who should have jumped in and when, and whether *near-death* experiences created a valuable learning environment.

The ongoing conversation was enough to distract her companions from keeping watch, but not Miri. She spotted two men, leaning against barrels stacked by the door, attempting to look casual. To their credit, they maintained relaxed posture and an air of boredom, but the way their eyes scanned the street revealed the fact they were clearly on watch.

*Of course, you went and got yourself some muscle,* Miri

thought to herself as she shook her head. Going on this little side quest for Dace was always a risk. He had never been one to give anything away for free. And now? Well, she knew him well enough to see that he was arming himself to take, by force, whatever she brought him.

"Honestly, Riven. I think you underestimate what we gained fighting the construct," Zyndraxis said exasperatedly. "If we have one or two more of those encounters, we will master our skills. I guarantee it."

"One or two more?"

"Sorry, you are right. I underestimated. Three should do it, though."

Resisting the urge to laugh, Miri looked back at the pair. Well, at Riven. It continued to amaze her that her childhood best friend now contained two unique consciousnesses within a single body.

That realisation made her steps falter and she glanced back at the guards outside of Dace's headquarters. Instead of warning Riven of the probable threat, she did not. It would only make matters worse.

If, somehow, Dace had been quick enough to put two and two together, he would be after Riven and Zyndraxis. From what Miri could see, he would not have near enough force to capture a being as powerful as Zyndraxis, but that did not mean he would not get hurt in the process of escaping.

Before they got much closer, Miri turned and grasped Riven's arm.

The conversation between the Shade and her friend stammered to a pause. "What is it?" Riven asked, suddenly alert.

A cavalier smile swept over Miri's features. "Nothing. I just remembered there is a wonderful bakery not far from here. Why don't you get some food for us for lunch, While I square things up with Dace?"

Riven blinked, and the set of his jaw changed. He arched an eyebrow at her. No, *Zyndraxis* arched an eyebrow at her. "Are you sure that's wise, Miri? He is dangerous, and we do not like the idea of him being alone with you."

Miri would never admit it out loud, but there was something slightly endearing about their genuine concern. "I have been dealing with Dace for years. What I have not been dealing with well, though, is my craving for cinnamon rolls from down the road." Patting his arm and batting her eyelashes at him, she added, "Please?"

The response from Zyndraxis and Riven was half-growl, half-groan. "Fine," he huffed. "Just stay safe."

Miri squeezed his arm. "Of course. You too. I will meet you by the docks soon." She released her hold on them and stepped back, making a shooing motion.

"You've spent far too long spoiling her, Riven," Zyndraxis whispered as Riven led them away.

"You only say that because you've not yet been privy to how angry she gets when she's hungry," Riven replied, shaking his head. "It is not spoiling. It's self-preservation."

With a soft laugh, Miri turned and looked back at Dace's office building. Luckily, the Revokers lurking around the place had not spotted the conversation she'd just had. So, she straightened her shoulders, summoned her swagger, and strode to the building.

The two men by the door noted her as she walked by, but did not reach for their weapons. That was a good sign. Perhaps Dace had only betrayed Riven, and not her.

Either way, it was not good enough.

Bypassing the queue of sailors wanting to check in with

Leiton, she pushed through the crowd. "Oh, Miri. You cannot go in there. Stop! Dace is—"

Despite his protest, the young man had no hope of stopping her as she made a beeline for the door to the back of the room. She pushed it open without knocking.

The room beyond was lit by a wavering glow that was muffled as Dace choked, "Shit!" and leaned back over the desk. He slipped, but still managed to cast the tail end of his cape over the surface to cover the source of that light.

Resisting the urge to yell at him, or hurl a ball of fiery Aedris at his stupid head, Miri reached across and ripped the edge of Dace's cloak from the communication orb.

Rage surged through her when she saw Gareth's face blinking back at her.

"Ah, Miri, you've returned earlier than I anticipated!" Dace said, raising his arms in faux welcome.

"And I see you called the Lorekeepers for me," she said, forcing a pleasant tone. "That was so thoughtful, Dace. Saved me the hassle of doing it myself." She gave him a look that told him he would pay for it later.

Dace could have disagreed with her, but then it would look like he had lost control of the situation. That was not something he could afford to do, otherwise the Lorekeepers would sense his weakness and crush him.

"Miriam, how lovely to see you again. I do hope you've been keeping well in Chafford," Gareth said.

"Chafton," Miri corrected. She ignored the way Dace's forehead creased at the mention of a city he had not heard before.

"Same thing." Gareth's arrogance was enough to have Miri's blood boil. "Your friend Dace here was just telling me that you stumbled across something rather ancient and interesting. Perhaps you took more from the temple than you disclosed."

Miri's heart skipped a beat as she realised her earlier suspicions were confirmed. She whispered, "Bet you left out the cache you sent me after."

Dace shrugged.

"Why didn't you contact me yourself, Miri? That doesn't look good, you know," Gareth tutted. "After Nina showed you such mercy, I had hoped you would have been more loyal to our cause."

"Oh, I was intending to call you when I got to an outpost," Miri lied. "But Chafford is so out of the way, there was none around."

Gareth's face twitched with annoyance as she purposefully used the incorrect pronunciation of her own town to mock him. He forged onwards, though. "Well, I am pleased you are doing the right thing and turning the Shade over to us. That is, if it really is one. It belongs with the Lorekeepers, not you."

"It's not that simple, Gareth," Miri said, straightening up and staring right into the part of the projection where his eyes were. "That Shade is bound to a friend of mine. A friend who would willingly give up that bond, mind you."

"Then I will research an unbinding ritual," Gareth said, speaking slowly and enunciating his words as if he believed Miri was a fool.

*What a brilliant idea*, Miri thought to herself. She hated how he had a habit of drawing conclusions from information she spoon-fed him and acting like he was clever.

"The only concern now is getting him to you," Miri said slowly.

"Then it is lucky you are in the office of a Wayfarer," Gareth said exasperatedly.

"I don't make enough money in Chafton to feed myself, let alone pay Dace's exuberant rates," Miri said, a bite to her tone that she could not repress. If it weren't for Gareth, she would not have been scraping and working for even the most basic of necessities for the past few months.

"I can settle the accounts directly with the Lorekeepers," Dace said. It was clear that neither he, nor Miri, wanted to tell Gareth about their quid-pro-quo arrangement to secure her passage on a boat. If they did, there was no doubt he would try and claim it all for the Lorekeepers.

She turned and gave Dace a tight smile that promised violence if he fucked her over again. He returned it with a cocked eyebrow, and stepped back to lean against the door, letting Miri take over the negotiations. Apparently, he had what he wanted. She had no doubt the bill he sent the Lorekeepers would be nothing short of extortion.

"The passage is only one problem. The real concern is getting him there safely, and unsuspecting. If the Shade senses that he may be removed against his will, he will not go down without a fight." Zyndraxis had already agreed to be separated from Riven, but Miri did not think Gareth needed to know that. It served her purposes far better to have him believe that it would be a difficult task, one that she was uniquely qualified for.

Gareth sighed. "And let me guess, you have a suggestion for that?"

"To quell any suspicion," Miri said, tamping down the danger in her tone, "I am willing to accompany my friend, and the Shade, to Southport. However, I will require a favour in return."

Any impatience on Gareth's face was covered by exasperation. "Of course you will."

"I want my parents."

Silence fell between them, and there was a moment of recognition behind Gareth's eyes. Still, he said, "They are dead, Miriam. You know th—"

"Don't fuck around, Gareth. I know they are still alive," Miri interrupted, not wanting to waste time playing stupid games. "I want them back. One ancient, and powerful Shade for two old, run-of-the-mill archivists. It's a pretty good deal for you."

"Getting your parents is beyond my capacity," Gareth said, shaking his head. The flatness of his tone indicated to Miri that he was telling the truth. "But I can tell you where they are."

Miri's heart skipped a beat. Sure, she would much rather have her parents and be done with this business once and for all. However, she had to be realistic. Thus far, she had not been able to locate them beyond the noncommittal, *"In Lorekeepers Possession."* This was not useful information, but rather vague words that could mean almost anything. If Gareth could find their location, then that was a step in the right direction. The amount of money Miri would need to bribe that level of detail was more than she would earn in a very long while.

"Fine," Miri conceded.

Gareth nodded. "In which case, this conversation is over. Bring your friend and his passenger to Warehouse Eighteen in Southbank. We will have eyes on the docks, so do not think you can betray us, or you – and your parents – will pay."

Miri was about to reply when the orb cut off and the pulsing, bluish, light died. She wasted no time wheeling around and storming towards Dace. She jabbed a finger into his chest, hard. "You duplicitous bastard!"

There was no sign of concern on Dace's face, or even shock, about Miri's outburst. "You've grown soft if you were not expecting something like that. To be honest, I did not expect you to finish so fast."

"I remember saying the same thing about you a few times," Miri retorted. She ignored the way he leered at her as she swung her pack off her back and let it slam onto his desk with a dull thud. She opened it so he could see the mundane items inside, such as blankets and clothing. Then she pulled out a drawstring bag. "You are lucky we had a deal. Here is your stuff. I assume you are still providing my companion and I with safe passage to Southbank?"

She held the bag out to him.

With an understandable expression of wariness, Dace took the sack. "Absolutely, the Lorekeepers will be paying handsomely for that service." He untied the strings and opened it before taking his time to observe the contents. He whistled appreciatively as he pulled out a solid gold chalice, encrusted with a variety of small gems. He turned it around in his hand, and Miri could sense the Aedris in it from where she was standing. It would fetch enough for him to retire on if he wanted. "And the rest of it?"

"There is more," Miri said. She pulled out the second decoy bag she had prepared, and jangled it in front of Dace, before shoving it back in her pack. "But that is mine. Consider it my cut, for not burning you where you stand, you two-faced bastard."

Dace watched her, his body tense and coiled like a snake, ready to strike. However, he let out a slow, measured breath as he gestured towards the door. "Your boat is at dock four. The captain is waiting for you. Do not come back looking for favours again. We are done."

"You said that last time, yet here we are," Miri teased, turning around and walking out before he changed his mind.

When Miri stepped back outside, she took in a deep breath of the fresh river air. She walked over to the edge of the nearest dock, leaning against a bollard as she waited for Riven to join her. After a few minutes, Dace appeared at the door of his shop and had a hushed conversations with his summoned cronies who beckoned for their comrades to join them before they turned and left.

Miri's wait time gave her an opportunity to go back over the deal she had made with Gareth. Granted, she did not have much of a choice when she had walked in to find Dace already speaking to him. However, it had never been her intention to turn Zyndraxis over to that slimy git. She knew several other archivists who were more intelligent and more empathetic who would have given her what she wanted... but the moment Gareth was aware of Zyndraxis' presence, she was on borrowed time. She had had no choice but to pivot. If she had done anything other than make a deal with Gareth, and give Dace an outcome he could be happy with, she would have had both the Lorekeepers and the Wayfarers hunting them down.

It was another fifteen minutes before Riven came into view, his crookedly worn, second-hand Lorekeepers cape hanging around his torso, his metal pauldron glinting in the late afternoon sun. His narrowed eyes softened as he spotted her and he held up a lumpy sack.

"All sorted?" Riven asked when he reached her.

"Yes, all sorted." Her stomach grumbled when she caught a whiff of the aroma of cinnamon and sugar wafting from the bag. Before she could dwell on the discomfort, she said, "Come on, let's get on this boat of ours before they leave without us."

It was not hard to find their ship, thanks to placards at the end of each dock saying what number it was. When they got closer though, Miri's footsteps slowed as she took in the low, heavily loaded river barge waiting for them. The crew of the ship were walking around, calling out to one another as they prepared to leave. Most of the people were dressed in comfortable and practical wool and linens. It seemed like they were an industrious bunch, and Miri hoped that it would be a swift, smooth trip. Just as they reached the end of the gangplank, the door to the cabin on the deck opened, and out stepped—

"Oh no..." Miri breathed.

The woman who emerged pulled the peak of a tricorn hat low over her black braids. Even though the movement cast shadows over her warm maple skin, Miri would know those carved features anywhere.

*Can this day possibly get any worse?*

Concern had Riven attending to her immediately. "Miri, is everything okay?"

Before Miri could answer, the woman caught sight of them, and the expression on her face brightened in recognition, her deep brown eyes warm. She strode over and extended a hand out over the gangplank. "Well, well, well ... it seems Dace was telling the truth after all. It is a pleasure to see you again, Miri."

Riven's footsteps halted on the plank behind Miri, and she could almost picture the look of confusion on his face. *"Again?"*

*Ah, another point for you, Dace,* Miri thought. She could just imagine the smug bastard being rather chuffed with himself for pulling off this set up. "Riven," Miri begun, knowing there was little else for it at this rate. "This is Aliandra Murano, Captain of the *Swiftwater*. Captain Murano, this–"

"*Captain Murano*?" Aliandra repeated, her voice as sweet and sultry as honey. "Really, Miri. Why so formal?"

Miri resisted the urge to shiver. She had forgotten how Aliandra's voice made her feel as though she was sinking into a hot bath. Then, Riven stepped up behind her, and the incredulous, hard-line set of his firmly set jaw made her shake out of it.

"Yes, Miri. Why so formal? From the expression on your face, Captain Murano is clearly a … friend?" Zyndraxis drawled.

Even if Miri could not have told it was him from the tone, she would have known because Riven would have never said that of his own accord. She ignored the implication – however true – and placed her hand over her heart. "You worked hard for a long time to get your own ship. It would be disrespectful of me to introduce you any other way."

Aliandra, of course, saw right through Miri's comment. She let out a soft, enticing laugh that Miri remembered all too well before saying, "Please, no need to pretend to be respectful around me, darling." She stepped forward, resting her hand on Miri's shoulder, and leaned in to kiss her cheek. "It has been a while. I was suspicious when Dace said he wanted me to take you to Southbank, but I was not about to turn down the offer of your company. He did not tell me about your handsome friend, though. Riven, was it?"

Tearing his gaze from Miri as Aliandra turned to him, Riven nodded. "That's right." He offered her a hand, and she shook it. "Thank you for having us aboard, Captain Murano."

"It's my pleasure," Aliandra replied, stepping back onto the deck, and moving aside. "Now please, feel free to come aboard. We have lingered here long enough as it is. We really should get going."

Eager to have the awkwardness over and done with, Miri led the way onto the boat. Aliandra called over one of the crewmates and had him show her and Riven to the quarters below deck. As they walked through the narrow timber hall, the boat creaked around them. The sounds from overhead hinted that the crew were hard at work getting them underway.

When the crewmate stopped at a door at the very end, he pushed it open and cleared his throat. "Cap'n said to give you the best room we got. Problem is, we only got one good room, with only one bed," he said with a shrug. "I expect you two'll make it work."

Then, he turned and walked back the way they came.

"So, how many of your *old friends* are we likely to run into on this trip?" Riven leaned against the doorframe.

Miri shrugged. "I've got enough that I can never be sure," she admitted. She patted his shoulder and walked past him. "Don't worry, though. Aliandra is lovely."

There was a pause before Riven scurried after her. "You mean, unlike Dace?"

"Yes, unlike Dace," Miri confirmed.

"And are all of your ex-lovers either vagabonds or swindlers?" Zyndraxis chimed in.

With a chuckle, Miri threw her bag on the end of the bed. "That's a good question." She unpacked the items she had set on top of their share of the loot. Then, she started checking and mentally cataloguing their new acquisitions.

She sorted it into two different piles; one with Aedris infused artefacts for herself, and another for mundane, but valuable, takings for Riven. She assumed Zyndraxis would not mind being left out of the distribution.

"No, I am not asking her again," Riven hissed beneath his breath. He turned his back on her and began pacing the few feet that made up the span of their shared cabin. "Because it was an inappropriate question in the first place! No, I—"

"—Miri, you did not answer my question." Zyndraxis burst through Riven's muttering.

Miri sang, "Did I not? Hmm. Interesting."

The pacing stopped and, after a moment, a hand settled on her shoulder. "I am not trying to judge you, dear Miri. I am just trying to do Riven a favour and gauge what type of lovers you enjoy."

That made Miri turn around and glare at the Shade. "Oh, really? Because Riven *really* wants to know, huh?"

The way Zyndraxis stared back at her made Miri's stomach twist. Apparently, Riven really *did* want this knowledge. She cleared her throat. "No. Not all of them were vagabonds or swindlers."

Hope sparked in Riven's eyes, and warning bells rang in Miri's mind. She could not afford to get invested in anything. Not right now. Not when she had to hand Zyndraxis over to Gareth in a few days. To ensure he didn't get the wrong idea, she added for good measure, "Just most of them."

Miri stepped away and let Riven's hand drop from her shoulder, then resumed her sorting. Riven and Zyndraxis returned to their pacing and secretive conversation, so she ignored them. Miri thought about who she could call on to aid her once she found her parents' location. Of course, it was a fruitless line of thinking because she had no idea where they were. Still, it was distracting, and it was the easiest way she knew to mentally push through the start of what, she had a feeling, would be a very long trip.

~

"So, how do you like the cabin?" Aliandra asked that evening as she, Riven, and Miri sat at a table on the deck eating a welcome meal of freshly caught cod, carrots, and flatbread.

The night crew moved around them, keeping the ship on course as they sailed down the river, while the dayshift sat on various crates and ledges enjoying their own food under the stars.

"It was very kind of you to let us have it," Miri said between bites, "although not necessary. We would have been fine in the crew quarters. We don't want to inconvenience anyone."

Aliandra glanced between Miri and Riven. "I assumed you two would appreciate privacy."

Riven choked on his bread.

Miri thumped his back as she met Aliandra's eyes. "You know how I feel about your assumptions."

"Would you rather I assume you'd want to take your spot back in my bed instead?" Aliandra almost purred.

Riven, who had been drinking water from his flask, to dislodge the bread, now choked on his water instead.

Miri stopped patting his back, figuring it was a lost cause at this point. She focused on the captain. "Ah, there's the unapologetic Aliandra I know best."

"And there is the evasive Miri I thought I knew."

Aliandra leaned against the back of her seat, clicking her tongue.

Setting her bowl down, Miri ran a hand through her hair. Her mind whirred back to the last time she had seen Aliandra, and the way that she had left the inn, promising she would see her again; someday.

Aliandra's shoulders had sagged, and Miri watched her heart break in that moment. *Better to leave now, before things get too serious*, Miri had told herself. However, it was a lie. They were deeply involved, and they both knew it.

"Why did you agree to pick us up?" Miri asked quietly.

"Because I owed Dace a favour."

*Liar.* Miri narrowed her eyes at the woman whose bed she had warmed for many long, passionate nights.

Aliandra turned away. "Don't make me answer that, Miri."

"Ah, now there are two evasive women at the table," Zyndraxis said, breaking the tension that was sucking the air out from between them. "Perhaps we enjoy our dinner and focus on the lovely journey to come, rather than the misgivings of the past?"

Aliandra forced a smile. "You're right, Riven," she said, oblivious to the different tone and vocabulary. Then again, Miri realized Aliandra may have little interest in her companion.

"Now, why don't you tell me how you met our Miri?" Zyndraxis suggested.

That made Aliandra perk up in a way that warmed Miri to her core. "I was a crewmate for one of Dace's favourite shipping partners at the time. Miri was sent along to help with handling more volatile cargo," Aliandra started, her voice brimming with wistfulness and nostalgia. "I was on night shift much of the time, and Miri tended to have a lot of trouble sleeping back then. She would join me on deck, and we shared stories about the stars."

Blinking away the emotions, Miri returned her attention to the cod. Her heart fluttered at the memories, of how it had felt to spend that quiet, intimate, time with Aliandra. It was a painful thing to reflect upon, especially with their hard ending. Out of the many, many, relationships she'd had, Aliandra's was the one she'd wanted the most. Which was exactly why letting her go had been the right thing to do.

It was not until Aliandra stopped her recount that Miri re-entered the conversation to find that Aliandra had turned Zyndraxis' question back on Riven. Riven would have made the story a simple, *"We grew up together,"* but that would not do for Zyndraxis.

If there was anything Zyndraxis enjoyed, it was talking about himself. He took the opportunity with unsurprising elation, as he launched into a dramatically told, yet heavily altered, version of how Miri and Riven shared a childhood friendship, only to be separated by age and fate. At times, he would pause and Riven would correct an exaggeration or misattribution, but no one seemed to notice. It seemed to come across as a natural flair for storytelling.

Miri had no interest in hearing this tale. She was grateful for the opportunity to take a break from socialising. The sound of the river water lapping against the hull was a rhythmic, hypnotising thing. She was not sure how long passed before she was pulled from her musings by the sound of laughter.

Several crew members gathered to listen to Zyndraxis oration. His and Riven's meal was sitting half-finished and cold on the table before him as he gestured around, adding real theatre to his accounts.

"Oh, but that was not enough for our Miri. Covered in a mixture of baker's flour and stewed apple, she could not help herself—"

Miri covered her eyes as she knew exactly what Zyndraxis was going to say next. She would kick Riven's arse for telling the Shade that particular anecdote. There was not a single person on the ship that needed to hear about how she had gone on to try to convince the baker that she had gotten covered in the ingredients because she was trying to chase a stray dog out of her shop, rather than sneak out the back and pinch some cinnamon rolls whilst Riven distracted her.

"Ok, that's enough now!" Miri jumped up, shocking Zyndraxis to a pause. He peered over at her and the wind whooshed out of his sails at the interruption to his punchline.

"I was just coming to the best bit!"

The crew let out a chorus of complaints, and Miri clapped her hands together. "You know what we need?" She pointed at the beaten-up lute, drum, and flute on top of a crate near the door to Aliandra's cabin. "Captain, it has been too long since I have listened to music and seen dancing on the deck of your ship. What do you say? Shall we have some music to carry us into the dark night?"

That earned a cheer from the crew, and with Aliandra's say so, two men and one woman made their way over to retrieve the instruments. They took a few minutes to ensure they were in tune, and then the deck was alive with the strains of their talents.

"Don't look at me like that," Miri said as she sank into her seat, ignoring the puppy-dog eyes Riven was making at her. "You know I hate that story."

"It was a good one. We had so much fun," Riven protested.

"And it is an even better one when it is our little secret," Miri replied, leaning closer and covering his hand with her own.

As she hoped, the gesture made him stiffen and gawk at her, his mouth flapping open and closed as he struggled to handle the closeness.

While he was off-guard, she rose from her seat and let out a loud yawn. "I don't know about you, but I am going to retire for the night."

"So soon? You just asked the crew to play music so you could dance!" Aliandra said, her eyes drawn to Miri's body as she stretched and shifted.

Miri shook her head. "No, I said it has been a while since I have *seen* dancing. My own dancing days are over... and it has been a long week. Good night, and thanks again for having us on board." Then, Miri turned and left before Aliandra could argue.

Getting some space from both Riven and Aliandra made Miri feel like she could breathe a little. Her earlier conversation with Gareth and Dace came back to her mind, and she wondered what Riven would say if he knew. Of course, he had been the one who started this whole adventure by trying to turn Zyndraxis into the Revokers, but unlike all the other truths she had kept from him, the one about her new deal felt particularly heavy.

Over the next two days, a pattern emerged on the ship. Aliandra was, blessedly, busy working. However, she seemed to ensure she took meals at the same time Miri did. Miri considered simply skipping them, but she had spent enough time in her life living on the streets to know that she should eat while she could. That meant that conversations at those times were unavoidable. In any other scenario, Miri would have been secretly grateful for the chance to see how her favourite ex-lover was faring. That was not the case now. Instead, she was more concerned about ensuring Aliandra remained unaware that Riven was carrying a stowaway. The only positive was that it was easy enough to do this after dinner, as the music and dancing had occurred each night, and given Miri a chance to slip away, despite Aliandra's best attempts to keep her on deck.

Riven and his stowaway, on the other hand, seemed to have reached some sort of truce in the confined quarters of their cabin. Miri was grateful that both Riven and Zyndraxis were smart enough to stay below deck as much as possible. Save for some strolls above to get fresh air or pick up food, they were spending much of the day in their cabin, training. At night, Miri fell into bed with them. After their travels overland, they had gotten used to sleeping in close proximity. She was not sure what Riven and Zyndraxis thought of the arrangement, and she did not ask. In truth, the answer would only complicate things, and Miri did not need that distraction.

In the void left behind when they stopped their incessant arguing, Riven and Zyndraxis had decided to learn to fight together. As fascinating as it was to watch, Miri found the cabin was too small for their level of action. With their weaponry, she escaped a close haircut more times than she cared to experience. Zyndraxis had offered to stop the physical training and turn to lecturing instead. When Miri saw the utter devastation on Riven's face at the thought of more talking, she had told him it was fine. So, in the afternoons, Miri spent time on the deck.

"And here I was thinking you were trying to avoid me." Aliandra's work-roughened hand settled on Miri's hip as she stepped past her.

Miri nearly jumped out of her skin at Aliandra's comment. "Me? Is that really something you think I would do?"

"Absolutely," Aliandra replied without missing a beat.

Pretending to be offended, Miri turned and widened her eyes. "You wound me. That is so unkind. After all the tender moments we shared, is that really the impression I have left on you?"

"Yes." Aliandra back against a nearby barrel. "But please don't think I view that as a bad thing. You have always been slippery, but never without reason. I only wish I'd found you again before you got yourself involved with whatever it is you've got going on now."

Before Miri could come up with a response, Aliandra pushed herself off the barrel and straightened up. Her expression changed, and whatever regret or longing Miri had been reading was gone, replaced by something more casual. "We'll be having dinner shortly. We have made good enough time that we should get into Southbank Port just after sunrise tomorrow."

Even though Miri was still caught on the implications in Aliandra's words, dread trickled down her spine. "Tomorrow morning? I thought we would be in closer to the evening?"

Aliandra shrugged. "We've had a good current, good wind, and we are lighter than usual. Will that be a problem? If you want to extend your time with me, then I can let the crew know to—"

"No!" Miri blurted, an image of Riven's face when he was being steered by Zyndraxis flashed through her mind and she bit her lip. She thought they would have at least until the afternoon to talk. She did not know what she was planning to say to him. She certainly was not going to tell him that she had turned Zyndraxis over to Gareth. Even though her plan was always to find someone to do the ritual to separate he and Riven, that would lead to his immediate independence. She was not sure what Gareth would do with him, and it was far easier to exercise wilful ignorance.

"Ouch." Aliandra toyed with the ties on her blouse and a deep crease formed on her forehead.

"Sorry, I didn't mean it like that." Miri shook her head, and took a step closer. She put a hand on Aliandra's forearm. "It's been lovely seeing you again. I just wasn't expecting our time to end so soon, is all."

The normally calm and unaffected captain looked down at where Miri's hand had settled on her forearm. She cleared her throat. "Truth be told, I am not keen on the idea of our time together ending, either." She reached up, tracing her fingertips over Miri's cheek.

It was a matter of pure instinct that Miri leaned into her touch. It felt good to have Aliandra's skin on hers again, and it reminded her of all the things she had been missing since warming the woman's bed. She still felt it was such a great pity that they had different goals in life. Aliandra had always been beholden to the call of the water, and Miri had vowed to not rest until she had rescued her parents.

"I've missed you, Miri," Aliandra whispered. She lowered her face to Miri's and their lips brushed.

A relieved moan slipped from Miri, and she kissed Aliandra back more enthusiastically. Aliandra slid the hand that was on Miri's cheek around to tangle in her hair, and tingles ran down Miri's spine. She tilted her head to the side to deepen the kiss, but suddenly that delightful twist in her stomach turned to nausea. The tingling in her limbs became a stone-cold tension that was impossible to ignore.

Pulling back with wide eyes and parted lips, Miri felt her cheeks heat. "Sorry, I—"

Aliandra's mournful laugh cut through any excuse Miri was about to make. She unwound her fingers from Miri's hair and gently patted her cheek. "So, there is something between you two, then?"

"What?" Miri froze.

"You and Riven," Aliandra said slowly, as if it spelling it out so Miri could not try and hide it from her. "I was wondering if you were workmates, or if you were more of a 'friends to lovers' kind of thing? I guess it is the latter, then?"

"No!" Miri spluttered. Her lips still felt warm from Aliandra's attention and, darkness be damned, she could not bring herself to kiss the woman again even though part of her wanted to so badly. "Darkness, no. We're just old friends."

Shaking her head, Aliandra let her hand from Miri's cheek. "Miri, darling, old friends don't look at each other the way you do."

Miri was sorely tempted to argue, but that would only make it seem like she was trying too hard. She and Riven were not a couple. She had never had more than a few stray, passing thoughts of anything more than friendship with him. Granted, those moments happened over the past few days with increasing frequency, but proximity with the best friend she thought had *died*, was bound to have some impact.

"Hey there." Aliandra squeezed her hand, "Don't go

getting lost in your thoughts. I am happy for you. How about we celebrate with one last dance tonight, after dinner, just for old time's sake?"

The tenderness in her voice was enough to make every bit of tension in Miri soften. She nodded. "That sounds nice," she said, without a hint of sass or sarcasm.

"Great. I am already looking forward to it." Aliandra kissed Miri's cheek before she finally resumed her trek to the other side of the deck to speak with her crew.

Miri took a walk before finding a spot between some crates. She settled down onto some old, folded sailcloth and pulled out her parents' notebook. As she did whenever she needed to clear her mind, she thumbed through the yellowed, well-worn pages of runes and notes. She was pleased her parents had taken the time to record their findings, as they had helped her on so many occasions. She just wished they had left behind clues that would help her find them. In a fit of frustration, Miri tucked the book away. There was nothing in there for her now, and the information about her parents was only one sleep away. She had been patient so far; the need for lies and betrayals was almost over.

With a renewed sense of purpose, Miri watched the sun sinking the rest of the way beyond the horizon, painting the sky with breathtaking tones of lilac and peach. Miri felt undeserving of witnessing such beauty. As the evening darkened, angry, thick clouds started rolling in from the west. The air was cool and tangy with the promise of rain. It was a signal to Miri that it was probably time to retreat below deck. She considered returning to see what Riven and Zyndraxis were doing, but she was not quite ready for their energy. Instead, she made her way to the kitchen to offer the chef her assistance in helping prepare dinner. She was not much of a cook herself, but at least she knew how to peel potatoes.

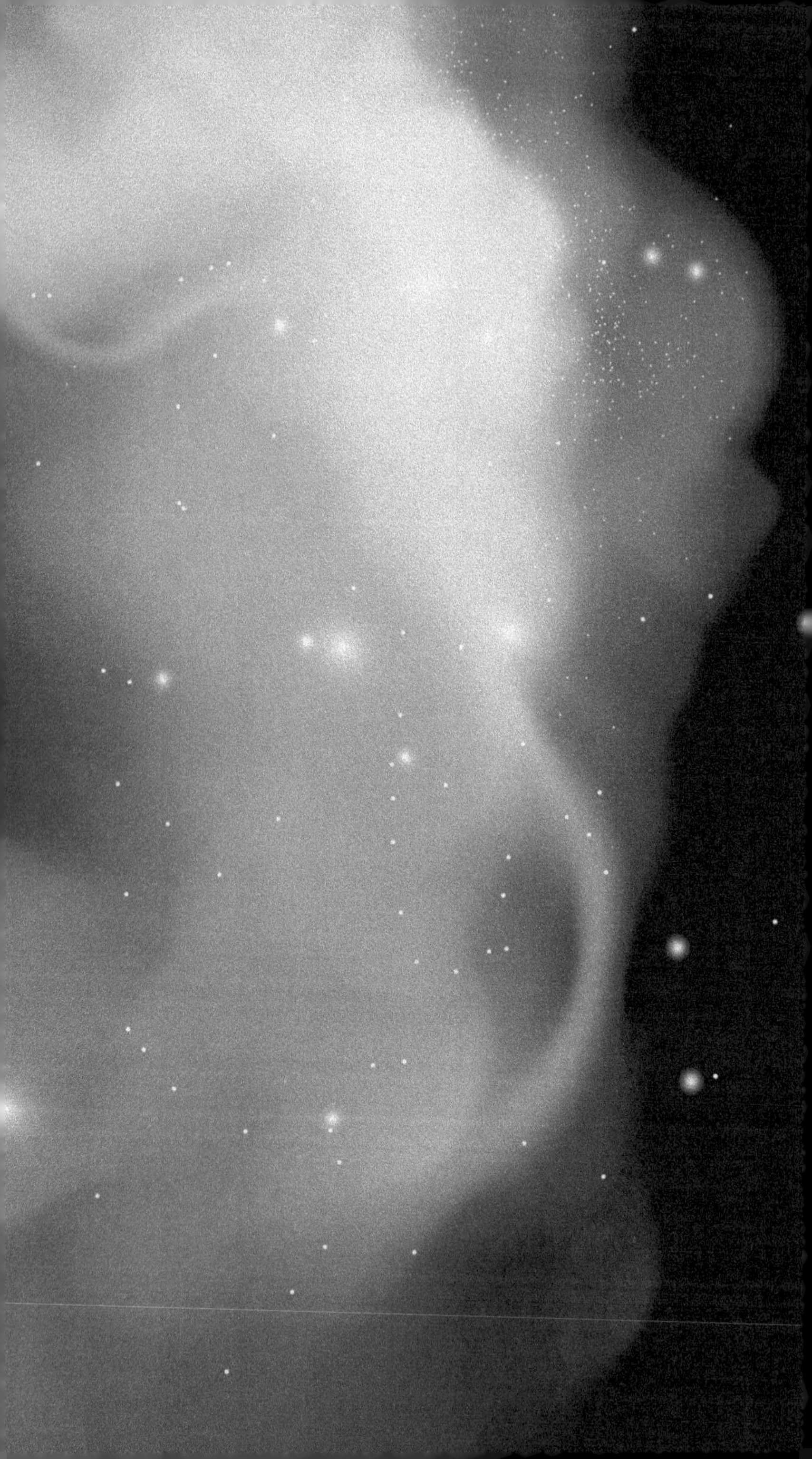

# CHAPTER 15

# ZYNDRAXIS

Miri left Riven and Zyndraxis in the cabin. It occurred to Zyndraxis they were cramped in their current accommodations.

"We need more space. This room is not sufficient for the magic I endeavour to teach you," Zyndraxis stated as Riven smothered out yet another spot fire, following a poorly aimed practice strike.

"We can't train outside. Remember, magic is not as accepted now as it was in your time. People are afraid of glowing swords and balls of fire being flung around."

"There must be somewhere on this vessel where no one else can see us."

"It's a couple of hours before dinner, let's have a look around," Riven suggested. Zyndraxis got the feeling the man was only saying as much to appease him, but he was not about to argue. He was longing to be free of their wooden cage.

Before his imprisonment Zyndraxis, had not spent much time on the water. Of the times he had, the vessels were much larger and far more extravagant. Aliandra's boat was reasonable considering the circumstances, but it was quite crowded and difficult to find personal space on.

In the evening, most of the crew hurried around the lower decks performing a variety of tasks. Riven zigzagged around them as he made his way through the belly of the boat. *"It's so busy down here."*

*"Indeed, and so very flammable,"* Zyndraxis replied. *"Perhaps we should venture to the top deck."*

Riven continued topside. A strong wind hit them as soon as they emerged from the protective confines of the lower decks. A light shower of rain battered the ship, and the side-to-side sway of the was far more pronounced.

*"Maybe we should head back down,"* Riven suggested when the droplets started dripping down the muscles of his bare chest and soaking the waistband of his black linen trousers.

Zyndraxis was about to agree, but then he surveyed their surroundings more closely. The crew operating here appeared to be very minimal. The only ones topside were all busy keeping them on course. Usually, crew members patrolled the main deck, but with the rain it was it was significantly less busy.

*"This would be the perfect time to train Riven, look they are all so busy with their work surely we can find a spot to continue."*

*"Are you crazy? It's storming out here ... and freezing."*

*"Pah, these conditions are perfect. Look near the stern of the ship. There is a section we can go that will be away from the others."*

Riven growled both inwardly *and* outwardly before trudging over. He passed some crates stacked up to find that there was a clearing at the very back of the boat. *"Is this good?"*

*"Perfect. Now, to protect yourself from the storm, we will need to form a barrier around us. It is like what you have done before with the shield, but this time it is bigger; but it does not need to be as strong. It only needs to block the wind and rain. Weave it into your clothing and armour to give the spell something to latch on to."*

Zyndraxis prepared the spell and Riven formed it around him. Though Riven's skill with Aedris was barely equivalent to adept level, Zyndraxis discovered that Riven was much better at using magic with implements he was familiar with, such as weapons, armour or, in this case, clothing. Several moments later the spell was complete and Riven was protected from the weather.

With that sorted, Zyndraxis continued with their lessons. He started as he always did when training beginners, only this time every spell would be channelled into the Revoker's shortsword. As they discovered before, the sword absorbed magic that could be used in physical combat, so when he channelled force energy into the blade, its strikes were incredibly strong. Riven swung the sword around with a flourish and grace that he had been unable to achieve in the cabin. Even Zyndraxis had to admit Riven's physical combat skills were impressive. He had only ever studied the theory behind the martial arts. He considered the actual practice barbaric and pointless. However, given their recent encounters, Zyndraxis was beginning to realise the benefits.

Also, over the last few days, Zyndraxis noticed their bond was increasing. When Riven used magic, Zyndraxis was able to guide him more fluidly and he, in turn, was able to feel the movements of his body as he swung the blade around the space. Despite the differences in their personality, skills, and literally everything else, they were beginning to forge a synchronicity. Perhaps their opposing styles gave them an advantage; while Riven focused on the physical, Zyndraxis could focus on the mystical.

*"Now let's move on to the elements,"* Zyndraxis suggested, sensing Riven was ready for more.

Zyndraxis infused Riven's blade with a mix of fire, ice, wind, and lightning. He ensured the spells flowed with his movement and complimented his strikes. Waves of elemental energy arced outward into the storm around them; they did not have as much of the range as his normal spells, but they made up for it in raw power.

*"I wish there was something I could hit, swinging at the air seems so pointless,"* Riven panted as they took a short break.

*"Interesting thought. You know, illusion magic is one of the most advanced forms of magic. Well, next to transmutation and restoration. Perhaps we could—"*

*"Please Zyndraxis, not another lesson. I only just managed to understand elemental magic without blowing us up,"* Riven muttered, reminding Zyndraxis of just how young, human, and impatient he was.

*"No, I think I can keep it much simpler for you."*

Riven slumped back against the railing of the ship. *"Gee, thanks."*

*"You're welcome,"* Zyndraxis replied. He was aware Riven was being sarcastic, but he felt like he had to let him know that his whining held no weight. *"What I am trying to tell you is that we can use a simple spell to create targets for you to hit. Illusion magic is not as taxing on Aedris as the other forms."*

*"Oh, in that case, let's do it."* The knowledge that he was not the one that had to do extra work seemed to create a hearty change of mind. Riven straightened and raised his sword, readying himself.

Zyndraxis prepared a basic spell for Riven to use. *"Now use your hands to form the shape of an opponent in front of you, don't worry about controlling them, once the spell is ready, I should be able to control them without any additional effort."*

Riven awkwardly waved his hands before himself, and a hue of magic followed the path of his actions, and when he was done, they had conjured several shimmery targets around them. The vague, humanoid forms shimmered with pearlescent light in the dying drizzle. They were fuzzy and relatively featureless but that was by design; anything else would be too complex for him.

Then Zyndraxis commanded the targets to attack.

Riven was quick to adapt. Despite their fake appearance, he treated them like real enemies, ducking, diving, and weaving. Zyndraxis used his theoretical and observational knowledge to give them strategy and techniques to challenge Riven. Because of their bond, he was also able to weave in force magic to give Riven the illusion of feedback when he struck his illusionary opponents' blades, armour, or shields. It made for a much more thrilling training session.

By the time they were done, both were thoroughly satisfied. Zyndraxis pulled his Aedris back to expose Riven to the refreshing coolness of the drizzling rain.

Riven took a moment to catch his breath, collapsing against the deck and letting his arms and legs sag against the timber. *"Wow, after all we've been through, that was the most fun I've ever had."*

*"You've never been invited to Nylamora's parties. Those were wild! I never thought a human body could do such things until I had seen them for myself,"* Zyndraxis

commented nonchalantly, needing Riven to understand there was more to life than swords and training.

*"I don't really go to parties. Not something mercenaries get invited to. Or when we do, usually we stay outside and guard the door."*

*"Well, maybe you can change that and ask Miri to dance tonight,"* Zyndraxis suggested.

*"I'm not sure that is a good idea."*

Through their bond, Zyndraxis sensed conflict in Riven's feelings toward Miri. *"There's something more, isn't there?"*

Hesitation coated Riven's consciousness, and he fell silent. Zyndraxis knew better than to push right now, so he gave him time to gather his thoughts.

Finally, Riven said, *"She is not the person I remember. She is more..."*

*"Adventurous? Outgoing? Outspoken?"* Zyndraxis offered.

*"Dangerous, cunning ... and promiscuous."*

*"That makes her all the more desirable. Don't you see, she is what* you *need. What* we *need,"* Zyndraxis *said wistfully,* wanting time to choose the right words, before continuing. *"Our entire lives we have just existed, never truly experiencing the world, content to drift from one place to another without any consequence or outcome. That goes for me as much as it does for you. Miri is a force for change! Does she invite more danger into our lives than ever before? Of course, but that is what living is; triumph in the face of danger."*

*"But..."*

*"No buts. I have existed long before you and will long after you. I can assure you that a woman like Miri is rare and you should not so easily dismiss her. Your natural desire*

*for her is not an accident. Deep down you yearn for the excitement she brings."*

It was a long while before Riven answered. Zyndraxis knew he was contemplating the revelation of the truth in front of his eyes. *"I can't believe I'm taking life advice from a Shadow."*

*"Shade,"* Zyndraxis corrected.

*"Right. Shade."*

*"Even if you are right and I do still want her, I don't think she is interested in me like that. Miri has only ever seen me as a friend. Nothing more."*

*"That is because you have not offered more."*

*"How do I do that?"*

That, Zyndraxis thought, was a good question. There was much work to do. Too much, perhaps. However, he was nothing if not resourceful. He needed to prioritise. *"First, we need to teach you how to dance. Unfortunately, we do not have the time to get you to where you need to be. However, over these last few days I have gained a lot more synergy with the way you move. If you will allow me more physical control, I can ensure you move with more grace than an Erkrellan swan."*

*"Firstly, I don't know what an Erkrellan swan is. Secondly, if I give you that much control, she will know it's you and it will be you that she falls for."* Riven argued, wariness now edging his muscles back to a tense state.

*"You misunderstand, Riven. My desire for Miri is a result of our symbiotic relationship. My only goal is to bring you, my consort closer to her."* Zyndraxis paused a moment to think. *"How about this... you will still be in control when you dance with her. Make your feelings known to me through bond and I will help translate them into your movements. It will be you dancing with her, not me, I promise. Please let me*

*help you with this before we are separated."* Zyndraxis allowed his feelings to flow through their connection. He gave Riven the unfiltered emotions of his intentions to let him see he was speaking the truth.

*"Very well, but you know I don't like that word 'consort'."*

*"What would you prefer? My human? My person? My meatsuit?"*

*"What? No! How about ... companion?"*

Zyndraxis let the word sit with him for a moment. Though he'd loathed to be separated from tradition, given recent events, it did seem more appropriate.

*"'Companion' it is."*

Riven clapped his hands together in triumph "All right then, let's dance."

"No, first we wash. You smell worse than a Baruvian duck."

"One day you are going to explain what all these made-up creatures are."

Riven brought them back down to the lower decks and into their stateroom where there was a jug of cool water and some washcloths. By the time they finished cleaning up, changing, and making their way to the galley, dinner had already started. Miri was seated at the regular table next to the captain. Their arms were touching and Zyndraxis admired the closeness they shared. With Dace, he felt a sense of jealousy at his familiarity with Miri, but with Aliandra it was different. Miri was more affectionate with her and less transactional. It was heart-warming to see, and he enjoyed the privilege of watching Miri enjoying her life and her love.

"Where were you two?" Miri asked, setting down some bread she had been tearing up and watching them with barely contained mirth.

Captain Aliandra paused mid-sip from her mug of ale. "Two?"

"Oh, Riven is such a party on his own; it's like travelling with two people sometimes. It's an inside joke. I suppose you had to be there," Miri said smoothly even if Zyndraxis saw the tinge of regret in her expression.

"Right ..." Aliandra seemed unconvinced.

"I was just finishing up my training. I found a more open area at the back of the boat," Riven said, trying to keep his tone casual. From the way his gut twisted, Zyndraxis got the idea that he was hoping Miri would be impressed by their commitment.

"I hope you didn't break anything on my ship," Aliandra warned, with a playful spark in her eye that Zyndraxis spotted but flew past Riven's notice.

"Of course not, we wouldn't dream of it."

Aliandra's eyes narrowed as her fingers twitched on her mug.

*"You said 'we' again. As much as I enjoy the recognition, I believe* we *are supposed to be incognito,"* Zyndraxis pointed out.

*"Maybe she didn't notice."*

Zyndraxis snorted in Riven's mind.

Before Aliandra could ask anything else, the entertainment for the evening started. The weather had driven them indoors for their meal, and the music sounded louder, and more joyous, in the confines of the galley. Like the other nights, Zyndraxis was not familiar with the exact tune, but the beat was something he recognised and could follow along. Before he had a chance to tell Riven to ask Miri to dance, Aliandra had already dragged her to the small clearing between tables that was serving as a dance floor.

The captain winked at Riven before she took Miri in her arms and started to move with her.

*"Darkness! I forgot that we would have to compete with her former lover. How can I? She is a woman; I do not have anything that matches,"* Riven griped internally as his eyes tracked the sensual sway of their bodies.

Normally Zyndraxis would argue that they had plenty to offer, but the odd gesture that Aliandra gave Riven before the dance suggested something else was happening. While Riven sulked in his chair, Zyndraxis observed the dance. Aliandra and Miri swayed against each other in time with the music, their bodies pressed close enough together there would have been no secrets between them. Even Zyndraxis found himself feeling envious. Arousal for Shade was different to how it was for humans; it was less physical and more emotional. It helped if the consort ... no, companion, was also aroused. Given the show they were putting on, he certainly was.

Aliandra's hands roamed up and down Miri's body, grazing her curves. Miri's actions seemed stilted at first, but she soon relaxed into Aliandra's touch in a way that spoke of sensual familiarity. Riven's inner turmoil at the sight thrummed through their bond; on one hand he seemed jealous of Aliandra and the ease at which she caressed Miri, but on the other hand, watching them dance together seemed to be highly entrancing for him.

As the dance continued, Aliandra slowly turned around and peeled her attention away from Miri. She made eye contact with Riven and seemed to think for a moment before her hand slipped off Miri's waist, and she beckoned him closer.

Zyndraxis seized control to force Riven off his chair,

but the movement shocked him and he quickly reclaimed himself. *"Uh, what is going on?"*

*"I believe our dear captain is trying to help us."*

*"How?"*

*"By lighting the fire, she warms the hearth. All we need to do is add fuel to the flames,"* Zyndraxis replied.

An internal thrum of arousal rattled through Riven's consciousness. *"What are you talking about?"*

Zyndraxis had to forgive Riven's inability to interpret dignified language. He was very distracted. *"Remember to focus on your feelings for her; I will guide your movements and I promise we shall have a raging furnace tonight."*

A moment passed before understanding dawned and Riven's stomach churned, but he cleared his throat. *"We're on a wooden boat. I am very uncomfortable with these fire metaphors,"* he thought. It felt like a last-ditch attempt at protest.

Despite any half-hearted misgivings, Riven allowed Zyndraxis the freedom to move his body. He did not have full control; that would require much more time and training with Riven, but it was enough for him to turn Riven's military-like march into a smooth, confident stride. Aliandra smiled at them, and Miri remained unaware of their approach until Zyndraxis stood behind her and rested his hand on the curve of her hip.

He purred in her ear, "May I have this dance, Milady?"

Miri glanced at her current dance partner, lips parting to speak, but Aliandra stepped back. She took Miri's hand and kissed it before winking at her. "Don't let another one get away," she whispered before she left them alone on the floor, with the music falling around them.

Zyndraxis stepped in before Miri could question the change. Not wanting to lose momentum, he pressed

Riven's body close to Miri, replacing Aliandra's timing and movements.

Miri turned in his embrace and draped her arms around his shoulders. "Zyndraxis?" she whispered, her warm brown eyes searching Riven's.

*"Don't answer. Keep her guessing,"* Zyndraxis told Riven.

Before she could ask again, Zyndraxis allowed the rush of emotion to fill him as Riven's body warmed with passion for Miri. Traditionally, he would demonstrate his mastery of dance and seduction, but tonight was not about him and his abilities. Instead, he ensured Riven's desires were translated through his dance. It was not the usual advanced footwork, grace, and flourish he preferred; instead, it was simple and to the point. *Just like Riven*, Zyndraxis thought, *but in a good way*.

The tempo of the song changed, trading liveliness for a smooth yearning. Despite his preference for choreographed waltzes, Zyndraxis kept his frame but held Miri against Riven's body. She whimpered, and he sensed she was almost theirs.

*"We've got her right where you need her,"* Zyndraxis thought to Riven, as he slid his hand lower down Miri's body, resting it in that delicious dip just above her rounded behind. He heard Miri's breath catch and he leaned in close as if to kiss her, stopping a hairsbreadth away from her lips. *"Do not forget to tell her how you feel. She's all yours, my friend."*

# CHAPTER 16

# MIRI

Miri's hand instinctively tightened against Riven's chest, her nails pressing into the thick fabric of his borrowed archivist cape. Their breath mingled in the scant space between them, and she felt the surprising, and overwhelming, urge to close that distance.

The moment lingered a beat too long, and Miri frowned as she pulled back. She looked into his eyes as something shifted behind them. She wondered what was going on between him and Zyndraxis in that moment, but she did not have long to think on it, as Riven cupped her cheek in his calloused palm.

Or was it Zyndraxis?

Her thoughts and emotions were in such a flurry after her dance with Aliandra and the partner swap. She could not make heads nor tails of the situation.

Riven cleared his throat. "Miri, I …. I must tell you … I-I …" Riven stuttered, his cheeks growing red as his voice became huskier.

A lifetime of interactions flashed behind Miri's eyes. In each moment she had shared with Riven, she felt such a deep connection with him. She had never been quite sure what to call it before, but as she watched him struggling to find his words, she knew Aliandra was right. The way he was looking at her now spoke of more than just friendship.

Strangely, the idea of "being more than just friends" with him felt like a warm blanket wrapping around her nervously fluttering heart. After almost losing him, it felt *right*.

"You see, ever since .... well, not quite the first moment, but—"

"Riven," she whispered, cutting through his rambling as they swayed on the spot, "you don't need to be nervous. It's just me."

Riven paused, gulped, and nodded. After a deep breath, he continued in a much more stable, measured manner. "For as long as I can remember, I have loved you in some way. Growing up, I just assumed we would stay in Chafton together for the rest of our lives." As he spoke, he seemed to be searching her face for something, for a sign or response. "Then you said you were leaving, and I wasn't prepared. In fact, I was scared by the idea of leaving town. It wasn't what I'd planned. But it became my biggest regret. I ... I should have gone with you."

Miri's eyes widened at that news. At the notion that he made a mistake all those years ago. She remembered vividly how crushed she was when he refused to come with her. Like him, she had just assumed that they would always be together. Only, she did not have that dream tied to a location. When he said he would not leave Chafton, she thought that perhaps she had been wrong about the depths of their friendship. That he was not quite as committed as she was.

Riven kept speaking. It was hard for him to stop, now

that the floodgates had opened. "When you came back and I saw you, it only reminded me of how much I missed having you in my life. I was going to ask you to stay with me once we had finished at the temple, but then I lost you a second time."

The world around them fell away as Riven unlocked a part of Miri that she had kept closed for so long. Aliandra had gotten close to opening it a while back, but then Miri had run before she'd had a chance. Now, though, her eyes stung and her vision blurred with welling tears.

"We've had a crazy few days. I have learned so much about the world, and about you. It's not what I expected, and I was thinking that I should just go home." He rested his cheek against hers, and his breath danced against her skin. "But Zyndraxis is right. I need you, Miri. I will not lose you again. I don't care where we have to go, or what we have to do, I want to do it together ... if you'll have me."

Blood roared in Miri's ears, and if she had not been clinging to Riven, she was not sure if she would be able to stand. It was not until this moment that she had realised just how hurt she had been when he refused to leave Chafton. When he had chosen the ghost of memories over the reality of her. Now, though, she looked back at a string of transience, casual flings, and self-sabotaged relationships. She saw a version of herself who refused to commit to anything because it would mean she would have something to lose. But now?

Miri pulled her face back and met Riven's gaze. The nervous tension in his dark eyes was a palpable thing. It was stretched so taut between them that breathing the wrong way would make it snap.

Even though her limbs tensed, getting ready to run, Miri kept her feet firmly planted on the deck. She did not need to ask herself if she wanted this. She knew it in her bones.

"Yes," she breathed, her cheeks warming.

That was all Riven needed to hear to close the distance between them again. He kissed her as he pulled her against his body, and she melted against him. The world around them disappeared, and the rhythm of the music merged with Miri's heartbeat. A thrill of pure, primal connection ran through her as Riven slid his hand into her hair while deepening the kiss. Relief echoed in his movements and, even though her feelings for him were a brand-new revelation, she understood. She may not have been pining after him in this way for long, but there was always a part of her that had yearned for contact with him. This felt like the natural progression of that, and she wanted more.

Finally, when her breath became ragged, Miri ended the kiss and rested her forehead against his. She closed her eyes as she drank in the sensations coursing through her body; its reaction to the taste of him was undeniable.

"We've lost so much time because I was scared to take chances," Riven whispered. "I hope you will let me spend the rest of our lives making it up to you."

In any other situation, Miri might have thought the confidence in his words was coming from Zyndraxis. However, she had seen Riven like this before. For a man who usually reverted to polite deference or tentative suggestion, his moments of steadfast determination were rare but always impactful. When he made a heartfelt decision, he meant it.

The implication in his tone made Miri's heart skip a beat but, for the first time, she did not feel the overwhelming urge to run. Reaching up, she brushed her fingers over the stubble on his cheek. "I still have things I need to do," she told him.

"I'll do them with you," he replied without hesitation.

She kissed him again. This time, she moaned softly against his lips and the way his hands grasped at her back told her he liked the sound.

Miri vaguely registered the fact that their bodies were still swaying slowly in time with the music. It sounded so far away and was the least important thing in her mind. Instead, she found herself becoming fixated on the smallest details of Riven. The way his chest radiated a solid, reassuring heat as it pressed against her. How the faint musk and metallic scent of him suffused every breath she inhaled. And then there was the slight taste of ale that still lingered on his lips.

"I want you to take me to bed," Miri whispered between kisses.

Riven's body froze against her, and he pulled back. His eyes, dazed and foggy with lust. "You do?"

She was just as surprised as he was, but her growing need was undeniable. She nodded. "Yes. Unless you're not ready for that?"

For a moment, Miri was concerned Riven would choke on his own breath. He recovered quickly, his palms sliding down her arms until he could take her hands in his own. "I've been ready for so damn long," he replied. He kissed her once more before he stepped back.

Cold night air rushed between them, and Miri almost regretted her request. She did not have long to think on it, as Riven turned and led her through the small crowd of dancing sailors. The music followed them all the way below deck, right up until they reached the small stateroom they shared. There, Miri became more attuned to the speed of

Riven's breath, and the way he let out a soft groan before crushing her body against his again.

It was hard to keep track of what was going on when Miri let herself get lost in Riven's kisses. At some point, she became aware of the presence of the edge of the bed just behind her legs. It was around the same time that Riven unclipped her cloak and pushed it off her shoulders. His hands slid around her back before settling on her arse. He gripped it and used the leverage to pull her tighter against him. She moaned in approval, and he let one hand roam around to her hip. It travelled over her waist and moved steadily upwards until he was cupping her breast through her dress.

Miri was never one for patience. The instant Riven's hand found her breast, she let go of him so she could start undoing the laces holding her overdress together. It was loosened in a flash, and she gently guided Riven away from her, so the fabric could fall down her body. Beneath the dress, she still had a shift and a skirt. It was far too much fabric between them. Riven seemed to agree as he looked down at her and started to untie the strings on the neckline of her shift, to loosen it, as she moved to unclasp his cape. In that manner, they continued to shed the layers of their clothing until there was nothing left between them. She dragged her eyes down his body her heart beat faster she noticed the dark, sinuous lines of the memento. The black, tattoo-like marking had grown from his elbow to his mid bicep. She ran her hand over it, marvelling at the very vivid reminder of the power he now contained.

"Do you ... do you like it?" Riven asked, uncertainty plucking at his tone. Now they were alone and away from the music, the crashing storm reverberated through the boat, setting the stage for an evening humming with anticipation.

"Like it?" She kissed the markings on his bicep. "I love it. It suits you. It highlights your muscles."

The radiating heat of Riven's skin and the way he groaned at her praise wiped away any questions Miri might have had about whether going down this path with Riven was the right thing to do. Her misgivings about the morrow faded to the back of her mind, and the only thing she could think about was how desperately she wanted more of him.

That thought spurred Miri into action, and she slid her hands from around his shoulders. She dragged them down his chest, leaving one there as the other travelled lower.

Riven covered her hand with his own and shook his head. He kissed her, leaning over her until she fell back to sit on the edge of the bed. He gently spread her knees so he could stand between them, as he helped her recline. When it was too hard for him to kiss her, he moved his lips to her neck and shoulders. Miri was grateful she was laying down, as the way he sucked at her pulse point made her head spin in the best way possible.

Then, Riven kissed even lower. He captured one of her nipples between his lips as he gently massaged the other breast with his calloused palm. Miri moaned and arched her back, craving more of that touch. "You like that, huh?" he asked, lips moving against the tender flesh of her breast.

It was Miri's turn to laugh. "Don't get too cocky, the night is still young."

"That sounds like a challenge to me," Riven murmured as he moved his lips over to the middle of her chest and started to kiss a path down her torso.

*Just how I wanted it to sound,* Miri thought to herself. She knew Riven could be hesitant at times, but he would always find the confidence when he had to prove his skills at something.

As Riven's trail of kisses continued, Miri did not notice the fact his fingers were creeping up her inner thigh until they brushed against her bare mound. She sucked in a shocked breath as her mind tried to split itself between focusing on his lips or on his hand. It became especially impossible as he sunk lower on his knees and the two paths met at her most tender junction.

"Oh, Riven!" Miri's hand flew to gently hold the back of his head as he pressed a kiss against her pussy. Her hips bucked involuntarily.

"Yes, that's it," he hummed against her sensitive skin. The satisfaction in his tone was *almost* enough to make Miri draw back, to pretend that his affection was not impacting her quite as much as it was. But ... this was Riven. Her oldest and dearest friend. As much as Miri didn't like letting other people have power over her, she would allow him this win.

Miri's determination to give Riven some leeway was rewarded when his fingers pressed against her entrance, and then pushed inside of her. She moaned, and he drew his fingers out, and then thrust them back into her, in time with a flick of his tongue.

"Darkness, yes!" Miri's inner muscles tightening around his fingers as anticipation sizzled through her.

Riven had the good sense to continue what he was doing. Every now and again he would experiment with a new tongue movement or pace of his fingers, and she would reward him by letting him know what she preferred. Soon enough, he found just the right motions to have her pent-up need growing in time with the increasing pleasure she was feeling.

"Oh, Riven. I'm so close," she murmured, her voice desperate, even to her own ears.

"Don't hold back," he whispered.

As much as Miri *wanted* more, she *needed* release. So, she gave him what he asked for and, in return, he fulfilled her craving. She forgot where they were, and how many other souls were on board, as she cried out his name until her voice was raw in her throat. Her cries were in fierce competition with the wailing winds outside, making the ship rock from side to side. Ecstasy rippled through her limbs until she was a shaking mess, and she sank into the mattress.

Miri was keenly aware of Riven's movements as he pulled his fingers from inside of her. She glanced down at him, bleary eyed, as he licked his lips and rose to his feet. He dragged his eyes over her shivering, flushed skin and watched her in a lazy, almost predatory way, as his hand drifted to his cock.

*Oh, fuck,* Miri thought to herself, as she saw him take it in hand. If she was able to do anything other than whimper pathetically, she might have let him hear her surprise at what he had been hiding from her all these years.

Instead, she watched, mesmerised, as he used the slickness from her orgasm to coat his hardness. She noted the way his chest stuttered as he gave himself that pleasure, and suddenly she was overwhelmed with the need to feel him inside her.

"Please," Miri begged, as she tore her eyes away from his hand to look into his eyes. Something behind them solidified at her soft plea, and he stepped forward.

Leaving her lying on her back, hips at the edge of the bed, Riven spread her thighs once more. Her body pulsed as it came down from her own release, and it was made all the more exquisite as he stepped between her legs and ran the tip of his cock up and down her slit.

Riven looked down as he settled the thick apex of himself against her entrance and leaned into her. The pressure was sublime, but it was only a heartbeat before he pushed through the tension and slipped into her. The sound he made spoke to something primal in her, and she reached down, grasping his hips and pulled him deeper.

"You have no idea how long I have imagined what it would be like to watch my cock disappearing into you," he said, voice gruff and alluring.

Miri felt herself tighten around him. "Then keep going."

Apparently eager to accept her invitation, Riven pushed and pushed until he was fully sunk within her. He fell forward, resting a hand against the bed, beside her head, to support his weight. Miri turned, kissing his forearm while he caught his breath. After a moment, his cock twitched and he said, "Ready?"

Miri cooed against his skin, not exactly sure what she should be ready for, given the fact he was already buried deep within her.

Then, he showed her.

Riven stood again, grasping her hips, and thrusting into her with the muscles that came from years of hard physical work and dedication. That was certainly one perk of his well-trained physique. Her pleasure did not build the same way her orgasm had earlier, but there was something intoxicating about his consistent, purposeful movements. Each time he bottomed out in her, he hit a spot within her that made the world go fuzzy. It wasn't until he found her hand, untangled it from the sheets, and guided it between her own thighs that she even considered a second release.

"I want to watch you touch yourself," Riven panted between thrusts.

There was such desire in his tone that Miri didn't dare deny him. After what he had given her—was still giving her—she wanted to give him something in return.

It was easy for Miri to find the pace of her own pleasure with her fingers, and each pass over her most sensitive spot only heightened their coupling. Soon enough, she could feel herself racing towards another release. The hunger in Riven's eyes only increased, and his grip on her thighs became tight in such a way that it nearly bordered on pain.

The sensations made Miri's head swim, and as each of Riven's thrusts became harder, she knew it was inevitable. This time, she did not need to warn him of her impending crest. He glanced between her face and her pussy as he drove into her. A shaking gasp emanated from deep in his chest as she rode the edge of her release.

"That's it, do it."

Riven's words coaxed her over the edge and she cried out once more. This time, his fingertips dug into her skin and he grunted as he joined her. Miri did not have the presence of mind to give him guidance of where he should finish, and she wasn't sure she wanted to. Each new slam of his hips brought a pulse of his cock that prolonged her pleasure, and made her grateful he was still inside of her, as he spilled his seed.

Riven kept going until Miri's moans turned to whimpers, and he collapsed against her in a sweating, panting mess. All Miri could do was wrap her arms around him as his cock spasmed inside of her and her own muscles twitched with delightful aftershocks. Riven led a trail of clumsy, tender kisses over her shoulder and neck until he could catch her lips. She kissed him back until their bodies settled.

Without a word, Riven withdrew from her and gently unwrapped her legs from around his waist. He pushed the sheets down the bed and helped her settle against the pillows. He laid on his back and pulled her against his body. He guided her to rest her head on his shoulder, as he traced his fingers over the freckle-like stars of her tattoo.

"I had no idea you had this," he said, voice gravelly from his exertion. Miri had to admit that she liked the huskiness of it.

"Probably because you haven't seen me naked before today," she murmured, while trying to catch her breath.

Riven laughed. "True." He kissed her forehead. "Are you hiding any other surprises around here?" he asked, the fingers that had danced over her tattoo now moving to caress her flushed, naked skin.

"I can't give away all my secrets in one night."

It took some time for their bodies to cool enough for Miri to pull the sheets up over them. As she did, her senses started to return and she remembered where they were and what they were supposed to be doing.

What *she* was doing.

Guilt surged through her, and she looked up at Riven as he laid back, eyes closed, a faint smile playing at his lips. "Zyndraxis?"

Riven squeezed her hand. "He withdrew to give us privacy," Riven whispered, the end of his words slurring a little with sleepiness.

Miri was not sure whether she was relieved or disappointed.

Either way, her stomach churned at the thought of

what the morning would bring for the Shade. She only hoped Riven would understand.

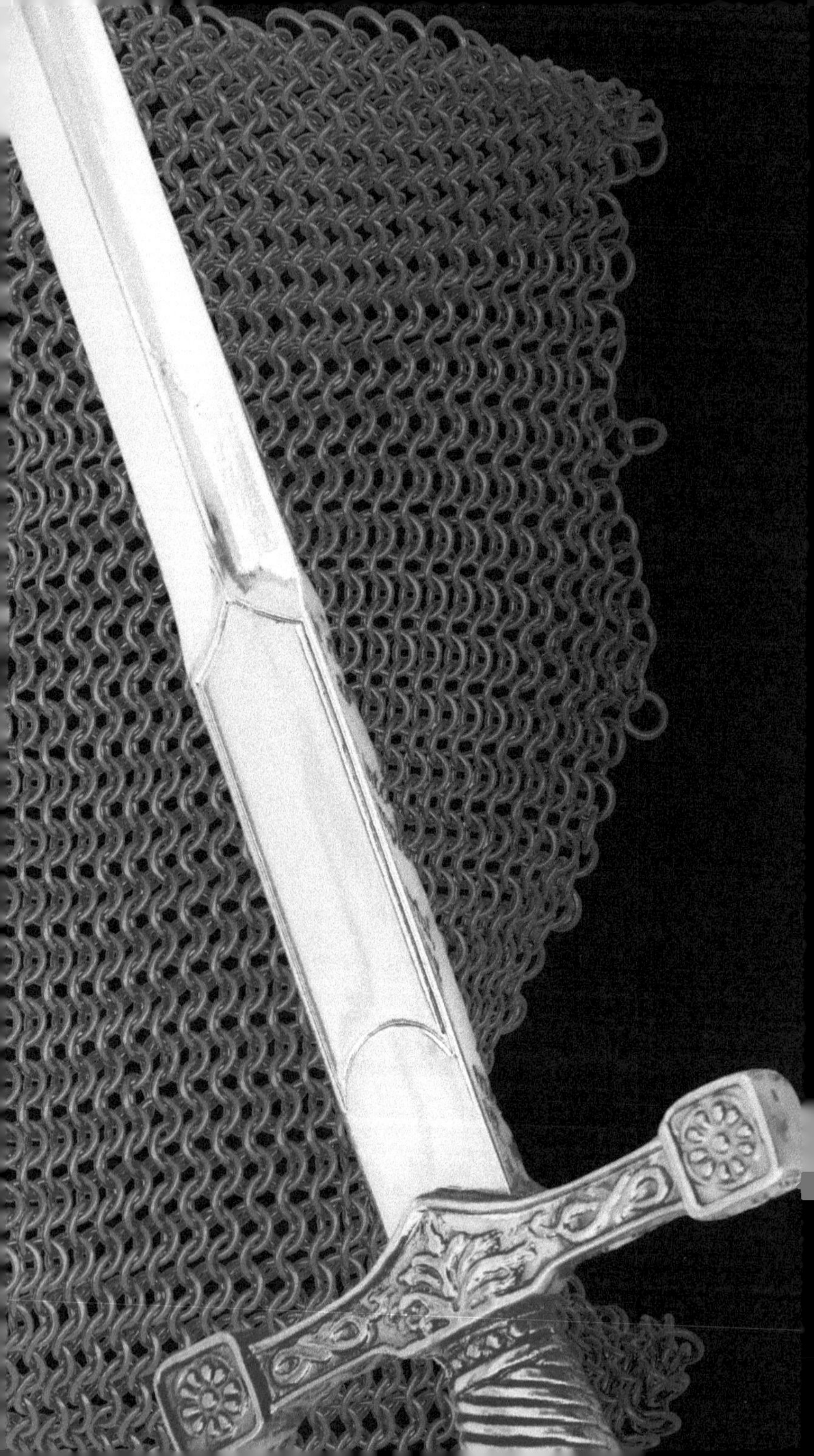

CHAPTER 17

# RIVEN

As consciousness returned, a strange sensation washed over Riven. It was as though he was a passenger in his own body, which was acting of its own accord. He stretched his limbs beneath the soft sheets and then felt the warmth of a naked feminine form next to him.

The memories of the previous night flooded back; he slowly opened his eyes. The room was dark and the details still hazy with sleep, but he was more interested in the beautiful woman beside him. He surmised that his mind was still waking up, because he did not feel like he was in control of his movements. All the same, he took great joy in pressing his nakedness against her smooth skin, his morning hardness laying against the crevasse of her butt cheeks.

She purred with sleepy pleasure and slowly turned to face him. He was about to cry out as the eyes that met him were green on a headful of pale blonde hair. That was not Miri, with her deep brown eyes and almost black hair.

Instead of expressing his shock, a voice that was not his own murmured, "Good morning, Aly."

The woman's face brightened, highlighting the cut of her angular cheeks. "Good morning, Zyn."

*Zyndraxis? Was this a dream?*

Before Riven could understand anything more, the door to their room burst inward. The light from outside blazed into the space. It was immediately clear that they were no longer in the cabin on the boat. The room was much larger and far more extravagant; there were pieces of furniture that looked completely out of place and far more decorative than functional. There was also a lot of clutter around the space, as if someone was working on several half-finished projects. The room was not rocking like the *Swiftwater.*

Three imposing figures rushed into the room, each of them wearing uniforms Riven had never seen before. They were equipped with outdated weaponry and armour that seemed inappropriate for the times. Zyndraxis sat bolt upright, and the power of Aedris filled his body. Orbs of power swirled to light in his hands and glowed brightly.

The intruders were not perturbed by his display, and instead took up a triangular formation blocking the exit. The man in the middle spoke with an unwavering authority in a deep voice that denoted him as their leader.

"Zyndraxis, Lord of Thymear, Grand Vizer to the Archmage Lorian, Keeper of the Hold. You and your consort are under arrest for treason. You are to come with us immediately."

"That will not happen," Zyndraxis snarled.

Aly placed a soft hand on his wrist. He looked over at her, expecting to see fear but instead saw an expression of apology. "I'm sorry Zyn, I told them you would go quietly."

The pain in his gut, in Zyndraxis' gut, was so intense that the bed felt like it was swaying. The room rocked back and forth and the groaning of the floorboards echoed all around him. His vision blurred and everything went out of focus. A loud bell sounded in the distance ...

And he awoke.

Riven gasped as he sat up, the age-worn sheets on the bed falling around his naked waist. He tested the movement of his body and found he had full control of himself. He let out a sigh of relief, but then turned to check on his companion.

The bed—no, the room—was empty.

"Miri?" he called, panic surging through him.

"*She is safe. She woke up earlier.*" Zyndraxis sounded uncharacteristically reserved.

"Did you ... was that ..." Riven trailed off, scratching his neck as he stifled a yawn. "That dream, did that happen?"

There was a long pause.

"*As our bond strengthens, so too does the melding of our knowledge and memories. What you saw was a memory. For a human, though, I suppose it would seem more like a dream.*"

"*How long ago did that happen?*"

"*Not long before I was imprisoned.*"

"*And Aly? Who was she?*"

"*She was...*" Zyndraxis began, but Riven sensed hesitation in his words. There was pain intermixed with longing.

Aly was not just a passing fling. She was much more than that. Riven could feel it. "*If you don't want to talk about it...*"

"*No, I should. Besides you will find out on your own anyway.*" Zyndraxis was more resigned than Riven had ever heard him. "*Alyxian—*"

"*Wait!*" Riven's eyes widened. "*Alyxian, as in the*

*Alyxian whose cache we raided? Whose automaton almost killed me?"*

*"Killed us? Yes. That very Alyxian. She was not only a brilliant Aedris Weaver, but also an on-again, off-again partner of mine. Because of our immortality, Shade do not have the same long-term commitments as humans. Especially since our consorts do not always get along. However, in Shade terms we'd spent more time with each other than most."*

Warmth and connection radiated through Riven again, and there was no doubt now that Zyndraxis had romantic feelings for his fellow Shade. It was the most genuine emotion he had felt from the ancient magical being yet. Well, save for his admiration of Miri.

*"In the dream she betrayed you."* When Riven said that, it was not a question. It had been abundantly clear that Zyndraxis' own lover had turned him over to the people who imprisoned him.

*"Oh that? Not in the same sense as humans perceive betrayal. We Shade tend to feud amongst ourselves quite frequently. Over the millennia there is not a single thing that either of us has not done to each other."* There was an odd mix of nostalgia and in Zyndraxis' tone. *"In her case, I think it was justified. Especially given how everything turned out."*

*"What do you mean? What did you do?"*

Zyndraxis paused for the longest time yet. Riven hung on patiently, hoping the Shade would share more. *"I will keep that one to myself for the moment. In time you will find out, and in time you will understand."*

*"Okay. Thank you for sharing ... Zyn?"* Riven teased, figuring that the time for pushing was over, and a bit of humour was needed to defuse the tension.

Aedris crackled in the air around them. *"From you, I*

*will only accept Zyndraxis or Milord. Anything else would be too informal."*

*"Sure, Zyn,"* Riven joked.

*"I could go back to calling you my consort."*

*"Okay fine, Zyndraxis."* He emphasised the name. *"Let's go find Miri."*

Riven eased himself of the bed and retrieved a fresh set of clothing before heading out of the cabin. Unlike the previous night, the lower decks were far less crowded. He did not spend long there because he assumed that Miri was on the upper levels.

Sure, enough he found her leaning against the edge of the boat with the captain beside her. Aliandra noticed Riven first and gave another knowing nod, and wink, before nudging Miri. His beautiful, troublesome archivist turned and graced him with the sweetest little wave. The warm morning light made her smooth skin glisten, and Riven's stomach churned as he approached.

"Good morning," Miri said quietly, her eyes flashing with what could only be the memories of the previous night. Riven had a feeling she wanted to say more, but Aliandra shifted beside her, and Miri kept her thoughts to herself.

Most likely sensing the awkward tension growing, Aliandra clapped her hands and straightened up. "We arc almost at the port. I think I will leave you two for more alone time." She hugged Miri and kissed her cheek before stepping away.

Riven felt a pang of jealousy at the gesture; after all they were past lovers.

*"Do not fret. Remember, she helped us last night,"* Zyndraxis reminded him.

Riven ignored the reassurance and turned to Miri. "I

need to talk to you," he told her at the same time as she said, "So, about last night."

They both laughed at the clash but Riven gestured to her. "You go first."

"Last night was amazing and we said a lot of things, but I want to be sure you know what it means. My life is not exactly simple, as you've already seen. It's dangerous and exciting all at once. If you've had trouble with the past few days, you need to know that the next few *years* will be more of the same. I just want to be sure it is what you want."

*"It's not like we hadn't guessed that,"* Zyndraxis offered quickly, as if trying to jump in before Riven's self-doubt did.

He was right, though. He had a growing feeling that this was the real-life Miri lived. Alongside her, he realised it was not as bad as he had thought. It would be even less bad if they continued doing what they did last night. "It is what I want. I promise Miri, I will not leave your side."

"Good, because once Zyndraxis is gone, then it'll be the two of us against the world." She winked at him.

"Now what did you want to tell me?"

Riven gulped. *The two of us?* That made his gut twist. After his conversation with Zyndraxis in the cabin, he was not so sure about that anymore.

*"Riven, what are you hiding?"* Zyndraxis quizzed, once more showing he was in tune with Riven's mind.

"I just wanted to reassure you that I'm in it for the long haul," Riven said, taking her hand and changing the subject. He stepped around to stand behind Miri, so that she was facing outwards, and his body was pressed against her back. He leaned in, pushing some stray hair off her neck, and tenderly kissing the soft skin there. Taking a deep breath, he consumed her scent and let out a satisfied "Ah."

that seemed to distract Zyndraxis, and it was enough to have Miri relax against him.

They spent the next short while taking in the sights and sounds as they approached the port. Compared to Weymouth, Southbank was positively thriving. There were more docks than Riven could count between the veritable armada of riverboats, and Riven could not see the edges of the town from his vantage point. Smoke rose from hundreds of chimneys along the waterfront; ramshackle buildings of two or three storeys that looked to be a mix of warehouses, homes, and shops. Farther back, on a hill that seemed to be the heart of the city, stood more expensive looking stone manors that oversaw the hustle and bustle of the town around it.

Having never been anywhere larger than the small country towns around Chafton, Riven felt it was a rather impressive, if intimidating sight.

"Everything looks so different now; hard to believe humans were able to do so much without us," Zyndraxis noted aloud.

Miri hummed in acknowledgement, but she seemed distracted as the ship was guided expertly into the port.

While Aliandra and her crew worked, Riven found he was thankful that they would soon be on solid ground. As much as he appreciated their hospitality, he was looking forward to getting away from the rocking of the ship, so he did not feel as though he had overdone it on the ale.

They disembarked and Miri gave Aliandra one last hug and kiss on the cheek. Riven reminded himself of his conversation with Miri, and was surprised, yet grateful, when the captain also gave him a warm hug. Despite Aliandra's own past with Miri, it was a mature gesture, and Riven could understand why Miri had been drawn to her. She was quite a pleasant person.

Miri led them into the town and gave them a tour. She indicated several different shops and brewhouses that were popular for tourists and locals alike, whilst also pointing out the hidden agendas and shadier operations that lay behind them. Even after the last few days, Riven was still surprised by the amount of back dealing and underhanded operations that were being carried out right under his nose. What made the lesson even more overwhelming was Zyndraxis' own commentary about the town and how it was so different when he was there; apparently, he thought the technology level of civilisation had fallen back to hundreds of years before he was imprisoned.

After an hour of a meandering tour through side streets and back alleys, they finally arrived at their destination. It was an unassuming, single-storey warehouse that sported the Lorekeepers' spiral symbol above the door. Miri took out an odd-looking item and prepared to use it on the door. As she did, Riven realised that this was it. He was about to have Zyndraxis torn from him.

Riven stopped and put a hand on Miri's shoulder. "Wait!"

Miri jumped at his sudden outburst. "What is it?"

*"What are you waiting for?"* Zyndraxis asked.

"It's just ... are we sure we want to do this? I mean, it hasn't been as bad as I first thought," he said, intending the words for both Miri and Zyndraxis to hear.

*"Riven? I had no idea you thought that. I must say I am surprised."*

Miri didn't answer; she looked at him with an unrecognisable expression. Her lips parted as if she was about to say something, and then the door opened.

"Gareth?" Riven cried with surprise.

The annoying man in the doorway was familiar, with an impatient expression on his face. Around him stood several other Lorekeepers in the general uniform, which was slightly different to the one that Miri and Gareth wore. There were four other Lorekeepers in total. One of them Riven recognised as Willis, the young man that had accompanied them to the temple of Thymear, and who had lost his mother in the process. The other three were more imposing. They stepped out of the building and flanked them on either side. Though they were wearing the same cloaks on the outside, Riven's experience told him they were equipped with weaponry and armour underneath.

"What are you waiting for? Get inside!" Gareth snapped. His three bulkier accomplices surrounded Miri and Riven and ushered them along, as Willis fell into step with him.

They walked straight into a room that spanned the entire width of the building. It was a wide-open area in the centre, with old, rickety pine shelves lining the walls. They held a variety of boxes and containers and from the way Zyndraxis shifted inside him, reaching out with a sense of curiosity, Riven got a feeling there were relics in them.

*"There is a lot of dormant power in this place,"* Zyndraxis said, confirming his suspicions.

The door shut behind them, and the Lorekeepers, with the weapons hiding under their cloaks, stood between Miri and Riven, and the exit. "You're late Miriam," Gareth noted, puffing out his chest.

"I'm exactly where, and when, I need to be," Miri replied through a clenched jaw. She did not seem surprised to see him there, and that worried Riven.

"I thought you would try to back out of our deal."

Riven looked at her, confused. He mouthed the word, *"deal?"*

She did not meet his gaze, instead focusing on Gareth. "I think you will find that everything is as expected. One Shade for my parents' location."

"Parents?" Riven asked, heart seizing in his chest. Miri appeared to *know exactly* what was going on. "Miri? Please, tell me what is happening."

*"Oh, dear. Our Miri really is a sneaky one, isn't she? Did she say anything about this last night whilst I was unaware?"* Zyndraxis asked.

All Riven could do was shake his head.

She did not answer him, either. Miri's expression still focused on Gareth, though her eyes darted around the room at the others that had now surrounded them.

"Ah, I see. Your friend was unaware of the arrangement." Gareth turned to Riven. "She is trading you in for her dear Mummy and Daddy. Once more, it seems you are just another piece of collateral damage in her long line of failures. Only this time, you will not escape."

"The deal is for the Shade, Gareth. Riven is not part of all this. Once they have been split, you will let him go," Miri growled, taking a step closer to Riven.

*"I wonder why she did not tell us about her parents or any deals made. I never disagreed to our separation."* Zyndraxis did not sound annoyed. If anything, he seemed to find the situation intriguing.

Riven gritted his teeth. *"I'm just as confused."*

"My recollection might be hazy; you said you would give me the Shade for information about your parents. We never said anything about letting your friend go." Gareth smirked.

"That is ridiculous! After you separate them, he serves no other purpose." Miri waved a hand in Riven's direction.

Riven might have objected to being purposeless without the Shade, but he realised the argument was in his favour and decided to keep his mouth shut.

"Ah yes, the ritual," Gareth said, sounding bored. "I don't think we will be performing that today." Standing just behind his shoulder, Willis' eyes widened at the betrayal. He glanced between Gareth and Miri, appearing upset by Gareth's deception.

Miri looked furious, and Riven feared steam would soon start whistling from her ears. "That was not the deal!"

"You merely told us to have the ritual prepared. I did not agree to complete it immediately." Gareth gestured around the room, and his colleagues stepped forward. They held an assortment of everyday items laden with Aedris. Their presence made Riven's skin prickle. Something felt *off* about them.

*"The items are, in fact, used for performing the bonding ritual. However, they also have the side effect of nullifying magic. Given the way they are wielding them, I'd say they are prepared for more than just a ritual,"* Zyndraxis spoke in his mind. He had been unusually quiet during this whole exchange, which made Riven even more concerned.

Miri's stance shifted subtly. Riven sensed the change immediately. She was preparing for a fight. Riven's hand slowly went to the sword at his hip. He sensed Zyndraxis conjuring a spell.

"And you held up your end of the bargain, delivering this creature so that the Lorekeepers can deal with it as we see fit."

Miri's hands disappeared beneath her cloak. "What about my parents?"

"Don't look so betrayed; I'm not a complete monster." Gareth reached into his own cloak slowly, so as not to alarm everyone, and withdrew a tightly rolled sheet of parchment. He held it up for her. "That is all of the information I could find."

For a split second, the determined look on Miri's face flashed with disbelief. Apparently not wanting to get close to him, she summoned some Aedris and levitated the scroll out of his hand. She unrolled it, her eyes darting between her old colleague and the parchment. When it was open, she glanced down and her eyes flashed with something Riven had rarely seen in her. Shock.

"And now for the last part of our *deal.* As far as the Lorekeepers are concerned, you are free to go, Miriam." Gareth gestured to his companions, and they rearranged themselves to surround Riven. Before any conflict could begin, Gareth yelled, "She's all yours!"

There was a heavy thud as the door was flung open, banging back against the wall, and shaking on its hinges. Several fully armed people burst into the room, the white of the shield and hammer logo seemed stark against their black tabards. Riven's jaw dropped as he recognised Nyrelle, one of the Revokers from Chafton.

Riven drew his sword, and the blade flared with light as spectral red flames licked the cutting edge; after all they had been through, after everything said, Riven would not let them take Miri from him.

The Revokers joined the Lorekeepers to surround Riven and Miri, weapons drawn and ready for a fight. Miri recovered quickly by jamming the scroll in a pocket in her cloak, and pulling an Aedris-laden, jewel encrusted, dagger from the pouch on her belt.

"As I said, the Lorekeepers officially freed me from any

obligation. However, the Revokers have a bounty on your head. Something about killing one of them?" Gareth shrugged and yawned, as if bored.

Time slowed to a heartbeat. Riven surveyed the room, the sheer number of enemies showing exactly why Gareth felt comfortable being so complacent. He had them outnumbered five to one. Unlike the last time Riven, Miri, and Zyndraxis fought the Revokers, their opponents now knew who they were, and what they could do. Riven had not seen how the other archivists fought, but if they were even half as good as Miri, he had a sinking feeling they were in dire trouble.

Still, Riven was not one to give up easily. *"Can we win this?"*

A feeling of concern washed over him through the bond. *"Not without major injury or death."*

*"We cannot lose her. I don't care what happens to me,"* Riven insisted.

*"We will not let anything happen to her, but we will need most of our Aedris reserves to pull this off. It will leave us weak."*

*"What do you mean? What are we going to do?"*

*"We are going to send her far away from here. They will not find her."*

*"Then let's do this."* The room seemed to snap back into place around him, and Riven captured Miri's gaze. "I'm sorry, I have to break that promise."

Her deep brown eyes widened. "Don't you—"

Riven stretched his open hand toward her. In that instant all of their opponents prepared for an attack, but it did not come. Instead, he released the spell that Zyndraxis prepared; it opened a maelstrom of Aedris with tremendous force. The tattoo that had slowly crept up his bicep during their training on the boat now blossomed, with tendrils creeping over his shoulder. The black curls of the memento glowed, and a pool of radiant crimson power opened at Miri's feet. It held solid until Zyndraxis twisted Riven's hand and the floor beneath her dissipated. With a cry, she fell into the portal, and it zipped shut behind her, sparks of red Aedris sizzling for several seconds, before the magic was completely gone.

Everyone looked at the empty spot where Miri once stood, then back at Riven. His shoulders slumped and he staggered where he stood. The feel of Zyndraxis' presence was unnervingly weak in his mind. Riven dropped his sword, fell to one knee, and then raised his hands.

"We surrender."

# CHAPTER 18
## MIRI

"-D are!" Miri cried out as she fell through blinding crimson light.

Her frustrations were quickly overshadowed as the red was replaced by a sunny yellow, and she landed on a wooden deck with a "thunk."

Pain flared through Miri's body, and she grunted at the sudden impact. Her back arched unnaturally as she landed on her pack, the contents clattering as she rolled onto her side and sprawled out. Her vision swam, and she tried to blink her way through the disorientation as footsteps echoed around her. There were garbled voices as she tried to sit up, not wanting to be entirely prone when she was so out of sorts.

Her view cleared, and someone leaned over her.

"Miri?"

Aliandra's dark hairline rose and she sunk to her knees, resting her hands on Miri's shoulders.

The world came back into focus, and Miri realised she was on the *Swiftwater*. The way the ground seemed to rock back and forth now made sense, and she shook her head to try and break herself from her disorientation. "Aliandra, where are we?" Miri croaked.

Miri knew she should be worried about having her body thrown through a portal made of a phenomenal amount of Aedris, but all she could see was the look on Riven's face as Zyndraxis sent her away.

"We're an hour out of Southbank Port. How—" Aliandra choked on her own words as she looked around, frowning so hard Miri feared the expression may become permanent. She shook her head. "That doesn't matter. Are you hurt?"

*That*, Miri thought, *is a good question.*

"Help me up, please," Miri said. She took Aliandra's hand, and the other woman helped her to her feet. It was a slow process, especially with the rocking of the boat, but whatever aches or pinches Miri felt were easy to ignore.

Standing, Miri remembered the information she had learned about her parents, and instinctively pressed her hand against her pocket to see if she still had the parchment from Gareth. At first, Miri wanted to cast it overboard. She did not want to read what was printed on it again. She didn't even want to think about it. However, she knew she would regret that later, after she had been able to process the feeling of betrayal sitting in her gut, so she left it be. She had more important things to worry about for now. Like getting Riven and Zyndraxis back. She was still shocked that Riven had suggested remaining bonded to the Shade. If she had known, she never would have—

"Are you okay, Miri?" Aliandra whispered, bringing Miri back to the present moment.

*Not really,* Miri thought. But she said, "Yeah."

Relieved, Aliandra looked over her shoulder at the crew who had gathered after the thump and were now gawking at them. "All right you lot, nothing more to see here! Back to work, please. We still have a ship to maintain."

There was a slight delay before the crew dispersed, and Miri took in a deep breath of the sharp river air. Her ribs twinged with pain at the movement, but it was bearable. Aliandra waited until everyone had moved away before she returned her attention to Miri.

"Now, what's going on?" Aliandra asked, voice hushed. She smoothed some stray strands of hair off Miri's face as she assessed her, apparently still wary of injuries.

"I need to get back to Southbank," Miri said, her body trembling at the thought of Riven and Zyndraxis being dragged away by Gareth and his cronies. "They're going to hurt them. I need to get back. Riven and—" She stopped and took a deep breath. "Riven's in trouble."

Aliandra watched Miri with a mixture of apprehension and empathy. She let out a huff before turning around. "Potts! Turn this baby around. We need to get back to port as fast as the wind and our oars will carry us!"

The first mate, who was at the wheel, gave Aliandra a salute and started calling orders. Their trip to Southbank had all been under the power of the wind and the current. This time, Miri knew Aliandra was pulling out all the stops to get her back quickly.

Before Miri could think, Aliandra had taken her hand and was leading her across the deck to the captain's quarters. It had been a while since Miri had been in the space, complete with a soft rug, a plush bed, and a desk full of maps and ledgers.

"What are you doing?" Miri asked, following along.

"You say you need to go back, then we're going back. But I am going to need more information," Aliandra said firmly as she shut the door behind them. "Now spill."

Miri knew better than to argue with *that* tone. "I made a deal with a dodgy archivist, and he screwed me over. He took Riven and Zyn—" Miri stopped and corrected herself, "Riven and I need to—"

"Don't do that," Aliandra raised a hand to stop her. "You've slipped up enough when saying Riven's name for me to know something is going on and, as much as I like Riven, he was a bit ... odd."

Instinctively, Miri glanced around, worried that they were being observed. There was no one to be seen, and the door to Aliandra's quarters was firmly shut. "You know how I have those little trinkets?"

"You mean your parlour tricks?" Aliandra asked, using her own affectionate term for the relics.

They were not parlour tricks, but Miri had given up encouraging her to call them relics. "Relics are Aedris powered artefacts. And Riven? Well, he found a particularly interesting relic and happened to become intimate buddies with a Shade," Miri explained, figuring that her abridged version would give enough of an idea of the forces they would be facing.

"A Shadow?" Aliandra spluttered, taking a cloak off a hook by the door and securing it around her shoulders. "That's not possible, aren't they—"

"He's a Shade, actually. Shadow is a derogatory term."

The death stare Aliandra levelled at her told Miri that she didn't much care for the semantics of it all.

Miri cleared her throat. "The point is, the Lorekeepers have him. They were supposed to separate Riven and Zyndraxis, but they took them both. I just gave them a damn package deal."

"Okay, so we'll have some Lorekeepers to deal with,"

Aliandra said slowly, taking stock of the situation. "And do they have their own little trinkets?"

"They do." Miri then scratched the back of her neck. "We can also expect a contingent of Revokers to be waiting for us, too."

"Revokers?" Now Aliandra sounded truly incredulous. "Darkness, Miri. What have you gotten yourself into?"

"Told you it was a mess. Riven tried to turn the Shade in, I had to save him from becoming gallows-fodder. We killed one revoker, left a couple more unconscious, and ran before we could get caught." Miri shrugged. "Feel free to back out now. I can handle this on my own, I swear."

"Oh, shut up." Aliandra pinched the bridge of her nose. "Look, I have to get my crew in order before we dock. Help yourself to any weapons or supplies you need. Take a nap. Whatever. We will be in port before you know it. My crew can row like the wind when they need to."

Knowing better than to push any further, Miri nodded and let Aliandra go. She looked around the cabin, noticing that the woman had fixed the broken shutters that had woken Miri too many times, and had acquired some new trinkets to put on her shelves. Miri did look in the chest Aliandra had referred to and found she had quite the cache of weapons. As a capable archivist, Miri did not really care for martial weapons, but she did take a sword and scabbard, figuring she may need to give it to Riven if his own weapon was confiscated.

After that, Miri walked over and pushed open the shutters that were still fresh with the scent of sawdust. She looked outside to see they were almost flying over the water, the rhythmic crash of oars hitting waves, setting the pace for their journey. She knew it would be a short while before she could see Southbank in the distance, but she had to plan to find Riven and Zyndraxis once she got back to town.

*Surely Gareth's moved them somewhere,* Miri thought. *The question is, where?* Out of all the ports and towns Miri had visited, Southbank was only ever a short stop on the way to Eldergate. She knew some people there, but she did not have enough sway with them to ask for favours. She would need eyes and ears on the street, and a significant amount of coin, if she was going to convince someone to tattle on the Revokers or Lorekeepers.

Miri considered which of her items she could sell for bribe-money when her mental cataloguing stalled on a particular item.

"The mirror!" Miri whispered to herself, remembering the small compact they had acquired from Alyxian's vault. She winced as she remembered the crunching and clattering when she had landed on Aliandra's deck. Shrugging her pack off, Miri turned and set it on the end of the captain's bed. She opened it and rifled through, trying to find the silver, sapphire encrusted item. "You better not be busted."

Relief flooded through her when she found the vanity item had slipped between the folds of a spare shift. She retrieved it and opened it. The mirrors on either side reflected a tired and frazzled looking version of herself. Ignoring the urge to tidy up the stray locks and wash her flushed cheeks with cold water, Miri focused instead on channelling some Aedris. As she did, she also concentrated on the feeling of being with Riven and the intense, unique signature of Zyndraxis' being that he had imprinted upon her. Her reflection swam in the mirror and an overhead view of Southbank formed on the surface.

"Don't worry lads, I'm coming. I'll teach those bastards for messing with us," she whispered, clutching the mirror tighter and hoping they are able to stay safe until she arrived.

~

"Are you sure this is the right place?" Aliandra whispered as she and Miri crept up along the side of the same Lorekeepers warehouse, Miri had approached earlier that day.

Miri was surprised that Gareth had chosen to keep his prisoners in the same location, especially given the fact that Miri escaped. Perhaps they had so little faith in her that they did not feel the need to move. Just as she was about to show Aliandra the location in the mirror, Miri spotted movement through one of the windows of the building. "Get back!"

Aliandra gasped as Miri grasped her arm to pull her back and pinned her to the wall, keeping her out of view of the people inside the building. Miri ignored her surprise and peered past her, watching the window. From her vantage point, she noted that the door at the back of the main room was slightly ajar, but guarded by several Revokers.

"Seems they're waiting for my return," Miri whispered, drumming her fingers against Aliandra's wrist as she considered their options.

"They were supposed to arrest you, weren't they?" Aliandra asked.

Miri nodded.

Without saying another word, Aliandra began to unfasten Miri's cloak.

"Uh, Aliandra, I appreciate the interest, but this is hardly the time to get intimate," Miri hissed, reaching up to still Aliandra's hands.

Aliandra shook her head. "Miri, the size of your ego never fails to amaze me. I'm not *always* trying to seduce you, you know."

*Could have fooled me,* Miri thought.

"I'm going to distract them. If I am wearing your cloak, they may chase after me. It should give you time to go in and get Riven and your Shade."

"But if they catch you—"

"They'll realise that they've got the wrong person and race back here. It just means you will have to be quick. You think you can do that?"

"No." Miri shook Aliandra off and refastened her cloak. "I'm keen to get Riven and Zyndraxis back, but I cannot do that knowing you are out there dealing with them on your own. I'll be too distracted. I would rather we fight side by side. It wouldn't be the first time."

A wave of tenderness washed over Aliandra. "I'm certain it won't be the last, either."

Memories flooded back, and Miri's demeanour softened. "That's exactly what you said the last time." The way Aliandra's eyes dipped to her lips made Miri swallow. She cleared her throat and stepped back, drawing her dagger with Aedris charged stones in the hilt. "Okay, let's do this. I can throw a few distractions in, but we will need to guard the door to make sure they don't escape."

"Why don't you go in the front, and I'll sneak in through the window while they're busy looking at you?"

"Perfect."

The natural urge to kiss Aliandra on the cheek flitted through Miri's mind, but she pushed it down. That was not their relationship anymore. Instead, she nodded firmly and squeezed the other woman's shoulders. Then, she turned and jogged around to the door before she did something stupid.

*Well, something more stupid than throwing myself into a room full of Revokers*, Miri thought as she pushed the door open.

The four Revokers in the room all froze as they looked up at her. Nyrelle held a hand up to have the others hold their position. "Come to turn yourself in quietly? That is a very wise decision, Miri."

Miri edged the door shut behind herself with her foot, and grinned as she settled into a defensive position. "It's cute you think I'm here to turn myself in," she said. "You have one chance to tell me where Riven is before I take you down."

Nyrelle merely laughed in response.

Without further warning, Miri summoned a deep pull of Aedris from her pendant and cast out a wave of kinetic shock. It knocked the soldiers off their feet and sent empty crates and other debris clattering to the ground.

From the corner of her eye, Miri saw Aliandra open the window and slip inside the room. Her free hand darted into her pocket, and she pulled out a handful of small, marble like orbs; normally they were used as a convenient way to summon water when required. She threw them onto the floor as the Revokers steadied themselves, then charged. They danced over the rolling orbs, but Miri modified the spell within, and the glass spheres exploded with thunderous rumbles, thick fog oozing from them.

The Revokers seemed to assume that the clouds being behind them indicated Miri had failed, but the fog obscured Aliandra's approach, as Miri backed towards the door.

"Drop your weapon, and we'll make sure you show up

at the gallows without any bruises on that pretty face of yours," Nyrelle sneered, eyes glinting in a way that Miri assumed was supposed to be intimidating.

Really, all the look did was make Miri realise just how much they underestimated her. "You mean, drop this?" Miri waggled her dagger. "A small price to pay, I suppose."

Then, Miri threw the dagger on the floor. It skittered noisily along the stone towards the captain's feet. Two of the Revokers tracked the movement of the blade as the captain reached for the cuffs on her hip. Miri took advantage of the distraction to reach for the pendant at her neck. She felt a rush of exhilaration as she connected with the Aedris within. With a cry of raw power, she extracted a thick rope of flames and flung them out with a whip-like crack.

The first guard let out an agonised scream as the flames struck his chest armour and turned the metal molten. As his peers turned to face him, Aliandra leapt out of the fog behind them and slammed the hilt of her cutlass across the back of Nyrelle's head. The woman clattered to the ground, and Miri summoned a fireball, catapulting it towards one of the other revokers. The acrid tang of burning flesh and screams let Miri know her fireball had hit its mark.

Aliandra engaged the other, swinging her blade to meet his Aedris-draining sword. Luckily, Aliandra was fighting with nothing more than steel and skill. She got locked into battle with the revoker, but he was too heavily armoured to keep up with her swift and sneaky strikes.

After a short scuffle, Aliandra wrestled her foe to the ground, and Miri had managed to subdue her own. Miri leapt forward, snatching the cuffs off the comatose Nyrelle, and throwing them to Aliandra, before summoning some water and splashing it over the other two guards before they boiled alive. As they lay, panting and groaning on the floor, Miri took the cuffs off each of their belts, and secured them with their own bindings.

Working in efficient silence, Miri and Aliandra worked to get the Revokers in different corners of the room, each bound, hidden behind some crates, and gagged with strips of fabric torn from their own uniforms.

With that sorted, Aliandra went about taking the weapons and any keys or other items off the Revokers, and Miri retrieved her mirror. The energy signal for Riven and Zyndraxis was just ahead. She surged forward, running towards the door at the back of the room. It was odd that no one had come out when they heard the noise, but she figured the Lorekeepers were more interested in enacting their own nefarious plans than helping the Revokers. They were self-absorbed like that.

However, as Miri made her way to the back of the room, no one came. She pushed the door open and grunted when she saw that it was completely empty save for a few stacks of chairs and a folded table, all pushed against one wall. At the far side of the room there were two doors, both shut.

"Where are they?" Aliandra asked, jogging to Miri's side, and looking just as perplexed as Miri felt.

"What the—" Miri spluttered as she glanced down at the mirror. She was standing right over the energy signal now, but Riven was nowhere to be seen. She steeled herself and fed some extra Aedris into the device, but it just glowed brighter. "There must be a damn basement."

With little time to waste, Miri ran over and pulled the left door open to reveal a storeroom containing stacks of chairs. At the right, there was a kitchen. She ran into that space and looked around. Another empty room. Miri huffed and kicked a barrel nearby. A hollow thud resounded through the room that made Miri's eyes widen.

"Let's get this out of the way," Aliandra said, diving right in to help.

Between Miri and Aliandra, the barrel was tipped and rolled aside in a matter of seconds, revealing the dusty hatch for what was most likely some sort of cold storage cellar. The edges were smudged with fingerprints.

"Gotcha," Miri hissed as she bent over and yanked the wooden panel back to uncover a steep, stone staircase. She tugged her pendant out of her shift and let it sit over her breasts, ready to use it to summon and transmit light if needed, and retrieved her dagger. The metallic zing of Aliandra drawing her weapon sounded behind her, and Miri was content knowing her friend and ex-lover would be able to hold her own in a fight.

Senses alert, Miri padded down the stone staircase. It was eerily quiet below, even when her feet reached the stairs that had to be visible by anyone standing inside. Miri gripped her dagger tighter and summoned some Aedris through her pendant, holding it there and ready to cast a blinding light from it if she spotted anyone.

But the cellar was empty.

"Are you sure that thing works?" Aliandra whispered, glancing around warily.

Swearing under her breath, Miri walked in. The damp, dirt-dusted stone below crunched under her boots as she walked around, noting closed sacks of flour, grain, and other long-term storable ingredients. She shook her head and pulled out the mirror again. Once more, the light of Riven's presence was just ahead.

"Well, they aren't upstairs," Miri mused as she walked

forward. She kept going until she hit the back wall, which was still a several meters away from where she needed to be.

Sheathing her dagger and tucked the mirror away, Miri inspected the wall. She ran her fingers over the seams of the rock but was unable to find any hidden latches or releases. She was just about to give up when she remembered she still had one of her favourite items with her. She rustled through her hip pouch and withdrew a small monocle.

"Let's see what my eyes won't show me," she whispered to herself, as she held the monocle up and peered through it.

Sure enough, when she was viewing the wall through the glass, a thick line of magical energy glowed through the cracks in the stone. The overall outline was a rough rectangle a foot taller than she was, and wide enough for a person to slip through. She summoned some Aedris and tentatively reached out, tracing her fingers along the seam line.

"I hope I don't need a password," she whispered, as she worked her way around the shape. She kept going until she had completed the outline, and a sinking weighed over her shoulders at the lack of reaction on the wall.

However, when she let go and stepped back, there was a low groan of stone moving on stone, and the solid rectangle slid back. Miri was relieved and figured that whoever made the secret door did not plan on many people being able to wield Aedris. That was a unique enough key of its own.

"That is amazing!" Aliandra said, stepping up beside Miri.

Beyond the door was darkness. The two stared into the void before Miri remembered they had a mission. She summoned light into her amulet and gasped when it only reached a few meters into the roughly cut rock tunnel.

At the end, or at least, what Miri thought was the end, was just *black*.

Well, not just black, but a complete and utter absence of light. The stones around it seemed to be trying to glow with power, but the depth of the void absorbed the light. It called to Miri, and she found herself stepping closer and closer. She was vaguely aware of the fact that it was right where Riven's signature ought to be.

A hand grasped Miri's shoulder. "I know I said that was amazing, but are you sure this is safe?" Aliandra whispered.

Miri focused on the symbols around the void, her mind whirring as it translated the characters.

"It's a portal," Miri explained. She held up the mirror for Aliandra to see, and then gestured to the void. "Riven's signature is hanging right there because it kind of snagged on the gateway between dimensions. I don't know what's waiting for us on the other side, but if we want to get them back, that's where we need to go."

Aliandra straightened her shoulders, held her weapon at the ready, and nodded. "Then let's do this."

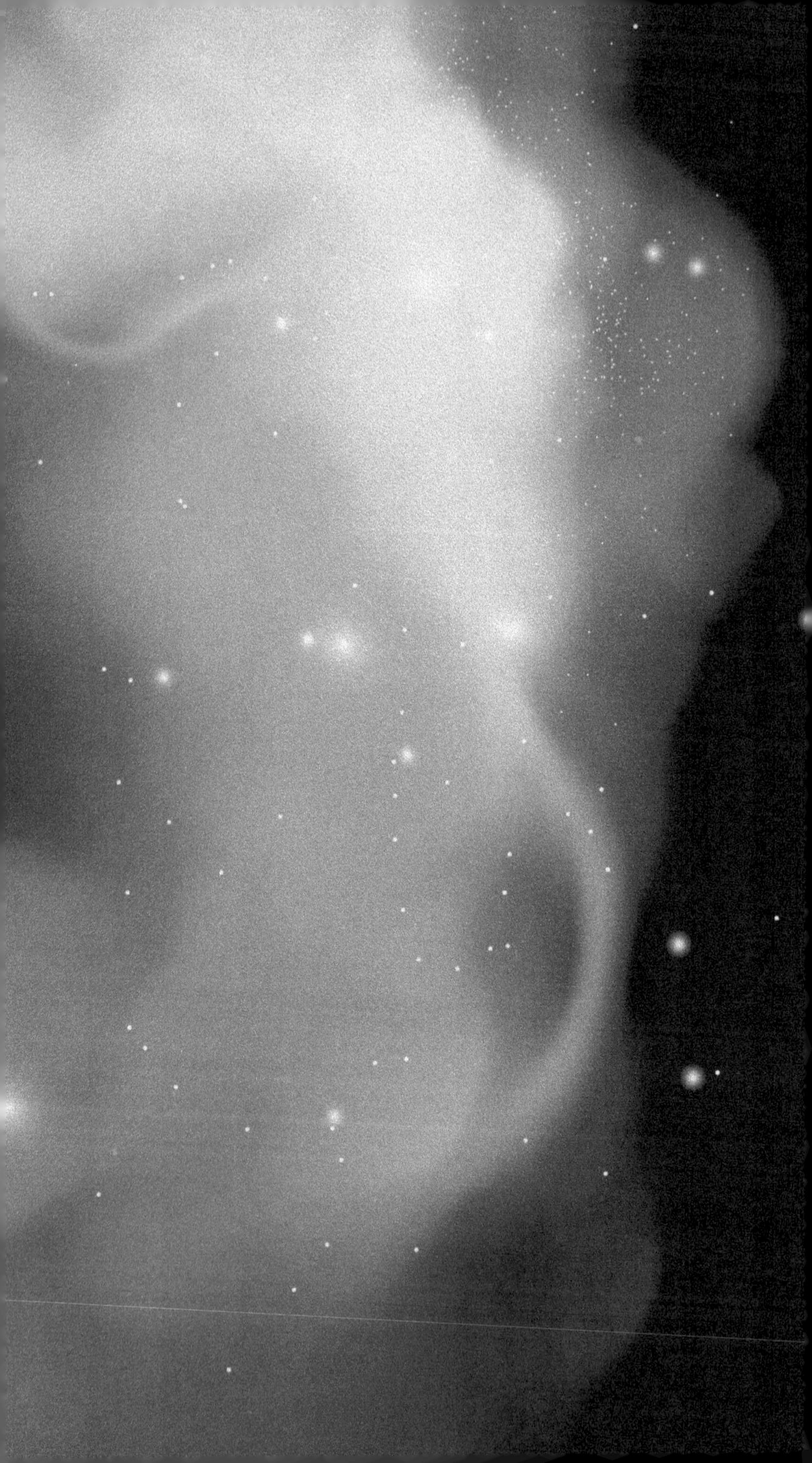

CHAPTER 19

# ZYNDRAXIS

As soon as he had cast the spell, Zyndraxis was drained, almost empty. Riven fell to one knee as his own energy had been depleted, too. In that moment Zyndraxis hadn't had time to be efficient with his expenditure. He focused on one task and one alone, getting Miri to safety. Given his limited exposure to this new world, there was only one place he could think of and visualise that would truly be safe for Miri: the *Swiftwater*.

After Miri vanished in a dazzling array of light and energy, the Revokers panicked. They dashed around the room looking for their prisoner. One was sent to summon reinforcements.

Nyrelle charged up to them, grabbed Riven by the leather strap of his pauldron, and yanked him closer. She pressed the tip of her sword against his neck. "Where is she?"

"I have no idea," Riven grunted before turning his attention inward. *"Not that I would tell her, but where is Miri?"*

*"Somewhere safe."*

*"Where?"*

Growing impatient, Nyrelle pushed him to the ground. She pressed her sword to his neck once again. "Tell me where she is!"

"You are wasting your time, captain. That simpleton has no knowledge of magic. It is more likely that the Shade cast the spell and is withholding the information," Gareth explained, sounding bored as he sauntered closer.

"Then maybe I can cut my way to the Shadow and make it tell me," Nyrelle pressed her sword firmly enough that the sharp edge started to bite into Riven's skin.

*"You may need to prepare to fight, my friend,"* Zyndraxis warned, unable to summon any extra Aedris so soon after such a drain.

Gareth reached out a hand towards the revoker, a warning flaring in his eyes. "No! This man and his *affliction* are under our jurisdiction. Punishment for the crimes against your kind was your jurisdiction, as per the agreement between our organisations. Your business is with the girl. Or do I need to take this up with your superiors?"

"You promised that you would deliver the criminals responsible for deaths of my officers." Nyrelle kept her sword right where it was.

"*Criminal,*" Gareth corrected, "And she was delivered. It is not my fault you lost her. Surely you and your officers are competent enough to find one stupid woman."

Zyndraxis could sense that Riven wanted to say something in Miri's defence, by how blood boiled. *"Calm yourself my friend, lest we reveal our hand."*

*"You won't even tell me our hand!"*

"She could be anywhere! Make him tell us. I know your

kind can do that," Nyrelle commanded, dragging Zyndraxis' attention back to his surroundings.

"Really? So, am I to understand this correctly; are you invoking article six, subsection three?" Gareth's tone held a note of amusement as he glanced down at Riven.

"Yes. I give my authority to perform the task." She spat at the ground with disgust as she stepped back.

Riven sucked in a breath of relief, even as a small drop of blood rolled down his skin.

"With pleasure." Gareth grinned, as if he had been given an early birthday present. Reaching into his robes, he pulled out a small artefact. Zyndraxis recognised it as a remembrance ball, something they used in his time as a way of recording events from a person's memory. Gareth manipulated the spell within and shaped it in such a way that it could be used more forcefully than its original intent, then he directed his attention to Riven.

"Gareth, is this really necessary?" Willis whispered, stepping between Gareth and Riven. He had been quiet up until this point, probably trying to avoid Gareth's attention.

Gareth callously shoved his apprentice aside, narrowing his attention on Riven with gleeful anticipation.

*"I'm sorry my friend, this will probably hurt,"* Zyndraxis warned. Had he been human, he would have winced at the knowledge of what was coming.

Before Riven could demand more information, Gareth channelled the Aedris within the device, and a sharp spear of silver magic struck Riven directly in the temple.

"Argh!" Riven cried out, body convulsing as he felt as if his skull had been cracked in two, and his brain lanced with a hot iron.

Zyndraxis shared the pain through their bond as the

spell ripped through Riven's mind. He focused on keeping his own thoughts and memories protected, while allowing Gareth to probe Riven. He did not enjoy allowing Riven to suffer, but there was little choice in the matter. They had to protect Miri.

When it was finally done, Riven was left panting and only half-conscious, lying on the cold, hard floor of the warehouse.

Gareth let out a huff as he tucked the device back into the pocket of his uniform. "He doesn't know anything."

*"And now you know why I didn't tell you where our Miri is,"* Zyndraxis explained, hoping to give Riven comfort with the knowledge he was not excluding him from knowledge out of malice.

Riven groaned as he rolled over onto his stomach. His arms and legs shook beneath him as he tried to sit up. *"You weren't the one having your brain torn apart from the inside."*

Nyrelle moved around to stand before Gareth. The pair seemed to be arguing as she jabbed an accusatory finger in his direction. Right now, Zyndraxis was much more interested in Riven. *"I felt as much as you, my friend,"* Zyndraxis assured him. *"But don't worry, our secret is safe."*

*"Are you going to tell me where she is now?"*

Zyndraxis considered it for a fraction of a moment before deciding it was still too risky. *"She is safe."*

*"Great…"*

"Fine. Separate them and we shall interrogate the Shadow. I'm sure we can dig out some of our old tools and make it talk," Nyrelle suggested, sheathing her sword, and stepping back. She gestured towards Riven with an aggressive sweep of her arm and two of her Revokers scurried forward.

"I'm afraid not. As I said before, the Shadow is under Lorekeepers jurisdiction. Perhaps when we have effectively neutralised the threat, we can turn over the host, but I can assure you that your organisation is ill equipped to handle the creature within," Gareth replied.

Nyrelle eyed Gareth for what seemed an eternity before grunting in acceptance. "Fine." She turned to the rest of the officers in the room. "If the criminal has not gone too far, then she will likely come back to try and save her friend. You lot, report back to command. I will stay here with these three and ensure that our friends hold their end of the bargain."

"You are welcome to stay captain, however we will not be performing any rituals on this level of the building. We have a more secure location below, and it might be some time before we are finished," Gareth explained.

"I can wait. Don't double cross us Gareth. I know who your superiors are," Nyrelle warned.

Gareth ignored the comment "Willis, put the cuffs on him and take his weapon. We don't want any more surprises. Edgar, Wrynn; take him to the cellar."

"Sorry Riven," Willis whispered as he leaned over and placed a set of metal cuffs, engraved with glyphs, around Riven's wrists. The other two half carried, half dragged him to a different room.

As they were travelling, Zyndraxis attempted to reach out to the different devices Gareth had on him, to see if he could sense any Aedris he could steal from them. There was nothing, though. *Or perhaps,* Zyndraxis thought, *the cuffs on Riven's wrists are preventing me from accessing any Aedris from the items.*

Any distractions fled from Zyndraxis as he saw Gareth trace his hand up, across, and down the stone of a blank wall to reveal a magic door. Zyndraxis mused that this building was likely once home to a former Shade and they had installed a surprise. Inside the long, narrow corridor there was an even more interesting surprise, a single translocation portal that likely led to a completely different location.

At this point, Zyndraxis realised that he needed to act. Heroic as it was to send Miri away to safety, he knew that she wouldn't just let it go. Miri would likely try to find them. He hoped she would remember the mirror she found in Alyxian's vault. The only problem was that they would be teleported out of its range the moment they stepped through the portal.

Zyndraxis modified the anchor charm on he and Riven already tethered to the mirror, he redesigned it so that it would be absorbed by the portal as soon as they stepped through, since it was not magic he was casting outwardly the power dampening cuffs would not prevent it from happening. At least, he hoped it wouldn't.

Willis activated the controls while the other two led Riven onto the platform. Gareth and Willis joined them before all five were transported to their new location. This time Zyndraxis did not have enough energy to shield Riven from the effects. This time when they stepped through, his legs gave way and he dropped to the floor. The two other archivists appeared behind them immediately after, and hauled Riven up off the ground.

"Keep moving!" one of them yelled.

Riven did not seem to have the energy to respond and instead spoke to Zyndraxis *"I hate these portals. Did you use them a lot during your time?"* Riven's mental voice was still groggy from the mental ravaging.

*"They're not as common as you might think. They require*

*an enormous amount of skill to design and Aedris to construct. Transporting a living being is not as simple as one might think. You felt how taxing it was to get Miri away from us. Usually only the most well-resourced Dyads could afford a luxury like this in their home. The greater the distance travelled; the more power required."*

As soon as they arrived, Zyndraxis observed their new location. A sense of nostalgia washed over him. Unlike Alyxian's vault, which was a simple pocket dimension, the antechamber they were transported into sported the Shade architecture he was more familiar with. Whereas the storage warehouse had been stripped down to a simple structure, this room still had the stylised grey stone and elegant scroll-work carvings of his own time period. The walls were covered in the intricate reliefs, and towering stone columns supported the vaulted ceiling, leading in a neat row towards the far end of the room. Torches with eternal Aedris flames danced on the walls, making the shadows of the columns waver through the space.

"Take him to the ritual chamber and get him settled in. They are going to be with us for quite some time," Gareth ordered, unclipping his red and black Lorekeepers cloak and sweeping it off his shoulders.

"What about the revoker captain? Isn't she waiting for us?" Willis asked as he walked over to Riven and helped him stay on his feet. The two guards holding him kept a tight grip on his elbows so he could not run.

"Do not worry about her. Those idiots have no idea how these things work." Gareth waved a hand dismissively as he walked towards one of three large mahogany doors at the far end of the chamber. They had symbols carved into them, each one covering the story of a different age in history. The accounts were rather accurate, so Zyndraxis guessed that a Shade must have overseen the creation of this place. Towards the time of his imprisonment, there were many humans trying to mimic the artistic flair of the Shade.

"You think she'll just forget all about us?" Willis sounded confused.

Gareth pushed the middle door open with both hands. "Just wait an hour and inform them that both Riven and the Shade didn't survive the process. We can give them one of our worn containment crystals and tell them this was all we could recover. They won't be able to tell the difference."

By this time, Riven was able to clumsily walk, so his captors guided him through the trademark, labyrinthine stone hallways of the Shade-built building. As they moved through the corridors, Zyndraxis was certain it was an aeons-old temple, likely hidden from the purge. The ancient, untouched atmosphere made him think that the only ones who had walked its halls in a long time were other archivists.

When they arrived at their final destination, it was the only space that had been modified. The room itself had been emptied of any furnishings, and a metal slab was set at a forty-five-degree angle in the centre of the room. Zyndraxis recognised it as a draktah. It was normally used to assist a cleric in healing injuries. Attached to it were manacles with leather straps that had been retrofitted to the sides.

As they moved closer, Zyndraxis spied unfamiliar Aedric symbols carved into it. On an initial glance, he surmised that they modified the draktah from its original intent, but he did not have enough time to decipher the difference. In the corner of the room there was a pedestal topped with a control panel. Zyndraxis was familiar with these, however from the angle he and Riven had, he was unable to determine its actual function.

*"What in the darkness is that?"* Riven asked.

*"I'm not sure. Normally this would be draktah. A medical bed. But given the straps and different symbols, I really don't know."*

*"Well, if you don't know something, it must be bad."*

Zyndraxis resisted the urge to thank Riven for that rather amusing compliment of his knowledge.

Riven seemed to sense the sentiment, so he forged onwards. *"I thought they were going to perform the bonding ritual in reverse. You mean this isn't part of that?"*

*"No, this is most certainly not part of the ritual. This looks to be more of a torture device."*

Riven's muscles tightened as Gareth draped his cloak over the edge of the control panel, and then started muttering to Willis in a low voice. Zyndraxis sensed the urge Riven felt to run, but given their recent draining, and the fact they were still being held by two guards, there was no way they would make escape. Trying would be foolish. Riven became serious and said, *"If I don't make it, please let Miri know—"*

*"Don't speak like that, Riven,"* Zyndraxis interrupted, not allowing Riven to finish the rest of the sentence. *"We cannot give in. Besides, you're not the one they are after."*

*"You're right, but just in case ..."*

*"I know."*

Riven was guided onto the slab forcefully; any physical resistance he provided was easily overcome. Gareth tapped the control panel and activated the device. A sinister grin disfigured his face. The symbols on the slab lit up. The other two Lorekeepers secured his arms and legs in place and the cuffs were removed.

"Well, Riven, I thought you were utterly useless when I first met you. A simple-minded brute who barely understood the world he lived in. I believed Miri to be such a fool to hire someone as basic as yourself, but now I see it has worked in my favour." Gareth rested his hand on the console and looked down at them as they lay on the slab, secured and unable to get away.

"You see, after the great war, many of the Nexus points around the world were destroyed, or buried, in the fear that the Shade would return and retake our civilisation. Our only supply of Aedris in the modern world comes from relics of a forgotten age." Gareth manipulated the controls on the panel and the device began to hum with energy.

"With the limited power available from salvaged artefacts, we needed a way to replenish our supply of Aedris to keep our business running. It was theorised that, should a living Shade be discovered, we could drain their essence and recharge our artefacts. This device's original purpose was to assess the status of a human and their bonded Shade to assist with any injuries they might have suffered; however, we've made some minor adjustments." Gareth manipulated the controls again.

A strange energy gnawed at Zyndraxis' core, at the place where he was connected to Riven. It was uncomfortable, but not painfully so. Sensing the energy, Riven struggled against the restraints.

"If I tune it just right, we can ..."

The soft whir of the machine turned into a deafening buzz, and pain sizzled through Zyndraxis' entire being. Riven must have felt the same because he screamed. Though Zyndraxis didn't know what the device did before, it was quite clear now what it was doing. The small amount of Aedris he had after teleporting Miri was draining away, siphoned from the very essence of his lifeforce. Zyndraxis had never known what it would be like to fall into the void; to cease to exist, but right now it felt awfully appealing.

Gareth was laughing.

"We can drain you and your Shade, little by little, and this bed will keep you alive just enough to recover, just enough so we can do it all over again." Gareth directed their attention to a small crystal at the front of the pedestal that Zyndraxis had not noticed until now. It had a slight glow to it; likely this was where his precious Aedris was going.

Gareth stepped away from the control panel and stood directly in front of Riven.

"I wonder, does the Shade feel what you feel? Does it feel the pain or is it completely devoid of any sensation at all?" He paused a moment as if contemplating the answer. "It matters not; we will get what we want. I've been told that the host can survive for many years before their body dies. You seem young and fit; I'm sure it will be decades before you give in. Willis, keep going. Use the standard rotation. I'll go and make sure the Revokers do not bother us any further."

Gareth rustled through his pockets and pulled out a crystal like the one at the end of the slab, only it had a gnarly crack straight through the middle. He gave Riven one last satisfied nod and then left the room. Willis looked over at Riven with a pained expression, then he continued. The other two stood by watching, and waiting, as Zyndraxis and Riven were tortured.

Zyndraxis lost track of how much time had passed. Being drained to the brink of his existence, and then slowly brought back, was a harrowing experience. He'd lost count of how many times they had endured it. All he knew was that he would fade out and then back in, and it would start all over again. Riven was doing even worse, every moment he was conscious, he was in agony. As a Shade, Zyndraxis could not fully experience what was happening for Riven, but Riven described it succinctly.

*"It's like having my skin ripped from my body, healed back, and then torn off again."*

After what seemed like an eternity, Zyndraxis and Riven regained enough lucidity to realise the device had not been activated recently. It was a slow return of their faculties that hinted at that fact.

They were aware of a quiet scuffling, and Willis held a cup to Riven's lips. Zyndraxis sensed the temptation to ignore the cup ripple through Riven, but in the end his basic human needs won out. Even though he tried, he barely managed to take a few sips.

"Quickly, the others will be back soon," Willis whispered.

Riven looked up and tried to make eye contact. Zyndraxis could feel the fatigue that Riven had; he could barely focus on the boy. "Willis, thank you," Riven said, the words filled not with hate or anger, but guilt. "I'm sorry I couldn't save your m-mother. There w-were so many rocks."

*"His mother? What are you talking about? This boy is hurting us. Killing us!"* If Zyndraxis had the energy, he would have choked the imbecile himself.

Riven groaned as he took another sip of water. *"His mother died, I tried to save her; he's scared, Zyndraxis. He's only doing what he needs to survive."*

Willis set the cup down. "Thank you, Riven. I know you tried, that's why I can't let them do this to you." He rushed back to the control panel and deactivated the device.

The menacing glow of power dimmed, and the room

fell silent. Willis returned to undo the straps and helped Riven to his feet.

"You need to get out of here. If you stay any longer, you will die. I'm sure of it," Willis explained. "Gareth might have said he would keep you alive for years, but the power setting is just too high."

"Escape? H-how are we going to escape? I can barely move. Unless you learned how to fight since the last time we met," Riven said, his head spinning as he tried to get his bearings. Zyndraxis wasn't sure how he would walk like that, but they would have to figure it out.

"Me? No, I'm barely an apprentice. Gareth just keeps me close because he knows he can boss me around without any push back." Willis snatched the crystal that had slowly been collecting Zyndraxis' energy, and then handed it to Riven. When Riven took it, Willis searched through the inner pockets of his robes and retrieved a second crystal; this one glowed much brighter, hinting that it stored more power inside.

"Here. I'm not sure if you can use these, but I'm hoping it will help."

Zyndraxis could not believe it. He was going to have to eat his own words from just moments ago. The boy was actually helping them.

*"Can we do anything with these, Zyndraxis?"*

*"Give me a few minutes and I will make something happen."*

At that moment, the door to the room was thrown open to reveal one of the Lorekeepers.

"Hey, Willis, you said it would only be a few minutes. That took — uh, what is going on here?" He had an exasperated expression on his face that slowly turned to alarm. He did not give Willis a chance to answer before he slammed his hand on a panel next to the door; a siren with a loud repeating voice saying *"Lundash! Lundash! Ekris Lundash!"* blared through the chamber and the hall beyond.

*"Forget a few minutes. You have a few seconds,"* Riven yelled loudly in their mind.

Zyndraxis hastily drew all the power from the first crystal. As he did, the power thrummed through him and Riven, and any residual pain or disorientation from the torture was gone in an instant. In fact, as Zyndraxis drained the last of the power, the crystal shattered under the high amount of stress.

"Sorry, Willis," Zyndraxis whispered, using Riven's voice. In such an emergency he didn't have time to explain this one to Riven. He then created a wave of force that knocked both Willis and the newcomer off their feet. Willis was flung against the control panel, and his colleague flew back out the door into the wall behind. Willis whimpered and pressed a hand against his head.

*"What are you doing? He was helping us!"* Riven rushed to the young man's side. For the most part he seemed healthy aside from a gash on his forehead that was bleeding, but it was not deep.

"Willis, come with us." Riven offered him a hand to help him stand.

Zyndraxis thought it was entirely too kind of a gesture.

"Us?" Willis stammered.

Riven raised his right arm, and the red cabochon gem caught the light.

"Oh, right. The Shadow."

"He prefers *Shade*, but yes. I meant that you should come with Zyndraxis and I."

*"Every second we waste here is another second we should*

*be spending getting back to Miri,"* Zyndraxis growled in Riven's head.

Willis shook his head before he hissed with pain, then seemed to think better of it. He took a handkerchief out of his pocket and held it to his wound. "I can't. I have important things I still need to do here."

"What happens when they find out you helped me?" Riven asked. Zyndraxis wanted to throttle him for sticking around. They needed to move!

"Actually, thanks to your friend and this nasty bump, they won't find it hard to believe that stupid, careless Willis accidently let the prisoner go."

*"All part of my plan."* Zyndraxis beamed.

*"Sure, it was Zyn."* Riven groaned, then spoke to Willis. "Okay, if, you're certain."

"Oh, don't forget your sword. It's over there. Not sure how a Revoker blade helps you, but I left it against the wall with your other things."

Riven dashed over to the wall perpendicular to the door and found the sword and his pack. He gathered his things and, with one final look of thanks to Willis, he ran out of the room.

As Riven attempted to find their way back, Zyndraxis focused on reclaiming his own energy from the final crystal. He didn't want to shatter the second one, just in case they needed it in the future.

The blaring alarm continued. Zyndraxis could tell that Riven was having difficulty navigating their way through the corridors. He could have sworn they were just running around in circles. He was about to raise his concern with Riven when they turned a corner and skidded to a stop, as they came face to face with two archivists. This place was such a maze, there could have been any number of foes hiding in the corridors.

"Stop. Return to the chamber or we will take you there by force," one of the archivists warned, raising his hand.

*"It seems we have an advantage, Riven. They need us alive."*

Riven's body tensed, poised and ready to attack. *"Good. How do we use this information?"*

*"Their attacks will be less powerful and lethal because they will focus on subduing us rather than killing us."*

That was all Riven needed to hear before he charged headlong at the pair. The archivists were prepared for combat, but not a reckless assault. They sent small waves of energy to keep Riven back, but Zyndraxis empowered Riven's muscles, allowing him to overcome it easily, he then prepared the next spell. Riven charged at the closest one first and slashed out in a horizontal arc unleashing a wave of force towards them and shattering both of their magical shields like glass.

The archivist who had issued them with that pathetic warning yelped as the force of the spell sliced a deep red line over his cheek. He turned and ran, leaving his colleague alone with Riven and Zyndraxis. The man reached into his robes to pull out a different item. With it he conjured a blazing ball of fire and threw it directly at them. Riven's superior reflexes allowed him to react in time and raise his blade. The specialised metal absorbed most of the attack, with the rest bouncing harmlessly against their energy shield.

Riven took the opportunity to hit the archivist with the butt of his blade. The man collapsed with a groan and Riven stepped over him. They continued down the next hallway and the next until an automated door system activated and closed off their exit.

*"What now?"* Riven asked.

*"We go back, there is likely another path we can follow."*

As Riven turned three more archivists stood in the hallway they had just come from. *"And how about now?"*

This time their opponents did not say anything. They already had their spells ready; a bolt of ice, lightning, and fire were headed directly toward them.

*"Now we fight."* Zyndraxis readied the shield spell, and Riven raised it.

Then he charged. They absorbed the lightning, dodged the fire, and slashed an ice bolt in two. Despite the onslaught, the archivists didn't let up. They flung spell after spell, causing Riven to fall back. After several minutes of fighting, the surrounding walls were charred and broken with battle, but no one had given any ground.

Unfortunately for Riven and Zyndraxis, two more archivists approached from another one of the corridors.

*"We're outnumbered. I hate to say it, but we need to retreat,"* Riven said as he sunk into a fighting stance as he continued to hold his ground.

Zyndraxis sensed that their enemies were carrying some well-charged relics. *"Agreed, direct the next spell that way as a distraction and then run down one of the other hallways."*

Zyndraxis prepared a smoke spell. It didn't require much finesse, so he figured that Riven could manage it; it covered the entire area, covering their escape.

Riven dashed down the nearest hallway, following it until they reached another three-pronged fork. *"Which way?"*

There was so much Aedris flowing through the walls of

this place that Zyndraxis was unable to sense how to get out. *"I'm not sure."*

*"What do you mean?"*

*"I mean this isn't the way we came and I'm not sure how to get back to the exit."*

*"Didn't you live in these kinds of places?"*

*"Secret hidden dungeons? No, not really. Although if I ever design one, I will be sure to include a sign that says 'exit'."*

Riven surveyed his surroundings, his shoulders falling. He sucked in a breath, and then chose a corridor at random. They kept moving; this time Zyndraxis tried to guide them based on the lack of signage. After a few turns, they stopped short and a loud yelp echoed through the room as they nearly ran into someone.

On instinct, Riven held up his hand and fell into a defensive position.

*"No!"* Zyndraxis warned, forcing Riven's sword down and mentally urging him to *look*.

Miri stood before them, panting, apparently trying to catch her breath. Whether she'd been running, or Riven had scared the life out of her, Zyndraxis couldn't be sure.

"Miri?" Riven cried, a surge of emotions flooded Zyndraxis through the bond; surprise, confusion, anger?

"Riven, thank the darkness." There was such relief and affection in the way that Miri said his name.

Riven, however, appeared to be frozen in place, so Zyndraxis spoke. *"Are you just going to stand here and stare at her? Kiss her, you fool."* Zyndraxis gave him a slight nudge. Riven nearly tripped before taking the hint and drew her into his arms and into a short, but passionate, kiss that Miri reciprocated with enthusiasm.

As soon as Riven broke for air he asked, "What are you doing here?"

"What am *I* doing here?" Miri asked, her eyebrows rose. "Rescuing you, of course. Well, that was the plan. I thought you'd be more ... I don't know, captured?"

"You're not supposed to be here. Zyndraxis sent you away, so you would be safe."

"There's no way I'd let that bastard take you two from me," she declared, fierce determination making her hold her chin high.

"Both of us?" Zyndraxis inquired. This revelation was new to him. When he enacted his plan, he expected she would return for Riven, but not for him. "Wasn't I your bargaining chip?"

A look of guilt flashed across her face, but before she could say anything further, they were interrupted as another figure appeared from around the corner. Aliandra. Her weapon was drawn, and she was out of breath. Zyndraxis didn't expect the captain to join Miri, but he was thankful that she did. The pair must have turned the *Swiftwater* around to come back and rescue them. He supposed they owed the captain even more now.

"Yeah, we aren't getting through that lock. Tried all my usual tricks," Aliandra stopped in her tracks and stared at Riven. "Oh, you're out? I thought we were supposed to be rescuing you."

"You are. Well, still are. We got some help from Willis. Turns out he's not as indoctrinated by the Lorekeepers as we thought," Riven explained.

"Willis?" Miri glanced around. "Where is he? Is he coming with us?"

"No. The boy elected to stay. I congratulate him on his

bravery," Zyndraxis informed her begrudgingly. He had not trusted the lad, but Riven had been right about him.

Miri considered that for a moment, before nodding and changing the subject. "As much as I am loving this reunion, we really should be going. The door to the teleporter locked behind us, but maybe we can find a way through."

"It's more than likely the alarm has locked us out," Zyndraxis explained.

"Zyndraxis?" Aliandra's mouth dropped open, most likely at the change in tone of Riven's voice.

Zyndraxis was surprised she picked up on his interruption. He glanced at Miri warily.

"She knows."

"Well in that case, I am pleased to make your acquaintance." Zyndraxis offered Aliandra Riven's hand to shake, and bowed low when she took it.

"It is good to meet you properly, too. I'd love to chat more, but we really must get moving," Aliandra said, as she took her hand back.

Miri and Aliandra then led them down the corridor until it finally opened into the vast, columned entry chamber that held the teleportation portal. It was concealed behind a solid door right now, but Zyndraxis could certainly sense it.

Miri immediately began work on the control panel near the door. Through Riven, Zyndraxis guided her efforts, assisting with the translations. "Argh why does that voice keep saying 'Concern, concern. There is a concern.'?"

Riven scratched the back of his neck as he was unable to answer her question.

"It's saying 'Emergency, emergency. There's an emergency'," Zyndraxis said aloud, correcting Miri's interpretation. For someone self-taught, her translations were actually quite good. In his time, even his consorts didn't bother learning their language, since a Shade was always there to interpret for them.

Aliandra hovered around them, watching the various doors around the room, and swishing her sword back and forth. It was several minutes later when she cried out, "Miri, it's—"

A voice interrupted Aliandra. "Couldn't keep away, could you?"

Riven turned, and Zyndraxis saw Gareth standing at the other side of the room, flanked by several more Lore-keepers.

"This is the end of the line, Miriam. You won't get away this time. And to think you were nearly free; you could have left this idiot to his fate, left the Shade to us, but you had to make everything so difficult. What would your parents think of you?" Gareth and his cronies stepped closer.

"Don't you dare talk about my parents!" Miri screeched, Gareth barely registered her response and turned to his retinue.

"Try not to make a mess, and if possible, keep the boy and the Shade alive. I don't care what happens to the girls."

Miri looked at Aliandra, then Riven, and by proxy Zyndraxis. Her face was full of determination as she then reached into her pockets and produced several sets of relics. Their opponents did the same, sinking into a low stance and walking into their room. They formed a semi-circle in a vague attempt to surround them. Miri, Aliandra, and Riven stepped closer, holding their chosen weapons aloft. Zyndraxis focused his attention at the renewed well of Aedris inside of himself and Riven.

Then, everything happened all at once.

Blasts of energy ripped through the room. Zyndraxis

and Miri coordinated their defences, deflecting every assault magically while Riven took a more direct approach hacking, and slashing, with his blade. They fought like they danced, in perfect harmony. It wasn't until two of the archivists began breaking parts of the room and hurling pieces of it at Riven, that things started to become unmanageable; one of the large boulders struck his sword arm, causing him to drop the blade to the ground. Riven had no choice now but to be completely on the defensive. Zyndraxis made sure he had adequate shield spells ready, but it was difficult to keep up with the assault. Riven had already received several large bruises in vulnerable areas of his body.

Miri could no longer defend him, as two of the other archivists had decided to flank her. Her hands were whipping about, retrieving items, and throwing magic, but it seemed to be getting tougher, as she was being attacked from both sides.

While all this was happening, Aliandra found a way to insert herself into the fight. She ducked, dived, and spun around the inferno of destruction, dispatching their enemies one at a time. Her surprise attacks made her especially effective since the archivists thought Miri, Riven, and Zyndraxis were the dangerous ones.

Gareth didn't fully engage in the fight until his side was starting to lose, and even then, his efforts were not enough to slow their progress. As the last two archivists fell, Zyndraxis noticed Gareth chanting a new spell. Zyndraxis prepared his defences, but too late realised Gareth's intended target was Aliandra.

The captain was unfamiliar with the spell and prepared to evade it like the others, but Gareth wasn't using a standard attack. Instead, he conjured a wide net of incapacitating energy that she could not dodge. She collapsed on the ground, and in the next moment he followed up by casting a lasso of purple energy around her and dragging her towards him.

By the time Miri and Riven could react, Gareth was yanking Aliandra off the ground and using her as a human shield. Zyndraxis snarled; the amount of power he was flinging around was indicative that he had to have a lot more of those cursed crystals. How many Shade had been drained for him to perpetrate these evils?

"Stop!" Miri hissed, holding her hand up towards Riven, even though he wasn't fighting. Zyndraxis knew she was speaking to him.

"You have always been a thorn in my side, Miriam, but no longer." Gareth held up a palm sized replica of an oil lantern, glinting with a ruby instead of a flame. The device glowed briefly and the lighting around the room immediately changed from bright and welcoming, to red and flashing. The constant droning alarm changed, and it chimed in with a new warning.

*"Dreska dorma! Dreska dorma!"*

"Portal Absence?" Miri looked over at Zyndraxis for confirmation, her brows creasing.

"Portal disconnect," Zyndraxis corrected, "and it's counting down. He means to trap us here forever."

When they looked back to Gareth, he was racing towards the door at the far side of the room, dragging a swearing Aliandra behind him.

"Wait, won't he be trapped down here, too?" Riven asked, not dropping his defensive stance.

"Not if he has an emergency exit portal that is attuned to him. Something only he can use."

"We have to get Aliandra from that bastard," Miri spat,

already turning to race after Gareth. "I should never have let her come with me!"

"We need to get out of here before the portal closes," Riven argued.

Zyndraxis used Riven's hand and summoned Aedris to open the door, covering the portal opening. Behind it, the edges of the portal were already fizzing away from the stonework. *That is bad. Very bad.*

"Only a person who has the override, or a Shade, can interrupt the process," Zyndraxis told Miri. "We can stay here and hold the portal open, but not for long. You go and get Aliandra. It will not be hard to find her. When Gareth activated the portal shutdown, it would have also locked all other doors expect the ones to the emergency portal. Just keep going until you find the one that's open."

She gave them a long look, the conflict behind her eyes evident and painful. She let out a frustrated breath before stepping closer. She slipped her hand behind Riven's head and pulled him down for a kiss.

Riven was dazed by the sudden, and forceful, show of affection; Zyndraxis couldn't help but be amused by his innocent reaction.

"That was for the both of you," Miri said as she pulled away.

It was Zyndraxis' turn to be shocked as she winked at them and then turned and ran after Aliandra.

Riven cleared his throat and turned back to the portal, tearing Zyndraxis' attention away from the way Miri's dark hair streaked behind her as she ran. What he wouldn't give to be present when Riven slid his fingers into her silky tresses again.

As soon as Miri was out of sight, Riven nearly collapsed to the floor. The injuries he'd sustained from their entire ordeal were finally catching up with him. Since their bond was much stronger now, Zyndraxis was aware of every cut and bruise. However, his greatest concern was Riven's left arm, as it hung limply against his side, perhaps broken.

*"So, about the portal,"* Riven thought rather pointedly, probably sensing Zyndraxis' assessment of his condition, and wanting to divert attention away from it. *"Can we really keep it open?"*

There was a sense of scepticism in his tone that Zyndraxis did not appreciate. *"Sure, it's just like holding back a tonne of stone while a whole temple collapses on us."*

*"Very funny."*

# CHAPTER 20

# MIRI

Miri's lungs burned as she raced through the labyrinthine stone walls of the void building. Gareth should not have had much of a lead on her, given the fact he was dragging Aliandra along with him. However, his knowledge of the corridors was clearly giving him an advantage, as it was becoming increasingly difficult for Miri to hear his thudding footsteps around the corners with her own heavy breathing, and the alarm blaring overhead. She was grateful Zyndraxis was right, though, as all the locked doors meant that she still had an easy path to follow.

After running down yet another stone corridor, lit by torches, she finally turned down one that stopped in a dead end, with a door on either side. She skidded to a stop, looking back and forth between them, trying to figure which Gareth would have taken. She noticed a sliver of light coming from the one on the right.

Her head was aching from the drama of the day, so her revelation took a moment to register. The alarm still blaring through the complex did not help, but just as Miri stepped towards the door, the sound of a loud scream pierced through the cacophony.

"Bastard!" Miri hissed under her breath as she reached for the door.

A powerful jolt of electricity shot through Miri as soon as she touched the handle. She jumped back and hugged her arm to her chest. The spell had paralysed her from the tips of her right fingers, all the way up to her elbow. She recalled spells with similar effects from her past. From memory, the injuries only lasted a few days, but she couldn't wait a few days to face Gareth. Miri swore as she realised, he must have trapped the door deliberately to weaken her; despite his bravado, his ability with Aedris was mediocre at best. He had to compensate with snake-like tactics such as this.

Experience told Miri she would need a way to bypass the trap without touching it. The door itself seemed very sturdy and solid. A simple force spell probably wouldn't work to push it open. She would need to weaken the frame first, to be able to knock the door off its hinges, and bypass the need to touch the handle, and therefore the trap.

Miri slipped her left hand into her cloak pocket to pull out a small silverware cylinder encrusted with a ring of opals. Its original purpose seemed to be making little balls of ice for drinks and what not. Instead of using it for a party trick, she summoned the Aedris within and twisted the ice magic to create a beam of cold energy that she used to freeze the doorframe. Once she'd traced the whole frame, hairline cracks began to spread through the wood.

Letting out a grunt of anger, Miri kicked the heavy door open. The room beyond was a small chamber that looked to be some kind of storage room. There were crates along the side walls, and the one opposite of the door was blank stone. She noted Gareth was grasping Aliandra's collar with one hand, and was running his other over the stone wall. He was so distracted when the portal he was trying to open flashed to life, that he didn't react to her entering. Aliandra was doubled over beside him, blood dripping from her temple, her now bound hands pressed against her head.

The injury that Gareth inflicted on her friend, as well as the fact that he could drag her away through the now open portal, was all Miri needed to see, to plunge into the well of Aedris in her pendant and send a heavy ball of force hurtling towards him. Given the ferocity of her interruption, Gareth did not have a chance to defend himself. The magic hit him square in the chin and sent him flying back from the wall. He was still gripping Aliandra, though, and she went tumbling back with him. Miri sent a blast of air towards Aliandra to cushion her fall, and to stop her from landing on Gareth.

After regaining his bearings, Gareth activated a device on a crate beside him. Dozens of razor-sharp icicle shards shot from the crate, and flew towards Miri. If Gareth had been the one controlling the magic, she would likely be able to deflect this easily, but whatever was in the crate was designed to kill, so it was not easily dodged.

Falling to a knee, Miri raised an arm and conjured a shield of fire. It flared just in time to stop the worst of the icicles, but one skimmed off her shield and sliced over her ear; the cold a stark contrast to the hot blood that beaded on her skin afterwards.

Another shower of shards came Miri's way, and she compacted herself further behind her shield. She moved on her knees, crawling closer to Aliandra. As the thuds and crackles of the ice shattering on stone rained around her, Miri threw a ball of fire in Gareth's direction. She knew he would be able to evade it, but her goal was not to hit him. She just needed him distracted, and moving away from Aliandra.

Gareth dove out of the way of the magical ball of flame. Miri snatched her dagger from its sheath. She would have helped Aliandra cut her bindings, but her right hand was still paralysed, and she needed to focus on Gareth. So, she slid the dagger across the floor so Aliandra could free herself. As her ex-girlfriend worked, the ice trap finally ran out of Aedris and Miri dropped her shield, wanting to save the reserves in her necklace. She retrieved a small steel hammer with rough amethyst strapped to it. The spell within usually allowed the device to break through solid surfaces, but this time Miri threw its energy at Gareth in an all-out assault. Wave after wave of kinetic force slammed into him, pushing him farther and farther back towards the portal.

After the seventh wave, Miri's timing slowed, and Gareth used the opportunity to pull a relic from his robes. Miri expected him to attack her directly, so she considered summoning a shield of force to deflect it. However, the Aedris welled between them and the middle of the room filled with a waist high, dog-like automaton. It leapt at her, immediately crashing into her raised shield; the force of which knocked her back with enough energy that she was thrown on the ground.

Because she only had one working arm left, she had to lower the shield to attack the thing. As the construct over-shot her, and skidded to a halt to turn towards her, Miri unleashed the remainder of the Aedris in her pendant in its direction. Unfortunately, just like the automaton in Alyxian's vault, when she tried to use magic against it, the spell was completely absorbed. The construct renewed its assault, and this time she didn't have any defences. Its long, razor-sharp claws slashed through her clothes and tore long, agonising gouges into her skin. With a cry, she rolled away, desperate to avoid a true attack.

Miri didn't have the martial prowess that Riven had, nor even a weapon to parry, but she did have one more thing. From another pocket in her robes, she retrieved the control crystal for the automaton in the vault. Through the pain, Miri summoned her own golem. It was a smaller version of the faceless, humanoid abomination that Alyxian had created, only this time, Miri was in control. She commanded it to fight the magicked dog. It launched forward, catching the hound-like creature in powerful hands, and flinging it across the room into a stack of crates. The timber shattered, sending splinters flying, but the two constructs resumed their battle, unperturbed by the chaos they were causing.

Using Miri's distraction to his benefit, Gareth edged towards his escape portal. He gave her one last look of triumph before he stepped through.

The portal snapped shut behind him and left behind a completely bland looking stone wall. If Miri hadn't seen it herself, she would have had no reason to suspect there had ever been a doorway there at all.

Keeping the low ground, Miri darted towards Aliandra while the two constructs continued to fight as commanded. It didn't seem to matter that Gareth was gone; the hound he had summoned would fight until it was destroyed or had run out of energy.

Miri didn't care about the constructs, though; all she wanted was to get Aliandra out of there.

"Come on, we need to get out of here," Miri whispered, not wanting to distract the beasts.

Aliandra finished sawing through her bindings and grasped Miri's uninjured hand. The instant Aliandra's warm fingers knitted with Miri's, they started to run. The sound of the summoned constructs battling clanged and echoed through the hallways, but as they made their way through the maze of corridors, those sounds became less deafening.

"Do you know where you're going?" Aliandra panted, rubbing the rope burn welts on her wrists as they ran.

"Yes." Miri wanted to stop, to help ease her wounds with some ice or something, but they didn't have time. Not when the alarms were still wailing. "Well, no. Maybe. Kind of."

"Not reassuring, love." Aliandra wheezed through her exertion.

"All the other doors are locked. The only way left is the path open to us," Miri explained as they hurtled down a new passage and took a sharp right. It wasn't long before they found the corridor that opened into the large entry room, to see Riven standing, with half of his body in the portal. It had shrunken down to his height, and where his body met the black magic, he glowed with the radiance of Zyndraxis' energy.

"We started to worry." Riven gestured for Miri and Aliandra to quicken their pace. "You need to hurry. We can't hold this much longer."

The two women ran over to him. Riven grabbed Aliandra's hand and guided her through the portal, then took Miri's. He pulled her close, and she felt the warm static tingle of the portal as he kissed her, before guiding her through.

A split second later, Miri and Aliandra were standing in the basement and Riven tumbled into the room. He fell to the ground and rolled as the last of the portal's energy ejected him out with a vengeance.

Miri rushed to Riven, clutching his shoulder, and helping him stop. She looked down, caressing his cheek as she met his eyes.

No. There was a deep seriousness in them that was not Riven.

"What happened to Gareth?" Zyndraxis asked, as Miri helped them up.

"He escaped through the emergency portal, which means he could be anywhere," Miri said, lips contorted in distaste. "In any case we need to get out of town. I doubt he would have come here without back-up. There are probably people waiting for him to bring you to them. We cannot let them find you."

For a moment, Zyndraxis held her gaze. Then, he nodded slowly. "So, you no longer wish to turn me over to them?"

Miri's stomach clenched and her cheeks burned. "I ... I messed up. I'm so sorry, I never should have—"

"As much as I like a good reunion," Aliandra interrupted, "If we don't get back to the *Swiftwater* soon, my crew may worry."

Zyndraxis' stiff posture and intense focus dissolved, and concern plucked at Riven's lip before he said, "Let's go, then. We can talk when we are safe."

After they made their way to the *Swiftwater*, Aliandra wasted no time getting the ship underway. Miri and Riven had slipped below deck to tend to their injuries. Miri had helped clean Riven's cuts and bruises with her working hand, and then conjured some ice for him to hold against his broken arm.

When the captain joined them, she needed little more than salve for the rope burn at her wrists, and a wet cloth to clean blood from her hair. Aliandra properly bandaged Riven's arm and helped him into a sling. She then checked Miri over, but Zyndraxis had told here there was little that could be done for Miri's paralysed hand. That would just have to resolve itself over the next few days. She hesitantly moved on to clean the cuts and grazes Miri had collected, and then the small group moved to the deck.

As they leaned against the railing and watched South-bank receding in the distance, Miri felt like she was finally able to catch her breath. The deck of the ship was alive with sailors getting the ship on course. Aliandra excused herself to check that they had not been pursued by any other vessels. The crew seemed wary as they looked around, eyeing Riven with renewed interest. No one dare ask what happened, though. All they knew was that he and Miri were on board once more.

"You know, when we sent you away, the point was for you to stay safe," Riven said, turning away from the view. He put his uninjured hand on Miri's hip. "You weren't supposed to return for us."

Riven's back straightened and, an arrogant smirk thinned his lips. Zyndraxis drawled, "Actually, she was. That was one of the reasons I sent her away. I knew she would return for you. I just didn't tell you that."

"You planned this?" Riven's entire body stiffened, aghast.

"What's done is done; no point arguing about it now."

Miri shifted to face him, looking into his eyes. "You can just say 'thank you' and leave it at that."

With a rumble of laughter, Zyndraxis took the helm. "Thank you, Miri, for rescuing us from a mess of your own making."

"You're the ones who wanted to get a bit of distance from each other," Miri said with an innocent shrug.

Riven cleared his throat. "Actually, about that." He scratched his chin. "We've decided that we'd rather remain bonded."

Miri's eyes widened. That was certainly news to her. She took it in and chewed it over. "But you argue all the time. It's insufferable."

"We have minor disagreements, but in the end, it works out," Zyndraxis said without missing a beat. Then, he nodded towards their arm, and Miri noticed for the first time since their escape how the memento markings now spread all the way up their bicep, and blossomed over their shoulder. She squirmed, liking the way the tendrils highlighted the shape of Riven's hard-earned muscles. Zyndraxis cupped her cheek. "It will also make it much easier for me to kiss you, if I am bonded with Riven."

Heart skipping a beat, Miri looked at him. Her mind slipped back to the mornings spent sleeping on their trek to Weymouth, and how she had woken up to Zyndraxis' intense flirting and intimate Aedris sharing. She was not sure whether that romantic familiarity was just in his nature, or if it was borne out of a genuine interest in her, but it was undeniable. Now that she knew he would not be leaving her life any time soon, she found that the prospect of getting to know him better in that way was enticing. It was an odd situation, but she wanted to make the best of it, if they would allow.

"Is that something you want, Zyndraxis? Riven?" Once

more, Miri was surprised at the blunt confession. "Even after I betrayed both of you?"

They stepped closer. Zyndraxis looked into her eyes causing her insides to melt and her skin to flush with heat. "We can discuss that later," Zyndraxis said. "For now, I need you to know that I stepped back when Riven made love to you, to give him privacy, not because I did not want to be there. Riven and I have an agreement to share this body now."

That was enough to make Miri lean in, closing the distance between them so she could brush her lips against theirs. She rested her hand against their chest and moaned softly into the kiss. Zyndraxis slipped their hand past her cheek and buried their fingers in her hair, gently holding the back of her head.

When the kiss ended and Miri retreated, there was a satisfied smirk on their lips.

"Take note, companion. *That* is how you kiss a woman. Not that overly sloppy tongue thrashing you did earlier," Zyndraxis crowed.

Riven knew better than to retaliate . He just returned their attention to Miri. "Are you sure this is what you want? The both of us?"

Miri laughed, but it was not a cruel thing. She rested her forehead against theirs. "I've done it well enough for the past few days. The real question is, can you two handle *me*?"

Riven's grip on her tightened and he groaned at her words.

Amidst the sound of the sails snapping into fullness and the river lapping at the hull, footsteps tapped across the deck until Aliandra stopped beside them. Miri stepped back, letting the breeze off the water cool the heated air between her and her bonded lovers.

"Apologies for the interruption," Aliandra said, her voice was pitched too high for it to seem entirely casual. Her eyes lingered on Miri's plump, freshly kissed lips for a beat longer than necessary. "I was just wondering if you had anywhere in particular you wanted to go? We dropped our cargo off at Southbank, so we are free agents right now."

"Oh, we can't ask that of you," Miri said, immediately turning towards her ex-girlfriend and shaking her head.

Aliandra placed a hand on Miri's shoulder. "We don't have much choice. We'll be on the Revokers' and the Lore-keepers' hit lists now. I think it's best if my crew and I lay low until that heat blows over. We might as well help you get where you're going in the meantime."

After years of Aliandra's friendship, and more, Miri knew there was little point arguing with the woman.

"That is a good question," Riven mused. "What *are* we supposed to be doing now?"

"Well, I have an idea," Miri admitted. She retrieved the scroll Gareth had given her and unrolled it, turning to flatten it out on a crate nearby.

"A passenger manifest?" Riven asked, pressing up against her back as he read over her shoulder. He draped his arms around her waist and rested his chin on her shoulder.

Miri looked at him. When she did, she noticed something different. It wasn't just Riven peering out of those eyes. The expression on his face was a merger of Riven's calm and Zyndraxis' intensity. As if both were presenting in that moment. It was new, and disorienting, but it was nice to see them learning to share their space.

"Look here." She tapped two names on the hand-written list.

*Evangeline Raxward*
*Darius Raxward*

Riven's arms tightened around her. "What were your parents doing travelling to Port Egress?" he asked incredulously.

"That," Miri said, glancing at Aliandra, "Is what I need to find out."

Aliandra's expression brightened, and she gave Miri a playful salute before turning away. She whistled to get the attention of her first mate, who was at the helm. "Set a course for Port Egress!"

"Well, Riven," Zyndraxis teased, "I guess you will be living your life away from Chafton after all."

"It's what I should have been doing all along." Riven hugged Miri tighter. "I feel like I'm making the right decision this time."

Aliandra let out a low whistle. "Careful, lads. Miri spooks and runs when she catches a whiff of commitment."

She and the bonded companions laughed.

Miri, for once, did not argue, because she knew the truth. She had everything she wanted; she was not going anywhere.

# TO BE CONTINUED...

# IF YOU ENJOYED THIS STORY...

If you enjoyed Return of the Shadow, please consider leaving a review on one of the following sites:
GOODREADS
AMAZON
Reader reviews are crucial for helping indie authors share their stories with the world.

If you would like more news, updates, sneak peeks, and bonus content, you can find it on any of the following sites:
www.livevans.com.au
@LivEvansWrites on Instagram, TikTok, and Facebook.

# ALSO BY LIV EVANS

**The Underground**

*Book One of the Derivates Rising Trilogy*

The Government rule the Hub with an iron fist, their strict laws enforced by Derivates, humans with psionic abilities. When one of these Derivates flees her post, they send KC-847, a powerful telekinetic, to bring her back. But KC-847 s is unprepared for what he finds when his mission goes awry.

Flit, a plucky teleporter, works for the Underground resistance, the last refuge for Derivates wishing to live free of the Government's control. On a routine security patrol, Flit comes across KC-847 and breaks all the rules to bring him back to the Underground.

However, KC-847's arrival brings with it a string of deadly events that threaten the safety of the Underground. Convinced the incidents are more than unfortunate coincidences, Flit refuses to fall back on a false sense of security and drags KC-847 on an investigation that will change the trajectory of Derivate-kind forever.

# ALSO BY LIV EVANS

**The Code of Us**

*"Some things are worth breaking for..."*

When Mia and Arden Drew are in a horrific car accident, the dreams they shared for their future balance on a precipice. As a talented neuropsychologist working for one of the world's foremost experimental human research facilities, Mia uses the resources at her fingertips to save her husband's life.

Mia's grief-fuelled decision catapults her into the depths of a messy court case. Her intentions, relationships, and career are put to the ultimate test as the people around her question how far she should have gone to save her husband, and whether he is still the man she fell in love with. Now, she must face the truth of what she's done or risk losing her husband once and for all.

# ALSO BY LIV EVANS AND JAY THOMAS

**The Voidstalker Extraction**

The galaxy is a dangerous place. Habitable planets are controlled by powerful factions, and the space between them is fair game for pirates and expansionists alike. The best way to get ahead in the Void is by hiring mercenary companies to use their mechs to claim and defend territory.

Most mercenary groups are run by morally gray upstarts. One company is the exception: the Triple C. Led by former mech pilot Henri Durroguerre, it has gained a reputation for honoring contracts and minimizing collateral damage.

Astera Ramos, a runaway turned mech pilot, is new to the Triple C. Eager to prove herself, she volunteers for a supposedly straightforward reconnaissance job on Baldalan that quickly turns deadly.

Henri realizes that the fatal contract was a ruse, and recruits Astera to help him uncover what is happening. When the pair investigate, the Triple C unwittingly become entangled in a sinister plot that threatens to disrupt the balance of power in the Void.

# ALSO BY LIV EVANS AND ZAC PILOT

## Magnolia

*"A girl worth fighting for..."*

One-hundred and thirty years ago, an alien race known as the Hunduns invaded Earth. The survivors of their brutal attack now live in space, aboard the *Worldship Honour*. Now their resources are nearly depleted, the Emperor has called a conscription draft for a final attack in hopes of retaking Earth.

Determined to save her father from having to fly in the Fenix army, Magnolia steals his flight suit, disguises herself as a man, and joins the armada to fight in the last desperate attempt to save the human race.

*Turn the page for your bonus preview of "Magnolia"...*

# CHAPTER ONE

"*Missiles locked and loaded.*" Magnolia "Mags" Hua announced as she locked her missile on her target. The simulator console vibrated beneath her as the crosshairs settled right over the slick armoured carapace of the alien Hundun.

"*I'm covering your six,*" Willow chimed in through the comms. "*We have two ships coming in from your seven o'clock. I've got eyes on them. You keep following the others.*"

"*Gladly.*" Mags observed the way the naturally armoured plates overlapped, and the stretch of its double pair of membranous leather wings made her stomach churn. It reminded her of a mix between the bats and cockroaches her Earth Studies teacher showed her as a child.

She fired her weapons.

A missile blasted from the launcher on her bird-shaped craft and through the foggy atmosphere, rocketing toward the beast and hitting it in a spectacular display of fire and sparks. The Hun's leather wing started to sizzle away, the creature letting out a low, resonant yowl.

Without hesitation, Mags shot a second missile. It hit

the alien beast right in the sweet spot. A shower of gore bloomed across her windscreen, and she grunted as she banked her own plane right to try and avoid the debris.

*"Watch out! One of the ships is—"*

Mags yelped, pulling to the side hard as her evasive move put her right in the path of an alien Willow was tracking. She tried to avoid it, but she was too slow, and the creature shooting toward her had a death wish.

*"Mags!"* Willow cried in warning as Mags peered at the alien and prepared to meet her doom—

*"Alert! All males aged eighteen and over are required to report to the meeting deck immediately. Alert!"*

The simulator whined mechanically as it powered down. The interface helmet Mags wore went black, so she tore it off and slumped back in the seat, placing a hand on her chest as her heart hammered beneath it so hard it hurt.

Red lights pulsed on and off in her living room, and all peripheral electronics around her faded to emergency reserves.

*"Alert! All males aged eighteen and over are required to report to the meeting deck immediately. Alert!"*

Catching her breath, Mags slid off the seat and staggered from the small, cluttered living room into her bedroom. It had a bunk bed in it and two wardrobes set on either side of a desk. The bottom bunk was stuffed with a pair of threadbare blankets, two pillows, and the pyjamas her siblings had discarded that morning. She ignored the fact that the twins hadn't made their bed, yet again, and climbed the ladder to her bunk, where she shoved her hands under the mattress and pulled out a back-up communicator. She plugged it into the charging socket in her headboard and opened a chat window with Willow.

Hey, you around?

Mags bit her lip and wiped a sheen of sweat off her forehead as the blasted alert hollered through her room. She hoped Willow hadn't left her communicator out in the open again. Last time she had, and her parents had been so scared that she had the contraband tech that they threw it in the trash cycle. Luckily, they'd been too scared to run it outside of their allotted time, so Willow was able to retrieve the device.

I should be asking you that. That was a
close call! If that alert hadn't shut the sim
down, you would have been in for a
nasty hit!

"Don't I know it," Mags grumbled under her breath. She sighed and collapsed against her bed.

Mags had recently decided to take advantage of her father's old training simulator while he and her mother were out for work and her siblings were at school. Her grandmother was asleep in a bunk in her parents' room, but lately she had been sleeping deeper than space. Mags had always hated the stupid rule that only men were able to fight.

Well, I got out before it initiated, so I'm
fine. Any chance you can get us eyes on
the meeting deck?

Rolling over onto her back, Mags blew dishevelled strands of hair off her face. Her hair was another thing she had always hated, envying how the boys and men got to cut theirs short. Not that she wanted it that close-cropped, but something shorter than the regulated minimum of fifteen centimetres below the chin would be cooler and easier to maintain.

> I thought you'd never ask! I'll work on it
> now. Can you connect to the wall
> screen? I'll put up a firewall so they
> won't know we're there.

A wide grin stretched Mags' lips and she forced herself to sit up. She didn't bother with the ladder, instead jumping straight down to the metal floor, then yanked the communicator from the charge port and ran into the living room. She plugged it into one of the ports beneath the large wall screen her family used to watch the evening news or research different plants or historical stories from Earth.

Her foot bounced impatiently against the deck of its own accord, the rhythmic drumming matching the pace of her still elevated heart rate.

It had been a while since those in charge had called an all-hands meeting. Willow and Mags had snuck into that one, too. Digitally, at least. That had been two days before her sixteenth birthday, which was just over two years ago now.

The wall screen flared to life, showing a little window in the top corner where Mags spotted Willow's smiling face. Her friend's dark brown eyes were bright as she gave Mags a playful salute, her hair also messy from the sim helmet.

*"Hey, you,"* Willow said.

Mags couldn't help but think she looked pretty like that. *"Hey."*

Instead of letting her mind wonder what situations they could get into together that would tousle Willow's hair, she returned the unnecessary salute with a lazy one of her own. Then she tore her eyes away from the excitement on

Willow's pretty, heart-shaped face and look at the rest of the screen instead.

The meeting deck was the largest empty space on the Worldship Honour. Ever other level was crammed with a mix of living spaces, community rooms, storage, or critical systems such as air purifiers, water generators, engineering spaces, and the like.

With walls barren except for a screen here or there, the wear and tear of humanity's hundred and thirty odd years in space was clear for everyone to see. The scuffs on the floor, however, were covered by the congregation of hundreds of men crammed in together. There was a range of uniform colours represented, from the pieced together grey of engineering overalls, the bronze-trimmed black of slick pilot suits, to the deep green of medical staff.

Mags leaned forward, taking great interest in looking at the proportions of different uniforms. Given that the Empire wanted every single fit and healthy male on flight duty, they made up at least seventy percent of what she saw. Engineering easily made up another fifteen percent. The rest was a hodgepodge of the rare few who were assigned to things like medical, leadership, education, and main-tenance.

It took about twenty minutes for the last stragglers to arrive, and just as Mags wondered why there were so many more engineers than she remembered seeing two years ago, a blast door to the rear of the deck opened. The emperor emerged, dressed in a resplendent suit of red trimmed in gold, with his eight cabinet members in white and two guards in black. He was taller than a lot of other men of his generation, his smooth, flawless skin free of the dark bags and stress lines of the pilots or the scars that were hallmarks of the more dangerous positions in engineering or maintenance.

Silence automatically fell over those gathered as the tall man stepped onto a dais at the front of the space. He raised his hand, and the blaring alert finally stopped.

*"I guess it's easy to keep your handsome looks when you don't have to lift a finger in your life."*

*"You think he's handsome? Seriously? You need your damn eyes checked, girl."* Mags shook her head. She could count on one hand the number of times she'd ever looked at a man and thought he was handsome. She had hoped Willow was the same but was too scared to bring it up.

Willow and Mags had been born a few weeks apart. Given their close birthdates, they were in the same year at school. They'd known each other since they were five and had been friends ever since Mags punched one of the boys in their year in the face for trying to steal Willow's lunch ration.

*"Why? Jealous, Magnolia?"*

Mags pressed her lips together and glanced at Willow. She wanted to wipe away the smirk she wore with a kiss, but...

If anyone caught them, they would both be sanctioned.

Mags' heart ached as she pushed any thoughts of a kiss or possible sanction aside. She would take whatever punishment was dished out if it meant being with Willow, but she would never want to drag her friend through that.

The emperor three generations earlier had decreed that same-sex relationships were to be outlawed, as they would be *fruitless*. Nevermind the fact that fertility or adoption options were available for heterosexual couples who were unable to conceive due to infertility or sex organ variations. Apparently, the rule was good for some and not others.

*Utter crap, of course,* Mags thought, but any dissenters were swiftly dealt with.

She was just about to hit Willow with an epic retort when the emperor lowered his arm as he peered around, surveying his minions with a chin tilt that spoke of the superiority complex he had been born with. "Greetings, men of the Worldship Honour. Thank you for assembling swiftly and calmly. It is with a sense of great regret that I gather you all today. But I come to you with dire news."

"Maintaining the remaining population of humanity was never the goal of the Worldship Honour. It was meant to be a temporary host whilst we fought back with the other nations to reclaim our planet." The emperor spoke clearly, slowly, but his tone grew deeper, which made something in Mags' gut twist. "As such, we have now reached a critical point. We are no longer able to manufacture the materials required to replace crucial parts in our oxygen and water systems. And, as you all know, without those two things, this ship cannot survive."

*"Oh, crap..."*

Mags internally echoed Willow's sentiment. That was terrible news. What were they supposed to do without those parts?

"The current estimates from engineering tell us that we have another two months, at best," the emperor dropped the new information as if it didn't hold the same destructive power as a nuclear missile.

Conversation tore through the room, the men all turning and speaking to those around them, yelling in shock and alarm, demanding more answers.

General Li, the leader of the Fenix armada, stepped forward and raised his hand for silence. "I know that this does not sound promising, but there is hope yet." Then, he gestured to the screens secured on the walls of the space, which flickered to life with a view of Earth. It rotated in space, a green and blue spheroid that looked far more innocuous than it was. Several generations ago, it had been filled with human life. Overfilled, some said. Regardless of the population debates, humanity thrived. Then, a hive of aliens warped into the system and overpowered the humans with a combination of surprise and air superiority. The creatures were like those of nightmares; with armoured bodies and leathery wings, they reminded the people of the destructive, chaotic Hundun from ancient Chinese mythology. The years of the Great War were a brutal, deadly fight between the Hundun, or Huns as they were sometimes known, and the inhabitants of Earth.

Millions had died during the war, but even worse, the Huns began pumping noxious gas into Earth's atmosphere to make it more liveable for themselves. It created a thick blanket of toxicity on the surface of the planet, quickly making it inhospitable to humanity. Scientists had spent months trying to find the devices they presumed were generating the gas, but none were found, and it was assumed the creatures themselves were the source. Plans had been made to evacuate humankind before they all perished due to the poison.

Humanity had captured fallen Hun to study and understand how they worked together, the nations of Earth combining their efforts to create their own fighter ships to take on the Huns. Ships that could survive in the toxic atmosphere and interface with the human mind and react organically so they could finally catch up with the alien's air superiority. The ships were a mix of stolen alien biology and human technology. To honour the collaboration between the engineers from different nations who created the bird-like fighters, they were named Fenixes. The name paying homage to the Fenghuan, the mythological ruler of all birds, and the phoenix, the avian fire creature that is reborn from its own ashes.

The Fenixes proved to be extremely effective in combat due to the addition of human weaponry; however, the Hun were too great in number and too spread out across the planet to effectively fight. When it was clear the Fenix fleet was not able to protect humanity, the nations panicked. Each continent had created its own Worldship to evacuate the civilians into space. However, launching through the Hundun-controlled atmosphere proved dangerous, and only the Worldship Honour survived.

The image of Earth on the screen zoomed in. It was a dizzying sight as the scope dove into the cloudy atmosphere and the ominous shadows of the aerial beasts shimmered through the toxic fog.

"The Hundun have started amassing in a single location. It is the first time their population has gathered in such a way, and it makes them prime targets for a full-scale ambush," General Li announced.

The cheers of reply were so loud that Mags had to turn down the volume on her device. The men pumped their fists into the air, and the cabinet ministers wore satisfied expressions at their enthusiasm. The emperor retrieved an electronic slate from one of his advisors as the cheers died down.

"As such," he said, continuing as if he hadn't paused, "All ship operations will be dependent on the needs of our pilots, and any ancillary operations will cease. All pilots, whether active or not, will be required to serve. Any retired pilots will be recalled upon the conscription conditions that at least one male of maturity must serve per household."

The emperor continued to rattle off conditions, but they all sounded like gibberish to Mags. Her stomach was somewhere on the floor, and her heart hammered in her throat.

*"Mags? Hey, Mags!"* Willow's voice sounded a million miles away. *"Magnolia, speak to me!"*

Mags blinked and looked at the corner of the screen. Willow's face was so close to the camera all Mags could see was her eyes and nose. It would have been comical if she hadn't just realised that her father was the only man in her family who fit the requirements of the conscription notice... but he'd left the corps years earlier. At first, the doctors had suspected that he may have suffered neurological damage from a mission injury—the cause of his night terrors, low mood, irritability, and the way he trembled every time he heard reports of a new loss in the armada. However, when all the medical tests were exhausted, the psychological experts on board said it was most likely a condition of the mind. Other people in his old social circle had a hard time understanding the concept that her father had no visible injuries but was unable to fly, and she knew he carried a heavy load of shame and frustration over this.

Mags never understood the shame. For generations, they had given men no chance but to go to war and die, or watch their friends die. It was a brutal life, and she couldn't even imagine some of the horrors he had lived through. As much as he might try to hide it, she knew he was still struggling. The thought of him being forced back into a Fenix...

*"Father!"* The word slipped from her before she could stop it. Her hands flew to cover her mouth.

*"Mags, it's going to be okay. He was deemed unfit to fly. They won't take him back!"* The conviction in Willow's voice didn't register.

Despite Willow's attempt at reassuring her, Mags knew that he wasn't officially deemed unfit. According to regulations, only a physical injury excused a pilot from serving. However, her father's reputation, and his continued emotional difficulties, meant that he had been offered an honourable discharge to save his reputation. During a conscription, though? His excuse would no longer be valid.

It was different for Willow, Mags thought. Her older brother, Onyx, was one of the star pilots in his year. He was fit and healthy, and her father had retired with honour after an injury to his arm made it hard for him to pilot effectively. Nothing would change for her. There would be no added risk to their family.

But Mags?

*"I can't lose him,"* she said, shaking her head. Her eyes burned as the emperor passed over to General Li to explain the training regimen they were setting up to account for the new and returned pilots.

*"You won't,"* Willow promised. *"We'll come up with something, I swear."*

# ABOUT THE AUTHORS

Liv Evans and Zac Pilot met when they were teenagers and never managed to shake free of each other. Deciding to make the best out of it, they got married, and now live in Sydney's Inner West with their feisty daughter, cheeky son, and menace of a pup.

When they are not wrangling the chaos that is their family (which they adore, by the way), they are working in their day jobs, playing games, reading books, and generally immersing themselves in the best that nerd culture has to offer.

Everything written above makes it seem as though they've had a pretty smooth run of things, but they have been on their share of adventures together too, and intend to continue doing so for many more years to come. They are looking forward to bringing the next instalment of the Shadebound series to readers, so stay tuned for more. Zac doesn't bother with social media, so if you want updates, just follow Liv. Her handle is @LivEvansWrites on all platforms.